...ts as she wants. When ... ... or reading she can be found walking her American Cocker Oliver in the great outdoors, or dreaming of her next research trip away with the family.

Shelley Rivers is a Bournemouth girl who spent most of her childhood reading. Married with a family, she now splits most of her time between reading, writing and pandering to the whims of her hilarious greyhound. Her hobbies include lopsided sewing, holey knitting, and collecting old stuff that no one else sees the beauty in.

FALLING FOR THE VILLAGE VET

RACHEL DOVE

THE MIDWIFE'S NINE-MONTH MIRACLE

SHELLEY RIVERS

MILLS & BOON

First published in Great Britain 2022
by Mills & Boon, an imprint of HarperCollins*Publishers* Ltd,
1 London Bridge Street, London, SE1 9GF

www.harpercollins.co.uk

HarperCollins*Publishers*
1st Floor, Watermarque Building,
Ringsend Road, Dublin 4, Ireland

Falling for the Village Vet © 2022 Rachel Dove

The Midwife's Nine-Month Miracle © 2022 Shelley Rivers

ISBN: 978-0-263-30133-5

07/22

MIX
Paper from
responsible sources
FSC® C007454

This book is produced from independently certified FSC™ paper
to ensure responsible forest management.
For more information visit www.harpercollins.co.uk/green.

Printed and Bound in Spain using 100% Renewable Electricity
at CPI Black Print, Barcelona

FALLING FOR THE VILLAGE VET

RACHEL DOVE

MILLS & BOON

I dedicate this book to Carly Byrne,
my amazing Mills & Boon editor.

Thank you for believing in my writing from day one
and pushing me to be a better writer.

You are an inspiration!

A special mention to Lisa Hall, thriller Queen,
for her Doberman insights.

CHAPTER ONE

'I JUST DIDN'T know what to do, Doctor—he's just not himself. He's so listless, and he doesn't eat like he used to.'

Mrs Chan looked mournfully at her beloved other half, who looked back at her glassy-eyed and defeated. This was the hardest part of the job. It took a lot of compassion, a lot of heart, and tact. These were all things, unfortunately, of which this particular doctor was in short supply at the moment. He found himself feeling nothing but irritation towards Mrs Chan; he brushed the feeling aside as best he could most days but he could still feel it there. Bubbling under the surface. He had thought that moving to a brand-new place would have lifted his mood a lot more than it had. He just felt angry and sad in a new place instead. Sure, Puddle Lake was a very pretty village, but he still felt the same as he did in the city. Angry, frustrated. He tried to smile at Mrs Chan, but it came out more like a toothless grimace.

'The problem, Mrs Chan, is that Gustav here is rather…well, he's rather fat, isn't he?' Mrs Chan's jaw dropped, but he had started talking now and he needed to get his point across. 'Now, I don't want you to misunderstand me, Mrs Chan. I know you love your cat. Unfortunately, he loves his food too, but a cat is incapable of saying no. He doesn't get onto the scales in the morning and worry about his waistline. If the food is there he will eat it. If he goes round to the neighbours and begs for food, he will eat that too. This is what cats do.'

Mrs Chan was looking decidedly miffed still, but her expression had softened.

'It's a common misconception that the giving of treats to pets is love. Sadly, often this is not the case. Dogs, cats, lots of animals need a balanced diet and it is the job of the owner to provide it. What I'm saying, Mrs Chan, is that he needs to stay on his diet food and nothing else. That's the way to show him love. He's an active cat but he's miserable because he can't move. He wants to lick himself and be able to reach all the parts that he could reach before and no longer can.' Gustav looked at the vet and meowed mournfully.

It's okay, buddy, Chris thought. *I've got your back. Just lay off the treats. Buy a little kitty treadmill.*

'So, what are you saying, Dr Jennings?'

'Basically, if you love little Gustav here any more with those treats of yours, then he's likely to run through his nine lives a lot quicker.'

Mrs Chan's incensed look told him that he'd gone too far, but in truth he would have gone further to stop the woman from feeding the poor feline to death. He did care about the patients he had, even if he was indifferent to everything else.

'I think we might need to speak to Dr Ingham, instead.' She looked him up and down, and her expression told him in no uncertain times that his curt words had fallen on deaf ears. 'Does Cheryl have his number?'

Chris resisted the urge to roll his eyes. The second

week on the job, and all but one of his patients had asked the same question. He suddenly missed his old practice, the rapport he'd built up with the families of the animals he'd spent years caring for. It was a different world there, familiar and comfortable. He didn't have time for this, with his full clinic. He sighed inwardly, focusing back onto Mrs Chan's disapproving face.

'I am sure that Dr Ingham would agree with my diagnosis, given that he was the one to put Gustav on the diet food, but you are of course free to get a second opinion. I am afraid, however...' He wasn't at all, but he had to at least try to keep up the thin veneer of being polite. Somewhat misunderstood even. 'Dr Ingham is on vacation at the moment, and he's not taking calls. Cheryl is of course taking messages, for when he's back.' Dr Ezekiel Ingham, the man who had offered Chris the practice here, was probably three sheets to the wind on the cruise ship with his family right now and wouldn't give a fig about Mrs Chan or Gustav.

Maybe I should have done that, he thought to himself grumpily. *Sold up and just travelled, instead of... well, this.* 'I'll see you and Gustav out, Mrs Chan. You can settle your bill in Reception.'

Gustav was already sitting back in his little carrier, throwing Chris a scowl that matched his owner's. Mrs Chan huffed, picking up her rather portly cat and giving the vet her dirtiest final look, and left the room. Poor Cheryl. He could already hear Mrs Chan moaning about his bedside manner, and his new receptionist giving out the usual apologetic patter that she had taken to since he arrived. It was all he'd heard. He felt a little guilty, but he couldn't help his moods. He wasn't interested in being a polite functioning human. He was always there for his patients. Work was always something he excelled at. Now that it was his *only* focus, it had only honed his skills further. At the moment, he got dressed of a morning, fed himself, paid his bills and showed up to the new practice. That was enough for now, surely?

The front door to the surgery slamming shut gave him an inkling that perhaps it wasn't. Sighing heavily, he washed his hands in the sink and started to prepare for the next client. He was just reaching for the door handle to call the next patient when it was barged open by a rather dirty and eager-looking snout. The dog, looking as if he had bathed in mud, bounded into the room, his lead flying in the air as the mad Doberman dashed around the room. It took all of five seconds before the dog caught the scent of where he was, and he tried to bound right back out of the door. The lead thwacked Chris in the leg as he passed, and, in the waiting area, he could hear a woman's panicked shouting.

'Hendrix, you daft dog! Calm down!' The woman entered the room, blocking off the exit to the dog with a well-placed knee. Hendrix was overjoyed to see the woman, whoever she was, and Chris was still rubbing at his trousered leg, where a nice red welt was now showing on his ankle from the whipping of the metal dog lead. 'Sorry, I'm so sorry, he's a bit…well…bouncy.'

'Indeed.' Chris grabbed at the lead and the big brown hound came to a stop at his feet. 'Hendrix, eh?'

'Yeah.' The woman, red-faced from wrestling with the dog, beamed at him. 'He's terrible at guitar though—all paws.'

She was standing there, grinning at him again while Hendrix wasted no time in saying hello by sniffing him closely, right in the crotch area. Chris gently pushed the dog's nose away and moved behind the surgery table. He was keen to keep his distance from the eager hound. Looking at the woman before him, who was dressed in every colour of the rainbow and still beaming like an idiot, he moved a little bit quicker. Hendrix's eyes followed him, but he didn't move from his owner's feet.

'So, what seems to be the issue with Hendrix today?'

'Oh, just the usual. He needs his jabs and worming, of course; the shelter checked for a microchip but nothing came up. He's probably an ill-thought-out Christmas present. These dogs get so big… I don't think people realise.' She patted Hendrix on the head, and he looked up at her with a goofy. adoring look on his face.

'So, you're adopting him?'

The woman laughed. 'Sorry, I don't think we've been introduced properly. I'm Susannah Harkin. I work with the local shelters. I lost my Labrador a few years ago, and I couldn't quite wrap my heart around getting another dog. I went to look round the shelter one tragically sad afternoon…' Her voice cracked, and the rest of her words didn't leave her mouth. They seemed to hang there, in the air, and Chris found himself wondering what they would have been. 'Anyway…' She seemed to shake herself mentally, and the smile was back. Chris almost squinted as he felt the brightness invade the room. 'Here I am. I foster some of the dogs that are a bit too much for kennels, work on a bit of house training, get them ready for their for-ever home.'

'Is there such a thing these days?'

'Such a thing as what?'

'A for-ever home,' Chris retorted. 'Our throwaway society seems to feel different.'

The woman looked a little thoughtful. A second or

two later, she bent to stroke behind Hendrix's ears and eyed the vet over Hendrix's head.

'Maybe, but you don't throw the baby out with the bath water. Not in Puddle Lake anyway. People do care. The way I see it, if I can help a few dogs get a better deal, then it's more than worth it. Bit of company around the house too.'

Chris found himself nodding despite himself. She did have a point—just thinking about going home chilled his blood. It was too quiet, devoid of life. He found himself sitting at home waiting for work to start, but then work started and his mood didn't improve.

'So, Hendrix here just needs the usual MOT. A bit of training, a good groom and he should be good to go.'

Hendrix looked up at Chris, a comical expression of horror on his features as though he could understand everything the pair of them were saying. Typical dog—they all loved the vets until they had some kind of treatment, and then the pooch soon wised up for the subsequent visits. Hendrix was looking at the door and Chris followed his gaze. Susannah was still staring at him when he realised he hadn't spoken for a full minute. In all honesty, he was with the dog. He wanted out of this room, right now. He snapped back into vet mode and pushed his own muddled thoughts aside. He was becoming a pro at it too.

'Okay, well, let's get him up on the table and see what's what.'

The scared Doberman, as though he had understood every word, suddenly pulled up on the lead Susannah was holding, her face registering the movement just a second too late. Hendrix, now fully aware of the impending doom that was coming his way, threw his whole body weight against the door, letting out a pitiful howl in the direction of the vet's waiting area.

'Woof—woof!' Hendrix was pulling at the lead with everything he had, trying to dig through the wood of the thick surgery room door with his overgrown claws. 'Woof! Woof! Woof!'

'Hendrix! Come…on…!' Susannah, knocked off balance by the terrified hound, ended up on the floor, partly beneath the dog, partly wrapped in his lead. She looked like a rainbow, her coloured clothing spreading out around her and Hendrix's brown chicken legs hopping all around her as the dog made a valiant but ultimately futile bid for freedom. 'Hendrix, please! Cut me a break. I told you this was coming. We had a deal, buddy! I bought you a pup cup in good faith, damn you!'

The dog paused for a moment, looking Susannah in the eye and giving her a long lick up her cheek before returning to his frantic scrabbling and high-pitched whines of frustration and fear. Chris looked at the bright and scattered woman flailing on the floor, and at the dog, and sighed.

'Hendrix, stop.' He didn't shout it, but his deep controlled voice stopped both Hendrix and the woman beneath him in their tracks. The dog looked at him and slowly turned away from the door, standing on Susannah in the process; he then sat quietly at Chris's feet. 'Good boy.' He patted the dog once on the head, and then, looking at his surrogate owner sitting on the floor agog, Chris held out his other hand. She eyed it warily for a long moment, Hendrix seemingly in awe of the vet now and obediently waiting for the next instruction. She wiped her now muddy hand on her clothing and slowly put her hand in his. Her hand felt warm, and surprisingly soft to the touch. His jaw dropped a little, the shock of the contact enveloping his body. He hadn't held a woman's hand in what seemed like a lifetime. He slowly pulled her to her feet, his other hand reaching for hers as she come to a stop right in front of him.

She's quite pretty. Beautiful green eyes, with that red hair. Sea glass and fire.

She slowly pulled her hands from his.

'Thanks. Sorry about him too.'

He grabbed his stethoscope from his desk and came to kneel by the startled hound.

'Not to worry. I think we've come to somewhat of an agreement. Hendrix, let's get this over with.'

Dr Jennings inspected Hendrix, noting things down on his computer screen as he went. Susannah watched him work his magic on the bedraggled canine, who was now allowing the vet to investigate his undercarriage without trying to rip his arm off.

'So, you're the new vet, then? Not some weirdo masquerading under his name?" He sounded nothing like the outgoing vet had described.

'Stating the obvious, since I currently have a thermometer in an awkward place.'

Hendrix's face was a picture, but Dr Jennings looked as if he were sucking on a lemon. Susannah pressed on undeterred.

'Settling in okay, then? Must be different for you, from a big-city mega vet to this little corner of the world.'

'It was hardly a mega-vet. We only had six partners in total.'

'Well, our whole village has *one*. Trust me, to us

that's a mega-vet. When we got Starbucks on the motorway exit everyone went nuts for weeks. We only had the tea shop in town before then. There was even a petition to get it closed down, but thankfully the caffeine seemed to fend off any real feuds. So, you liking it?'

'I've been a vet for a while now,' he rebuffed, his face stony. 'Hendrix is fine, and his jabs are now up to date.'

'I know that.' She ignored his attempt to shut the conversation down. 'I meant living and working here.'

What was this guy's problem? She was only trying to be nice. It was like trying to talk to the dogs at home. Hendrix had a better line in conversation than this sour-faced man. He was rather cute though, she noticed as he got to his feet and went back to his computer. He was tall, dark-haired, and would be handsome if he didn't scowl all the time. Dr Ingham had made a strange choice for his practice. Ezekiel Ingham was like Santa Claus compared to the tightly clenched man before her. She knew Ezekiel had been looking for a while, and the last time she'd been in to talk to him about her dream of an adoption drive, he'd been excited for his successor to arrive in order to give him some much-needed time off. He'd been a stalwart of the local community for years, but now his children were all flying the nest and raising chicks of their own, he was looking to slow down. From the way he'd spoken to her about Dr Jennings, it had seemed as if he was going to be a perfect fit. Now, as she watched him tut at the screen, banging at a couple of keys a little too hard, she couldn't really see what Ezekiel had been thinking.

'Are you having a bad day or something?'

He ignored her, his face lit up with the glare of the computer screen.

'Hello? Earth to Dr Jennings.'

'What?' He almost snapped his reply at her, and she felt herself frown for the first time that day. Even Hendrix hadn't annoyed her to nearly the same degree as the man standing in front of her. He finally turned to look at her, and she noted a touch of regret cross his features. 'Sorry, did you say something?'

'I asked if you were having a bad day.'

He frowned, his almost black brows forming a tight frame around his dark brown eyes.

'No worse than any other day.'

'And?'

'And what?'

'And is that good or bad?'

'It's just a day. It's a dull Wednesday afternoon, my clinic is full, and I got assaulted by a Doberman.' He looked at her, his face pulled into a sour expression.

'Well, a day is what you make it. I find that if you try to find the joy, it's there.'

She could tell from his expression that he thought she was some kind of 'Be Kind' hippie. Which she was, in many ways, but it still irked her.

'Not always. Are you having Hendrix fixed?'

Great, and now he was talking about dog testicles. He really didn't want to be spoken to, did he?

'Yes, please. I am hoping to get him rehomed as soon as his training is done.'

The vet said nothing, turning again to the screen.

'I can do the operation next week. Monday morning?'

She frowned, getting her diary up on her phone.

'I can't, I'm on shift that day. I can do Tuesday and Wednesday?'

He sighed heavily, squinting at the screen and tap-

ping a few keys just that little bit harder than was required. Susannah and Hendrix were both watching him,
and from Hendrix's unamused face, she could tell he
wasn't impressed by the new vet's mood either.

'Tuesday I can fit him in first thing. That suit?'

Susannah nodded, making a note in her phone diary.

'Perfect, I'll be home to look after him then. So
what's the verdict?'

'He's fine, a little underweight, but that should correct itself over time. He's quite healthy for a stray.'

'Oh, he wasn't a stray; he was surrendered to the
local dog shelter anonymously.'

'Ah, the behavioural issues make more sense now.'
His jaw flexed. 'I do hate how people think these animals are disposable.' He printed a quotation sheet off
the computer, coming around the desk to give it to Susannah. As he passed the paper to her, he knelt down
and gave Hendrix a rub behind the ears. To his credit,
the hound for once took it in his stride, and gave the
man a lick. He laughed, and Susannah saw the vet's demeanour change. His shoulders relaxed, his expression
changed from a deep-seated scowl to show a handsome
face, and his eyes now looked less like a shark's. The
change in him surprised her.

*What was wrong with him? It seemed like more than
a bad day, but looking at him now, playing with Hendrix, it was hard to reconcile the two men.*

'Do you have any pets?' she asked, suddenly interested to know more about him.

'No, sadly not. I never had the time before I moved.'

'And now?' she pressed.

He looked up at her then, Hendrix sitting with his
tongue out, clearly loving the ear scratch that Dr Jen-

nings was giving him. *Fickle,* she said to Hendrix in her head. He had been trying to bound out of the door a second ago, and now he was shamelessly leaning into the vet's touch. From the look on Dr Jennings's face, she realised that the thought of having his own pet had never occurred to him.

'Well, now I guess I have more time. I've never thought of it like that.' He gave Hendrix a last stroke and stood up straight. Susannah had to look up at him, given his tall stature, and she found herself looking at his body. Just for a sneaky second, before she caught herself. She wasn't here for any of that. She was here for the dogs. Which reminded her of the charity drive she desperately wanted to get up and running.

'So you might be in the market for a dog, then? Maybe you can get one at the charity drive.'

'Charity drive?'

Susannah's heart sank. She could tell it was the first he'd heard of it.

'Yeah, I did have an arrangement with your predecessor. We have a bit of a backlog with the rescue dogs in the area, and I'm a bit overstretched. Having a charity drive would be a great way of matching some with new owners and raise some funds too.' She had eight dogs at home, including the overexuberant Hendrix, and she was starting to feel a little stretched. Her job was emotionally and physically draining too, and although she only worked part time, it was still a lot. There was barely room for her in her own house, and it was getting costly. The shelters she worked with were amazing, but she tried to chip in with the costs when she could. Non-profit charities cut costs where they could, but the money still never seemed to stretch far enough.

'Right, and Dr Ingham agreed to this on my behalf, did he? He never mentioned it, and as he's away...'

He trailed off, standing there in silence. He was dismissing her! Susannah felt her hackles rise.

'Well, yes. He's away, but he did say that the practice would help. I was actually hoping to start the ball rolling today.'

His eyes were on the clock before she'd finished speaking.

'Well, I don't have the time today, I'm afraid. I have a patient waiting.'

'It won't take a minute. I just wanted to check you were on board. Perhaps arrange a proper meeting time, so we can discuss it in more detail. If we could have vet support, it would make a real difference.'

He made a kind of squeaking noise in his throat, as if he were being strangled.

'Well...er... I am new to the place, and my caseload is full. I really don't think—'

'Tuesday, then, you'll have the time. I can sign the consent paperwork beforehand.' She wasn't about to let this drop. He looked put out, but she smiled at him and turned to Hendrix. 'Right, you, home we go!' She turned to leave, the image of him staring at her open-mouthed etched into her memory.

This drive is going to be more of a task than I thought. I wish I were on a cruise. So I could beg the nice vet to come back and sort this sourpuss out.

He was going to say no, and she wasn't about to let him do it without a fight. Her house was packed to the rafters, and so were the shelters. They were having to turn dogs away now, sending them further afield. It broke her heart, and a man who acted like Ebenezer Do-little Scrooge wasn't going to put a kink in her planning.

The door closed behind her, and she walked into Reception, Hendrix's lead pulling as he spied the main door. She gave him a look, and he sat down at her feet. The waiting room was quite full. Maybe Dr Jennings was just busy, tired even. She wasn't one to be down; it wasn't her way. That didn't mean she didn't struggle herself some days.

'Everything okay, Suze?' Cheryl asked her from behind the desk. 'You look like you've had a bad day.'

Cheryl's choice of words made her cackle with laughter.

'You could say that. It started well.' She nodded her head towards the door. 'I need to book in for Hendrix here.' She made a snipping movement with her fingers. She never liked to talk about it in front of the dogs. She felt a bit sorry for them really, but it was for the best. Less chance of any more unwanted puppies to rehome down the line and fewer health complications in later life. 'Tuesday first thing, please.'

Cheryl clicked on her keys, nodding along.

'All booked in. Sixty-five pounds for today on the account, okay?'

'Elvedon Shelter for this one, please.' She had accounts running at the vet's for the shelters she worked with; she was the dog whisperer in this little corner of the world, and it was easier than paying out and having to claim it back. She wasn't broke, but she wasn't flush either. She owned her house and land, and loved her job, but she still had to be careful to watch that she didn't spend all her money saving dogs. 'I'll see you Tuesday.'

* * *

She was about to put Hendrix in the car when Cheryl called her name. She was jogging across to her, a furtive look on her features.

'Sorry, did I forget something?'

Cheryl waved her away. 'No, no. I just wanted to catch you to ask something. What did you think of the new vet?'

Susannah wasn't one for slating people she had just met, but she did find it very hard to bite her tongue without ripping the whole thing off.

'Well, I think bad days are catching,' she said diplomatically. She hoisted Hendrix into the back of her car, waiting for him to settle down with a treat she'd lobbed in before carefully closing the boot. 'Why do you ask?'

Cheryl looked back at the practice before answering. 'It's just…he's been a little bit…'

Susannah saved her from speaking. 'Moody? Surly?'

Cheryl nodded in relief, her eye still on those front doors.

'You did notice, then. He's a nice bloke, but…the transition is a little tricky, especially when Ezekiel went away. He needed it though—I'm just not sure the locals are accepting it very well.'

'The charity drive is dead in the water now too,' she muttered, more thinking out loud. 'What's his problem?'

Cheryl, never one to gossip either, looked uncomfortable again. 'It wouldn't be for me to say, but…'

'But?' Susannah found that she really was interested in the answer. She leaned in, and, looking into the boot, she could see that Hendrix was regarding them both rather intently too. 'You know I won't say anything.'

'It's his wife…' Cheryl gave in. 'I think she left him or something. When he was talking to Ezekiel about the job a few months ago, I'm sure Ezekiel said he was married. No wife, no ring.' Cheryl bit her lip, obviously feeling very guilty about her admission. 'I think it's because of her. He never gets any calls, you know? Nothing personal. The closest he got was when we had a kitchen firm call him about something about his house. I think he's a bit lonely perhaps. I just hope he settles in soon.' She gave Susannah an odd look, and then it dawned on her. She knew why Cheryl had been so eager to talk to her. She wanted her help. The resulting groan from the very depths of her soul made Cheryl wince.

'I know but come on! You make everyone happy around here! And…and…'

'Need a hand, clutching at those straws?' Susannah's mouth twisted into a tease. 'I can't help on this one.' She looked back at Hendrix, who had now settled down in the back, as if butter wouldn't melt. 'I only just met the guy, and he didn't exactly roll out the red carpet. He shot down my charity drive and—'

'The charity drive, that's it!'

Cheryl jumped in the air like an overexcited meercat.

'That's what? He practically threw up when I mentioned the idea. He is not on board.'

'No, I know he's probably a bit reluctant…'

'A bit reluctant? He walks around like he could sweep the floor clean with every tight step he takes. He doesn't give a fig about the charity drive, and why would he?'

'He loves animals!'

Susannah rolled her eyes theatrically.

'Rather a given, with his job.'

'No, I mean he really loves animals. He's been be-rating the patients' owners since he got here for not looking after them properly. He's a bit of a stickler for animal care, and he shows real passion.'

Susannah couldn't help but frown. The guy Cheryl was describing didn't sound anything like the angry vet she had just had the displeasure of meeting. He was curious about Hendrix's background though. Maybe he did care, just a little. 'I don't know, I don't really have the time.'

'That's what the charity drive was about, wasn't it? Getting more dogs rehomed, enticing more foster carers. It will all help, right?'

Susannah soon felt very tired, leaning her head against the back window. Hendrix jumped up and tried to lick at her forehead through the glass.

'I'm not sure I'm the best person for this, Cheryl. Me and men...'

Cheryl patted her on the shoulder. 'I know, but this is just business. It won't do you any harm to get out of the house a bit more either.' Susannah was ready to cut her off, but then she thought of her last weekend off. She'd not left the house, other than to walk the dogs. Even that had been on her land. She'd done it in PJs and wellies. It was hardly packed with action. The closest thing she got to excitement these days was when her Amazon book orders came. Cheryl had a point, but she couldn't help but feel irked by it. Cheryl could tell, judging by her face. 'Please? For me?'

Susannah snorted. 'The last time you rang me and said that, I ended up with a three-legged dog.'

'Yeah, and he got you moving again! Come on, after Beau, you needed some company.'

And the rest, Susannah thought.

When Beau, her old Labrador dog, had passed away, she had been lost. That was true. Cheryl had thrown her a lifeline asking her to foster a dog for the practice, and it had gone from there. Company in her house, but she was still not sure how she would get on with Dr Jennings and his stunningly rude bedside manner.

'I'll give you that, but you will also remember that I do better with male dogs than with their human counterparts. I'm not sure I can help this time.' She was slowly edging to the driver door, but Cheryl was clearly torn between trying to rope her into her plan and heading back to work to keep the chaos caused by Dr Mardy to a minimum. Susannah half followed her, one eye on the surgery door.

'Just think about it, okay? For me? One little chat. Maybe take him out for a coffee.' The look on her face was all gentle smiles and begging eyes, but even with the help it would generate, not to mention making her life easier, her mind was still screaming at her not to get into bed with this man. Metaphorically speaking, of course. She couldn't really imagine any woman wanting that little slice of delight—well, not with his scowling demeanour, anyway. It would no doubt be rude and perfunctory, just like his dog bedside manner. She did wonder what was under his clothing though—she could still appreciate a good-looking man when she saw one. If he smiled, he would be rather attractive, she thought.

'I'll think about it,' she said eventually, but she saw Cheryl's shoulders sag. 'Come on, Chez, you know me and men.'

'I knew you and one man,' she said softly. 'You

can't keep measuring all your experiences with the same yardstick.'

'Well, I've heard my ex called other things before, but never that.'

Cheryl laughed, and Susannah smiled. She loved making people happy—making them laugh, even. Even if it was as a result of poking fun at her marriage and the subsequent rather messy divorce. Still, that was in the past. She wasn't as affected by things as she once was, but Cheryl's comment did make her think. Did the people who were in her life really think that? Sure, he'd cheated on her, and treated her as second-best pretty much the day after the wedding—a whirlwind wedding at that. She'd been a fresh young nurse, and he'd been the powerful, commanding doctor. He'd wooed her, married her, and then promptly forgotten about her. She'd been the idiot who had fallen for it, but it had been first love. She'd never met anyone she cared about like him. He had tamed her free spirit, but then just assumed that she would take life, and his shenanigans, in her stride. It was a huge shock to them both that this simply wasn't true.

'I'm well shot. Happy as a lark.'

CHAPTER TWO

As SHE DROVE away from the surgery, Hendrix looking out of the window excitedly, Susannah thought over her encounter with Dr Jennings. She knew now why he had irked her so much. Oh, sure, his mood was sullen, and she didn't gel well with people who lived under a cloud, but it was more than that. He'd reminded her of *her* doctor. Commanding, a little bullish when it came to work, condescending even. *Handsome.* She mentally crossed that last one off the list in her head. Her husband had been handsome and look where that had led. The nurses she'd worked with had loved it, much to his delight and her disbelief. The thought of dealing with a man who made her feel like that reminded her of him; it drained her energy. Even Hendrix seemed a little subdued in the back. The pair of them travelled in silence, till she clicked open her electronic gates, and drove the car up the long drive to her house.

She loved Solitary Cottage. An odd name to be sure, and not really a cottage either. Not by traditional standards anyway. It was a huge place just for her really, but when she'd been reeling from her divorce, and wanting to leave her job in the city hospital where he reigned supreme, the local hospice in the little-known Yorkshire village she'd grown up in had been looking for a nurse. And when she'd first gone to the estate agent's, looking for a home to replace the one she'd shared with Duncan, Solitary Cottage had immediately caught her eye.

It wasn't just the name, of course, although that had screamed out to her when she'd first been told of the listing. It had been in a good state of repair, just a little unloved. It had only stood empty for three years, after the former occupants had aged and left for something more manageable. With their children living abroad, the house had been put up for sale, and eventually forgotten about. Too much of a fixer upper.

In those three years though, standing empty and forgotten, the few acres that came with the land had really come into their own. Now, as she let Hendrix out, free to roam the secure grounds, she opened her front door and was hit by a wave of nostalgia. The first time she'd got the key from the agent and driven up here, she had been met with resistance. Not from the neighbours, who were all quite happy behind their own fences and friendly from the off. From the house itself, it had seemed. Ivy had been growing through a crack in the window. The vines had slipped in, and eventually pushed through the rest of the glass to wind around the hallway. A pile of post wrapped in these vines had rendered the door firmly shut to visitors, and it had taken her a good twenty minutes to cut and rip and squeeze in through the door frame. She'd taken one look around the place and offered on it the same day.

She put her keys into the dish on the hall table, and, drawing breath, she went straight through the house, Hendrix in tow, heading to the back of the kitchen. Opening the back stable-design door, she walked out with Hendrix and closed the bottom half of the door off. Her back yard was more than a back yard, with the land that sprawled from her property, but it was welcoming. She felt safe here, even on her own out in the sticks. She liked that the place was a little out of the way in Puddle Lake.

She had divided the grounds into two sections: one for her to grow vegetables, read in, have a glass of wine in and sunbathe, the other for the dogs in her care. She had a row of heated plush kennels, a wash area, a separate kitchen and even a grooming room. She had made it her project over the years, with help and funding from charity events and the local council. Even now, sometimes it took her breath away at how much she had achieved since walking into this house, her old Lab in tow, and the ink on her divorce still fresh. It had been the start of something new. Which made her think, what was Dr Jennings here for anyway? The same reason? To live a quiet, easy life in this beautiful backwater? If it was a change of pace he was after, as he had alluded, then he didn't seem happy about it. Maybe he was regretting leaving his city life?

The wife thing was odd too, but she knew first-hand that saying *I do* wasn't a guarantee of a happy relationship that lasted for ever. Not every love could be like *The Notebook*, after all. Frogs and princes looked exactly the same with rose-tinted glasses. Experience took the blinkers off, but by then the damage was done. Maybe he was just dealing with stuff. Or not, as the case may be. She'd turned into Nurse Dolittle after her failed relationship. If she hadn't had her rescue dogs to fill the hole, maybe she wouldn't be as sunny as she was now.

Opening the door to the run, to which the dogs had

access from their kennels, she beamed as she was engulfed in a happy reunion with sloppy tongues, waggy tails and the sense that, in their world at least, she was important. She wasn't second best. She won first place in their hearts. And they in hers. Although, she did wish she could share it with someone, a man who saw her through their puppy-dog eyes and vowed to put her above all others. She sighed, the dream of a man popping into her head once more. He never had a face in her daydreams, and that depressed her even more than the thought that it would never happen. She wasn't even dating, so it was hardly a surprise. She got to work sorting the dogs out and tried to forget about her day.

'Cheryl, I do appreciate what you're saying, but as the new owner—'

'As the new owner, I of course defer to you. However, the clients are not happy.'

'The clients are the animals. How many complaints have you had from them?'

Cheryl's head snapped back as she digested this.

'Well, none, of course. You're very good with the animals; I'm not disputing that.'

'So this conversation is over. Yes?'

'Yes. No!'

Cheryl puffed out air from her cheeks and put one hand on her hip. Chris resisted the urge to smirk. He was annoying her, and it gave him an evil thrill. Till Susannah's face popped into his mind. Her comments earlier on that day had got to him over the course of the day, and he felt a tinge of guilt for winding up his assistant. He didn't make a habit of abusing staff. It was something he disliked intensely. He pulled his face into an apologetic expression, showing that he was listening.

'The thing is, Dr Jennings, the clients are happy, but they don't pay the bills. Their owners do, and the level of complaints is getting a little much. I just wanted to address it, and I did have an idea.' She looked up at him then, getting into her stride now she had his ear. 'The charity drive with Susannah.'

Chris felt his gut sink into his boots. 'Oh, God. No.'

'Susannah needs the help. She's had such a lot of new dogs come in recently, and the shelters are full. She's overworked, and it's not cheap, what she does.'

'Is this her job?' He slapped himself mentally. Why did he need to know? He wasn't going to do it. Not a snowball's chance in hell. He was pretty sure they would annoy the heck out of each other. She was far too…happy.

'No, no. She works at the hospice; she's a nurse.'

Chris felt as if the blood were being sucked out of his body with a straw. He felt a little wobbly on his legs. 'The hospice? Really.' A thousand images assaulted his brain, but he turned his back on them all and plodded on. 'Well, if's she's so busy, she must have help from somewhere.'

'She doesn't. It's just her. Her house. She does everything for the dogs, and her patients. She needs a break. It's not been easy for her. She could employ someone part-time eventually, I suppose, but that's a way off. Especially without a cash injection.'

'You seem to know a lot about her—are you friends?'

'Yes, I guess we are now. She came to us at a difficult time, losing her old dog, but then she fostered one for us.' From the look on her face, Chris surmised that she'd had something to do with that as well. He would have to watch his back. 'It grew from there, but now she needs this charity event to come off. And you need a little bit of goodwill in this village. People talk around here, you know. There are other veterinarian surgeries too, and although they're a little further afield I would hate for us to lose out on any clients.'

Chris frowned. 'Am I really that bad?'

'One client, who shall remain nameless, called you a bullish oaf. Another one said that Dr Spock was friend-lier than you, and just yesterday I overheard a conversation in the post office. Your name was mentioned, and it wasn't a recommendation.'

Chris winced, and she fell silent.

'I'm sorry for that. Who called me a bullish oaf?'

'Client confidentiality, I'm afraid. The charity drive could be the perfect way to turn it around. Show the villagers your other side.' She cocked her head to one side. 'You do have one, yes?'

'Have what?' he retorted, much less grumpily than he felt. Her words stung him, but it was a sting of shame. He had been numb for a while now, but he'd obviously overstepped far more than he cared to.

'A good side.'

He nodded his head, just once. 'I have. Somewhere, in the back.' He pointed to his head, and Cheryl laughed.

'I thought so. Will you think about it?'

'I will. I'll discuss it with her when she comes back with Hendrix.'

Somewhat satisfied, Cheryl left him to it after that. She was his ally with the patients, and he didn't want to alienate her or make her job harder than it was. The news that Susannah worked as a hospice nurse had lev-

elled him when he'd first heard. Now he could see it.
She was so happy, so colourful. Maybe that was why she
was able to do what she did. She obviously had a caring heart. He knew he couldn't do it. He never wanted
to set foot in one of those places again. He could still
remember the smells, the sounds, the staff. The nights
of watching his wife sleep, till her final slumber. It was
like another lifetime, but he knew every detail, as if the
memories had plugged themselves into his skin, pump-
ing constant reminders into his thoughts, his senses.
All it took was the scent of her perfume on a pet owner
in the clinic and his memories zapped into life and his
movements grew shaky and stilted.

They'd not been perfect, Chris and his wife. They'd
had to work at their marriage, like everyone else, but
broadly they'd been happy. They'd had their lives sorted,
together. They hadn't been waiting for the next step, or
lacking something. They hadn't talked about their future, or about what might come next. They'd married
in a low-key affair, after an easy and short engagement.
They had met, and just clicked. Like a key into a lock.
No flash of passion, just a recognition that they were
good together, happy in each other's company. Their
sex life had been good, comfortable, and not lacking in
passion. They'd both loved their careers, yet still made
time for each other. They'd brushed in and out of each
other's lives, had a great big circle of boozy friends to
go out with on a weekend. They had been busy living
their lives, working away, or staying overnight at their
jobs when it was needed.

When the cancer had come for her, he'd realised just
how much she'd meant to him, and they'd spent every
last moment together. And he'd grown angrier by the

day. Not at her, not at the cancer. At himself, he supposed. At them both. They'd had such a busy life together that when they had nothing but each other, and
endless treatments, and time off work, they'd stalled.
He'd been there, a constant by her side, but he'd realised,
with an overwhelming clarity, that they had needed
more than each other. They hadn't known each other as
well as he'd thought, and as they'd sat there, day after
day, waiting for some hail Mary that never came, they
had known that they never really would. He'd buried a
wife he didn't really know, and his anger was complete.
He'd wasted time, not fully loving the woman he was
married to, and now she was a memory.

His life was over too. Not in a devastated Cathy and
Heathcliff way. He was grief-stricken, of course, desperately missing his wife and crying over her pain at
the end. Life was cruel, and impossible for those left
behind. His life was over because he didn't fit into it
any more. He was the widower now, in a high-flying,
high-living bunch of friends who were all either dating serially or were married off. He was something that
they didn't understand now. His house was empty, his
calendar the same. Work didn't quite hold the same appeal. He found himself wondering why he'd taken so
much on, always working when he hadn't really needed
to. They hadn't had any children to provide for; they
had been more than comfortable. Now that he didn't
have any reason to rush home, he realised just how
much he wanted to. Wanted to get home early and meet
his wife in the hallway. Strip her bare and say hello
properly, take his time. He would have cherished her
more, learned more about her, and never put work before her. Ever.

It always taunted him. Hindsight was an honest and rather bleak realisation, and it kept hitting him over and over.

When he got home to his empty house later that night, the house his legal-eagle wife would never have wanted to live in, he pondered his own madness once more. He'd changed his life, slowed down, moved across the country and set up in a small village, cashing in his ticket for the fast lane once and for all. He had all the time in the world now, but he still had nothing but work. So he worked, and studied at home, keeping up to date with practices and techniques, but he knew it was a distraction. He'd created the kind of life he thought he should have now, but he only felt as if he'd got angrier. After all, what was the point? He was still alone, with his work and his house, and his money. Sure, he was comfortably off, but that was because he never spent a penny. Now that he wasn't even going out and enjoying his free time, the only thing increasing was his bank balance. His mood had dropped lower than a snake's belly, and now he was a mean boss to boot. His clients and neighbours hated him, and he felt as though he was being hogtied into helping the last woman in the village he would ever want to spend any time with. Mrs Sunshine-on-a-Stick.

The more he thought about Susannah Harkin, the more his mood soured. It just categorically could not happen. He would rather face the wrath of the likes of Mrs Chan before he would agree to working with that woman. The surgery would put up flyers, and that would have to be enough. A nice gesture of support. He shuddered, thinking of how happy the flyers would be. He had visions of his windows looking as if a rainbow had vomited on them, and his resolution to stay out of the charity-drive business hardened. He'd just have to be nicer to his clients, and find something to change his dark moods when he felt the familiar flickers of frustration and hopelessness erupting within him.

CHAPTER THREE

'I'LL GIVE YOU anything you want if you do what I say. Please. I'm begging you.'

Susannah tried her best alluring look, keeping her gaze fixed on the big, dark eyes in front of her. 'You know it's going to happen. I know it's going to happen. Let's just do it, get it out of the way. I can't bear this, us pussyfooting around each other.'

The eyes stared back, silent and unreadable. Susannah groaned in frustration, her head dropping onto her knees. She was sprawled outside the surgery doors, half hanging out of the bush into which Hendrix had just pulled her. He was sitting in the bush next to her, his lead loose, his flappy ears drooped low with his head.

'You won't feel a thing. My uncle Alan had the same operation, and he was fine in a day or so. Bit sore, but it's for the best. We don't want lots of little Hendrixes running around, do we now?' Ever vocal, Hendrix made a disagreeing growling sound beside her, and darted back into the bush when they heard footsteps approach.

'Everything okay?'

'Oh, great, it's Mr Sunshine.' She said this under her breath, but when she peeked out from behind a clump of leaves, she could tell he'd heard her.

'I prefer Chris most days. You are aware that you're late for your appointment, yes?'

Susannah clenched her teeth. She didn't have access to her watch right now, given that she was hanging like tinsel in the bush, but she knew she couldn't be more than a minute or two late.

'Technically, I am on the premises. And arrived perfectly on time.'

'Yes, but the council tends to object when I castrate animals in the car park. Do you need help?'

Of course I don't, not from you. I would rather take up residence in the bush than ask you for help, but I'm pretty sure that the long lead is unravelled and wrapped around my feet.

'I might. Is Cheryl inside?'

She could have been wrong, but she thought she heard him laugh. It surprised her that he knew how.

'No, Cheryl went on break right after she informed me of your arrival. She sent me to get you.'

Cheryl, I wish you a crappy break. I hope your biscuit drops into your tea, you meddling little witch. Maybe she had more than Earl Grey in her teabags. Eye of newt, perhaps.

'Right. Brenda, then.'

Given that Brenda was the cleaner, and only worked when the surgery was shut, she didn't expect an answer.

'Am I really that bad? I am going to be operating on your dog today. I do prefer my customers not to be terrified of me before I pick up a scalpel. Come on.'

He helped extricate her and Hendrix from the bush, half tangling himself up with her at one point when Hendrix realised he'd been scuppered. He made a last dash for freedom just as Susannah found her feet, but her legs were suddenly lassoed to his rather lithe trouser-clad limbs, and Hendrix was very vocal all the way through. She heard Chris curse as he reached down and gave a good strong tug on the lead to free them both up. He put his hand out, and she took it while she steadied herself. Chris pressed the release button on the retractable lead, and it sprang taut. Hendrix came to a stop and sat at his feet.

'Oh, now you co-operate!' She turned back to Chris. 'Thank you.'

'Training going well, then?'

Susannah bristled. 'It's a work in progress. Any hot-blooded male would fear today's procedure.'

Heading into the surgery room, Hendrix subdued but somehow calmed by Chris, she gave him a pet and Chris gave him to the nurse on duty to take into the back, ready for surgery. When the door closed, they both stood in silence.

'Do look after him—he's a good boy really. He just needs a bit of discipline.'

'He'll be fine, don't worry. I'll make sure to call you when he's in recovery.' He paused for a moment. 'Nice to have a day off work though, eh. Are you working later in the week?'

Susannah answered him without even questioning why.

'Not till the weekend. I have another possible foster dog to look at over at one of the shelters. They just got a stray in from the local RSPCA inspector.'

'Right.'

'So let me know if you know anyone wanting a dog. I think I'll have to bring this one home too, to be honest. Bit of a sad stray.'

'Mm-hmm. Shame.'

He didn't say anything else, so she really had no idea how to broach the subject of the charity drive. Normally, she could slip anything into the conversation. Given that she didn't even want to have the conversation in the first place, she was feeling more than a bit put out.

'Yes, it is a shame. Lots more like him too. Me and all the fosterers I know are packed to the rafters. The shelters are cracking under the weight of all those unwanted, unloved little doggies.'

'It is a problem.'

'Yes, but a problem that we could fix. Right?'

'Wrong. There will never be a home for every dog, given that things don't change. It's the system that's broken.'

'I agree with you there, but there is another thing we could do. Other than going all Targaryen and breaking the wheel. We could do the charity drive, for example.'

'I did already say that I would put the posters up. Didn't Cheryl tell you?'

'She did. We need more than that though, and Dr Ingham did say that the practice would help.'

'And I plan to uphold that.'

'We need more than posters. We need people to help, real support. If we could get the surgery there, offering advice, meeting the dogs, it would really help.'

'We have a busy practice.'

'It's planned for a Sunday. When the practice is closed.'

His eyebrow rose.

'I am on call.'

'You also have cover. It's just a day.'

'Of unpaid work, yes. On my day off. I might have plans.'

'Unpaid, but those brand-new dog owners will need a vet, and who better than the one they met on the day?' She'd thought of that one herself, hoping that the prospect of new clients might just give him the push he needed. 'Think of all the brownie points you'd score with the locals too. Puddle Lakers are big animal lovers.' Cheryl had told her about the complaints. Mrs Chan was telling all and sundry that he was a haughty fat-cat-shamer. It wasn't the best look for the only vet in the village, especially given that the practice relied on the villagers as much as they did on the practice.

'You've got a point there,' he admitted with a peevish look to his features.

'Exactly, and it's only one day! You can do whatever you were going to do another day. What were you going to do?' Silence. 'Well, you don't have to tell me if you don't want to, but—'

'I don't really want to, to be honest, and now I have surgery to perform.'

Susannah took one look at his haughty face and something inside the colourful, upbeat woman she was snapped. Just a little, a crumbled corner perhaps, but the damage was there. He was thoroughly ticking her off now. She narrowed her eyes at him, giving him her best steely glare, and he mirrored it right back.

So annoying. He looks quite sexy now.

She focused on her glare, and not his penetrating gaze.

'Well, I guess there's no point in taking up any more of your time, then, is there?' She gave him a final look up and down, as if to sear her dislike to his stupidly arrogant and rather hot body. 'I'll let you get back to your patients. No doubt they're all missing your wonderful bedside manner.'

She half yanked her bag out of the room in her hurry to get away from him. She was halfway across the reception area when she realised that every animal and adult in the waiting room had been listening to the entire exchange. They all jumped guiltily when she looked in their direction, many pairs of eyes swiftly avoiding her gaze.

'Bye, Cheryl,' she called, and then she was out of there. She heard the door swish closed and open again behind her, but it wasn't Cheryl's eyes she met when she turned to see who'd followed her. He started to walk over, but she didn't let him open his mouth.

'What is your problem, exactly?' She rounded on him as soon as he neared her.

'I don't have a problem. I just can't help, and I don't appreciate the disruption to my surgery either.' Following the thumb jab he aimed behind him, she could see the blinds at the surgery windows moving. At one point a little black dog snout poked through but was swiftly pulled back through the gap. 'I have enough on, being new to the place.'

He crossed his arms, bringing her attention back, and she found the move insanely haughty. He was so arrogant! The flicker of attraction was doused out. She could almost hear the sizzle as the fire was extinguished.

'I apologise for the scene, but you're so frustrating! You *won't* help, more like. Not can't. You've been like

a bear with a sore head since I met you, and I know I'm
not the first villager you've annoyed!'

'Ha!' he scoffed loudly. 'You've managed to deduce
my entire character after a couple of short meetings,
have you? The jungle drums of the village been playing
my sodding tune, have they? Well done, Agatha Chris-
tie!' Mrs Gallagher walked past them, her Schnauzer,
Herbert, in tow. Neither of them had noticed her coming up the road, nor seen the flickering of the blinds in
the surgery waiting room.

'Morning,' Mrs Gallagher trilled out to them both.
'Nice day, isn't it?'

'Lovely, yes,' Chris managed to stumble out.

'Yes, lovely,' Susannah replied, continuing to wave
and grin like a robot at Disneyland. Chris nodded dis-
tractedly at her, both of them standing there awkwardly
waving until she reached the surgery doors and went
inside. From the corner of her eye, she was pretty sure
she saw Cheryl's arms yank the pair of them through
the doors. Chris hadn't noticed a thing. He was too busy
tearing a strip off her. 'You see, this is the problem with
these villages. People are too...'

'Nice? Friendly?' She spat the words at him as if they
were bullets. 'Caring?'

'No.' He stuck his bottom lip out as a toddler who
had been denied ice cream might. 'Nosy. Cheerful.' He
levelled that word right at her. The way he said it, the
way he locked onto her eyes... The bullet word he fired
hit her right between the eyebrows and incensed her.

*Who the hell did this misery-guts think he was, diss-
ing her village?*

'Well!' She folded and unfolded her arms wildly. 'It

doesn't take a genius to spot a newcomer. Voldemort has more warmth than you!'

He unfolded his arms and followed her as she got closer to her car, keys in hand. 'Oh, so my mood is your business too now, as well as what I do on my day off? What's *your* problem?'

'*My* problem!' She gasped, leaning in closer and brandishing her key bunch at him. 'I don't have a problem. I'm just trying to do my job!'

'Oh, your job, how holy of you! It's not even your real job!'

How the hell did he know that? God, he was annoying! She had never wanted to slap someone other than her ex before, but her palm was tingling at the prospect.

'And? You have two vocations in life, do you not? Being a vet, and being a curmudgeonly old fart to boot! What are you, forty? My nana has more crack than you!'

'What *are* you talking about?' His hands slammed onto the car bonnet as she reached the other side, and she banged hers right back on the other side, mirroring him. They were circling the car bonnet now, leaning in with their clenched fists and getting right into each other's faces as they bickered. 'I don't have two vocations; I'm happy to just do my job and be left the hell alone. I'm not trying to be Mary sodding Poppins, like you! Swooping in, trying to save everyone. Give me a break and join the real world!'

'The real world! What would you know about the real world? You hide behind your table in there, with your foul moods and your scowling bulldog face. You do know the village thinks you're hard-faced, don't you?'

'I don't care what the villagers think!'

'You will when they all head to the surgery in town,

and you have no one to bellow at. The charity drive would help us both.' They were both nearly screaming at each other now, the air heated and thick. 'You're just too thick or too stubborn to see it. Look after Hendrix.' She gave him a final glare, telling him in no uncertain terms that she was trusting him with one of her dogs, and she wasn't a bit happy about it. 'That *is* your job, after all. Even if you do hate the world, don't take it out on him. No wonder you're alone, when you act like this!'

'Oh, really?' He folded his arms as she got into the driver's seat, stomping round to her side door and leaning into her window space like an annoyingly sexy traffic warden. She hated herself for noticing how cute he looked when he was mad. He tapped on the window, and the moment was gone. As she wound her window down, she considered winding it back up and catching his tie in the process, but then decided against it. Dragging the vet behind her car, annoying as he was, wouldn't be a great look. Besides, he had Hendrix to operate on. She could plot his demise another day. She could hear him chuntering away, but the words were cut off till she had wound down the window.

'What did you say? Sorry, I had my window shut. Never heard a thing.'

Given that he'd been ranting like a mime against her closed window, she knew she'd missed the highlights but the satisfaction she got from seeing his impotent rage was a balm to her stressed soul.

'I said,' he retorted, his face a picture, 'that I might be alone, but some of us are happier that way. You obviously are. Despite being an annoying busybody.'

'I am not a busybody, and you set the bar for annoying!' She went to wind her window up again, narrowly missing his face. Through the gap in the glass, he got the last word in. 'I just think that the villagers and their animals deserve more than the Grinch in vet form. You suck!'

'Yeah, well so do—' The rest of his comeback was muffled by the window, and she cupped her ear dramatically, motioning with her fingers that she couldn't hear him. He gave her a finger of his own as she pulled away, and she gasped in shock. All she saw before she focused on her driving was him laughing at her shock.

God, I could just smash his smug little face in!

'Horrible man!' she shouted as she pulled out of the car park, smacking the steering wheel for good measure. 'I mean, the gall of him! I am *not* Mary Poppins!' She ranted to herself half the way home, and silently seethed for the rest.

It wasn't till a few hours later that she got her nerves to stop feeling so jangly. She wasn't easily irked, but Christopher Jennings was the type of man she detested. Haughty, work-driven, rude and selfish. He epitomised everything she couldn't stand. And had been married to, once upon a time. The charity drive would just have to go ahead without him. After today, she wanted nothing more to do with Dr Moody Pants. He could keep his help, and his ruddy finger gestures. His laughing face would be in her nightmares for the rest of the week.

'Hateful man!' she shouted out into the ether. She saw to the dogs, made herself a cup of tea, and headed out into the garden with them. A bit of violent weeding would be just the thing to quell her rage towards a certain veterinarian from hell.

* * *

Chris checked Hendrix's vitals for the third time, and then cursed himself for allowing the argument and Susannah's barbs to get to him. The finger gesture had definitely been beneath him, but she got under his skin so much his fingers had tingled with the sudden urge to flip her off. He felt a twinge of shame at his actions now, which was only heightened by the fact that the whole surgery had obviously seen the free show. He'd lost himself in his work for the rest of the morning, switching his brain off and focusing on the medicine.

Hendrix's surgery had gone smoothly. The hound was now stable and awake, and looking more than a little fed up in his large cone collar. Chris had no appointments for the moment, so he sat down on a little stool they used in the back area, next to Hendrix's open cage. Hendrix moved a little bit closer to him, and Chris gave him a nose rub.

'She's quite mean, your foster mum. Did you hear what she said to me?'

Hendrix let out a low groan. Chris nodded at him.

'Exactly. You get it, right? I'm a good vet. I do care.'

Another low moan.

'And I'm not alone. I'm just...'

He trailed off. He couldn't even lie to the dog. She had a point. He had been a bit of an ogre. To everyone. No one had had the gall to say anything to him though, back home or here. Being called on it by her, of all people, was more than a little annoying. She didn't know him at all, yet here she was, making him feel bad for merely living his life.

'The point I'm trying to make, Hendrix, is that your "mother" is the one in the wrong here. I would help, of

course, but I don't have the time.' Her comment about
what he did on his day off came back to haunt him. She
did have a point there. In all honesty, other than work
at the surgery, he was home, rattling round his empty
place. *She didn't have to know that though.* It wasn't any
of her damn business, for a start. People like her only
ever saw the good, never the bad, and that happy-clappy
way of thinking just wasn't something he could do.
What was the point? People were horrible to each other
all the time, and they survived. A bit of dog-fat-shaming
and abruptness didn't suddenly make him Voldemort.

He knew it was more than that; he knew it was that
her job made him feel sick to his stomach. The fact
that she could be so happy to boot, well, it just made
no sense to him. He'd spent his fair share of time in a
hospice, and he couldn't imagine working in one. Selfish though that might make him, it didn't mean that he
didn't care. Looking at Hendrix, he sighed heavily. The
dog mirrored him with a sigh of his own, and reached
out his long tongue to give his hand a lick. Chris gave
him a pet, and leaned in close.

'You're not a bad dog really, are you? I hope you
do find a home, no matter what people might think.
No one should be lonely. You have a kip now; I'll ring
Cruella for you.'

He chuckled at his own joke as he went to look on
Hendrix's file. All of the dog's known history was
there, which wasn't much. Just a rudimentary profile
really, along with flags for challenging behaviour. As
he looked up Susannah's number, his gaze fell on the
details of the shelter, and something else popped into his
head. Looking back at Hendrix, who was now snooz-
ing in his quarters, he had an idea.

CHAPTER FOUR

SUSANNAH WAS IN no mood to hear from Chris, but she wanted to know about Hendrix. She let the call from the surgery number go to voicemail, listening as soon as the message popped up.

'Er…hi…huh-huh…' There was the sound of throat-clearing. 'It's Dr Jennings…er… Chris here. Just to let you know that Hendrix's surgery was very successful, and he will be ready to collect when you're ready. I… er…hope the visit today went well.'

Susannah's eyes widened. He sounded quite…*nice* for a change. Genial, even. Asking about the new rescue dog she had told him about too.

Strange. Maybe he's given himself a personality transplant at the same time he removed Hendrix's crown jewels?

She was in the car park of the vet's already, the timing of his call not lost on her. She had a very scrawny and matted dog in the back, and Cheryl had told her by text to bring her straight up. She didn't even have room in her kennels for the poor little dog, whose breed she wasn't even sure of at this point, due to the muck and the leaves matted in its fur. The poor thing was wrapped in a blanket, shaking like a leaf. She'd need a lot of care, and Susannah already had Hendrix on her plate. She was getting to the point where she would have to say no to taking a dog in, and she didn't relish the thought. It left her cold.

The dog burrito she was carrying sniffed the air of the surgery waiting room and retreated further into her cover. Cheryl took one look at the bundle in her arms and came around the desk.

'Come straight through to the back,' she instructed, smiling at the people in the waiting room to allay their shocked faces. Susannah saw them, and felt a fresh surge of anger at the people who had neglected the poor animal in her hands. Cheryl pushed through the door, and led Susannah straight to the room they kept in the back for longer consultations. Susannah's phone chirruped in her pocket, and Cheryl gently took the dog from her.

'You get that; I'll get this little one registered,' Cheryl said.

It was her colleague from the Elvedon Shelter. They normally called to check on their dogs when operations were involved.

'Hey, Adam, everything okay?'

Adam said his hellos and got to business. Chris came out of one of the consultation rooms, his gaze falling on hers. She gave him her best scowl as she listened to Adam's excited ramblings. Chris's lips twitched, and then he smiled at her before heading into the room.

'Ugh,' she said out loud.

'What? Are you not happy about it?' Adam's confused tones filled her ear.

'No, sorry, Adam. I was distracted for a minute.' *By an oaf.* 'What did you say about Hendrix?'

* * *

When she went back into the room, the little bitch on the table was now lying on top of her blanket while Chris inspected her. Susannah stood at the back, and Cheryl was nowhere to be seen. Probably in Reception dealing with the other patients.

'She's got a strong heart. Lungs are good.' Chris took a wipe and cleaned the poor dog's eye area, inspecting them and her teeth. 'She has a few teeth that are too far gone. I would put her at about eight years of age, so the oral care hasn't been maintained.' He checked every inch of her, tutting occasionally when he noticed something he didn't like. 'She has fleas, which we can treat here. Angie will bathe and treat her.' He began clipping her nails, but the dog had other ideas. She emitted a sudden high-pitched scream that didn't let up and got higher and higher the more he tried. The poor thing suddenly tried to take a leap off the table, and they both jumped to catch her. She ended up half in his arms, and half in Susannah's.

'God, she's a livewire, isn't she?'

Chris nodded, a broad smile across his face. 'Certainly is. She'll be fine. She just needs a little care, and time to gain a healthier weight. Are you taking her home, or back to the shelter?' Susannah sighed, the tiredness taking her over. She was back at work all weekend, and she didn't quite know how she was going to pull it off.

'My house, I think. I have asked on the WhatsApp group chat for a foster, but everyone is already up against it.'

'WhatsApp group?' he asked, a jovial tone in his voice. 'What do you call it, Fosterers Assemble?'

She looked at him, confused. 'What?'

He stammered a little, trying to go for the nails again but the dog was not having any of it.

'Like the Avengers? Can you do me a favour, please? Hold her? The nurse is busy.'

Susannah stepped forward, cradling the dog in her arms and comforting her while Chris swiftly treated her. 'There, all better.' He lowered her back down onto the blanket. 'She's a beautiful-looking dog.' He leaned in and scratched her behind the ears. The little dog, now discovered to be a very shaggy Pomeranian, leaned into his touch. Running his wand over the scruff of her neck, he sighed. 'No ID; she's not chipped.' Susannah's heart sank, as it always did, but it wasn't entirely unexpected. 'We'll get her cleaned up and treated for fleas, de-worm her and get her some food. I'd like to keep her in overnight, for observation. She's a bit dehydrated for my liking. I'd like to put her on a drip.'

'Thank you,' Susannah replied, earnestly this time. She was glad of the extra night to get organised.

'Do you think she has a shot of being rehomed?'

Susannah could see the dog shaking on the table, and she knew that it would be a hard sell. 'Well, her age isn't great for rehoming, and with her appearance and issues, it might be a while. I have work this weekend too; I'm not sure how much help I can be. With her and Hendrix and the others, it's all been a bit much of late.' She realised he was looking at her intently, and she brushed her melancholy away. 'Sorry, just a bad day. Preceded by a really hard few months. Hendrix has a home, though—the shelter came through, so that's a silver lining!' She said it a little too shrilly, and he noticed.

He didn't say anything. He nodded, taking the dog

wordlessly into his arms. 'Give me a second. I'll just settle her in.' He paused. 'Do you have a name? For her records?'

Susannah always named the dogs, the ones that didn't come in with one anyway. She never changed the name of the animals; they had been through enough, without an identity crisis to boot.

'I…er… I…' She scrambled in her head for a name, but he cut her off.

'Don't worry about it.' He looked down at the little dog, who looked right back at him with such sorrowful eyes. 'We'll take care of her. Give me a minute.'

He headed out of the back door towards the quarters, and she could hear him communicating what needed to be done to Angie. Angie was the best veterinary nurse around, and she was more animal herself than human. Susannah could hear her talking to the dog, telling her everything was going to be okay. Susannah sagged against the table.

Would it be all right? All the time she took these animals in, found them homes, but there were always more. More puppies, more owners who were ill-educated and unprepared for what owning a dog really meant. More family issues that led to the heartbreaking and unavoidable decision to rehome their fur babies. There were so many reasons, so many animals.

Her hospice job was her main passion, but she knew that her 'hobby' had turned into much more, and it was running away from her. She thought of Hendrix, cheered by the fact that the Doberman was sorted at least. The new owner had even elected to take him home from the vet's, and deal with the recovery. She felt relieved, but she knew the space was filled already by the bundle of fur she'd just brought in.

The door opened, and she didn't bother to look up. Her head felt nice in her hands, heavy. It was all she could do to stand up, she was so tired.

'Susannah?'

She met Chris's eyes, and straightened herself up, smoothing her rumpled clothing down. She smelled of the dog now, and she knew from the stinging in her own eyes that it wasn't exactly pleasant. 'Yes?'

He looked her up and down, and she bristled under his gaze.

'I know I look a mess.' She gestured to herself. 'Is she okay? How's Hendrix?'

'They're both fine. Angie is bathing Loki as we speak. She'll get the matted hair clipped off, then we can see what we're really looking at. Hendrix is a little tender, but he's happy enough. Wolfed his food down. He's got an appetite.'

Susannah snorted with laughter. 'You're not kidding. I hope his new owner is prepared.'

'I'm sure they'll manage.'

'Yeah, the shelter said that they'll collect him themselves. A bit unusual, to be honest, with him healing. I'm a bit worried, but they said he'll be in good hands.' Her own hands were wringing together now, her bag strap getting twisted between her fingers.

'I'm sure he will be well cared for. Would you like to see him before you go?'

Susannah blinked rapidly at him.

'Susannah? You okay?'

'Yeah, sorry.' She frowned, feeling her whole forehead crease down to her eyelids. 'No, I'm not sorry. We don't exactly get on. What's with the nice act?'

His lips pursed tightly. 'It's not an act. I'm not a complete jerk.'

'Not complete, no.' This was supposed to have been said under her breath, but it reverberated around the room. 'I would like to see him.'

He nodded, his arm sweeping towards the door. 'Ladies first.'

They headed straight to Hendrix's quarters, and Susannah's heart swelled. He looked so happy to see her, his tail wagging, his talkative voice in overdrive.

'Okay, it's okay! Gentle, Hen. Gentle.'

She sat down on the floor in front of the cage, not wanting Hendrix to get up and rip his delicate stitches. His cone was off now, but he was sporting a rather cute T-shirt.

'For his healing,' Chris offered. 'I do hate those cones. Some dogs do better without; Hendrix wasn't a fan.'

'Fireman Sam though?' she asked, clocking the decal on his T-shirt. Chris blushed.

'I buy them from charity shops, to keep in stock. It was either that or Angelina Ballerina.'

'Good choice.' She laughed, imagining Hendrix in such a shirt. 'That would only add insult to injury.'

'Exactly. More street cred with this one.'

They laughed again, and Hendrix was wagging his tail with gusto now. *He's quite funny,* she thought absently. She focused on Hendrix, who was still making noise for her to give him more attention. She leaned in, looking at his big brown eyes. She hated this bit. She always tried not to get attached, but Hendrix was one of a kind. She'd even considered keeping him, but she knew it wouldn't be fair or practical. He needed a lot of attention, as well as love. She had her neighbours and the other shelter staff to help, but he needed to be top dog somewhere. He deserved the best. She leaned in and dropped a kiss on his nose through the bars.

'I'll miss you. My skirting boards won't, but that's another story. I hope your new home is everything you want it to be, my darling.' She felt her lip start to wobble and pushed a hot tear away before Chris saw it. She was being silly. He wasn't dying; he had a new home! It was the best-case scenario for him, but the shock of it happening so fast, coupled with the month she'd been having…well, it was enough to make even the most chipper of people feel a little bit emotional. 'I wish I could have had you longer,' she whispered, wiping her eyes and standing up again. 'Okay, so if the little one is staying here, I might as well get off. Will you let me know how she is in the morning?'

Chris nodded, looking at her in a way she couldn't quite read.

'No problem. Hendrix will be fine—they both will.'

She smiled at him, before remembering their earlier quarrel. 'Sorry about before. What I said was a bit harsh.'

He studied her, his eyes narrowing. 'But you don't regret it.'

Foiled. She had attempted to smooth things over without dredging things up again, but this man was as stubborn as she was, clearly. 'No, I don't. Not all of it.'

There it was again. That raised brow.

She steeled herself for another heated exchange.

'I'm sorry for my part too. I know what you're up

against. I should have been a little less…well, surly. I'm not really one for getting involved in things. Not lately, anyway.'

'I get it. It's just, in my line of work, and with the dogs I care for, you tend to get mad when people moan about their lot in life.'

His jaw clenched, and she stopped talking.

'When did I ever moan about my lot?' he spat back, his whole demeanour changing.

'I didn't mean it like that.'

'Yes, you did. I haven't known you long, but I know that you say what you mean. I still have scars from the last tongue-lashing. You know nothing about me.'

'Neither do you know anything about me, but you still dismissed me as some kind of hippie weirdo. Judgemental much, or just plain mean?'

His meaty hand banged against his chest.

'Me! Judgemental? Mean I might give you, but I am not judgemental.'

'Oh, come off it, I only told you what everyone was thinking. Life's too short to be such a Dennis downer all the time. If you could see my patients, you'd soon understand.'

His face dropped, and his eyes went glassy. With rage, or something else, she didn't know. He looked as if his whole body was vibrating.

'I have seen patients like yours. Many of them, in fact, and it's not something I'd like to relive any time soon.' He looked straight at her, and she wanted to cut her own tongue out.

'I didn't know.' Her voice was devoid of anger, softer. 'I am really sorry to hear that. Someone close?'

'I don't want to talk about it, if you don't mind,' he

retorted, a little kinder this time. 'It's not something I like to talk about.' Susannah watched the utterly grim expression he had and decided not to press further. The pieces were clicking together in her head, and they added up to one word.

Widower.

The mystery of his wife, his sullen outlook.

He's grieving. And not very well, by the looks of things.

She'd never picked up on the signs before, but now they were flashing at her. She'd made a right dog's dinner of this, and she felt awful for her part in that.

'I understand. Well, I'll be off, then. Thank you for looking after them.' She lifted her hand to give him a pat on the arm but left it hanging awkwardly instead. It would have been too much. For them both. She was still stung by their argument. She understood him a little better though, and that unnerved her a little.

She went to check in with Cheryl.

'The dog's all booked in now, another one for the Bluebell. Chris named her Loki.'

Cheryl nodded, making a note on her computer. 'Aww, I like that. A nice strong name. Thanks, love. I hate it when they don't have a name, let alone a history. Poor thing. Good news about Hendrix though, eh?'

Susannah felt a pang. It reminded her that she wasn't leaving Hendrix here for the night, she was leaving him for ever. It made her grey mood even worse.

'Yes, losing his testicles and gaining a for-ever home, all in one day! He's had quite the adventure. I'll really miss him,' she admitted. 'I'm happy for him, of course.'

'You have plenty of wagging tails to keep you occupied,' Cheryl cheered, but she gave her a searching look. 'Are you okay?'

'Yeah, fine, you know me.' She went to leave, but what Cheryl said next stopped her in her size eights.

'At least you'll still get to see him. Old Frosty Pants says he's going to bring him here.'

'What?' Susannah's head whipped round so fast her neck clicked in protest.

'He's— He's not—' She jabbed her finger towards the room she'd just exited. 'He's never adopted Hendrix!' She jabbed at the door again, the keys in her hand flying around like spikes on a tumbling hedgehog. She bounced on the spot, glaring at Cheryl till she answered. Cheryl was up and out of her chair, looking at her as if she were currently talking to a demon. 'Tell me.' She half growled, and Cheryl's eyes went wide.

'Well, he has a soft side. Who knew?' She shrugged, and Susannah resisted the urge to scream.

Sitting in her car, she gave herself a minute to collect her thoughts.

Well, she had tried to put her key into the ignition, but her hands were shaking so much that she was still no nearer to sliding it in than she had been the first twenty times. She pressed the lock button on the dashboard, locking herself in, and pushed her seat button to full tilt. Lying flatter now, her seat belt off, she closed her eyes and crossed her hands over her chest. It was a little trick she'd learned just before she filed for divorce—and the week after she'd lost her temper and almost thrown a brick through her ex's Porsche window. He had been parked outside a restaurant at the time, eating inside with one of her former friends from the hospital. It was probably the one and only time in her life when she had felt such pure hot rage. The realisation had shocked her. She'd known then that the feelings would only get stronger, and the residual anger needed to burn out in a healthier way. So she'd learned techniques to quieten her mind, to zen her out, and to stop her from kicking people who annoyed her, like the vet, as a reflex. She was feeling murderous again at the mere thought of him.

Back to the technique. Slow your breathing. Everything is okay. You can't change everything. You can't save everyone.

It was a weird little mantra, to be sure, but it worked for her every time. Even on the truly dark days. She always got through it. When she thought about it, she was happy. She was glad for Hendrix. Chris did calm him; she'd seen it herself. Even she didn't have that bond with him. It was as though Hendrix had chosen him, she realised. That was the moment every person in her position hoped for. That look of love and 'it's you' between them, and she knew that they would be fine. She'd missed the signs with the two of them, because he had acted like Mr Darcy on arrogance hormones, and that had riled her from the off.

Hendrix had seen it though, and she laughed. A small little chirrup that burst through from her lungs and didn't stop. She laughed hysterically, so confused and amused by the unexpected news that she just had to laugh. Maybe Hendrix would be great for him—some company to laugh at, something living to tend to. It was pretty perfect, and she realised that her interaction with the vet was meant to be. She'd helped him without even meaning to. With a bit of luck, that crazy, loveable dog might just be the thing to thaw out Mr Frosty. Which meant her charity drive might happen after all. Especially if she let slip how much of a 'hero' Dr Chris Jennings was. She could see the headlines in the weekly parish news now. This was going to be great.

'Mr Frosty Pants and Hendrix,' she said out loud, and then she laughed even more. By the time she got home, greeted by happy faces and wagging tails, she was positively jovial.

'Hello, my babies! I have so much to tell you...'

'For God's sake, will you just shut up?'

Chris rolled over onto his back, pulling one of his pillows over his face and yelling curse words into it till he felt better. Another resounding howl sang out from downstairs, and Chris threw the pillow across the room. It hit a canvas on the wall opposite, knocking it to the floor with a thud.

'Okay, foul beast,' he growled, pulling the covers off himself with force and stomping to the stairs. 'I'm up! What's the problem now?'

Entering the kitchen, something hard, yet also crunchy, jabbed into his bare feet. Yelping in pain and confusion, he flicked the light on. A raw piece of penne pasta was stuck to his foot, as well as a fair few crushed cornflakes, and something sticky.

'Oh, no, please!' He turned to the open cabinet, noting the dripping honey bottle, complete with teeth marks. There were cereal containers lying on the floor open, half of their contents crushed into dust. Hendrix was sitting in his basket, covered in honey and cornflakes and looking as though butter wouldn't melt. In his little T-shirt, he looked like a naughty toddler coming down from a sugar high.

'Hendrix!' Hendrix lowered his head, groaning loudly. 'Don't you try to get out of this. I know it was you.' Another low moan. 'I mean it now, no back talk.' Hendrix lay on his side in his basket, looking at Chris out of the corner of his eye. 'You are in trouble. Shower time. Upstairs now, but wait—'

The second Chris opened the kitchen door, meaning to turn around and explain that he would get a sheet to cover him, Hendrix was up and out of the door, cornflakes and goo flying behind him. Chris took one look at his cream-carpeted stairs, and tried to reason with the hound.

'Hendrix, stay still. Your stitches. They could tear or get infected. It means more time on my table, buddy, and neither of us wants that, eh?' He held the sheet like a matador would to a bull, his steps slow. Hendrix had bolted straight to the top of the staircase, which he had decorated in what could only be described as a whitewashed colour scheme. It was all whites and creams, a nice bright colour to let the light in. Chris hated to feel trapped indoors, but right now he wished he had embraced some goth chic, or something nice and dark to hide the damage. As if Hendrix knew what he was thinking, his head started to move from side to side. Chris's steps were getting faster as he tried to corner the dog and carry him into the fully tiled and easy-to-clean bathroom. The whole room slowed down, and Chris took one step closer. Hendrix's head moved faster, and he shook himself out in the corner of the room.

'Hendrix, no!' Chris tried to dive onto the recovering monster, to stop the contents of his kitchen cupboards being spread any further. Hendrix saw him coming and jumped right over Chris's back, bouncing straight into the bedroom, where he promptly sat down on the bed. Chris hit his head on the wall, ending up in a heap in the corner, only just avoiding the stairs. His leg was wrapped in the sheet, and he had a cornflake stuck to the end of his nose. And from the smell of it, it wasn't honey that held it in place. It was dog slobber. He looked across at Hendrix, who was licking the food off his paws and leaving a Doberman-sized print on the bed cover.

'Right,' Chris said, sighing heavily. He plucked off the cornflake, threw the sheet into the laundry bin, and looked right at his new charge.

'I'm going to get a good stiff whisky, and then we are going to try this again.'

He headed down the stairs, crunching through the cornflakes and Lord knew what else on the floor. He headed to the liquor cabinet, and when he couldn't see a glass, he shrugged and took a deep gulp from the bottle.

He waited a minute or two, and then shook his head angrily and brought his phone out of his pocket.

'Cheryl? Yes, it's Chris. No, everything's fine. Sorry for calling a little late, but I wondered…did the er… shelter have any care advice for Hendrix?'

'Care advice?' Cheryl checked, her voice tinged with confusion and amusement. 'Er no, nothing but the usual on diet and exercise. We don't know much about him. Susannah deals with all that; she knows what to do. Is there a problem?'

'No, no, all fine. Sorry to have bothered you, Cheryl.' He ended the call, sighing heavily.

A second later, Cheryl sent a text message.

Call the dog whisperer. Be nice

She'd put Susannah's number at the bottom.

'Be nice,' he muttered, tutting. 'I *am* nice. Someone needs to tell Cruella to be a bit friendlier, if you ask me.' He took another deep burning swig of the liquor, and, after weighing up his options, he picked the phone up again with a huff. Dialling a number, he held his breath.

'Hello?' The tone was more confused than friendly.

'Er…hi.' He tried to speak again, but he realised he didn't know what to say. Heavens, this woman!

'Was that all you wanted?' she asked, an amused tone creeping in. 'To say hello in the middle of the night? What's wrong, did you miss me at the surgery?' Sarcasm was there too.

'No, I…just a second.' He pulled the phone away from his ear and took another swig. 'Look, I hate this more than you do, but I need your help, please. I'm out of my depth here. I'm desperate, to be honest.'

The line was quiet, but he could hear the television in the background.

'Hendrix making himself at home, is he? Say goodbye to your skirting boards.'

'Oh, it's worse than that.'

'Oh, that bad, eh? Do you want me, or Mary Poppins? I'm sure she could turn her brolly in your direction if you asked nicely enough. Goodnight.'

'Wait! Okay, I'm a jerk, all right?'

'Sorry, what did you say? The TV's a bit loud.'

'I said I'm sorry.'

'And you're a what?'

'A jerk. A big jerk. I am desperate, Susannah. Would I have rung you otherwise?' He didn't go as far as telling her Cheryl had told him to.

'Okay, you've grovelled enough, I suppose,' she

replied, a happy tone in her voice. 'Need anything bringing?'

He was so surprised by her response that he didn't filter his reply.

'Yes. A bottle of whisky wouldn't go amiss.'

'On my way,' she replied, sounding very amused indeed.

'You rang?' she quipped when he answered the door, a once-white towel in his hands.

'Oh, thank God you came. He's running around in the bedroom now. I've had to shut him in to get the door.'

She didn't need to ask what was wrong. She could see the paw prints and battle scars from the doorway. She held aloft the bottle of good whisky from her home stash.

'Oh, you are an angel!' He ushered her in, keeping his distance.

'I would offer to take my shoes off, but…'

'Don't. I stood on a piece of raw pasta in the kitchen, and it felt like a skewer. You ready for this?'

'Bathing a dog?' she asked dumbly, somewhat enjoying the night's events. There was definitely more than one side to this man. She found she rather liked him like this. 'Of course! Easy-peasy.'

Three hours, half a bottle of dog shampoo, and several meaty-flavoured bribes later, the house and Hendrix were as clean as they were going to be. The offender in question was now farting and snoring in his dog basket, which was lined with one of Chris's best bath sheets. Susannah and Chris had deposited him there wrapped in it and had not had the energy to get off the couch since. Chris had gone to get the whisky bottle at one point, and the two of them were sitting there, passing it between each other like bootleggers after a rough day at sea.

'I knew Hendrix was hard work, but that was something else.'

Susannah nodded, pointing her finger in the direction of his kitchen.

'Lockable cupboard catches on everything in my cottage. You have to treat them like toddlers. But smarter.' There was a slight slur to her words as she said it, and she hiccupped. 'Eyes in the back of your head.'

'I think next time I'll just move,' he deadpanned back. Susannah giggled, straightening herself up and getting ready to stand.

'I need to go. I'm on shift for the next week. Need my beauty sleep.'

'You're not driving, surely?'

Susannah shook her head. 'No, I'll call a taxi. Okay if I get my car in the morning?'

'How about I pick you up and drive you back here in the morning? I don't have surgery till later—we're having the new computer system installed at work.'

'Bet Cheryl will love that.' Susannah thought of her annoying receptionist friend and couldn't help but smile. She would love it, but she would never give Chris the satisfaction of knowing how much she'd wanted the surgery to modernise. She was still very loyal to Dr Ingham, and Susannah loved that about her, but neither of them had been about to ask him about it. His way had worked for many years, and he was an excellent vet in his own right. 'You sure you don't mind?'

'Well, I did drag you over here and ply you with drink; it's the least I can do.'

'The very least,' she mused, feeling her tired bones relax into the overstuffed couch they were sharing. 'I still smell of wet dog and honey.'

He chuckled beside her, holding aloft the bottle and looking at her questioningly.

'Go on, then, before I call a taxi.'

He passed her the bottle, his fingers brushing against hers on the glass surface.

'Why don't you come to see me at work, and see where we want to hold the charity drive?' She was lubricated by the whisky and, given that she had just helped him out of a huge mess, he did owe her. 'Come on!' She ignored his groans and choruses of, 'Oh, no, not this again.'

'Just one afternoon—you don't even have to stay long. I could just take you round the grounds, show you what I had in mind.'

'It's not necessary, really. I said I would help.'

'With posters, yes, but you know we need more than that. Seeing the hospice, and the staff, you will realise just what we're trying to achieve. Both sets of charities are so underfunded, it's a joke.'

She stopped talking the minute she looked at him. All easy traces of the man before her were gone. He abruptly stood up and stomped out of the room.

Oh, nice one, Susannah, she said to herself. *Way to overstep.*

He came bounding back into the room seconds later, thrusting a framed picture into her hands before he sat down again and focused his stare on the wall in front of them.

'My wife, Karen,' he offered as she looked at the frame in her hand. It was a wedding photo. Chris with an attractive blonde woman on his arm. They were both smiling at the camera. She looked every inch the doctor's wife. Elegant, well put together. Happy. 'She died in a hospice. She had tumours.' He swallowed, his jaw clenching and unclenching. 'It wasn't expected. Or quick.'

Having her suspicions proved didn't make Susannah feel any better.

'I'm sorry. I didn't mean to push.'

He waved her away with a shake of his hand.

'I get what you're doing, but I just can't go to one of those places. I get it, but I can't… Why are you holding the drive there? To split the profits?'

Susannah nodded. 'The dog drive will help the shelters, and they will be fundraising on the day. The hospice staff run stalls too, and they have an army of volunteers who all bake, sew and make things for the hospice to sell. Them having the gardens, with all the space…it just makes sense. The dogs will pull far more crowds in, and it will cut the running costs down for everyone.'

'Bringing your two worlds together, I guess.' He didn't look entirely happy with the statement, and Susannah knew he wasn't going to help. 'I get that.' He swallowed hard and reached for his mobile phone. 'I'll call you a taxi.'

She got up off the couch and gathered her things. Hendrix was still in his basket snoring, so she leaned in and dropped a whisky-smelling kiss on his snout.

'Enjoy your new home, mate,' she whispered to him. Looking across at Chris, who was watching her as he spoke to the cab company, she smiled at him. 'Look after each other.'

She thought she saw Chris smile at that, but he finished the call and was tidying up before she could blink. She followed him into the kitchen with a couple of empty plates from the sandwiches he'd whipped up earlier. She put the plates in the sink, but he wasn't in the kitchen. The back door was open, the light spilling out onto the lawn. It was a grand house, one of the best in the village. Dr Ingham had lived there for many years, raising his family in that house, like many other vets before him. It was an unspoken rule that once the departing vet wanted to retire, he would sell the house along with the practice—a way of ensuring that Puddle Lake always had a vet in residence. The house was a stone's throw from the surgery, and central in the village.

The lawn was huge, looking inky black in the dim light reflected from the windows of the house. It tapered right down to the few acres of land that came with the property, and wrapped around the house. It was gorgeous. It reminded her of her own land: peaceful, out of the way. In the dead of the night, she did her best thinking. Her best worrying too. She wondered what Chris did, when he was alone here. Did he feel it, as she did? Probably not. She stood in the doorway, lost in thought, and jumped when Chris spoke beside her.

'I have all this land.'

'I know,' she murmured. 'It's a lovely place. I've always loved walking the dogs round here.'

'Have the charity drive here,' he said suddenly, as if he would change his mind if he didn't say the words quickly. 'Have everyone come here.' He pointed off into the distance, where the field was empty, the bottom having a thick treeline that denoted the boundary of the neighbouring farm. They could just see the edge of the trees in shadow in the pitch-black night before them. 'I know you can't see it now, but there would be the space. You could have a marquee there, under the trees. The dog show could be in the field, and I have plenty of parking. His long drive had grass on either side. She could see it suddenly, all there. The stalls, the dogs, her friends from the hospice running their family-friendly games and selling their wares. It would be perfect here, but she didn't want to speak yet. Chris was looking at her now. 'So, what do you think?'

'We'd have to bring the patients who can be transported here, so they don't miss out, but I guess we wouldn't have to be so quiet here. Will you help? On the day?'

'I'll be here,' he offered, his eyes the only thing she could make out clearly on his face. 'I'll do what I can, but it has to be here, and I don't want people knowing why.'

Susannah reached out her hand, and Chris shook it.

'It's a done deal,' she said happily.

'Yes,' he quipped, 'I think I just have been.'

The taxi beeped at the front of the house and he waved her off from his front step.

'It's not that funny.'

'Oh, I think it's hilarious.' Roz's laughter was as wild as always. Whenever Rosalind Ormsby found something funny, it was as if the joy had to burst from her, and it was quite infectious. She was sitting doing her charting in a quiet minute on the night shift. A quiet night was a good night; it meant everyone was settled.

It meant that she could catch up with her colleague too. Not everything was discussed at handover, and Susannah sometimes felt out of the loop when she'd had a few days off—how the patients were, and their families, and the shenanigans of the staff on their days off.

'I bet he was rueing the day that he ever signed his name on those adoption papers.'

'By the look on his face, I could tell it was pretty bad. It worked out well enough in the end though.'

It had been nice, sitting outside with him. Oddly comfortable.

Roz snorted and gave her a shove across the table with her elbow.

'That was it? You drank together, and then he just waved you off? How come he offered his land so easily? I thought you said he was some kind of Scrooge about it? Wasn't it awkward when you went back for the car?'

'No, I woke up really early, so I just got a taxi up there.'

'Chicken.'

'I am not! I put a note through this door explaining why the car was gone. You know me—once I'm up, I'm up. Rodney doesn't care for alarms.' Rodney, her rooster, was a bit of a warbler of a morning, but the truth was she'd been reading in bed when he'd made his first cock-a-doodle-doo. She looked around her, trying to avoid Roz's mutterings of being too independent and missing opportunities. The hospice nurses' office was as bright and cheerful as the rest of the place. In here, one wall was filled with photos and cards, well wishes and little keepsakes sent in thanks. She hadn't told Roz the story about Chris and his late wife, Karen; she had kept her promise. It wasn't her news to share anyway. She knew better than to add this to the idle gossip around the village.

'Ha. Rather ironic given that you're a total chicken. Fancy blaming the rooster. So that was it? He's just in now? I thought he was dead against it. Last time we spoke you were chuntering about turning him into a poster.'

Susannah sucked her breath in through clenched teeth. 'I know, but that was before. He *was* dead against it,' she said vaguely, 'but I think Hendrix changed his mind.' She did believe that her furry friend had made it a little easier to win him over. 'He's a good owner, you know. Hendrix seems really happy with him.'

That wasn't a lie; every day since that night she'd seen the pair of them walking around the village when she was on her way to or from work—Hendrix bounding around, Chris laughing as he threw the ball. It was normally very early, before the surgery and her shift started. She had started to look for him on her drive to and from work, and she was always so confused by what she saw. He was laughing, smiling. He looked happy. She felt a flicker of something whenever she tried to assess it in her mind. The only conclusion she could come up with was that she reminded him too much of his wife, with the job she did. There was nothing she could do about that, but she could abide by his wishes and not spread his personal struggles around the village. His wife wasn't her patient, but her duty of care still applied. If she had nursed her herself, she would not have discussed anything with outsiders.

'They make the oddest pairing but, looking at them together, it's nice to see.'

'Another one less to worry about, eh?' Roz signed the bottom of the sheet she was working on, depositing it into the in-tray. 'Speaking of which, when are we going to get this show on the road?'

'I have a meeting with him and Cheryl tomorrow morning. If I can stay awake long enough.'

She was coming off the back of a set of night shifts, which meant that her body clock was more than a little skewed. She'd booked the meeting for half eight that morning, not even thinking about the fact she would usually just be getting home to sort out the dogs before heading to bed herself.

'Eager beaver as always. You do so much for everyone—you need to remember to have some fun too.' Roz's eyes were on her, the black frames of her glasses making her look like a stern librarian.

'Telling me off again? I have fun.'

'Really? When?'

'Well, I took the dogs—'

'No, without the dogs. I'm talking about fun with other adults who can talk back.'

'We had that meal the other month! You were there! That was fun.'

'That was Sandra's retirement party, and she's tee-total. We were home by half eight!'

'So?'

'So, hardly living it large, were we? Did you ring that bloke?'

'The bloke with the crazy moustache who gave me his number on the back of a betting slip?' Susannah checked sarcastically. 'Oh, yeah, I slid right into his DMs. What a dish.'

Roz laughed, but she was like a terrier with a chew toy. 'Fair enough—he was a bit dodgy.'

'He looked like an e-fit from a nineteen-eighties crime photo. I've taken lumps off patients that were more attractive.'

'They're not all like that though, come on! Get on one of those dating apps, get yourself out there.'

'No, thanks. I live in a country cottage on my own.'

'So?'

'So I don't fancy getting murdered and my dogs eating me, thanks. Far too scary to risk.'

Roz guffawed with laughter. Helen, one of the nurses, popped her head around the door.

'Mrs Sutcliffe's family are here, Roz.' Roz nodded, getting up on her feet in an instant. She nodded at Helen. 'I'm just coming.' She looked at Helen again, and her eyes scrunched up.

'Oh, God,' Susannah said.

Helen, who was watching Roz eye her warily, looked at Susannah. 'What? What's wrong with Roz?'

'Helen,' Roz declared, right before she put her face on and headed to do her job, 'show her your app. I'll make sure the floor is covered.'

She closed the door behind her and left the two women to talk. Half an hour later, Susannah left the office. The second she was out of sight, she deleted the dating app her mate had shoehorned onto her phone. Her friends meant well, but she wasn't about to put her heart out there to be trampled on again. Sure, Helen had met her now fiancé through the app she'd raved about, but still. That was one in a million, surely? She'd read enough bad stories to put her off dating full stop. Online was just too much right now. If ever, being honest. She watched the app uninstall and breathed a sigh of relief.

The fun barbs from Roz had stung though. She thought back to the last few events she'd been to, and she had to admit that they were all work trips, and things to do with work or the dogs in general. She hadn't been on a date in for ever, and the thought of lying naked next to a man had her reaching for the latest romance novel instead. She had to admit, her reading style had got a little more flirtatious, to say the least, but a woman had needs. It was just that she had been so hurt the last time, so broken, she didn't think she could do that again. She didn't have the emotional energy, or the sticky tape. She was whole now. She had her work, and her dogs, and her lovely little smallholding. She had friends, and even she and Chris had forged a sort of alliance. A weak one, but he smiled when he saw her now. He had a nice smile. She wouldn't dare to tell him of course; she just smiled back and carried on being herself. He still gave the odd eyeroll—normally at her brightly coloured outfit of the day—but she had been in and out of the vet's enough times to feel comfortable going. The clients seemed a bit happier too.

She headed along the corridor, calling into Derek's room. He was here on respite, and he had fallen asleep with the television on. She left the lamp on, tucking him in a little better, and turned off the television. She liked the night shift, and the peace it often brought her when it was like this. She thought about Chris then and tried to see the place she worked in through his eyes.

When people thought of hospices, they thought of cancer, or death. She knew that, and often it did mean that to the people coming in through the doors. It meant a step had been taken, and often those steps could not be retraced. She understood that; she'd held many hands, shed many tears, in private at home, or with her nurse colleagues in the break room. Some of the bleakest times in her professional life had been spent in that room, she and her colleagues holding it together for their patients and then later crumbling on each other. She knew that they were perceived to be like hospitals, but there was so much more than that to the work that went on.

She could hear Derek snoring softly, and she headed along the corridors, checking the rooms as she went. Chris categorically disliked her job and her workplace, but she knew enough about grief to realise that he was bottling up his emotions. Thinking about the dating app she'd just booted out of her phone, she knew he wasn't the only one. She thought of her meddling colleagues, the best women she knew with the kindest and largest of hearts. Just being around them might be enough to help her make that next move.

By the time she'd done her rounds, she had her plan in hand. She would help the hospice, the kennels, and Chris. It would do her some good too and distract her from the dating scene. Or lack of it. Expanding both of their social circles wouldn't be a bad thing, after all.

As she went to answer a call button, she was already looking forward to getting everything planned.

CHAPTER FIVE

'YOUR HOUSE?'

'Yes,' Chris said patiently, addressing his surgery team. Cheryl and the two veterinary nurses, Angie and Keeley, were both sitting in the staffroom looking across the table at him with faces agog. 'My house. Well, the gardens really. I will have St John's Ambulance there, portable toilets, the whole nine yards. The local pub will probably not mind people using the toilets either, given the extra custom it will bring. So that's the facilities covered. I know you all have contacts in the community, so do feel free to let them know what we're planning. And to contact Susannah Harkin. She should be here soon to talk to you all.'

He looked at his watch. He knew she'd been on a night shift. He felt a sudden flash of worry at the thought of her driving when tired. The woman never stopped. She made the Duracell bunny look like a monochrome sloth. She wasn't quite late yet, but he knew she'd finished her shift some time ago. He'd somehow along the way worked out her shift pattern, and he felt oddly comforted, thinking of her out there. She was his friend of sorts, he guessed. They clashed, sure, but he was finding it harder to be so melancholy with her in his life.

'So Susannah's in charge?' Cheryl pressed, a wry little smile across her face. Chris raised a brow.

'When isn't she?' The staff all laughed in response, and it gave him the push he needed. 'It's no secret that I wasn't exactly on board with this, but circumstances have caused me to have a rethink.' He looked across at Hendrix, who was currently on his back getting his tummy tickled. 'I know I haven't been the easiest person to work for since I arrived.' None of them said anything, which made him cringe on the inside. 'I just wanted to say that I am happy to be working with you all, so if you could bear with me a little longer, I promise we will get this place working well again, just like Dr Ingham wanted when he sold me the practice.'

'Hear, hear,' Cheryl said, lifting her coffee mug to salute him. 'Come on, ladies, cuppas up. Three cheers for Dr Jennings!'

The ladies all lifted their teas and Hendrix bounded around their feet, joining in with his own little vocal tribute. Chris blushed right down to his shoes, shuffling awkwardly from foot to foot.

'Okay, okay. Thank you very much. Till Susannah gets here, let's get opened up and get on with the day then, eh?'

The staff all started chatting amongst themselves, Cheryl heading off to open the main surgery with Hendrix in tow. He usually sat behind the reception desk with her, and he had access to the gardens outside. He'd slotted in really well, and as Chris watched him get a fuss from Cheryl he realised that Hendrix had saved him too. Sure, he was a nightmare around the house. He went to the toilet as much as he ate, which was a lot, and Chris's pristine furniture was now covered in dog hair and teeth marks. There was a rose bush by the back door that would never recover from being used as a toilet, and his grass was now patchy in places from where Hendrix had hidden his many toys. Some of the pet-owning villagers had brought in presents when they'd somehow heard that Hendrix was now a permanent member of the veterinary team.

Chris still had a full box out back, which he was going to donate to Susannah and her brood of furry charges. He owed her that much. Bringing the dog into his life had thawed out his customers for the better. He'd seen a few of them on his dog-walking travels. Some had even stopped to say hello. It was a slow process, but he was finding that he was a bit less of an ogre at work these days. No more flipping off in the car park. Thinking about Susannah's shocked expression behind the wheel made him smile despite himself.

He found he was eager to see her again, but he couldn't for the life of him fathom why. When she was around him, she annoyed the heck out of him. Her enthusiasm was exhausting, she dressed as if she was afraid of the colour black, and she was just so…happy. He'd never realised what a contrast he was to her until they'd spent some time together. The other night, at his house, it had been different. She'd been calmer, and he hadn't expected to see that side of her. Or that he would like it. She was intriguing, and the more he learned, the more he liked. It was quite annoying, and if there was one thing Chris hated, it was feeling as if things were happening out of his control.

'Roz, come on! Give me back my phone.'

'Are you kidding me?' Roz was swiping her finger

across Susannah's phone, her face like thunder. 'You deleted it already? I knew it!'

'Roz, I tried, I really did!'

Roz's eyes pinned her to the spot over her glasses.

'Prove it. How many matches did you get?'

'What?'

'How many matches did you get?'

'I don't know. I've no idea what I'm doing on those things!'

'The match is when you both swipe right on a person's profile. Did you swipe on anyone?'

Susannah looked at her friend and considered what the best way to lie was. Roz shook her head, and Susannah rolled her eyes. Putting her hand out, she pouted back.

'Please, just give me the phone. I deleted it, okay?'

'How quickly?'

'As soon as I left the room.'

'Susie!'

They were preparing a room for a new client, making sure the relevant equipment was installed and that everything was ready to go upon their arrival. The patient incoming was Beryl Richards, who regularly came in to give her husband respite. Errol was devoted, of course, so keeping him away long enough to give him the rest he needed would be an issue, but Susannah was looking forward to seeing her patient.

The two of them always gave her hope. Their love for each other had got them through a car accident that had left Beryl with life-changing injuries, yet the two of them were the epitome of love's young dream. Beryl came here to give Errol a break, but she would always joke that it was a break for her too. She'd been a busy person before the accident, and that hadn't changed now; she was always helping with the fundraising. Errol had run his own timber-mill company at one time. He'd sold up for the most part, after the accident, but their sons still ran it together, and he was still known as the boss man.

The pair of them were so inspiring, and Susannah always filled her well of emotional caring just by being around them. It gave her hope for her own future. An abstract future, to be sure, but still. They were the couple she thought about when she considered dipping her toe back into the game of romance. Something that just worked, two people who put each other first, and rolled with the punches together. Tightening against the strain of life, rather than bending and shattering as her marriage did. She absently rubbed the space on her finger where her rings used to sit as she waited for Roz to stop talking about what a waste it was. How her friend should be living her life while she could.

'I know all that, Roz, you know I do! It doesn't make it any easier, does it? Dating apps just seem so cold. People use them for random meet-ups—how am I supposed to tell the difference? Plus, the first profile that came up made me want to throw my phone at the wall.' Roz raised a brow in curiosity. 'It was Neville.'

Roz emitted a little gasp.

'*Neville*, Neville?'

'Neville, Neville.'

'Well, well, well.' Roz looked quite impressed. Susannah shook her head.

'Don't even think about it, Roz.'

'Oh, come on.' Roz jabbed her jovially in the ribs with her elbow. 'Neville from up on Oak Farm is lovely!

He's not been single that long either; Claire from the post office said he was considering going to Turkey for hair plugs. He used to have a nice head of hair, you know.' Roz fluffed the curtains so that they draped nicely in their matching tiebacks, staring wistfully out of the window onto the manicured gardens below. 'He was quite the dish back in school.'

'Yeah, when he was in short trousers, and he was always with Nancy Carrick anyway, remember? Since school!'

'Yeah, well, they're divorced now.' Roz leaned in, the way non-gossipy women did before they were about to gossip. 'Nancy's dating someone from Manchester. He comes in his flash car and takes her away for the weekend. I heard her say in the salon the other day that if she never smells horse muck again, it will be too soon.'

Susannah bunched her nose up. She didn't fancy Neville, but he was a lovely man. Having his wife up and leave him after twenty years had changed the man, and she just felt sorry for him now. He was trying to change himself for a woman he would never get back. She knew enough about heartbreak to realise that the dating apps and the hair plugs were just a way to appear as if he were moving on. Neville Rochester was a broken-hearted man, and she didn't see them hitting it off.

The truth was, she didn't see herself hitting it off with anyone. When she'd married, it had been for ever. When she'd realised that wasn't going to happen, she'd understood that she hadn't just lost a husband; she'd lost herself too. Her wardrobe had been muted down over the years, much like herself. She laughed a little too loud for his liking or wore something too eye-catching. She'd shaved off little pieces of herself, over time, for him. To fit into the world that had started as theirs and ended up being his. By the time he'd cheated on her, she hadn't known who the hell she was without him. She'd had to learn about who Susannah Harkin, née Danvers, was, and she wasn't about to offer her life up again for anything less than perfect. Since life and dating were far from perfect, it stood to reason that she would never find it.

'Ugh, that's awful. She was always a bit up herself at school. Poor Neville.'

'Exactly, poor Neville! On the dating app, looking for a nice woman to share his life with. He loves animals too!'

'He breeds lambs and has chickens—he's hardly David Attenborough. His dogs are all sheepdogs, and he refused to sign my anti-fox-hunting petition the other week—said he didn't want to ruffle any feathers. I don't need a man like that. What on earth would we talk about? I don't fancy him either!'

'Well, that's what the date's for! To find out, to take each other for a test drive. Some romances are slow burning. It's not always about ripping each other's togs off on the first date, is it?'

'He wears dungarees, Roz, not some silken Lothario shirt and sexy trousers. I'm a PJs and Jeep type of girl, and he's all tractor and double denim. Not compatible, and I don't want to date in the village! Too many people will know.'

'So? Everyone has a life, Susannah! Who gives a toss if people know? They'll figure it out one day.' Her eyes narrowed. 'Unless you were planning to just slip off into retirement with your bevvy of hounds…'

Susannah blushed. She hated being called out when she was being evasive. Roz always knew how to read her. It came easily after the years they'd spent working together, side by side. They knew just what was going on with each other, and it was extremely annoying at times. Times like this one.

'Well, what if I was planning to stay as I am? I'm doing okay: I have my own place, I can wire a plug and change my own tyres. I make my own money. Why bother looking? Come on, Roz, you're divorced. You get it. What's the point of doing all that again?'

'Because life is meant to be shared! Everything you just told me about is the boring stuff, Suze. You don't fall in love to split the gas bill or have someone to take the bins out.'

'Oh, I took the bins out when I was married.'

'Exactly. You can do everything on your own, sure, but why the hell would you want to?' Roz jabbed her finger towards the closed door. 'We see it here, every day. People wanting to live their lives, and be loved, and give love. Not everyone gets that. We see time being lost every day, Susie, and it's heartbreaking. When I got divorced, I was the same. You know I was.'

'I remember the gin and the sweatpants.'

'And the nights of crying on the phone to you, wondering what the hell was wrong with my life.'

'I remember.' Susannah nodded, making a sympathetic face to her long-time friend. 'It was rough.'

'We both had rough divorces, and, sure, I might think that my ex-husband is an amoeba on the backside of humanity now, but it doesn't mean I want to be alone for ever.'

'You're not alone though; you have all of us.'

Roz stared her down.

'I know, but it's not the same and you know it. Listen, I don't want to nag you—'

Susannah tried to cut into the conversation but Roz continued, shutting her down by talking louder over her.

'But I will! I'm happy dating Eric now, but I kissed a lot of frogs on that dating app first. It's life, Suze, and I'm not being funny, love, but you could use some.'

'I have a life!'

'Really?' The head tilt with the glasses again.

'Oh, come on, Roz, the bloody stern librarian look is getting on my wick now! I have a life.'

'I'm only "stern",' she bristled, throwing in a couple of hefty-looking air quotes, 'when I need to be. You sent me knitting patterns for dog blankets the other week.'

'And? I thought they might sell well. The knitting posse we have love new challenges.'

'The writing on them, Suze.'

'It's funny!'

'My mummy loves her doggies?' Roz was aghast. 'It's one knitting needle in the brain away from *Live Love Laugh* blankets.'

'I've got a pattern for those too,' Susannah retorted, before biting her lip fiercely. 'Okay, point taken. I have let work take over a little bit, but I am happy as I am.' *Another lie. Wow, she was racking them up lately.* Roz harrumphed in response.

The two nurses headed to the next rooms, turning down beds, checking equipment as they went. Seeing to the patients and chatting to them, making sure that they were all happy, that rounds had gone smoothly and everything was on course. It ran well when the two of them were on the floor. They were two arms on the same body, they'd often joke. The team was so close-knit, they were never flappable even when under the greatest pressure. Unlike her current scattered panic at the thought of seeing another man naked. Or another man seeing her.

'I know you're happy, and that's great. You're complete; you don't need a man. I know all that.'

Susannah signed off a medication sheet after checking it over for the fifth time. They could natter, but they were always on the ball.

'I just think that having a man in your life would enhance it. You'd have someone to share it all with. The vet's quite nice, by all accounts. I'm hearing good things.'

'Oh, yeah, he adopts one dog and he's expecting his sainthood through the post.' Susannah always bit when he was mentioned. She pursed her lips. 'He's good with Hendrix though. He's not all bad, but I won't be dating him.'

'You don't know that. Anything can happen on all those late nights, poring over stall plans and best-in-show entries.'

'It's hardly going to be all *Dangerous Liaisons* and whispering by candlelight. We're meeting in the village hall, with the others.'

Roz pulled up her lip, Elvis style. 'That sounds like torture. Can't you bin the others off and change the venue?'

'Roz! It's a big event; we need people to man things, to sort everything out. We have to sort out a beer tent, food stalls, the whole lot. Chris apparently pulled his staff onto it, and now half the county wants to help. Which is great, but I feel like I might have a small stroke at times, and the dogs are all great at mine, but now I have a pregnant bitch. I wasn't expecting it—the intake vet at the shelter missed it. The foster I had lined up can't have a pregnant dog in the house because her husband's off work with a twisted disc.'

'Breathe.'

Susannah stopped talking and took a deep breath. 'You see? I don't even have time for a stroke, let alone a date.' She clamped her lips together when she replayed her words and put a finger up to shush Roz.

'I heard it. Don't say it. Let it go. You know what I meant. I can't date, Roz. I'd have to get dressed up, and shave, and…get naked! I can't get naked with a man, I just can't.'

Grant, a member of staff, came walking into the room at that exact moment, brandishing a set of forms on a clipboard. The two women looked at him, and he squeaked in panic.

'Leave the forms on the bed—I'll just be a minute,' Roz instructed him in a kindly way, and he sagged with relief, throwing the contents of his arms onto the bed and power walking his way out of the room. The door clicked shut behind him.

'Well, that was embarrassing. Very professional of me.'

'Oh, give over. Grant's heard a woman talk about sex before.'

'I wasn't talking about sex. I was talking about being naked. I can't have sex if I don't want to take my knickers off, can I?'

Roz half pulled her out of the room and on with their duties.

'Listen, you never know. You don't want to get on the apps, the vet's nice. Single…'

'Wow, nice. Single. What's next? Has a pulse?'

'You'd be surprised. I dated a few zombies myself—you know, the obsessive types.'

Susannah nodded; she knew all too well. Work was the 'brains' her zombie ex-husband craved.

'He gets under your skin—I think that's worth exploring.' They headed to the office.

'If every man who got under my skin annoyed me, I'd be shagging half the neighbourhood.'

Grant was sitting in the easy chair, eating a yoghurt. He put it down and left wordlessly, putting his head down as he passed between the two women.

'Oh, dear God, I did it again.'

Roz's laughter exploded the second he closed the door. It took her a good three minutes to pull herself together, and that was even after Susannah had tried to kick her under the table, hitting the metal pole with her own toes instead.

'Damn you, I broke my toe!'

'Serves you right. Now go and ask the guy out, before I ask him out for you. Get him to look at your broken toe.'

'He's a vet!' She grimaced, pulling off her shoe and feeling relief when her toe wasn't splattered across the inside of her shoe. It felt more dramatic than it was. 'Not exactly his field.'

Roz clicked her ID into the computer, bringing up her email.

'You always had chicken feet—he'll have a look.'

Susannah's eyes narrowed.

Best mates always know what to say to wind you up. I don't dance like a chicken! I'm a swan. Especially after a couple of whiskies...

'Hey! My chicken feet stay in the best-friend vault, remember?'

Roz tapped away at her screen, but Susannah knew she was listening.

'I don't want to make it weird with the vet. He's not...'

'Hot? Single? An animal lover?'

'Available,' she ventured.

'Well, you won't know till you ask him.'

'No, Roz!'

Roz stood up suddenly, pulling her glasses off and addressing her friend with a steely glare. Her eyes were sparkling with mirth, giving her away as always.

'Oh, yeah? You ask him out before the next village meeting thingy, or I email him the tiddly chicken video.'

Pure horror filled her.

'You wouldn't dare show him the tiddly chicken video. You promised to take that to the grave.'

'And I will, but this is for your own good.'

'How is showing any hot-blooded man the chicken video going to get me a boyfriend?'

'We'll see. I'll give you two weeks. Don't bother asking the girls to override me either—I'll fill them in. It's time to get your feet wet, Susannah Harkin. You are dipping those toes back into the dating pool whether you like it or not.'

Susannah ground her teeth like a petulant toddler. Roz was unmoved.

'You're a rubbish friend, you know that.'

Roz laughed again. 'Oh, yeah, I'm the worst. Good luck.'

That afternoon they were too busy to talk, and as Roz drove away after her shift, leaving Susannah open-mouthed in the car park, she knew her friend wasn't going to let it drop. The parting comment was crystal-clear.

'Tick-tock, Harkin! Tick-tock!' Roz had made a noise like a chicken and laughed like a gurgling drain all the way to her car. Susannah muttered something about friends and enemies under her breath, wondering how she was going to get out of asking Chris on a date without Roz carrying out her threat. She had warmed to Chris now, but dating? No. It just wasn't going to happen. They were far too different. She found him stuffy, and too reserved at times. He thought she was eccentric and gave out such mixed messages that even when she thought she might be feeling something, before she could sound it out in her own head, he was different again—seemingly irritated by her, and showing another side of himself that seemed to come from nowhere. Or he was back in himself again, hidden from her understanding. It had been like Jekyll and Hyde at the beginning, but now she knew more about him, about why he might be like that, it annoyed her that she found him more fascinating as a result.

Two days later, the foster carer called again. Susannah had space now, and the pregnant dog was close to delivery. She needed to be moved now, and Susannah knew just what to do. She would call Chris and have him come to the house. A date of sorts, to keep Roz off her back. Once Susannah had collected the very pregnant and nervous-looking golden retriever—a three-year-old bitch called Melody—she'd already planned the conversation in her head. Once the dog was settled in the utility room, in a large makeshift birthing pen filled with blankets, Susannah left the exhausted and slightly stressed dog to sleep, keeping the door open so she could observe her.

When her friend Trudy came over a couple of hours later, Susannah was on her hands and knees scrubbing the kitchen tiles with a hard-bristled brush. Trudy was another animal foster mum and actual mum of Isabelle, who was fifteen and puppy mad. They looked at the sparkling floor, and back to Susannah.

'You okay? I think it's clean.'

'Oh, hi! Thanks for coming. I don't want to leave her for long but the dogs need a good run outside.' Isabelle was already peering into the utility room, over the safety gate.

'Aww, she's beautiful.'

Trudy smiled at her daughter and peered over the gate at the sleeping dog.

'Aww, yes, she's lovely. Don't you rush; she'll be fine with us. We've got some schoolwork to do, haven't we, Issy?' Isabelle groaned. 'Home-schooling, don't you just love it?'

From the look on Trudy's face, Susannah knew it was a bit of an ordeal for them both. Isabelle struggled at school, and, with her autism, the outdoors and animals were the only things that made her really happy, that made her feel like herself. She was going to be following in her mum's footsteps, that was for sure. Trudy had a horse stable, offering full livery, and her place was always booked out.

'Well, my computer is in the study, if you want to use the Internet, and I have all kinds of stationery in there. You just help yourself, okay? I made oat muffins too, there on the side.' Isabelle grinned at her, and

Susannah winked back. Issy had been a sucker for her oat muffins since she was little.

Trudy walked into the hall, leaving Issy to boot up the computer and log into her online lesson.

'What's with all the nervous energy?' she asked as soon as her daughter was out of earshot.

Susannah finished scrubbing the rest of the kitchen floor and snapped off her Marigolds.

'Me? Oh, nothing. I just thought I'd make sure it was ready for Melody, that's all.'

'Uh-huh,' Trudy said non-committally. 'I'm pretty sure *you* could give birth on this floor, never mind Melody. What's eating you?'

'Oh, nothing much. I have to ask a man out, and I don't really want to, but Roz—'

Trudy went to flick on the kettle, getting a can of Coke out of her bag and giving it to her daughter, who was busy rolling her eyes at the teacher on the screen in front of her. She closed the study door a little, and then rounded on her friend.

'Right, we have at least half an hour. The dogs can wait. Spill. What man?'

Trudy had drunk half her tea by the time Susanna had told her all about the vet, the issues hampering her charity-drive rollout, and Roz's threat to out her if she didn't ask Chris out.

'And what's the dirt she's got on you?' Trudy pressed, a wry smile across her features.

'My dancing.'

Trudy tried not to laugh but failed miserably. 'Oh, that Roz, she's a wily one.'

'She's evil incarnate, and she has video evidence.'

Trudy whistled through her teeth.

'Oh, then you're just going to have to do it! It will be fine, I'm sure. You get on, right? You and Chris? I've only met him once. He came to check on Misty. He seemed nice. Misty liked him well enough.'

Misty was her mare, a black horse with white markings that was a bit of a character around the village, known for picking apples off people's trees on her hacks out.

'Well, yeah, now I suppose we do, but there's more to this. He's not in the right place to date anyone.'

Trudy frowned. 'But you are.'

'Yes!' Susannah exclaimed. 'I mean, no! No, well, not on an app anyway. Oh, God, Trude, I don't know.' She sagged down in her chair, hating her own indecision. She wished she could rip it out, like the grey hair she'd yanked out earlier that morning in the mirror. 'Roz has a point, but I'm okay on my own.'

Trudy pointed to the pristine kitchen floor. 'Yeah, sure you are.'

'I was only cleaning!'

Trudy shook her head. 'This isn't cleaning, this is… something else.'

'A bit of obsessive bleaching is hardly a sign of sexual frustration, Trude.'

'No, but it's not as much fun as the alternative, is it? You look great; you're athletic, independent. You have your own house and car. Why wouldn't a man love to meet someone like you? You don't have to go mad with it. A couple of dates won't kill you, Susie.' She eyed the closed study door, where the two women could hear Issy's teacher instructing the class. 'Listen, I would love to have a night out. One where I can dress up and not be Issy's mum. Just for one day. It's not good to be isolated, trust me.'

Susannah felt awful for offloading about her problems to her friend. She knew that Issy's condition meant that Trudy often preferred her own company, and the comforts of home. Trudy was a foster carer because she wanted to keep busy at home. Susannah suddenly felt awful for appearing so selfish.

'I'm sorry, I didn't mean to moan at you.'

Trudy waved her off. 'Don't be daft! I'm happy with my lot, Susie. I have my house, and my work, and Issy is my priority.' She looked around her at the immaculate home that Susannah had cultivated since her divorce. 'You have a lovely life too. I just sometimes wish you would realise that you don't have to be alone if you don't want to be. I'm happily single for now.'

That was the difference, Susannah realised. Trudy was busy with a full life, just like her, but she didn't need anyone else in her life. When Susannah thought of the long winter nights ahead, cosied up indoors with her dogs, she knew that, while it seemed idyllic, it soon lost its appeal. The animals were great, but they didn't talk back. They didn't hold her in their arms after a bad day at work, even as comforting as they were. Hell, even Hendrix had thawed out the vet's heart. If a bit of company could do that for him, surely she could see the merits in trying.

Trudy and Issy went home for lunch once the lessons had finished and Susannah was back from walking the dogs. The long, brisk walk had really helped to clear her head. Trudy and Roz, Helen, Cheryl…they were all so bent on getting her out there. Maybe they had a point.

It had been a long time since she'd looked at a male. One without a hairy snout anyway.

She checked on Melody, who was now eating quite happily in her room, and reached for her mobile. The surgery would be closing in half an hour, and she needed to stop talking herself in and out of what she was about to do.

Chris had just waved off the last patient of the day when the mobile in his coat pocket rang. Susannah. He jabbed at the button.

'Don't tell me,' he said with a grin. 'You've rescued a wild cheetah from your back garden, and you want me to clip his nails.'

'Ha ha,' she retorted. 'Very funny.'

The line went quiet, and Chris looked at the display in confusion. 'Susie, you there?'

'Yes, sorry! I'm here. Less of the Susie too. No one calls me that.'

Good, he thought to himself. *I like hearing that. Susie will be sticking, if I have anything to do with it.*

'I think it's rather cute. So, what's up?'

'Nothing.' She sounded weird, and Chris wondered if work had upset her. 'I just wanted to ask you if you would come and check one of the new dogs I have. This one's pregnant, due any day.'

'Well, congratulations! Grandma Harkin, eh?'

Her reply came through gritted teeth. 'Again, very funny. I thought if you were free tonight perhaps I can make a bit of dinner, if you have time.'

'Dinner?' he checked, wondering if his ears were suddenly playing up. 'At your house?'

'Tonight, yes. Only if you have the time, of course.'

Chris looked at the phone display again before answering. He was so shocked he felt the need to check he wasn't being pranked.

'Er, no… I mean, yes, I have the time. That would be great.'

'Really? Oh, that's great, then.'

A lot of greats being thrown around. Awkward.

'Do I need to bring anything?'

'No, just yourself. Maybe your kit bag, for Melody.'

'Melody? Will she be joining us?'

'She's the dog, Chris.'

'Oh! Okay! Just the two of us, then.'

He heard her slight hesitation on the line and pondered for the fifth time that minute what was happening.

'Yes, I guess it is. Just the two of us.' Another long pause. 'Seven, then?'

'Seven's great.'

'Great, see you then?'

'See you then.'

'Bye.'

'Bye.'

'Bye.'

The phone line went dead, but not before he heard the start of what sounded like a groan coming from the other end. A minute later, she rang back.

'Changed your mind?'

'What? Er…no. Why, have you?'

'No, it's been a while since I had a night away from the TV. I do need to come and assess the dog.'

'Of course, yes, I was just ringing back to tell you my address.'

She reeled it off, and he pretended to note it down. The truth was, he'd already looked her up on the computer. Nothing in the realms of stalking, but he had found himself intrigued whenever she'd spoken of her house. Solitary Cottage wasn't a name he was likely to forget.

'Okay, I'll see you tonight, then.'

'Okay, see you soon.' She rang off again, and he was still standing there staring at his phone when Cheryl walked in, coat on and keys in hand.

'Chris, everything okay?'

'Yes.' He smiled. 'Actually, I think I've just been asked on a date.'

Cheryl's face was a picture.

'Really? That's...amazing.'

Chris chuckled, shutting everything down and heading out to Reception with her. Hendrix was already sitting there by the door, his lead in his mouth. He had got to know the drill of working together, and now you could set a clock by the dog.

'Who's the lucky lady?' Cheryl asked as he walked her over to their cars. 'Anyone I know?'

'Melody,' he said with a smile. 'I don't think you've met.'

CHAPTER SIX

HE KNOCKED AT the door and smiled at the cacophony of dogs barking. It was quite remote, he noted, but friendly-looking. The whole place reminded him of her: bright colours everywhere and little homely touches to the gardens and outside of her home that made it easier to walk towards. The place felt like a warm hug, and then the door opened, and she was there.

She looked a little more muted that evening, but that didn't stop her from lighting up the room. He hardly noticed what she was wearing at first. It was her he saw. Her white dress was casual, but fitted her so well it clung to her skin in all the right places. Chris forgot who he was for a second as he took her in. It had a vee neckline, showing off her pale, freckly skin. Her hair was brightened by the white of her dress, and her green eyes stared right at him.

'Hi,' she stammered, hopping from foot to foot. He followed the motion, taking in a pair of shapely legs, long and beautiful. Her slender ankles were encased in...in...

'Hi. I like your slippers.' Her face dropped, and she looked down in dismay at her novelty unicorn slippers. 'Cute.' She had flushed, and it made her eyes all the more noticeable. He had to keep looking away to keep his balance.

She doesn't always look like this. What's the deal?

'Yeah, present from a workmate. I forgot to change. Come on in.' She noticed the wine in his hands, and the kit bag. 'Oh, is that for us?'

'Well, the kit bag's for the dog, and this is to say thanks for the meal.'

'You haven't eaten it yet.' She beamed, taking the wine and kicking the slippers off her feet into the corner. 'Do you want to sit first, or see Melody?'

He knew she already knew what he'd say. 'Lead the way.' He lifted his medical bag.

The utility room was nice and warm, and the bedding she'd kitted out was pretty plush. He sat next to the pen for a moment, letting Melody make her way over and sniff him out. Animals didn't like feeling cornered; they were much like humans in that respect. He could already tell from a visual inspection that she was due any time, and looked healthy and well, if a little underweight. She'd already been bathed and treated for fleas. Her bites were healing nicely, the fur starting to grow back well. He'd need to carry out all the checks to make sure the delivery would be a smooth one. A thought occurred to him.

'Do you have a birthing partner in mind?'

If Susannah was startled by the question, she didn't show it. 'Well, it depends on the shifts I'm on. Most of my cover options have people at home they care for, and others work shifts too. We make it work, but I might be a little bit stuck on this one.

'When are you working next?'

'Tomorrow. First of four night shifts. We've had a

few people promoted or gone to other jobs. HR messed up, so we're all pulling in extras when we can. Melody was checked over but the pups weren't spotted so this is all a bit of a last-minute situation.'

Chris rolled his eyes. 'What vet missed that?'

Susannah shrugged. 'I don't know. Not as easy as peeing on a stick, I suppose. Some of the dogs are so traumatised when they come in, and…' She trailed off with a smile. 'Of course, you know. I'll let you get on; she seems to have accepted you.' Melody was now licking Chris's hand, much to Susannah's surprise and delight. He did have a way with the animals. It made her think of what her mother used to tell her. Her father had always been a huge dog lover, and it had always given her mum such joy to see them together. She'd always said that animals were a great judge of character, and Chris, even with his moods, had charmed every animal she'd seen him with. He definitely didn't tally with the first opinions of the villagers of his bedside manner.

When he'd finished, he headed into the kitchen, where Susannah was at the stove.

'Do you think she'll last till after my shifts?'

'I don't think so. It'll be any time now really. Have you not got a foster that could take her?'

'No, I took her as an emergency case as it is. I can make it work. You ready to eat? It's just my beef stew, but I have been told it's quite tasty.'

The table in the kitchen was laid out simply, not romantic as such, but it was certainly cosy. She placed a stew pot at the centre of the table on a warmer, putting down hunks of buttered crusty bread. The wine was on the side in an ice bucket, and as he entered the room and washed up she lit a couple of candles around the room. He felt his eyebrows rise. Candles? With him? Maybe this was something. A real date? No, couldn't be. Could it?

'It smells amazing, thanks. I'll get the wine.' He'd already noted the empty wine glasses on the table. His stomach was gurgling, and the smell of her home, coupled with the tempting food, made him feel rather comforted. It was a while since he'd spent an evening like this.

'How's Hendrix?' she asked as she sat down next to him at the table. He was pouring the wine, and he gave her a cheeky grin.

'I left him with the remote. Told him not to try to watch any pay-per-view.'

'Ha ha,' she retorted. 'Will he be okay on his own?'

'He'll be fine. I would have brought him but I figured you have enough on.' He held his wine glass aloft as she started to spoon the stew onto their plates. 'God, that looks amazing. Shall we have a toast?'

Susannah, already confused by his rather chipper mood, looked at him quizzically, her own glass raised now.

'If you like. What are we drinking to?'

'Oh, I don't know. Good food, good company. We have the village hall meeting on Monday evening.'

'So you want to say cheers to an event that I basically forced you to take part in?' she said drily. Chris looked at her amused face and blushed.

'Well, yes. I say we cheers to the charity drive, and to the dogs.' He pinned her with his gaze over his glass. 'I know we didn't have the best start, but I do see how valued your work is. The kennel work, I mean.' He cleared his throat, pushing his glass closer to hers in the air. She didn't touch her glass to his, holding it away instead.

'Well, I would say that all the work I do is valued.'

His eyes didn't leave hers when he answered.

'I didn't say it wasn't.'

'Well, it was implied. I know you have an issue with my being a nurse, but—'

'I don't have an issue with you being a nurse. When did I say that? I don't pick on other professions.'

'I know, but with your wife and everything.'

'Karen? What does she have to do with this?' His nostrils flared, and Susannah lowered her glass.

She felt like necking the whole thing down. It had started so well. She'd cleaned the house, put on a nice outfit. She had reasoned with herself that while she had been a bit shifty about this 'date' with Chris, she could use the opportunity to see how dating would feel. Judging by the fact that they'd not even lifted a fork, and were already quarrelling, she knew the evening would be a bit less fun than she'd thought. Mr Hyde was here again, it seemed, and he was ripping a slice of bread into smaller and smaller pieces with his fingers. As if it were a murder victim he were disembowelling. He noticed her watching, and huffily he stilled his hands. She took a sip of her wine and picked up her cutlery.

She'd only just taken a mouthful when he spoke again.

'I'm sorry. I didn't mean to make things awkward.'

'I know.'

'I just don't like talking about any of it.'

'I know that too.' She lowered her fork. 'The thing is, sometimes you have to.'

His jaw clenched, but she pressed on.

'Tell me something about Karen—nothing medical or sad. You must have good times you remember.'

He sat back in his chair, running his hand through his hair. It left it tufted up at odd angles, softening his look now he'd seemingly lost his flash of anger. Susannah watched as he composed himself, practically seeing the grief winding around his body like a wisp of smoke. He needed to talk about it, realise his anger.

'She wouldn't have liked it here, in Puddle Lake.'

Susannah smiled, sitting back and eating some of her stew. She wanted him to talk and not feel gawked at. 'Really. City girl, eh?'

Chris smiled. 'Oh, yeah. She would never consider something like this to be interesting enough. She needed top Wi-Fi, good coffee shops, and access to work. We were both like that really, but I always thought about slowing down.'

'What did she do?'

'She was a solicitor. We met at university. We ended up with a bunch of mutual friends, and we all just kind of went through it together. A few of us paired off.'

'Driven woman; I'm impressed. Sounds like you had a lot of fun.'

'We did.' He seemed to be remembering that himself. 'We did, yeah.'

'Good. Eat your stew; it'll get cold.'

They sat and ate in silence for a while, the dogs all seemingly asleep now. Chris checked in on Melody, and Susannah refilled her wine while he was gone. She held out the bottle in his direction when he retook his seat. He took it from her and filled his glass.

'Thanks. She's fast asleep. I think we're safe for tonight.'

Susannah puffed out a breath, blowing strands of hair across her face. She blew again to dispel them and saw that he was smiling at her.

'What?'

'You make me laugh.'

Susannah's brows were up in her hairline, and that made him laugh again. 'You do! It's true. I'm used to you now.'

'You make me sound like an old sock or something,' she countered with a huff.

'You're very expressive.' He pointed his finger in a circle in front of her face. 'Like Jim Carrey.'

'Jim Carrey is a man.'

'I'm well aware of that. I only mean his rather rubbery face. You look like that.' The finger ran in circles again. She pretended to snap at it with her teeth, and he jumped back, sloshing his own wine over his shirt. He cursed loudly, grabbing one of the tea towels hung up nearby and dabbing at his chest. Susannah watched the whole thing and tried not to giggle.

'Sorry,' she tried to get out, but the end of the word dissolved into laughter. 'Oh, God, sorry! I always laugh at things like that. Nervous response. Take your shirt off.'

'What?' Chris was trying to rub the stain into submission.

'Your shirt will stain, you're all wet, and you stink of booze. Take it off, put your jacket back on. I can bob it in the washer.' She looked towards the utility room where a sleeping Melody could be seen. She nibbled her lip. Too noisy. 'Or I can hand wash it?'

Chris had no shirt on when she turned back to him, and for a second she couldn't breathe. The shock of his naked chest, in her kitchen, with the candles and the 'date' vibes, hit her all at once. He was ripped underneath his shirt. She'd kind of had an idea that he was well toned. He walked a certain way, with a confident stride. She had once thought it was a swagger, but she knew now he was just built that way. And he had the goods to back it up.

'I'll just take it home.' He grinned, and then he covered himself up with his jacket, leaving it unbuttoned. When she sat back down across from him she could still see a bit of his rather sculpted torso. It was very distracting. 'Thanks though. I didn't mean the Jim Carrey thing as an insult.'

'Oh?' Susannah forced her eyes back up to his chest. 'I don't have a rubber face, then?' She'd forgotten about his awkward observation. She was still lusting after his body. There was so much more to this guy than she'd first thought.

I'm actually enjoying myself.

'Yes. No. Wow, I am always tongue-tied around you.'

She snorted when she laughed this time. 'What? As if!'

'I am—you're too quick sometimes.'

'Well, you mumble.'

'I don't think I do.'

'Sorry, was that doo-doo-tink-a-do?' She held her hand over her mouth, speaking through it and muffling her voice. He laughed, giving her a playful shove with his hand.

'Sarcasm is the lowest form of wit, you know.'

'Yeah, but it's worth it for the laugh. You're not tongue-tied around me; I could say the same though. You were rough when I first met Hendrix.'

'Rough? I don't think I was that bad. Not oafish, anyway.'

Susannah's eyes narrowed. 'Oafish?'

He waved his hand, reaching for another slice of bread to mop up the remnants of the gravy. 'Oh, yeah, apparently one of my clients called me an oaf.' He clicked his fingers. 'A bullish oaf, that was it.'

She cleared her throat. 'Well, I bet whoever it was thought their feedback would have been kept confidential. Cheryl has a big mouth.' She huffed under her breath, and Chris's eyes snapped to hers.

'It was you!'

'Yes!' she admitted, covering her face with one of her hands and transferring gravy onto her cheek. She rubbed it off with a napkin. 'I did. I'm sorry. You were a bit of an oaf though.'

He opened his mouth to argue but smiled instead. 'Okay, yes. I'll give you that one.' He continued to mop up the last of the gravy. Susannah rose to her feet, reaching into the fridge for dessert.

'Thanks. I will kill Cheryl when I see her next.'

'Oh, no, don't do that. I couldn't run the practice without her. Why don't I help with Melody?'

He was collecting the dishes from the table now, and he opened the dishwasher to start stacking the empty plates.

'You? I can do that.' He shrugged and kept going. 'You can't help really; it's nights I need the help for.'

'Don't be daft. It's the least I can do. Goodness, that

looks nice.' She was cutting slices of the Oreo cheese-cake she'd made for the evening. 'Did you make that?'

'Yep. It's full of sugar but it tastes like heaven.' She grabbed a fork, spearing a corner of one slice and holding it up for him to try. He came closer, and she could smell the spicy scent of his aftershave. It suited him. Woodsy, strong. He leaned in, taking the morsel of cake from her fork. She found herself watching his lips, and he groaned in pleasure.

'Wow. I can feel my arteries hardening already, but what a way to go.' He waggled his eyebrows at her, and she giggled, taking a bite herself.

'Mmm, that is good.' They took it over to the table, not bothering with plates. Chris took another big scoop on his fork and tucked in. 'I wish I'd made two now. The girls at work would love this.'

'Do you often bake for the hospice?'

She raised a brow at his mention of the hospice, but she answered quickly.

'Yeah, I get bored some evenings.' She looked around her home, which was neat and bright, just like her. 'I love the cottage, but it's not exactly on a busy street. Once I'm in for the night with the dogs, the time can be a bit hard to fill.'

'I know what you mean. I have my work, of course, and Hendrix now. He's a little turd, but it has made me realise how introverted I've become. Walking him round here, I've met more people than I did in the city.'

'Well, that's Puddle Lake for you. We all live in each other's pockets, but we're nice to each other. It works. What do you do when you're not working?'

His blank face said it all. 'Not much, to be honest.

Which is why I can help with Melody. I can watch her while you're on nights.'

'I can't move her though. It would be too distressing for her to move again.'

'I know, but I can come here. If you don't mind me sleeping on your couch of course.'

A man on my couch. That sounds so alien.

'I have a spare room, but I couldn't ask you to do that. What about Hendrix?'

'I can bring him with me. I'm sure he won't be any trouble. It means I'll be here if the pups come in the night. You can concentrate on your work.'

'I can't ask you to do that.'

He put his hand over hers. 'You didn't ask, and you did feed me tonight. Throw in another cheesecake when you're baking next, and we'll call it quits. Cheryl and the girls will love me if I bring one of these in.' He waggled his loaded fork at her, but she was looking at their joined hands. Chris coughed and pulled his away to reach for the wine bottle. 'We're nearly out. Just as well—I have the car.' He hiccupped. 'I might get a taxi anyway, actually. Mind if I leave the car?'

Since she'd already done the same to him, she nodded. 'No problem. Are you really sure about Melody though?'

'Of course. She's my patient. It will cost you to keep her in the practice overnight, and I have nothing on. As long as you don't mind me being in your house alone.'

She had a sudden image of him taking in her rather eclectic decorating, but she did need the help. The thought of having a vet in her house, looking after the dogs and Melody, flooded her with a great sense of relief.

'I'm okay with that, but I couldn't ask it of you.'

'You didn't ask, remember? I'll come after work tomorrow night and you can show me what's what.' He'd demolished two large pieces of cheesecake, and he patted his non-existent stomach with a frown. 'I'll have to walk that lot off. I'm stuffed. Thank you.'

'You're welcome. It's the least I owe you, what with the charity drive.'

'I know, we haven't even talked about that. Don't you think we should get our ducks in a row before the meeting?'

Susannah groaned. 'I have a huge file—it's in the sitting room.' She looked at the time; it was still quite early. 'Do you need to get off? We can go through it now, if you like.' He was still patting his stomach and stifling a belch. She tried and failed not to laugh. 'I have more wine, and some Pepto if you need it. I am grateful, you know, for all your help. I know I'm stubborn.'

'Me too. I know I wasn't my best when we first met. I was a bit mad.' He tilted his head to the lounge. 'Shall we get some planning done, then?' Rising to his feet, he took the glass from her hand with his.

Her lounge was as neat as always. A book lay across the arm of her reading chair, the blanket lying haphazardly across it. She had two lamps lighting the room, and the fire was lit. It looked rather cosy, and she caught his expression as he took in the room. She took a seat on the large couch, the oversized cushions all bearing funny slogans.

'It's very you, this room.' He seduced her with a slow-burning smile before sitting down next to her. She spread the file out on the coffee table in front of them. 'Wow. So is that file.'

She rolled her eyes at him. 'Yeah yeah, I'm slightly bonkers and highly organised. I've been told. Do you want to do this or not?' She jostled him with her elbow, laughing when he pretended to be mortally wounded. 'Stop being a jerk.'

'A jerk now, eh? That's an improvement from oaf.'

She nudged him again, and he nudged her back this time. They were nose to nose now, and she was laughing her head off. It was a minute before she realised he'd stopped laughing. He'd also moved closer.

'This might be the wine talking, but I love to hear you laugh.' He looked at her in a way he never had before. 'You irritate the hell out of me—' he ignored her pout '—but you brighten my day, Susannah. Your laugh, it's something I always look forward to.'

She didn't quite know what to say, but he did.

'I've really enjoyed our date. I wanted to say that before we start talking about Portaloos.'

She burst into guffaws of laughter. He watched her with a very amused smile on his face. His hair was a little messed up, making him look more casual than usual. Ruffled.

'You're a goofball deep down, do you know that?'

'Yep. Just like you.' He looked her up and down slowly. 'Minus the colourful clothing.' He bit at his lip. 'I'm not all bad. I wish you'd known me before, when I was younger. I was different then.'

'Things change us in life,' she soothed.

'Nothing's changed you.'

She laughed again. 'Not now, no. It took me a while after my divorce to lick my wounds. I bought this place and just hid away at first.'

'Doesn't sound like you.'

He spoke as if he'd known her much longer than he had, but it sounded right to her too. They had seemingly been studying each other. Judged each other, yelled at each other, but yet here they were laughing, working on the charity drive together and enjoying the evening.

'It wasn't,' she breathed. 'I'm glad you came to live here. I'm not sure if anyone's actually said that to you yet.'

'It is nice to hear.' He was so close now. His eyes were taking her in, and she felt the stirrings of attraction sparking. 'Especially from you.'

'Your harshest critic,' she near whispered. They laughed again. 'What a battle-scarred pair we are.'

He laughed softly again, and something changed. It was so slight, so minuscule that she could easily have missed it, but he tore his gaze from hers, and poured them both a glass of wine.

'We'd better get on with the planning, then—I need to get back to Hendrix.' He wasn't rude, or surly. He was the man she'd come to know. The man who was so buttoned-up, she didn't think he'd ever get free. She hid her red face behind her wine glass, taking a good long pull. Trudy was coming to sort the dogs tomorrow, so she could sleep all day and then hide in work. Then she hid her disappointment at the date that wasn't a date. The non-date that had turned into a hot date and then back into a non-date. Just as she was starting to feel…

Well, it wasn't anything, obviously. She sat up on her couch, pulled a pen from the pile on the table, and flipped open her notepad. Closing her heart at the same time.

'It was just a planning meeting and a meal, Roz.'

'It went well. Must be off, busy day!'

'Roz, mind your own beeswax, you nosy co—'

Maybe not. Susannah huffed into the mirror. The staffroom was compact but neat and she was alone. She was very early for the start of her shift, driven out by Chris arriving to look after Melody. She'd been writing and deleting texts cancelling him all day, but she had to admit that it was pretty stupid to turn down a free overnight vet on call. She had to put Melody first, and what would she say as an excuse anyway? The rest of the night had been cordial enough—they'd even laughed— but there was an awkward distance between them now. Him hiding his obvious pain and her smarting from the rejection. She didn't even think he knew it was a rejection, and that was the worst part. He'd had a moment with her—she'd been able to tell when he'd looked at her that he'd felt something like she had—but they had both taken very different paths with the information.

And so, she'd been ready when he'd arrived at her house, bag in hand, instructions on the counter with her work number and other information. She'd gone overboard, but when she'd woken up that late afternoon, she'd been possessed with a need to get organised—her old trick for helping cheer herself up, and to feel in control. She knew her own behaviours well enough now, but it had given her the resolve to be normal around him. She'd been nice and friendly, laughing and joking, thanking him. She'd even cooked for him, labelling everything up in the fridge. She'd set out a basket for Hendrix too, so he'd feel at home at the cottage. She couldn't be mad at a man who didn't even know he'd upset her, let alone an innocent dog caught in the crossfire.

She'd always known he was grieving. She didn't have

an excuse for feeling a bit sorry for herself. She'd gone against her golden rule of never being second best again, but he was someone she liked being around. He'd told her the same that night. They had the dogs and the charity drive together; it was too complicated to just ignore the man for the rest of her life. She'd have to move out of the village, and she wasn't about to overreact like that. Not yet, anyway.

She'd felt the same flicker of attraction as she'd left her house. He'd leaned in to kiss her cheek, wishing her a happy shift and telling her to be careful driving. It had felt so nice to see him again, and he had looked good. So she'd fled to work, smiling and waving like an idiot as he'd stood there outside her house, waving her off with her dogs and Hendrix milling around his feet. She'd driven away so fast she'd nearly chipped her windscreen on the shale. Once she was out of sight, she'd cursed herself for being such a goof over the complicated man again. Now she was here at work, and she knew that Roz would try to interrogate her after handover. She straightened her curls into a bright green hair tie, and made herself a cup of tea before the other night staff arrived.

As it went, handover was quite busy. They'd had a lot to report, and Roz had been so tired she'd just hugged her and left to get home to her bed. The night shift was busy too, with lots of monitoring and care needed, and she'd not even thought about anything else other than the job since her shift started. She took her break in the staffroom, wishing she could have the coffee in her hand administered by drip. She retrieved her phone from her locker, checking her messages. Friends, a few junk emails for dating sites and dog-food offers. Damn the intelligent advertising these days; you looked up something once, and that was all they tried to sell you for the next six months. It was depressing. She noticed a message from him.

Melody is comfortable, but I can tell she's getting a bit moody. I think she'll deliver tomorrow night. How much do you bet? Dogs all fine. Thanks for the food. That pasta thing was amazing. Hope work is going well.

It was nice to think of him texting her from her little house, keeping the dogs company. She rested her tea next to her snack on the table next to her, and tapped out a reply.

Thanks for looking after them. I know better than to bet against a vet on matters like this. You're welcome. Chilli tomorrow night?

Sour cream?

Sure. Sorry if I woke you. She'd belatedly realised the time of night, or early morning, it was.

You didn't. I'll bring dessert.

Deal.

That was all she wrote back, after deleting her rather saucier reply. It was easy to fall into that easy to and fro with him, though. It was nice.

A deal or a bet?

Oh. So he was teasing now.

Deal for the pudding, no bet on Melody. I think you're right.

She'd seen enough pregnant and labouring dogs in her time to recognise the signs.

Can I get that in writing, please?

You just did. That's all I can do. How come you're still up?

Woke up. The spare room is choking me with its sunshine décor.

She laughed. It was a little bright, but it was a guest room. Obviously she wanted it to cheer her guests up. She giggled at the thought of him in it. Mr grey suit. She tapped back, checking the clock.

I need to get back. Don't moan about my taste, your house could use a splash of colour. Ha ha.

He replied straight away, and she felt the thrill hit her when her phone pinged again.

You shall have to teach me. We could go shopping? Lunch in it for you.

What? Was this a date? After last time… She only had a couple of minutes left. She rammed everything she had left into her mouth, trying to think of a quick reply. One that would find out the situation without *asking* about the situation.

She was still chewing when her phone beeped again. She jumped, scrabbling to read the message.

It doesn't have to be a date.

That was it. So he had picked up on the change in the air the other night. She knew it know. He was giving her an out. And now she was due back, and she still hadn't replied. She didn't open the text on her phone this time, so he couldn't tell that she'd read it. She'd pretend she was back on shift instead. It would give her time to think of an answer. Turning her phone off, she tried to push it out of her mind. Back to work.

No reply.

Chris woke up in Susannah's spare room and the first thing he did was check his phone. She'd not replied to his last two texts, and he had a feeling that whatever this was, he'd just messed it up. He wasted no time in getting ready for work, making sure he left everything clean and in order. He went and saw to all the dogs, checking in on Melody, who tucked into her breakfast with encouraging gusto. Hendrix was as loopy as ever, running around in the yard with the other dogs like an utter nutcase. He sat on one of the chairs on the patio area to drink his coffee and watch them, waiting for Susannah to walk in to relieve him. He'd used her coffee machine, long neglected in the corner, and had a bubbling pot of the fresh good stuff waiting for her. He knew she liked her caffeine. He'd even put the teapot on standby in case she wanted that.

He was feeling good about helping her, and the realisation that he did care had loosened something in him. They were friends, so why not date? She was so nice; they got on. He knew without a shadow of a doubt that he was attracted to her. Being so close the other night had spooked him, but only because of the depth of his feelings. He'd wanted to take her into his arms and kiss the hell out of her, but he'd screwed it up. It was becoming a pattern: she'd get close, he'd gnash his teeth and snap at her ankles. He was like a battle-scarred rescue dog. Maybe that was what she saw in him. It wasn't a good look to have, especially given the fact that he did want to kiss her. In fact, it was pretty much all he thought about. Which then brought on the guilt spasms in his chest, and made him think of Karen, and then he was angry and glum all over again. And so the cycle continued.

He checked his phone. Still nothing. He sat watching the dogs till he saw her car come up the long driveway, and then he girded his loins and went to meet her.

'Hi.' She yawned in his face. 'Ooh, sorry.'

'You look really tired. Bad shift?'

'Not bad so much as busy. We had a lot on and the call buttons were pretty continuous. I hope the day shift got some sleep. It was still a bit manic when I left.' She walked into the kitchen, spotting the coffee and half running to it. 'Oh, my God, I love you!' She whirled around, a fresh mug still in hand, her face a picture of embarrassment. 'You know what I mean. I didn't even know how to work this thing. This is amazing!' She was lifting the coffee pot on and off the hot plate in wonder. Filling her cup, she sipped at it with both hands wrapped around the mug. 'Dear Lord, that's the stuff.'

'You really like your coffee.' His lips pulled into a smirk.

'The darker the better.' She nodded her head at her mug. 'This should just about give me the energy to climb the stairs. How's Melody?'

'Still pregnant, and a bit flatulent as well. She ponged out your utility room.'

Susannah smiled, stifling another yawn.

'I'll let you get to bed. I'll see you tonight.' He bent in and touched his lips to hers. It was so quick she didn't get time to respond. 'Sleep well.'

He threw her a sexy final look and then, calling to Hendrix, he got into his car and headed off down the drive. She watched until he lost sight of her. It had been impulsive, the peck, but he hadn't been able to help himself. He'd needed to do it, and he hadn't regretted it. Before he got home, his phone beeped. He read the text from its cradle on the dashboard as he neared home wearily.

Yes, it's a date.

She'd texted back. The second he was parked on his drive, he grabbed his phone and typed one back, grinning like an idiot.

Glad to hear it. You looked beautiful this morning. See you tonight.

CHAPTER SEVEN

'MRS CHAN AND little Gustav! How lovely to see you today!'

Mrs Chan set the cat carrier on the floor and picked up her chin. She gawped at Chris as he smiled back at her.

'What's wrong with you?'

'Me?' Chris gestured to himself with his thumbs. 'Nothing, why?'

'You're so…cheerful. It's weird.' She flipped open the cage door, and hoisted Gustav onto the table. Chris took in the cat's new slightly thinner frame and his smile grew.

'Well, I'm just so happy that Gustav here is finally on the way to being able to reach his little kitty bits. Well done, Mrs Chan—he looks great.'

'Are you being sarcastic? It's been really hard—he gives me these big sad eyes—but I stuck to it. I gave all his treats to the shelter; he didn't speak for me for two days.'

'No sarcasm here—it's the lowest form of wit. You are looking after him really well, Mrs Chan. I mean that. It's only been a few weeks, but I can already see the difference. He's going to be one happy cat come bikini-wearing time.'

She was looking at him quizzically one minute, and then he was being cuddled over the table.

'Thanks, Doctor. I thought you were a bit of a git when you first came, but you're not all bad.'

'Thanks, Mrs Chan. Tell your friends, eh, ask them to lower their pitchforks?'

'Ha!' she exploded. 'That's pretty funny. I will see what I can do.'

She was still chuckling when he'd finished the examination. His day went like a breeze. All of his clients and their owners were happy. He was the best veterinarian he'd ever been, and he hoped this feeling would last. It was Susannah, he realised. She'd quite literally come bounding into his life and sprayed it with colour. He was looking forward to seeing her that night, before she left for work. He liked staying in her house too—not that he was snooping or anything untoward. He just felt peaceful there, with her stuff all around. She made him food and left it for him. He felt cared for, and it was rather nice.

Karen had been fiercely independent in that way too, but she'd never showed her care for him that way. Both driven by their work, but expressing it in different ways. But unlike Karen, Susannah found joy in other things—in people and animals. She seemed to want to help the whole world, and he wondered who showed her care. He knew her friends and the community loved her because there were photos of them all around and little notes on the fridge from them. She was obviously loved, but alone. As he was. It was just them and their dogs, and now each other. He didn't know how to process the feelings he was having, but he wanted to go with them. She was changing him, changing his world, and it felt good.

As he locked up that evening, seeing his colleagues to their cars and heading off to his with Hendrix, he found his brain picking at his happiness. He had compared her to Karen. He knew he'd done it before too, which was only natural since he was now effectively dating Susannah. The problem was, he was comparing them, when they were total opposites. It wasn't that he was finding one woman better than the other; that was not even in the equation. He'd loved Karen dearly, and they had been wrapped in their own happy little life, busy, ever moving, ever achieving, but then she'd got sick, and when she passed, he'd known that that life was done. It was another life entirely, compared to the one he led now.

Karen had never been one for pets, with their work schedules, and now he had the loopy Hendrix at home. He was living in a picture-postcard village. He'd changed, he realised. His wants and needs had sharpened and were now focused on a quiet life, and work. Then Susannah had come along, and they'd skirted around each other, and now he was dating her, and sleeping in her house to be on puppy watch. Was it the affection she showed to everyone that he craved? Was she a rebound? He didn't know, but he knew his feelings for her were growing stronger. He needed to work it out before he hurt her, or even himself. It hadn't exactly been plain sailing to get to this point. The irony was that he and Karen had talked about work too much, and he and Susannah didn't talk about it at all. There was a part of her life that he didn't want to know about so much. It was a barrier he didn't know how to cross. He gunned the engine for home, eager to get changed, and get to Susannah's. He knew that looking at her would sort his feelings out. He was different around her, but he was still himself. He just needed to be woken up. She'd certainly done that.

'Hendrix, I think we have a lot of work to do.'

Hendrix barked in the back, and it felt like approval.

'Hello? Susie?'

'In the utility room! Oh, thank God you're here. Can you keep Hendrix away?'

Chris dropped the shopping bag, grabbing his kit and shooing Hendrix outside to play in the back garden. Running to the utility room, he saw Susannah in a very short nightrobe, and a pair of silky white slippers. Her hair was pinned back haphazardly, and she looked stressed.

'Everything okay?' He dropped to his knees by her side, snapping on a pair of gloves and sanitising both his hands and hers. He noticed she was shaking.

'I couldn't leave her to get my phone. There's too much blood, isn't there?'

Chris shushed her. 'It's a little more than I'd like, but don't panic. You go and get changed, and I'll assess her.' She didn't take her eyes off Melody, and he could see the worry on her face. 'Susie,' he said again. His eyes finally caught hers. 'I've got her. You get ready for work.'

Once she was out of sight, he got to work. The minute he examined Melody, he knew she had a problem.

'Oh, Melody, you poor girl. Let's get your baby out, eh? He's got himself a little bit stuck.' The bleeding was from the straining around the pup. He got to work, being as gentle as possible and checking for any more blood loss. When the pup was out, he put it in front of the mother for her to work her magic. She was panting far less now, and started licking the new arrival. The puppy was out of its sac and cleaned up by the time the next one came. Susannah walked in, looking put together but terrified.

'She's okay. Two so far—Melody's a champ.'

'Really? Thank God for that. She was making some awful noises; I didn't want to touch her and make it worse.'

'You did the right thing. The bleeding was caused when the first little pup got stuck.' He pointed out the bigger of the two healthy-looking puppies. 'I've called him Tank. He's a bit of a beast.'

Susannah grabbed Chris and dropped a very grateful kiss on his lips.

'Thank you. I was worried.'

'Thank you. That was nice. Do I get one for each pup?'

She smiled, rolling her eyes. She leaned in all the same, and when her lips touched his, he pulled her into his arms a bit closer. This kiss was a little longer.

Melody was feeding her pups when they looked in on them. Tank really was living up to his name, guzzling away with his siblings.

'You do know your top's on inside out, don't you?'

She looked down and groaned.

'Oh, God, that would have been bad. Turning up to work like that. Roz would have had a field day. Do you want a coffee, before I go?'

Chris closed the door to the utility room a little but stayed close by to monitor them.

'Please. I brought some bits; I'll just nip and get them from the car while you're here.' He was almost at the front door when he turned back.

'Why would Roz have a field day about a wonky top?'

'Eh?' She was studying the kettle now as if wishing for a genie. 'Oh, you know.'

She could tell from his words that he was smiling.

'No, you'll have to fill me in.'

She sighed dramatically. 'I thought you might. She knows you're helping with Melody, that's all.'

'Ah, and of course, any vet call ends in a wonky-top situation.' His voice was closer now.

'No, I didn't mean that.'

'What did you mean?'

He was teasing her now, and his voice was closer still. She was pretending to be a barista-level coffee-maker to avoid looking him in the eye but he was beside her, and the jig was up.

'Do your friends know about me, then?' He was grinning like a schoolboy, and she didn't know whether to kiss or slap the smirk out of him. 'Me, you and possible wonky-top scenarios?'

She giggled, trying to push her lips together to stop the laughter. They were both so close now, the coffee forgotten. Almost nose to nose.

'Well, we haven't talked about that.' Much.

'But you do talk about me?'

'Well, yes, we are dating. Right?' Her confidence seemed to wane with the end of the sentence.

'Right. I do think we need to talk a little more about what that means at some point.'

'I agree.'

'Definitely more talking about wonky tops too,' he murmured. 'I'll nip to the car.' His eyes flashed as he leaned in to kiss her. She drew him in for a longer caress. Having his mouth on hers thrilled her every time, and she deepened the kiss, testing her feelings. And his, if she was honest. He responded to her fire with fire. They were both snogging, hard, against the kitchen counter. His arms were everywhere, her hands were on his, and only the ringing of her mobile stopped them… after a minute of trying rather steadfastly to ignore it.

'It might be work.' She groaned, pulling away reluctantly. She answered, panting, and he was looking at her, so full of ardour and surprise, the same emotions she was feeling. It made her want to throw her phone over her shoulder and run at him like a sexually starved vixen. Wonky top going the same way as her phone, over her shoulder.

'Hello? Roz?'

'Hi, love, any pups yet?'

'Wha—? Er…yeah…' Chris looked at her ruefully and headed past her to check on Melody.

'Roz!' she whisper-shouted, with that great talent women had. 'What's up?'

'Nothing! Why are you panting?'

'I was er…busy.'

'Busy or *busy*, busy?' She positively leered over the last two words.

'Busy with new puppies.'

'Hmm-hmm. Okay, well, I was just checking in.'

'Checking up, more like.'

'That too. See you soon!'

'Bye. You suck, by the way.'

'Ah, come on. You needed a nudge, yes?'

She heard Chris come back into the room, pulling the shopping out of the bag he'd brought.

'Yes,' she said begrudgingly into the phone. 'I did. I'll be there for handover.'

They ate a quick early supper together. He'd brought some bread and cheeses, thick local ham, olives and local pressed juice to wash it down with. Everything she loved to eat. When she left for work, he kissed her softly at the door, and waved her off. She couldn't even remember driving to work, but when she got there, she couldn't stop smiling. Roz was thrilled, and she didn't even try to rib her friend. Roz was too busy congratulating her on how good and happy she looked.

She did feel great. He was so different from who she'd thought he was. The passion earlier… Well, she had no qualms in that area. Not any more. She fancied him rotten, and she knew the feeling was mutual. When she went on break, he'd already texted her some photos. The puppies had now increased to seven, Tank still being the easily recognisable one out of the bunch with his bulk and the shape of his rather meaty head. Melody was looking good, and Chris had reported that she'd done really well. She messaged him back as she ate a fruit salad as fast as she could. She was still a little full from the supper he'd brought.

So cute. Thank you so much, Chris. I really appreciate it. Will buy you lunch when we go shopping.

As ever, he was quick to text back.

Sounds like a plan. Does that mean my bill won't get paid? I have a hungry dog to feed now you know. Do these little ones have homes lined up?

Susannah laughed, but it didn't last when she thought of the seven new homes she'd have to find. The charity-drive meeting couldn't come soon enough.

Nope, Melody has but the pups will have to be the star attraction of the drive. Another load of homes for us to sweet-talk our way into.

We can do it. Have a good shift, I need to get some shut-eye. Drive home safe.

I will.

She knew it was a slip of the thumb, him calling her home 'home' like that, but it gave her a warm, cosy feeling all the same. She'd forgotten what it was like to share her space with someone. He'd only been there two nights, but it was making her think that this dating thing wouldn't be that bad after all. In fact, if she didn't over-think it, she was actually pretty stoked. Enter Helen.

They'd been working together on a patient, a quiet little gentleman called Freddie, who needed regular through-the-night turns and care. They chatted to him as they worked, telling him what they were doing at every step.

'You have a pressure sore here still, Freddie.' Susannah softly tapped her finger twice on his left hip, and he turned slowly to look where she was pointing. Fred was a man of very few words—near silent, in fact. He used to be a jazz musician before he got ill, playing in venues around the world. Now he spent hours listening to the radio, playing songs on his iPad and filling the room with guitars and strings. He nodded once, wincing as the two women removed the dressing, cleaned out the wound and applied barrier cream to make him more comfortable. 'It's healing well; another week or so and you'll be back on your feet.' Early onset Alzheimer's had caused him to have a fall at home, resulting in a hip fracture and a lengthy stay in hospital. He was mending well, and Susannah could see his colour was looking better. It gave her hope that he would be on his feet again, if only for a little while with his fast-failing health.

Freddie nodded away at her with a distant smile on his face, his ears filled with the sound of his songs. Once he was settled in a comfortable position, and they were cleaning everything away, the chatter turned to all things men.

'So, Roz said you deleted the app, but you still look like the cat that got the cream,' Helen said.

Susannah pulled Freddie's door to a little, heading to the medication cart to ready for the next patient. As she double-checked her list as always, she tried to studiously ignore the question.

'Earth to Nurse Harkin!'

She lifted her eyes over the clipboard. 'I heard you, and now I'm ignoring you.'

'Oh, come on! I know something's going on. Roz has been cagey all week and you look like you've been inhaling fairy dust. Who's the guy?'

Susannah rolled her eyes, but gave in.

'Okay,' she said, finishing her task and heading to the office with Helen at her side. 'It's Chris, the vet. We're dating.' Helen's eyes were like saucers when she sneaked a peek. 'It's new; I don't really want to talk about it. You know Puddle Lake. It's not the greatest place to keep a secret. It's complicated, okay?' She rambled on about privacy, and the village gossip mill. All the while Helen was looking as if she was holding herself together. Rather unsuccessfully too. She looked half mad.

'Do you need to pee or something?'

'No!' Helen jigged from one foot to the other. 'I'm just so excited for you! Another doctor too!'

'Well, that's not really anything to do with it.' Susannah could feel her hackles rise like a cornered animal.

'No, but can you imagine, going from doctor's wife in the city to doctor's wife here, in your home village? A dog doctor! I mean, you couldn't write it better if you were a romance novelist.'

Susannah was well aware of the romance of it all, but the doctor's wife bit? That left her cold.

'He's not exactly like my ex, though. The two of them couldn't be any more different if they tried.' It was one of the many reasons she was attracted to Chris in the first place. 'Is that really what you think?'

They were in the office now, the floor covered to give them time to complete their paperwork for the incoming patients that week. They had to make sure that they were catering for their needs as best they could, making sure the rooms and equipment were ready to use and their individual care plans updated with all relevant information. Helen looked up, pen poised.

'Is what really what I think?'

Susannah played it down, but it had stung. Helen's comment had knocked her to her core, and now it was all she could think of. Was she repeating history? Was she destined to be a doctor's wife again, like before?

'That, you know, I have a "type".'

'Well, doesn't everyone? I know you've had it hard, but it wasn't all bad, was it? You were happy with him for a while.'

Susannah's face was scrunched up so tight she could barely speak.

'Helen, I barely survived the last time. We were happy, but that was because I didn't know who the hell I married.' It didn't matter that he was a doctor. She hadn't gone out and set her cap at him. He'd pursued her. They'd got on, he was good at work, easy to be around. She'd thought he was the one, and she'd changed herself to allow him to follow his dreams. And then, like a shifty pigeon, he'd gone and pooped all over the patio, full of the food she'd provided. It was a pretty rough analogy for a relationship ending. She was the one who'd got pooped on, and she wasn't about to offer herself up for more of the same. She realised Helen was staring at her open-mouthed, and she felt bad for a second. Helen's words had been a little close to the bone though. She'd been there; she knew what a toll it had taken on Susannah.

'Look, Hel, I—'

'No, I'm sorry. I didn't mean for it to come out that way.'

'It's fine. I need to go and check on Heather. Cover the floor?'

Helen knew she was being dismissed, and Susannah ignored her hurt look. She was butting in, and Susannah wanted to crawl away and inspect her wounds. She *never* liked to think of the good times with her ex, and Helen knew that too. It was getting too much, even for village life.

She wished she'd never started this whole dating thing. She knew Chris was wanting to take things slow—he hadn't said it, but it was obvious. He was still half in love with his wife, and grieving was like taming a monster. Monsters lurked in the shadows, and they came and went as they pleased. She'd grieved in her time. For patients, for their families. For her marriage. Being a divorcee was never on someone's life wishlist, after all. She was just mad that she had ignored the glaring signs that he wasn't the one. That he'd wanted *any*one, and his wife sitting at home waiting for him. Now look at her. Five minutes ago she'd been thinking about a future with Chris, now her armour was firmly back on. She shuddered, and put on a brave face before she entered Heather's room.

Heather Anderson was a stalwart of the community, but her time was near now. Her husband, Wilfred, had passed the year before, and Heather was pragmatic to say the least. She had been one of Susannah's favourite neighbours growing up, and her own parents had been friends of Heather's. She'd seen Susannah grow up, and now Susannah felt privileged that she could be there for her, as her family and parents would have been if they had been able.

Her soft tap on the door was unnecessary; even at this hour Heather was up, watching her favourite crime shows. She did love a box set, and she didn't sleep much either.

'Hello, love.' Heather raised her hand to usher her closer. Susannah took a seat close to her, taking her hand and checking her vitals. She was comfortable, and pain free, which was a good sign. 'You look bothered by something.' She nodded towards the monitors. 'If it's that, don't you worry.' She smiled, settling back down on the pillows. 'I'm fine.'

Susannah gently rubbed her finger along Heather's arm with her gloved hand.

'I know, I can see that. No pain?' A shake of the head.

'No, love, Wilf's waiting. I'm ready.'

'I know you are,' Susannah said softly. She'd said it before and Susannah knew it was the truth. She was tired, in mind and body. 'Can I do anything for you?'

Heather patted her hand, pausing the already muted TV. Gil Grissom stood frozen on the screen on the wall by her bed.

'You can tell me what's wrong. You don't look happy.'

Susannah rolled her eyes. 'I'm fine.'

Heather stared at her till she caved.

'It's nothing really. Dating has been a bit of a learning curve, and Helen just said something that's got me thinking.' She got on with the job of checking Heather's vitals, checking her charts and noting down her pain levels. 'So, you have some visitors coming, I hear?'

'Not till later. Go on, tell me what's wrong with this new man in your life.' Heather's eyes sparkled as she smiled at Susannah.

'Really? You really want to hear this?'

'Almost as much as I want Gil Grissom to come visit.' Susannah smirked.

'Okay. She said something about being a doctor's wife again, and it just left me cold.'

'I bet it did. Tell me about him.'

'Chris? He's nice. He was a bit prickly at first, but he's widowed.' She bit her lip but the words were already out. 'Not that it's a bad thing, he's just…dealing with stuff, I guess. We keep clashing on things, and his temperament is a bit up and down.'

'Makes sense. I was a dragon when Wilf passed. So, he's the new village vet? That's great, isn't it? You love your dogs; it makes sense.'

'It does, and that's the problem, I think. John and I made sense at first, and this is my home. Imagine how awkward it will be when we break up? We're not even in a proper relationship yet and it's just so draining trying to work out what to do for the best.'

'Do you want to break up?'

'Well, no, and we're only dating.'

'That's like saying you are nearly a couple; it's the same thing if you're only seeing each other. Do you like him?'

'Yeah, but he is a doctor.'

'So?' Heather leaned forward, producing a flash of pain across her features. Susannah resisted the urge to run up and comfort her. She waited till Heather had settled down again, checking her monitors whenever Heather wasn't looking. She didn't want to take one ounce of dignity away from her friend. It was ingrained in her nursing skills, and Heather was a proud woman, illness be damned. 'That's not why you like him, is it?'

'Oh, God, no. I met him at the practice, and he was rude and all coiled up. I didn't like him one bit.'

Heather said nothing, but she spoke volumes with

her expression. Susannah filled the silence for her. 'But he's not like that really. He's all bluster, and he's so soft with the animals. It's ridiculously cute. He's at my house now, looking after a litter of puppies he helped deliver.'

That got a reaction. 'So, Solitary Cottage isn't so solitary any more, and you're freaking out that you're repeating your past.'

'Yes!' Susannah prodded out with her finger. 'Exactly! And what if I am, and then I've got another messy break-up and it's all played out in front of the village?'

Heather shook her head. 'Listen to me, John wasn't it, and there's no shame in that. Divorces aren't what they used to be! Oh, if they had been back in my day, lots of marriages would have crumbled. Wilf and I were lucky, but we had to work hard to keep it that way. This village will see everything, I know that, but don't let it stop you.' She squeezed her hand, and Susannah's eyes brimmed with tears. 'Don't waste it. Your mum and dad would break their hearts if their little fireball wasn't happy.'

Susannah snorted through her tears. Her dad had always called her *fireball* because she had been a force of nature from the minute she could get around. The name had stuck within their little circle of friends. Heather was one of the last, and it saddened her more than she could ever let on.

'It sounds like they are two very different people. Having a medical degree doesn't make him a bad choice for you. I think you've already made up your mind what to do. All I can say is that everything you have done makes you the person you are, and I'm so proud of you. I know you'll be just fine.'

The two women wept together for a little while, till

it descended into laughter. Susannah was soon back on the floor, her face back on, and she worked like a Trojan for the rest of her shift. It wasn't until she was on her way home that she realised Heather was right. She had made her mind up. She'd get through the meeting, and then speak to Chris. See once and for all what they had.

CHAPTER EIGHT

CHRIS'S ALARM WENT off on his phone, and that was when things went downhill. His calendar notifications popped up on the screen, and when he read them he felt sick. It was such an innocuous reminder, but it felt as if someone had stuck a scalpel straight through his heart.

Anniversary—make arrangements

That was it. Hardly heartfelt, but it was there. A remnant from a former life, but as he was reading it in Susannah's spare room, the timing felt all wrong. He'd thought he'd deleted them all. He opened his calendar and deleted it for ever. He sank back under the covers, remembering when he'd put the reminder in his calendar in the first place. He'd forgotten their second anniversary. They'd both been so busy with work, but he had blanked the whole thing. It had caused a row, but an empty one. She'd remembered just in time, but not enough in advance to get him a card either.

It should have shocked them, but it was just their life. He'd of course made an effort since, hating the feeling that something so special could be forgotten so fast, but it had been more of a perfunctory obligation written like that. He always kicked himself for how distracted he'd been, how distracted they'd *both* been. They'd been happy, but then when she'd become sick, their happiness in their careers had been all but on hold, and the void had been palpable without the work, and the noise, and the swanky nights out, and the scores of friends.

He'd missed most of his marriage.

The bit he missed the most was sharing a life with someone. He wasn't lonely per se, but reading that notification had made him think of all the other times he'd received little reminders that he'd had a life, and now he was trying to live another one. A more centred one. He'd spent three nights at Solitary Cottage now, and today, the anniversary, was the day of the charity-drive meeting with the volunteers. Bad timing, given that it would be the first public event in the village where he and Susannah would be together, on show. It felt like bad taste, but it was just business. He could get through the night and take her out later in the week. They had that shopping trip planned at the weekend—perhaps he could extend it to dinner too. It would be nice to spend more time with her.

He went to get dressed and see to the dogs. He had an early appointment, so he was leaving half an hour before she got back. Trudy was coming up to hold the fort and tonight she was taking the night shift for him as her daughter had begged to spend time with the puppies.

He'd not wanted to say no, but he was secretly gutted that he wouldn't be there longer. He quite liked being part of Susannah's world. They just needed to get the village meeting out of the way, get the event organised, and then they could focus on them. After Monday, things would be much easier.

* * *

'There's quite a lot of people out there,' Susannah murmured from the position behind the curtain. Her hands clasped around the velvet were shaking, sending little ripples all the way up the fabric. 'I didn't think so many people would come.'

'I know. I feel like Bon Jovi,' Chris said beside her. He looked grumpy, as he had when they'd first met. 'Shall we just go out and get it over with?'

He wasn't looking at her, his gaze focused on the people through the gap in the curtain, so she didn't have to try to hide her hurt.

'Sure,' she said, clapping her hands together to keep them from smacking him around the face. 'If you're ready.'

He huffed in response, but she was already through the curtain and down the stage steps. She took a seat at the table at the front of the stage. What looked like the whole village was sitting in front of them, talking amongst themselves on the plastic chairs set out for the meeting. Hendrix was being fussed over by Cheryl, who was sitting with the other nurses on the front row. When Cheryl saw her, she motioned to everyone there and gave her an enthusiastic thumbs-up. Chris took his seat next to her and placed his hand on her lap—just for a moment, and then it was gone. She felt the heat from his body seep through her jeans. He was shuffling papers around on a clipboard now, looking both stern and official. She wanted to roll her eyes at him, but when she glanced back at the chairs, she knew that their every move was being watched. She almost wished that Heather could be here, just so she would see it. It really was something to marvel at. The residents of Puddle Lake, and their rather long bird-like necks, leaning close and sticking their metaphorical beaks into everything new and shiny.

She straightened her top, and called the meeting to order by standing up and introducing herself. The hall fell silent as she detailed her plans for the first ever charity drive being held in the grounds of Dr Jennings's home. Chris blushed when they applauded him, and she tried to catch his eye, but he was looking everywhere but her.

What's his deal?

His mood was making the doubts in her mind scream louder. Once the introduction had been done, the shelter teams all had their introductions to make, detailing their work and what they would need on the day. As the two of them sat at the top table, listening to the people come up and talk, the awkward feeling between them seemed to grow thicker around them. She put her hand on his knee, and he jumped. She snapped her hand back as if she'd been burned.

'What's wrong?' she whispered across to him, keeping an eye on the crowd for onlookers.

'Nothing,' he whispered back. 'Just trying to concentrate.' He leaned in closer to the front of the table, as if the extra half-inch would give him bat-like hearing. She started clicking her pen and heard him tut. 'Do you mind?'

She put the pen on the table with a clatter.

'Nope,' she said briskly. 'Not at all.' She stood up and headed to the refreshments table. There had been some wine donated for the meeting, to try to get the volunteers to be a little forthcoming with offers of help on the day. There was half a bottle of white left, and she drained the contents into the biggest glass she could see on the table before heading back to her seat. Chris was watching her return, and she waited for him to react to her. His face was pure stone. Expressionless. Giving nothing away. Solidly closed off from her. She'd drunk half the glass by the time her bottom hit the seat pad.

'Sorry. I just feel a little on show. It's been a bit of a weird day.'

She heard him, but she didn't acknowledge it. She focused on the meeting for the rest of the time, and then they were busy mingling, chatting to people about dogs they might be interested in, and introducing the shelter teams to the villagers that would be helping on the day. Before too long, they had a solid plan and she could see things start to take shape. The volunteers all had jobs before and on the day, and the rest were co-ordinating with each other. Chris had dealt with the legal side of the hosting duties, and Susannah had made sure medical, first aid and facilities were covered, and safety would be maintained on the day.

The dogs would be a little stressed if the schedule was too overwhelming, but by the looks on some of the faces of those in attendance this evening, the homeless hounds would be able to melt a heart or two. It was all coming together, but she just felt wretched about having had the idea in the first place. There was no getting out of this now, and as it was now being held in his grounds, it was even worse.

Once the last person left, and she and Chris were saying goodbye to the hall warden, she was desperate to get home.

'I am sorry, for earlier.'

Damn. Almost got to my car, too.

She turned and he was standing behind her, car keys in hand. She was hauling her handbag, her file for the charity drive, and a rather cumbersome portable pin board. Her keys were between her teeth. Reaching out an awkward hand, she dropped them into it and braced herself for an awkward chat. The contents of her arms suddenly felt a lot heavier.

'Sorry for what?'

Does he even know how mad I am at him? For being so aloof, when I was already having mixed feelings and swirling doubt. He doesn't see the doubts, and I know I can't blame him for something he knew nothing of, but... oh. It just shouldn't be this hard. I feel like I'm going to get hurt here. I need to protect myself. There's just too much baggage on both sides. We'll never be able to fit it all under one roof.

Helen's words were etched on her brain.

'Being a moody so-and-so.' He stepped closer and lifted the heavy board from her hands. 'It's been a weird day. I just wanted to get the meeting done.'

'I know, I get it. I do too, but these mood swings, Chris? I don't get them.' She turned to go to her car, clicking the doors open on the key and trying not to drop everything. He was there, right beside her, opening the boot.

'I know, and you don't have to get them. It's just a weird day, like I said. I needed to focus on work.'

Susannah put everything into the boot, taking the board from him and shoving it on top. She shut the door up and headed to the driver seat.

'Wait, Susie.'

'Susannah. I'm really tired, Chris. It's been a rough few days…my friend is…sick. Can we talk tomorrow?'

'I just wanted to say sorry.' His words were a little clipped. His jaw tensed when she focused her eyes on his. 'That's all. I know you've been busy, and I'm sorry about your friend. You know that. I just think we need to talk, soon. I can explain.'

And there it is. His opener or mine? Am I going to be dumped before I can get in first?

'We do need to talk.' She nodded, not looking away. 'I have some things I want to say.'

'Me too.' His face had brightened, but then he bit his lip. 'Just not today; I can't today. I have to work late tomorrow too—the surgery is offering some later sessions now. Some classes, things like that.' He was rambling now, and he looked flushed.

'Okay, later in the week is probably better anyway.'

'Saturday, then?'

Saturday? Something jangled in her memory, but it was wily. She couldn't quite remember. Her blank expression gave her away, and Chris straightened up a little taller.

'Er…yeah. Our shopping trip.'

'Oh, yes!' She slapped herself on the forehead, wanting the ground to swallow her up. Or better, for her to get in her car and drive home as fast as she could. 'I'm sorry! Er…yes, we could do that.' It would give her time to work out just what the hell she wanted to say to him. How she would be able to look him in the eye when they worked together. 'I'd better go.' She couldn't look him in the eye, so she knew that wasn't going to be easy.

'Susannah, look at me.'

She could barely hold her keys, she was so sweaty-handed. Gripping them tighter, she turned and leaned her back against the car door.

'Chris, I don't think I can do this.'

His jaw flexed.

'I know you're tired, but Saturday is a way off…'

'No.' She swallowed. 'I mean, I don't think I can do…this.' She pointed her finger between her and him. He took a step closer and she yanked her hand back before he could grasp it.

'Susie, I know I've been grumpy, but I really like you.'

'I really like you, but it's just not going to work.' She flexed her jaw to match his. 'I promised myself that I would never be second best again. We're already so in each other's lives, I just don't think it would end well. For either of us. Puddle Lake is a small place. People talk.'

'Screw the people.'

'What, all of them?' He didn't respond to her failed attempt at humour. He was mad, she realised. She could see it in his eyes.

'You know what I mean. I would never put you second best.'

'You're still grieving for your wife.'

She'd never said it out loud to him before, but she'd always known it. He was half consumed by it, but his grief was twisted around his gut, hidden from view to most people. Even himself, at times.

'That's not fair. Or strictly true.'

'Of course it is, Chris, and I don't blame you one bit. You should never feel bad for loving your wife.'

'It's not that. It's more than that.'

Susannah didn't want to hear him trying to explain something she understood only too well. She knew grief; it was a silent companion of hers. It had walked the hallways of the hospice many a time. Sometimes, she'd fallen into step right along with it.

'I just can't risk it again, I'm sorry.'

'Risk what again? Susannah, this is madness. Why are you walking away?'

'I'm tired!' she half shouted back at him. 'I'm tired of doing things for everyone else, and not expecting anything back. Okay? Spoiled princess, eh? My ex-husband treated me like I was an accessory to his life, and utterly disposable. Just like the poor dogs that I look after. I am sick and tired of people taking me—or anyone—for granted, and I just can't be in a relationship like that again.'

Chris was ashen, his mouth in a frozen grimace, his head turning from side, to side, to side.

'You've read this all wrong, Susie.'

'Are you grieving for your wife, yes or no?'

He crushed his lips together. 'It's not that simple. We were very different—'

'Please,' she half whispered. 'Just be honest.'

His eyes shuttered closed. 'Yes. Surely you don't judge me for that?'

'Of course I don't! I just mean that it's still too fresh, and with everything else...'

'Like what?' He wasn't getting it, and she wasn't explaining herself well either. She couldn't say everything she was feeling. One half of her wanted to tell herself to shut up, that the man in front of her was getting hurt by her words, and that was the last thing she'd wanted to do. The problem was, the other half of her, the one still smarting from the epic and messy divorce in her past, wanted to run back to her cottage, lock the door and never leave again. This was exactly what she'd feared.

'I don't know.' She shrugged weakly. His eyes flashed with frustration and she gabbled on to fill the silence, to stop him from saying something nice to change her mind. 'Lots of things. Your work is important to you, just like mine is.' He winced when she mentioned her job again, and she found the resolve she needed. 'See, you can't even stand me mentioning work! And with us working together, your wife, my ex-issues… it's just too much. I don't want to lose your friendship.'

He snorted at that. 'We were never just friends, Susie, and you know it.'

She looked at his chest, rising and falling rapidly. Was his heart racing as fast as hers? She could see Roz now, and Helen, being all sympathetic to her face but lamenting her love woes to each other when she wasn't there. They wouldn't be mean, but they wouldn't understand her reasons either. Her divorce had put her through the wringer too much already. She would not let Puddle Lake become a place she wanted to leave. Even if it meant pining for the vet from afar. It was safer that way at least.

'I just think it's the timing, Chris. I'm sorry.'

She looked straight at him, trying not to see the tight clench of his jaw, his beautiful eyes that were scanning her face urgently for any sign of a chink in her armour. She had opened her car door by the time he spoke again.

'So that's it? You've decided that it won't work, and that's that?'

She sat down in the driver seat, and when she went to close the door he didn't stop her. He just stood there, watching her pull her belt on and start the engine. She was about to put the car in gear when there was a tap at her window. She wound her window down but kept her eyes on the view in front of her.

'Susie, will you look at me?'

When their eyes locked, she felt the familiar pull of him. The jolt of electricity that ran through her when she looked into the eyes of the man she had once thought so bullish. They were marked with hurt now, and she shook her head.

'I'm sorry, Chris, but I really think it's for the best. I have to go.'

She managed to keep the tears at bay till he was out of sight. He didn't move when she drove away. She'd left him standing there, watching her leave. She couldn't take the look in his eyes, and when she wiped at her tears in the rear-view mirror, she saw the same reflected in her own watery globes.

When she got back to Solitary Cottage, she spent the night looking after the dogs, crying over her own cowardice and fear. Chris called her twice; each time she let it go to voicemail. The third time he tried, she turned it off altogether and shoved it into her nightstand.

Chris called again, and it went to voicemail without ringing once. He growled in frustration, throwing his phone onto the couch next to him. Hendrix jumped up from his bed, gripping the phone in his mouth and plonking it back on his lap, a string of dog spit now splatted across the screen. Chris rolled his eyes at the eager hound.

'Hendrix, I tried. She doesn't want to speak to me.' Nothing but a head tilt and a groan. 'Oh, come on, that's not fair. It's not my fault.' Hendrix lifted a paw and covered one of his eyes. 'It's not! She called it off.' Hendrix dropped his paw and jabbed the phone with his slender snout. 'Oh, come on, what makes you the dating expert? You don't even have testicles.' Hendrix omitted a low howl that made Chris cringe to the tips of his toes. 'Okay, sorry.' He leaned forward to stroke him, and Hendrix nuzzled into his hand. 'That was mean, and we both know I'm not really mean. Not that it matters now. She thinks I'm some damaged workaholic city boy.' Hendrix barked once, and Chris tilted his face to the side to match the dog's. 'Listen, I know you're not really talking to me, but that felt like a low blow. I'd say we're even now.' Reaching for his phone, he tapped out a message.

I hope you got home safe. I want to talk about this, I have things to say. Think about it?

He thought about adding a kiss, or even a funny dog emoji, but instead he slapped the silly thought away with a swift tap to the forehead. He deleted the message and threw the phone back into its original discarded spot. Hendrix groaned and headed to his bed. Moments later, a loud snore filled the room. Chris sighed heavily, reaching for the remote and putting the TV on. There was a vet show on, one of the good ones, and he watched the rather jolly vet on the screen explain what he was doing to the camera. His left arm was shoulder-deep in a rather bored-looking Holstein-Friesian cow, who was known on the farm as Mrs Butterfield, with a suspected prolapse. As he watched, he remembered a conversation he'd once had, back in his old home, on his old couch…

* * *

'This show again? That vet is far too happy sometimes.'

Chris chuckled, frowning as he turned and saw his wife's pale face.

'Are you okay? Warm enough?'

Karen rolled her eyes from under the layer of covers she was wrapped in.

'I'm like a blanket burrito. I'm warm enough, trust me.'

'You look a little pale. Do you want a drink?'

'I want you to stop fussing. You know what chemo's like.' He nodded grimly. He'd seen her go through it enough times to understand she was feeling ill. They watched TV for a while in silence. There were far too many silences between them now. It was as though they'd just run out of things to say. The things they'd spoken of before didn't feature much in their lives any more. Karen pointed at the screen.

'That's what you should do.'

'We don't get many pigs at the practice, aside from the odd pot-bellied house pet.'

'No.' She reached for her water. Chris's hands itched to help the straw to her mouth, but he knew she would ask if she needed it. *'Open a practice in the country.'*

Chris's head snapped to hers.

'That's not funny.'

'I'm not being funny.' The water she'd sipped went down the wrong hole, and she coughed. He went to help her, but she coughed again and held up a hand to stop him. *'I'm fine.'* She wiped her mouth on one of her burrito blankets. *'Please stop fussing.'*

'I'll stop fussing when you stop making bad jokes.'

'It's not a joke,' she retorted, smiling at him. 'I could see you doing that, living in the fresh air. Stress free.'

'He just got kicked in the knee by that goat; it hardly looks stress free. You hate the country anyway!'

'Well, that doesn't really matter, does it?' His jaw clenched, and she smiled apologetically. You know what I mean.'

Chris reached for her hand, clasping it between his. 'I'll be fine. I love you so much.'

She squeezed his hand tight, and he moved it to his lips to bestow a soft kiss on her pale skin. 'You're a rubbish liar, you know that, right? I love you too,' she said, giving him the smile she always did. The smile he only saw when she gave it to him, and him alone. 'I just want you to enjoy your life. That's all I want for you. Please don't bury yourself in your work again.'

'I won't, I promise.'

He'd promised that to her often since that night, over and over every time she asked it of him. He'd done it too, not just to fulfil a promise, but the more she'd spoken about it, the more it hadn't seemed so alien to him after she'd passed. His old life had moved on and left him behind. He'd still failed though. What was it that Karen had said? Something about being happy. He was the village vet now, but he was lacking in the jolly part. He'd upped and moved, but then work had been his focus. He'd grown mean, and scrunched in on himself, like a tricky tumour, hiding between organs and tissues, throwing out its poison and not being touchable. Unreachable to the light, and hard to identify where work started and he ended.

Till Susannah had walked in, with the hound that

was now snoring like a walrus beside him. They'd both bounded into his life, colourful and gleeful and optimistic. He'd felt irritated by her that day, incensed that someone could be that full of joy.

'She woke me up, you know,' he said to the dog. Hendrix retorted with a snuffle and a flick of his paw. He was probably after a dream rabbit. Maybe he was talking to the empty room. Maybe he was hoping Karen would hear him. As odd as it was, he knew what she would have said.

A promise is a promise.

It was what she'd always said, when he'd asked her to change the subject on LAH. Life after her. It had seemed so abstract at the time, like a child thinking about being their grandparents' age. Like something far away in the future. When the time had come, he'd turned on the autopilot. He'd got through the funeral; he'd tried to carry on as before. His old routines. Her words had come back into his mind so many times before he'd finally decided to go for it.

He'd been meant to come here—he knew that now. He wanted to be here. He liked his new life, and he was ready to share it again. The whole day had been a bust, the anniversary triggering his guilt. The guilt that he'd felt alone when he was sitting by Karen's bedside. The guilt that he'd put not his wife on a pedestal but work instead. Work didn't cuddle you after the loss of a patient. It didn't call to tell you it loved you. He'd chosen wrongly, and he'd tried so hard to make it up to Karen before she died. He'd chosen her, but it had been too late. Their time had already been cut short. Given an expiration date.

Second best. That was what Susannah had said to

him. Her ex had neglected her too, in a different way. He'd strayed. Taken her for granted in his own cruel way. It was ironic really. He'd been half twisted with grief and guilt over not realising what he had, and she was too scared of him hurting her to realise that he would *never* do that to her. Work was important, yes, and he'd fallen back into his old ways that day to cope with the significance of the date. That was it, he realised. She'd seen a glimpse of the old him, and she'd had déjà vu. He wanted to kick himself for not realising sooner. Why did he never work things out till it was too late? He stood up off the couch, grabbing his phone and keys.

'Hendrix, I'm going out.'

As he pulled his car up to Solitary Cottage, his headlights picked up a flash of something brightly coloured coming out of the front door. He parked next to Susannah's car, pulling the handbrake on. He could hear keys jingling, and Susannah's voice, full of panic.

'I'm coming, okay? I just need to lock up.' She ended the call, shoving her phone into her coat pocket and cursing loudly as she dropped her keys.

'Susannah? You okay?'

She whirled around, and his heart missed a beat. She was crying, shaking, fumbling to find the right key on her chain.

'What are you doing here?'

'I came to— What's wrong?'

'My friend, in the hospice...' She dissolved into sobs once more, and shook her head, a look of anger crossing her face. She was mad at herself for being emotional. 'It's nearly time. I have to go.'

She turned and tried to lock her door again. Chris stepped forward, taking the keys from her gently and locking up. She tried to take the keys from him, but he held them back.

'You can't drive like this, Susie.' His heart pumped when he realised what he needed to do. 'I'll drive you to the hospice.'

Her jaw dropped even through her sobs, but he'd already wrapped his arms around her and steered her to his car. He got her inside, and drove wordlessly to the hospice, listening as she called Roz back. Heather was asking for her. Chris reached for her free hand with his. She didn't let go till they pulled up outside.

'Thank you,' she said, distracted as she left. 'I know this was hard for you.'

They were both standing at the front of the car. Close enough to touch, but he didn't try.

'Anything for you.'

She smiled through her tears, and, stepping towards him, she stood on her tiptoes and touched her lips to his. *Zolt!* He kissed her back, pulling her close and wishing he could tuck her into himself. To save her from the pain she was in. She kissed him till he tasted the salt of her tears, felt the tears on his cheeks, his hands as they embraced.

'I won't forget this,' she whispered, leaning up for one last touch of his lips. 'You're a good man.'

Then she was off, running towards the doors. He stood there for a while, touching his fingertips to his mouth and wiping away the evidence of her sobs, and then he turned to get back into the car.

Twenty minutes later, he was still there, standing at the doors to the hospice, willing his feet to move.

'Work, damn you!' he said to his un-cooperative feet. He paced up and down. 'Come on!'

He punched himself in the leg, as if to wake it up. 'Get in there, she needs you!'

He was still chuntering, taking steps forward and back, when the door opened. He noticed a woman watching him.

'Chris, is it?'

Embarrassed by what she might have observed, he nodded his head dumbly. 'Er...yes. Chris Jennings, pleased to meet you. Roz, is it?'

Her lips quirked. 'Yes, that's me. Can I help?'

'I don't think so.'

'You might be surprised. You coming in?'

'I'm still trying to decide,' he admitted. 'I want to.' He swallowed, and straightened himself up. 'My wife passed away in a hospice, back home. I...don't do well going down memory lane. Is Susannah okay, and your friend?'

Roz nodded. 'Bearing up. I'm sorry for your loss.'

'Thanks, it was a while ago now.'

'Doesn't make it any easier. I'll leave you to it. There's no shame in admitting defeat today. Susannah would never judge you for that.'

'I know, and that makes it worse. I can't even make it through a door. I don't know how you do what you do. Either of you. I lost one person in a place like this, and that was more than enough.' He ran his hands through his hair, trying to ground himself into the moment. 'I want to be there for her.'

'Well, you're here, so that's a start, right?'

There it was again, that look. Roz looked as if she

was in on something that he wasn't aware of. He caught sight of the doors behind her, and his legs turned to jelly.

'Yeah, but a start of what? At the moment, it feels like a panic attack.' Roz leaned closer, but said nothing.

'Well, I think that's for you to decide.' A buzzer went off in her pocket, and she turned to leave. 'Cup of tea?' she asked over her shoulder, a brow raised in query. 'I can bring you one out, and a sandwich maybe. If I come out and you're gone, I won't tell her you stayed.' She gave him a friendly smile, one that reminded him of Susannah. 'It's nice to put a face to the name.'

Chris's heart swelled. Susannah had been talking about him to her friends. Maybe all was not lost. If she was talking about him, she was thinking about him. As was he her. He knew he couldn't get her out of his mind, despite his best efforts. The chance that she might be feeling the same preoccupation that he was for her gave him a warm glow.

'Nice to meet you too.' He stepped forward, and held out his hand. She shook it, and when she went to walk back inside, he took a deep breath, and followed her over the threshold.

CHAPTER NINE

HEATHER PASSED AWAY peacefully mere hours later, Susannah and her friends by her side as she slowly took her last breath. Susannah managed to keep her tears in till she had kissed everyone goodbye, and it wasn't till she got into the break room that she allowed herself to feel it. She cried herself to sleep on the couch, and that was where Roz found her sometime later.

'Hey,' she said softly once Susannah's eyes opened. Both women could tell the other had been crying, and Roz sank down beside her as she sat up. Roz passed her one of the mugs in her hand. Susannah thanked her and took a deep gulp of coffee.

'I've called Erika to cover for me today. I can't concentrate enough on the job.'

Susannah squeezed her arm. 'Good call. I'm glad I have a day off, to be honest.' The two women sat and sipped at their drinks, feeling drained and sad. 'It doesn't get any easier, does it?'

Roz shook her head. 'No, it doesn't, but I take some peace in knowing that we do everything we can. This place…' She looked around her, at the wall of thank-you cards and messages from grateful families, the pictures of them sitting with their loved ones punctuating the heartfelt, tear-stained words they wrote. 'It's not just a place of endings for them. It's a place that makes an unbearable time bearable.'

She was so right. Susannah felt exactly the same. Heather's loved ones couldn't thank them enough, and she knew that Heather had been comfortable and in a place filled with love and care. They did make a difference, to everyone who passed through those doors. She found her mind wandering again to her other source of pain. The fact that she was newly single, having walked away from the vet who was grieving for his wife and falling for her. She knew he was falling; she could tell. She felt the same way, and that was the problem. It sounded crazy, them being so different, but she just knew in her gut that she had more feelings for him than she should have. If she allowed herself to fall…

It was too late, she knew that. She took another deep gulp of her coffee, sighing so hard she pushed all the air from her lungs. Roz misread her melancholy a little and wrapped her arm around her.

'She's free now, love. Heather was ready to go, bless her. Are you going to be okay? You can come to mine if you like; we can watch some rubbish daytime TV and eat some major carbs.'

'I wasn't thinking about Heather, not just about her anyway. I was thinking about Chris.'

'Oh, yeah? Well, that's good, isn't it?'

'Not really. I think we're done. Too many things against it, I think.'

His face last night… I bet there are gravel tracks up the drive from his quick getaway.

She'd just wanted him with her, but her job was coming between them again. She wanted to share her whole life with someone, but the fear in his face had haunted her, even at Heather's bedside. This was the job, or a huge part of it. Being there for people in the dark times gave her comfort; it fulfilled her even more than placing a foster dog. Could she really ever share that with him?

'Okay.' Roz's delayed reply distracted her from her own wishy-washy thoughts.

'Is that all you're going to say? Okay?'

'Well, you didn't give me much to go on.'

'Sorry. I'm tired. I don't think my decision-making skills are quite up to par.'

'I know, but that's never stopped you before. You got scared, didn't you? With the vet.'

She glared at her friend, but that only made Roz laugh. 'Oh, come on, I'm not evil. I've been a pushy so and so, maybe…'

'Definitely. And Helen.'

'Okay. I pushed because you needed it. Helen loves you too. I was just saying that I think you got scared! You changed when you met him.'

'I despised him when I met him.'

'No, you didn't. Not really.'

'Yes, I did. I wished every type of pox upon that man. I was livid!'

'Because you fancied him.'

'No—'

'Yes! He annoyed you, yes, but you have never talked so much about a man who you supposedly despised. You fancied him, and you were glad he was a massive idiot, because it scared you into thinking about dating again. That's what the app was about! To give you a shove.'

Susannah shook her head, but she was smiling. 'Am

I really that stubborn? I really thought you and Helen were being cows, you know.'

They both giggled, and the tension that Susannah had been feeling around her fell away. She had read it wrong.

'Helen was really scared you were going to flip,' Roz confided with a titter. 'I had to convince her it would work, and that I'd take the rap. Heather was in on it.'

The two women fell silent when they realised her co-conspirator was no longer here to share the moment. Of course, they still felt her in the room.

'Well, thank you, Heather,' Susannah said to the ceiling. 'I flipped out on him though, spouted on about being second best.' She put her head in her hand. She could have fallen asleep right there and then. 'Oh, my God. And I talked about his wife too. I'm awful.'

'Hey! That's my friend you're talking about.'

She sat up, putting the now half-empty mug on the side. Coffee slopped onto the table. She mopped at it with the sleeve of her coat.

'I messed up, I think. We could have been friends, but I handled it wrong. I really like him, but I just can't go through it again. This might sound stupid, but I want the fairy tale, I guess. You know? Someone who puts you first, and makes you feel loved?'

'That's not stupid. It's just far less easy to find in the real world than in a book. It's no coincidence so many women read those books you love. They want the same. Everyone wants to be cherished, Suze. It's human nature.'

'He reminds me of John sometimes. He'll feel something, and then it's all locked up again. Like he found a leak in his heart and plugged it quick. John did the same, and he just buried himself so deeply in work he never came out the same. Geez, I'm here moaning, and Heather... I just think it's best if we stay apart for a bit, till I can get my feelings sorted out.' She didn't even sound as if she meant it to her own ears. She looked to see if her friend had bought it. Roz said nothing, but she had that look about her. The one that meant she was fooling no one. 'Spill it. I know you have something to say.'

Roz pretended to look surprised, but Susannah raised a brow and she crumpled like a cheap suit.

'I think you read him wrong, to be honest. He's here. I put him up on a cot in one of the family rooms.'

Susannah laughed. 'Very funny. He wouldn't set foot in this place.'

Roz squeezed her friend tight. 'You are dense sometimes. He never left the car park. I found him standing outside. He wanted to be here, for you. That's not putting someone second best in my book.'

Susannah had so many questions.

'Which family room?' was the one that burst from her mouth.

He was fast asleep, sprawled on the sofa with one hand over his face. The blanket he was under was half on the floor, and she bent to straighten it up. As she covered him, he awoke. He looked tired, drawn. She wondered how long he'd been sleeping.

'Hey,' he murmured. He sat up and motioned for her to sit next to him. She sat, and he pushed the blanket aside. 'Can I do anything to help?'

She smiled. 'No, but thanks for asking. She passed peacefully. Thanks for bringing me too. You were right;

I wasn't in a fit state.' He didn't reply. 'You didn't need to stay.'

'Roz put me up. She's a character, isn't she?'

Susannah nodded, laughing despite her exhausted state. 'Yep, she's one of a kind all right. I can't believe you're here.'

He stood slowly, stretching out his limbs and tapping his foot on the floor as he walked around the room. He looked dishevelled, crumpled and utterly adorable. She was about to embrace him, to thank him for being there for her, but something stopped her. It was the look on his face. He was looking around the room as if he was looking for a rip cord somewhere.

'Neither can I. I almost vomited in the bushes at one point. Listen, I have to get back to the surgery, but I just wanted to be here.' His eyes inspected the room once more, and she wondered what he was seeing. What was going through his mind? He'd put himself through a night there, for her. The thought made her heart soar, but it brought something else into crystal clarity. Life was evil like that, sometimes.

His eyes zeroed in on hers, but she could tell he wasn't fully with her. He'd tried so hard, but he wasn't there yet. Would he ever be there? She played every scenario over and over in her head. Her work with the shelters and the dogs, her seeing him all the time at the surgery. She was in his life, she knew his colleagues, his patients even.

'Are you okay?' she made herself ask him, and she begged for the answer to be that he was healed. That he'd conquered a demon. 'I know last night must have been hard for you.' She wanted to say more, to tell him how much it had meant. *Everything.* He'd put her first, even over his own pain. She knew the cost was dear to him. When his eyes locked with hers, she knew it was too much.

She knew she was begging the Almighty for something impossible, but she held her breath and willed it into being anyway, with everything she had. They couldn't do this now. They were so close to…to…

'I'm fine.' He yawned, checking the clock. He rubbed her shoulder softly. 'I should go though. I'm sorry to leave you like this.' He was up and halfway across the room before she could blink. 'Do you need a lift?'

'No, thanks. Roz's here. Chris—'

'You don't have to thank me, Susie. We're friends, right? I wanted to help.' He smiled, but when she searched his eyes, they looked right through her. 'I'm really sorry about Heather. Look after yourself today.' He was looking at her as if she were a chipped china doll. His forehead was shiny with sweat, and his eyes kept finding the clock. 'I'll call you later, okay?'

He leaned in for a kiss, but she turned so he got her cheek instead. He stilled for a moment, his lips meeting her forehead this time. She didn't dodge that one; she closed her eyes and cherished it. All the moments weren't nearly enough, and now there would be no more.

'It did mean a lot, you coming,' she said. She'd waited like a chicken for him to get to the door before she spoke. 'You don't have to worry about me though. Thanks for being a friend.'

She looked down at the floor, at the spot on the tile she'd planned to search for before she spoke. She knew her head wouldn't move an inch till he'd left. She couldn't take his face. Relief or disappointment would have crushed her to see on the face of the man she loved. 'I will always worry about you,' she heard him say.

The door closed behind him with a click.

'Well,' she said to herself, long after her vision had turned the spot on the floor to two blurry ones and his steps had faded away. 'Looks like that's that.'

CHAPTER TEN

EVEN IN PUDDLE LAKE, time didn't stand still. Days turned into weeks. The season changed, bringing with it the sunnier weather. Heather's funeral had taken place, and life was moving on as it did. People went about their days, and Susannah's life fell into the old pattern of work and her dogs. The puppies were nearly ready for homing now. Tank was the liveliest of the bunch, and he kept her on her toes when she was at home. The name Chris had bestowed on him had stuck, and he certainly lived up to it. She found herself wanting to send him pictures, but she always stopped herself. He'd been at the funeral—she'd seen him sitting at the back—but when she'd gone to find him at the wake, Cheryl had told her he'd been called away on an emergency. It was the same when she visited the practice. The times when they did cross paths, they didn't speak much other than about the dogs, or the charity drive.

The drive was well under way now, the villagers all pulling their weight in their own ways. The pub had agreed to allow access to their toilets and were opening up their beer garden for the visitors. The local shops were all on board, advertising the event in their windows and donating prizes to the raffles. The hospice volunteers and crafty clan were working away, their knitting needles warm from all the things they were making. At one point there was a cotton shortage in the village, and the local craft shop was practically stripped bare. Everyone had gone all out, and Hendrix and Chris were one of the star attractions on the day. He was everywhere and nowhere in the village, like a will-o'-the-wisp. Now that there was a week to the event, the time had come to have another meeting. This time, at the venue itself: Chris's house.

She'd left work a little earlier that day. Trudy was on dog duty for her, and she wanted to be prepared for the meeting as best she could. It was one thing him keeping his distance but being at his house wasn't going to be easy if they were barely speaking. She was just getting into the car when she spotted what looked like Chris's car pulling in. He drove through the staff car park, heading round the building to where the visitors kept their cars.

'That's weird,' she mumbled. She waited for him to come to the front door, but there was no sign. She gave it another ten minutes, and then dismissed it in her head. She was imagining things now. She thought she'd seen him there the other day too, in the corridor, but when she'd finished with her patient and gone back to check, there had been no one there. 'You're hallucinating, woman,' she said out loud. She started her car and headed for home. The sooner she got over this, the better.

'Do you think we've got enough nibbles?'

Hendrix was sitting at the foot of the table, licking his lips. He'd already swiped half a pork pie off the order from the butcher when Chris wasn't looking so he was in the doghouse. Hendrix woofed once.

'Yeah, that's what I thought. I did too much, didn't I?'

He'd been on tenterhooks all day waiting for the meeting. Half of Puddle Lake was descending on his house, many of whom remembered the past vet living there. The other half, the non-attending half, would no doubt be fully regaled of the evening's events. He'd never been so nervous in his life. He normally didn't really care what people thought; after all, he'd spent the last few months being the worst version of himself. Now, he wanted to fit in here. He wanted to help Susannah. He might have screwed things up when he first arrived, but he was changing.

His world wasn't devoid of joy any more. Sometimes, when he woke alone in his bed, the old feelings of despair would be there, right behind his eyes, and he'd have to resist the urge to pull his head under the covers and stay there. This morning, Hendrix had awoken him by jumping on his torso like a kid on a bouncy castle. His first moment had been laughter, and company. Watching the hound eyeing the food as if he was planning his next theft attempt, Chris couldn't help but smile. In the last few weeks, he'd made himself go out. He wanted to heal himself and give Susannah time to grieve for her friend. He knew she'd be there for everyone else, and he wanted to work on himself. For her and him. He'd forced himself to see the village as she did.

Walking the dogs, he'd met more locals and their hounds. Mrs Chan had brought a pineapple upside-down cake into the surgery. A sugar-free version, to thank him for Gustav's new vigour. The now rather slender cat could not only lick his man parts, but he was out terrorising the local mouse population like a sprightly kitten. She'd even brought a fat-free treat bag for Hendrix.

The villagers were slowly coming around to him, but he still didn't have the one person he wanted. Susannah was like a ghost now. He avoided her at the practice when he could, wanting to give her space. She didn't ask Cheryl about him, and his loyal receptionist was very quiet on the subject. Loyal to Susannah, probably.

Heather's funeral had been a real event. Quite different from the ones seared into his memory. The church had been full of colour, and Susannah the brightest one in the crowd. He'd stayed in the back, watching her take care of everyone around her. When she'd gone to the pulpit to say a few words, there had been no sadness in her tone. She'd spoken of Heather, to Heather. She'd shared memories that had the villagers rolling with laughter. The whole church had seemed to fill with love, and joy, and Chris had been amazed by her all over again. He couldn't imagine one person looking at her and making her second best. He wished he could meet her ex-husband, to tell him what an idiot he'd been.

It was hypocritical, in a way, he mused. He'd taken his wife for granted too. They'd both been guilty of that. It was the way of modern life, he thought. Moving here, meeting Susannah and the other people who lived their lives so differently, he felt as if he'd finally woken up. There was more to life than work, as rewarding as it was. Hendrix shared his life, his home, and quite often his bed. Even the dog he'd taken in knew the value of life better than the city version of himself had. He had a big house, a good salary, a thriving practice. None of that had altered, but it wasn't what he measured his achievements against any longer. His old friends had happily let him slink off, uncomfortable in the presence of such reality. Money couldn't cheat death, and being reminded of their own mortality had caused them to retreat, just as he had from them.

Sitting in the church that day, he'd seen it all. People laughing at memories they'd shared, holding each other as they cried. Being a supporting arm to a sobbing woman. A mother holding her child that bit closer. Susannah, standing with the other nurses, saying goodbye to the friend they had loved and cared for till the end.

He wanted this life, more than anything. He wanted the colour, and the fresh air. He wanted to be mourned when he died, by a church full of people who knew and loved him. People he'd helped along the way. He wanted to be Mr Rogers, damn it. He wanted to be the person that Susannah deserved. He'd known that day that he'd fallen for her. Watching her speak of her friend, not shedding a tear or letting her voice waver, he'd longed to walk to the front of the church and throw his arms around her. He'd been so close, that night he'd driven to tell her how he felt. He'd been so close to telling her how she'd started to heal his closed-off, gnarled and battle-scarred heart, but he'd missed his chance. He couldn't do it now. At first she was grieving, and then time moved on and she still kept her distance. When they were in the same room, she was kind and polite. Friendly.

'I hope we can be friends,' she had said.

Yeah, that hit like a ton of bricks. Were we ever friends, really?

She'd cited his grief, but his wife was gone. He had

loved her, yes, but his grief was about the life he'd had as much as the person he'd lost.

The life he didn't fit into any more. The one he didn't miss now. He was the village vet, Puddle Lake was his home, and now he needed the woman to go with it. The new love he'd never thought to look for. The rainbow to his rain cloud. The light to his dark. Hell, he'd even stepped through the hospice doors for her. To be there, in case she needed him. When Roz had found him in the car park tying himself in knots, she'd given him the choice to go in with her, and he'd not even questioned it once his feet had finally moved forward. His hands had been shaking as he'd pushed open the foyer doors, and he'd waited for something to trigger his memories. A disinfectant smell, a poster on the wall. The beeps of the machines. There had been nothing. The minute he'd stepped in, all he'd seen was her. The place was a cacophony of colours too, the warmth of the painted walls filled with quirky art. There were no banal *Live, Laugh, Love* slogans to be seen. The whole place was built like the embrace of a loved one.

'Hang in there,' Roz had said to him as she showed him to one of the empty family rooms. 'Don't give up on her yet, okay? Heather is special to her. Her mother's best friend. It's a bit like losing her parents all over again, I think. Her work means such a lot to her.' She had given him a warm smile and patted him on the shoulder. 'Just hang in there, okay? You're good for her.'

She'd meant the words kindly, but they had hit like shrapnel. Ripping into him and leaving him bloody and shell-shocked.

You're good for her.

Am I?

He'd played those words over and over in his mind, and he didn't like the conclusion his tired brain kept coming to. He wasn't good for her, because if he were, wouldn't they be together now? He'd been mean to her since the minute he'd arrived, his anger and unprocessed feelings coiled around him like the bars of a prison. She was light, and caring, and happy. He'd dulled her light. He'd made her feel second best. He'd done it without meaning to, but it still stunned him. He didn't want to make the same mistakes all over again. He wanted to share a life with her, not have her on the periphery of friends, and possessions, and working every hour as though racing to some impossible goalpost that he would never reach anyway. Her friend had just passed away before her eyes, and when she'd come to the family room to find him, he'd walked away.

He'd had to get out of that room. When he'd known she was suffering, and going through that process just a few rooms away, it was all he had focused on. Being near her had felt so important, even if he couldn't be by her side to comfort her properly. She wasn't his, so that wasn't his place. He'd ignored the smells, the memories prickling at the corners of his brain. He'd coped, till he saw her.

She had looked so broken and sad. So tired. He'd known the nurse in her would feel relief for her friend, that the pain and the suffering had passed. He'd felt it too, and that was when the walls had started to close in around him. The smell had become noticeable once more.

He'd seen the hurt on her face, but he'd known in that moment he couldn't give her what she needed. What she deserved. Not quite yet. He hadn't been ready.

The day after, he'd called Roz, and now here they were. He'd thrown himself into village life. He'd bonded with his patients and their owners, he'd been seen out at events and eating in the café. Sitting in the pub beer garden after a long walk with Hendrix, chatting to the other pubgoers and swopping dog stories. He'd made an effort and, to his surprise, he'd actually enjoyed every minute of it. Even going to the hospice had exorcised some of his demons. Roz had helped him there too, allowing him to read to some of the lonelier patients when Susannah was out of sight. Many families still needed to keep the wolf from the door, even when their loved ones were sick. He'd filled in for them, reading books out loud, and playing cards in the games room. He'd even suggested that a therapy animal might be something to look into for some of the people who came through the doors.

He'd felt her presence on those corridors too. The place smelled like her. He could see first-hand how much the people in her life thought of her. She wasn't second best to anyone, and he needed her to see that.

They were now mere days away from the charity drive, and it had to go to plan. He wanted to do this day for her, host it in his house, show her *and* the village the real him. The new Chris, who cared, who wore his heart on his sleeve. It had to work. After the drive was done, the opportunity would be lost. She'd sent Trudy the last time she'd needed a vet for one of her rescues, and it was obvious that Trudy was well aware of their situation, as diplomatic as she was. He needed to get this right, and he needed every bit of help he could get.

The doorbell rang, and Hendrix bounded to the door, his nails click-clacking on the wooden floor as he jumped up at the door. Roz, Helen and Cheryl were all standing there, looking a little like the Sanderson Sisters, furtively looking around them for onlookers.

'Come in, ladies, thanks for coming. I really need your help.' He moved aside for them to come in, grabbing some of the bags of goodies they'd brought for the drive. Roz and Helen asked where the kitchen was, and hurried off. Cheryl loitered behind a little, and then surprised Chris by reaching out to hug him.

'Oh,' Chris said, surprised. He hugged her back. 'What's this for? Being a good boss?'

Cheryl pulled back laughing, picking a bit of dog hair off his shirt.

'That, and you finally asking for help. Honestly, Chris, I never thought you'd get it together.' She eyed him up and down. 'Well, you look smart. Are you sure you're ready for this?'

Chris thought of everything that had brought him to this day. To this village, to this practice, to Susannah and her army of amazing friends. These women would do anything for her, and he knew that feeling very well. It had consumed him for weeks.

'Not even a little bit, but I'm done with letting life happen. Are you sure you're ready? She'll be mad, you know.'

Roz cackled from behind them, Helen joining in.

'Oh, Christopher, you have no idea. She'll be livid! Which is precisely why you need to do it. It's perfect, Chris. Trust us.'

Chris laughed, looking at the three friends he'd come to know quite well. He could see why Susannah loved them.

'I do, ladies. Come on, we don't have long. Everyone else is briefed—do they know to keep schtum?'

'We natives can hold our own water, you know.' Helen was grinning at him now, patting Hendrix, who had decided that she was the one that would give him the most fuss. 'Can't we, Hendy?'

Roz chuckled, and Helen rolled her eyes at her.

'Okay, we all live in each other's pockets, but they won't spoil it—don't worry. They know what's important. You should see the sign-up sheet; it's going to be amazing!'

'I know. I still can't believe you came up with it.' That was from Cheryl, who was busy setting up a flip-chart in the corner of the dining room.

'Thanks. I'm not that much of a bore, surely?'

The three women looked at each other, and he could tell that they were deciding how diplomatic they should be.

'Oh, come on! I know I was awful when I first came.'

'Mrs Chan was talking about getting a petition together to run you out of the village at one point. She said you were too political and curt.'

'Her cat was overweight—a petition wouldn't have sorted that,' he retorted huffily. Cheryl's lips clamped together, and she went red. He side-eyed her. 'You know I'm right.' She shook her head, but she was laughing.

'I'll give you that. Bygones, eh?'

The doorbell went, and all four of them jumped.

'Ready?' Chris asked. 'Not a word.'

The three women were now poised for action. For a second he felt like Charlie did when he had his angels in tow.

'We're ready.'

* * *

'What? Why are they here?'

Susannah jerked up the handbrake on her car and stared at the familiar vehicles that were parked outside Chris's house. Roz, Helen and Cheryl were already here? They'd not said anything to her. What was going on lately? Chris seemed to be everywhere these days; all she heard about was the kind village vet and his funny dog. *Her* funny dog, she thought childishly. *She'd* named him; *she'd* nursed him back to health. Now he was some kind of doggy celebrity, and everyone was singing his praises from Puddle Lake church to the outskirts of the village. Irony was a cruel mistress sometimes. When she'd liked Chris, the village hadn't and now, when she needed to keep her distance, it seemed as though the village had adopted him like a lucky stray.

'God, you sound bitter.' She was talking to herself in the mirror again, which only proved how bothered she was. It made it all the harder for her to keep her distance. He seemed better though, happier even. He was out and about, living his life. She was happy for him. She could lie to herself in the mirror all day long about how much of a chicken she felt for cutting loose before things really got started but she couldn't quite pull off deceiving herself about her feelings for him. She'd fallen for him, white coat and all, and she was miserable. She'd even told the shelter she wanted to keep Tank. She couldn't bear to let go of the dog he'd saved and named. Pathetic? Maybe, but Tank was staying put and that was that. She'd already taken him off the list of prospective dogs for the charity day.

The door opened before she even got to the front pathway.

'Oh, hey!' Roz exclaimed, heading out with Helen. 'You're early.' She passed something behind her back to Helen, who headed off to her car. Susannah didn't even register the movement.

'Er…yeah.' She checked her watch, even though she knew damn well what time it was. 'I got off early for once.' Roz nodded, but she was acting off. 'How come you're early?'

'Oh, Helen and I have something on tonight.' She was already retreating to her car, Helen already driving off with a wave. 'We'd better get off, see you at work!'

'Roz, wait…where…' Roz's car door shut with a click, and her engine roared into life '…are you both going?' she said to the retreating car. Roz held up a hand to wave goodbye, and she was gone.

Susannah got her phone out to ring her but, tutting, she put it back in her pocket. She had been a bit of a cow lately. It was no wonder her friends were not in a mood to stop and chat. Seemingly, the nicer and more sociable Chris got, the more she went the other way. Come to think of it, the people she had seen in the village lately had been a bit standoffish too. She looked at her drawn expression in the mirror, and, with a deep sigh, she slapped on some lippy and headed to the house. She was almost to the doors, when the other villagers started arriving, taking with them the chance of any alone time with Chris. She had the dogs to get back to, and her foster cover to relieve.

Before she knew it, she was back home with the puppies and the minutiae of her daily life. Giving Tank an extra kiss before she headed to bed, she wondered why everyone around her was acting so weird. Maybe it was just her. Not being Miss Little Sunshine for once had been out of character for her, but she couldn't help it. She could feel the green-eyed monster pipe up at times too. Stupid really, but it did tick her off. Right when she'd decided to be a grump, the once-hated village vet had transformed himself into a pillar of the community. This time next year he'd be a national treasure, and she'd be one of those women who got videotaped losing their temper in traffic and going viral for being a 'Karen' meme, whatever that meant If she wasn't so confused by the whole thing, she'd probably get a kick out of it.

CHAPTER ELEVEN

WHEN DAWN BROKE on the morning of the charity drive, Susannah opened her bedroom curtains and squinted at the first rays of sun. It was a beautiful summer's day, the ground dry and firm. Perfect conditions for an outdoor charity drive. She could scarcely believe it was here. Turning away from the window, she felt Tank nuzzle against her feet. She picked up the rambunctious puppy, who was still chewing on one of her fluffy white monogrammed slippers. She went to take it out of his mouth.

'Leave, Tank. Got out of your pen again, I see.' The stocky little puppy released the slipper, and a small trail of slobber slid from the mangled fabric, down the sleeve of her nightshirt. 'Ugh.' She gave it back to him. 'Ah well, guess these are yours now. Just leave my wellies and pumps alone. Do we have a deal?' The little puppy was already eviscerating the slipper again. She kissed his broad little face and set him down in his basket under the radiator. 'Trudy will come get you later, okay? I'll see you up there.'

The morning went even faster than Susannah had expected, and before she knew it, people were heading up to Chris's with their stalls and wares in boxes. Trudy and her daughter were on their way to collect some of the dogs at the cottage. There were three at her place ready to home, a Westie called Ricky, a beagle called Dynamo, and a rather nervous Yorkie called Neville. She had high hopes that these dogs, and many others from the shelters, would get a home today. It was what the whole thing had been for, and Susannah was hopeful it would all come off without a hitch.

As she drove through the village, her boot full of stuff for the day, she saw scores of people walking or driving up to Chris's house. When she turned the corner onto his property, she was taken aback to see all the activity. The place was crawling with people. The shelter vans were all there, setting up their areas for the dog shows and the meet-and-greet tents for prospective owners to bond with their possible new fur babies; the stalls were all around the front of the house, running like a ribbon the whole way around it.

'Wow,' she breathed, taking it in. She could scarcely believe the day had arrived, but here it was, looking even better than her wildest dreams. She pulled into a space in the trees, and, getting everything out of her car, she got to work.

'Morning!' Mrs Chan trilled, walking past her with a couple of cake tins stacked up. 'Doesn't it look great? You've done so well.'

'Thanks.' She smiled. 'It takes a village, right?' Mrs Chan laughed with her.

Everyone was bustling around inside, Hendrix barking at everyone from his position at the living-room window. Chris had obviously rather wisely decided to keep him away from the bustle. And, knowing the Doberman as she did, away from the food too. He'd once wolfed down a large pack of mince that had been defrosting on her sideboard. One that she had been planning to cook up for the dogs anyway. She laughed at the memory.

Heading straight down the side of the house, she stopped dead in her tracks. If the front was more than she'd expected, then the back gardens were like stepping into paradise. Everything was fantastic, and just as they'd planned it. There was a large area for the dog show, with obstacles in place in the centre. It looked amazing. She headed over with her piles of stuff, making a beeline for the hospice stall areas first. Everyone was in very high spirits, and raring to go.

'Hi! Almost time!' Helen was sitting at the information stand, ready to get people to donate via a regular monthly direct-debit payment, or give what they could as a one-off. 'It's really come together, hasn't it? Roz is over the moon.'

'Where is Roz?' Susannah asked, but Helen appeared not to hear her. She dropped off the supplies and checked in with the shelters. They all had information boards about the dogs, with some of the more sociable and less nervous ones there, ready to wag their tails and charm their way into a new life. She spent the next hour weaving around, making sure everything was on track and accounted for. Chris was nowhere to be seen, but she knew that he was running a tent for the practice, and would no doubt be busy. She looked around for Cheryl and Roz again, but, without finding them, she resumed her clipboard full of things to check off. She'd see them soon enough.

The day went so fast, and the crowds of people that showed up could have filled the village twice over. Peo-

ple were laughing, having fun on the tombola stalls and
the games. The local radio station had come, and they
were plugging the event for them, interviewing visitors and the shelter staff, talking about the dogs, and
the hospice, and why they were all there, pulling together. The dog show had been a resounding success,
and Hendrix had picked up an award for completing the
circuit in record time. Cheryl had run him around the
event, and Susannah found her mind wandering once
more to their host as she listened to the DJ make another announcement.

'So, folks, as we know, the day has been great so far!
People are digging deep for these charities, and, at the
last count, we have made matches for over twenty dogs!'

Susannah, sitting on a camping chair at the corner of the fenced-off green, clapped, whistling with
her fingers. Twenty dogs in just a few short hours! It
was working. She felt the relief overcome her, and she
wiped a tear from her cheek as she hollered with the
rest of the applauding crowd. *Chris.* She looked for him
in the crowd again, but he wasn't there. In the corner
of her eye, she suddenly spotted Cheryl pulling out a
large square object on a set of wheels. Neville from Oak
Farm, complete with some fresh-looking hair implants,
was helping her. A couple of women in the crowd giggled and waved to him.

Good for you, Nev. He does look good. More happy,
confident.

He pushed the large object, which was covered in
a sheet, into the centre of the field and winked at the
ladies as he made his way back to the crowds. Susannah was just wondering what the heck the box was for,
when her world went dark.

'Hey!' she shouted, but someone clamped a hand down over her mouth.

'Shush, it's me,' Roz said into her ear. She tied something round the back of Susannah's head, and she found herself being dragged off. Another set of arms reached for her, and she kicked out.

'Ow!' Cheryl cried out.

'Cheryl? Roz? Get this off me now! Argh!' She was silenced again, and felt her feet leave the floor. Her bottom was plonked into a rather hard chair, and then the hands were gone. She reached forward, trying to grab at them, but her hands hit something hard. *A wall?* She tried to stand, but then she heard Roz's voice over the microphone.

'What did you do?' Susannah growled under her breath. She tried to get the blindfold off, but felt someone slap her hand away. When she tried to turn around, realising that the walls were only on three sides, she was shoved back into her chair. 'When I get my hands on you, Cheryl, it's not going to be pretty. What are you doing?'

Roz's voice was booming across the crowd, the odd ripple of applause from the crowds erupting when she named and thanked the various people in attendance. Susannah folded her arms, and glowered beneath her blindfold.

'And now,' Roz said theatrically, 'we have a very special guest, with a very special surprise event! Can you put your hands together, please, for our host, our very own village vet, Dr Christopher Jennings?'

The crowd whooped even louder than the other times, and Susannah swore she heard Mrs Chan shout, 'That's my boy! Go, Chris!'

'Yay, Christopher!' she whooped along sarcastically. 'Jennings for mayor!' She held both hands up and waved tiny imaginary flags in his honour. 'Woo-hoo,' she monotoned. *Kill me now.* That one was just for her.

'Thank you.' Chris spoke into the microphone now, and the crowd hushed. She could hear Hendrix bark, and he sounded close. 'And thank you, Puddle Lake, for giving me such a warm welcome to the village. I am only too happy to offer mine to you all today, and we're here now to celebrate one special lady. Cheryl, can you do the honours?'

Susannah felt Cheryl tug at the fabric at the back of her head, and she dug her nails into the soft flesh. Cheryl jumped back. 'Hey! Knock it off.'

'Knock it off? What's going on?'

'Trust me,' Cheryl said, right into her ear. Susannah sighed heavily but put her talons away. 'And get a manicure too. Geez.'

Susannah chuckled. 'I hope I drew blood. I'd better not be on a dunking stool. I mean it!' Cheryl just laughed, smoothing her hair down and retreating.

'Oh, it's much better than that. Hold tight!'

There was a series of bangs around her, and the blindfold fell away. Susannah opened her eyes, and the whole village was staring at her. The 'walls' she'd been beating against were gone, leaving only a wooden frame. There was a sign at the front of the structure, but from her position she couldn't read what it said. She was still taking in her surroundings when Chris spoke again, and her eyes were on nothing but him.

He looked so handsome, so…peaceful. He was wearing an open-neck white shirt, a pair of dark blue jeans with wellies on. His hair was ruffled, and she knew he'd run his hands through it many times that day. Hendrix was sitting by him. She felt the old flicker of attraction burn in her chest. He walked over to her slowly, and, when he was close, he gave her a wink. The movement was so intimate, in front of the world, so sexy, that she was suddenly glad she'd been shoved onto a chair.

'Nothing that we see before us today would have been possible without our resident nurse and dog rescuer, Susannah Harkin. Now, if you don't know Susannah, she's pretty easy to spot. She dresses like Joseph in her Technicolor clothes, and she gives her heart and soul to this village, and to the people in it. I've never met a woman like her, and personally I'm very grateful that she crashed into my surgery one day, with this little monster in tow.' He nodded to Hendrix, who barked loudly, delighted to be mentioned. The crowd laughed along with Chris. 'I'm sure it's not a secret that when I first came, I was a little…sullen.'

Mrs Chan piped up. 'Understatement of the century!'

Chris threw her a wry look, his gorgeous brow raised, and Mrs Chan blew him a kiss. The crowd whooped.

'Yes, thank you, Mrs Chan. Well, I was a little lost when I first came here. Susannah was the one who made me realise just how much life has to offer, especially in this corner of the Earth. So I wanted to honour Susannah, and everything she does for her patients, her dear friends, and the animals she works with. I am sure you can all agree, and know even more than I do, that without her this village would not be quite as bright.'

His eyes were burning into hers now, and she looked right back at him. She couldn't tear her eyes away. 'What people might not know about Susannah is her love of romance novels, and how she loves matchmaking those gorgeous dogs with their new owners. So in honour of the day, and in the spirit of matchmaking…' Susannah groaned, and a ripple of laughter burbled around her '…what better way to honour her than to have our very own…' he pulled a sheet of cardboard she hadn't seen from the sign '…Village Matchmaker?'

The crowd gasped, applauded and whooped as he bent to take a bow at her feet. When he raised his gaze, her look of shock didn't seem to register with him. He flashed her a devilish look.

'The rules of the Matchmaker are simple: a person looking for a match signs up to see if they can find their match from the suitors in the audience!' He did a little gameshow host sweep of his hands, before cupping his mouth around the microphone. 'Keep it clean—we have animals and children present.' The crowd rippled with laughter, and Susannah was glued to the edge of her seat. Any trace of surly Chris was gone from the man she was observing.

'So, before we get started with our lucky contestants, starting with our resident and newly single farmer—give us a shout, Neville!' He turned in Neville's direction, and Neville stood from his seat, flexing his muscles and making the females in the crowd all cat-call loudly. Susannah spotted his ex-wife, sitting with her new partner and looking very much put out that he was getting so much attention. Susannah saw her look from Neville to her new partner, and she looked a little disappointed in the new comparison.

Good for you, Nev, she thought. *Good for you. Maybe there is such a thing as second chances.*

Chris waited for Neville to retake his seat, and then he reached into his pocket, and pulled out a wad of notes.

'Neville will be here shortly, ladies, but first of all, I would like to make the first match of the day.' The crowd oohed collectively, and Susannah's heart melted. 'Susannah,' he started. He leaned down in front of her, so his elbows were on the booth counter in front of her. 'Susie. I have here in my hand a thousand pounds for the charity pot, for the chance to match with you.'

The crowd went mad, shouts of 'Go for it' and 'Grab it, you fool!' ringing out in the crowd. Chris grinned, and she found herself grinning back. Quietly, so the microphone wouldn't pick it up, she whispered to him.

'What are you doing?' she asked, half in shock, half delighted.

He leaned in close, and she caught the familiar scent of him. God, she loved this man. He was insufferable, and stubborn. Sometimes she wanted to slap him; other times she wanted to grab him and never let go. He whispered back, and she was lost for ever.

'I'm proving that, to me, you will never be second best. To anyone. Ever. You healed me, Susie. I couldn't imagine wanting to devote the rest of my life to anyone or anything else, but you. You are it for me. When you walked away, when I came to the hospice… It was all just so obvious to me once I saw it. You irritate the hell out of me, and I want you to do it for ever.' He leaned closer, and the crowd grew louder. 'I know you think I'm stubborn, and surly.'

'Don't forget oafish,' she quipped, and her lips twitched. He broke out into a broad grin.

'That too,' he acquiesced. 'I was all those things, but it wasn't just about losing Karen. It was the fact that we'd realised, too late, that our jobs were our main loves. We cared for each other, but it wasn't like this.'

He pointed his finger from his chest to hers, mirroring the action she'd used on him all that time ago. 'I was meant to come here, for you. For this.' He turned and waved his arm across the crowds, who were all waiting with bated breath for her answer.

'So,' he said, putting the money in the glass jar Cheryl had brought up, 'this money is in the pot, whatever you decide. I just want you to know that, to me, you will always come first. I love you, Susie. With my whole heart.' A single tear ran down her cheek, and he brushed it away with his hand. 'So,' he said into the microphone now, addressing the crowd once more, 'the money is in the pot, whatever you decide. Susannah Harkin, will you make me the happiest vet in the village…' he waggled his brows at her, turning her tears into laughter '…and be my match?'

The crowd went nuts, but Susannah didn't hear them. All she could see was Chris, and the whole village watching him woo her. Right there, where her parents and Heather had lived and died, where she'd grown from a girl into a woman. From a broken divorcee, to an independent woman, who now had a man who cherished the things in this simple life just as much as she did. They'd both had their hearts broken, and seen grief close enough for it to leave a mark on their souls for ever. They'd still found each other though, and she thanked her lucky stars for it. She stood up, taking the microphone from him.

'Dr Jennings,' she said, liking the feel of his name on her lips. She wanted to shout it from the rooftops. 'I thought you'd never ask.'

The crowd went crazy, and as he pulled her close, taking her mouth with his, she could hear everyone cheer. Hendrix was going mental, zooming around the booth like an excited child and leading the dog chorus, and she could hear the yells and whoops from Cheryl, Helen and Roz even above the din of everyone else. Chris pulled her into his arms, and kissed her as if he was afraid to stop. Which was ridiculous, because one thing she would never want him to do was stop kissing her.

When they eventually pulled away, the crowd rejoiced, and Roz took the microphone, calling Neville up for his chance. As Chris came and pulled Susannah towards the house, they could just make out Nancy elbowing her way to the front of the queue, pushing the other women out of the way to be the first to get to Neville. Chris saw it too, and laughed. 'Good for you, Nev,' he said.

Once they were in the house, he pulled her in for another long kiss.

'You're mad—you know that, don't you?' she said breathlessly when he finally let them both come up for air. 'You paid a thousand quid for something you could have had for free.'

He laughed heartily. 'Ah well, it's only money. I was thinking of the tax write-off anyway.' She went to slap him on the arm, and he grabbed it, linking her fingers through his, looking down at her. She felt so seen under his gaze. So cherished. 'I would have given the shirt off my back for the chance to prove to you how much you mean to me.' Another kiss, this time on her jawline. She shuddered with delight. 'God, I wish we didn't have a million people to look after. We could have a lot of fun, just the two of us.' He lowered his lips to her neck, tracing a line of kisses along her skin to her collarbone. 'I love you so much.'

She drew back to look into his eyes. 'I love you too, Dr Moody Pants.' The look of relief and delight on his face made her love him all the more in that instant. 'I'm so glad you came to Puddle Lake.'

'Not half as glad as I am,' he replied, touching his forehead to hers as he pressed his body against hers. 'Now, what do you say, shall we get this over with? We have some dogs to save and some money to raise.' He dipped his gaze to her body. 'And tonight, I would like to revisit the wonky-top situation, if you're up for it.'

She blushed as desire and love flowed through her.

'In the interests of medical science, I'm sure that can be arranged.'

His smile lit up the room, brighter than anything she'd ever worn.

'That's what I like to hear. Let's go.' Reluctantly letting her loose from his embrace, he took her hand in his, and together they headed back out, to enjoy their special day with the villagers.

Hendrix was waiting by the door, wagging his tail in delight as he spotted the pair.

'Do you think he'll get on with Tank?' she asked. 'I adopted him.'

Chris's eyes snapped to hers, and he grinned. 'You did?'

'Yeah. I couldn't let him go, not after you saved him.'

Hendrix jumped up at them both, but Chris clicked his fingers and he settled back down.

'You know what?' He smiled. 'I have a feeling the four of us are going to get on like a house on fire.' As they headed out onto the lawn, the villagers cheered their arrival.

Chris didn't leave her side all day, and every day after that. Susannah never felt second best again, and she would be grateful for ever for the paws and waggy tails that had brought the two of them together and helped them to find each other. They had found their for ever home, just like the furry souls they'd helped along the way.

* * * * *

THE MIDWIFE'S
NINE-MONTH
MIRACLE

SHELLEY RIVERS

MILLS & BOON

To Don,
whom the family lost during the writing of this book.

I hope the dog walks in heaven
are as good as the ones down here on earth.

And to Jean, one of the silent army of carers
who are often forgotten. You did good, girl.

CHAPTER ONE

Mart's Medical Clinic, London

GILA WRIGHT RUBBED a hand over her stomach and tried not to laugh at the appalled faces being made by the seven teenage girls viewing the film depicting a birth scene. But every time she gave this class, the horrified expressions on the faces of the young mums-to-be as the reality of impending labour hit home always made her chuckle.

'It's a bit grim, isn't it?' one expectant mother commented with a deep frown, her fingers flipping the braided strap of her purple handbag.

'Don't worry,' Gila soothed with practised ease. 'You'll be too busy pushing your child out into the world to be concerned with anything else. It's all perfectly natural and survivable.'

None of the girls appeared overly convinced by Gila's reassuring words. Each eager to do everything correctly during their pregnancy, while secretly dreading the actual event of impending childbirth and new motherhood. Gila understood their concerns. In less than a month, she too would be going through the whole process for the first time. Though at thirty-two years old she was far from being an unmarried teenager.

Since Mart's had opened two years previous, the walk-in clinic had run antenatal classes especially for teenage mothers. It had begun as a pilot scheme to help relieve the strain and workload on several of the area's local health practices. A place where young women could find help and information no matter what their circumstances were. Somewhere welcoming where the teenagers received no judgement or criticism. Just help, information and caring medical advice. The classes had proved so successful that a decision had been made to run them permanently, having become an important service to the neighbouring community, and many of the medical staff who worked at Mart's were actually volunteers who lived in the area and fitted in shifts around their main hospital jobs.

Gila had joined the staff two months ago, after taking maternity leave from her position as a midwife at the local maternity unit. She spent two days a week volunteering at the clinic, rather than sitting around on her uncle's narrowboat, lonely and bored, with too much time to dwell on things she'd prefer not to.

Rubbing her hand lovingly over her baby bump again, she sent a silent prayer of thanks as the film ended, signalling the end of the week's session. Her back ached, her slightly swollen feet pinched against the insides of her flat black shoes, and she yearned to head home. And for the last hour she'd also craved sliced apples and thick toffee sauce with ridiculous intensity. Both of which she envisaged eating while lying in a warm relaxing bath.

'So, any questions?' she asked, returning her full

attention to the circle of young women. 'This is our last group together before I leave to have *my* baby, so if you do think of anything before your next class with my colleague Sarah, who's taking over from me, remember you can speak to your individual midwives or family doctors. They are there to help. Nothing that is worrying you is silly or unimportant. I promise medics and midwives have heard everything before, no matter how crazy-sounding, so don't let embarrassment stop you. Okay?'

'I have a question,' asked a teenager, sticking up her hand as though still at school. 'How long before we let our partners back? You know, physically. Because after watching that—' she pointed at the now blank screen '—I'm thinking seriously about asking to be sterilised after the birth.'

Gila laughed and quickly mollified her. 'Depending on the birth, but usually we advise six weeks before resuming making love. I promise you'll soon forget about the messy side of giving birth the minute your baby settles in your arms. And if you want, I can suggest to Sarah that she talks about birth control options for after your babies arrive, at the next session.'

Several young mothers murmured their enthusiasm for the idea, before they all stood and shuffled towards the door, chatting and laughing as they filed out of the room. Each airing their opinion of what they had just watched.

Gila slowly rose from her chair, as a too familiar heavy silence and melancholy moved through her as the last young woman waved goodbye and closed the door. The difference between her and those seven young girls was that Gila knew for a fact that they would each be sharing the births of their first child with a partner at their side. Whether a boyfriend, mother or even a brother, each one fortunate to have someone with them cheering them on through the long hours of labour. Whereas Gila would face the birth of her child alone. The father of her baby would not be reassuring her with encouragement and loving words. Or holding her hand and whispering praise as the labour intensified. No, her child's father would be absent, just as he had been for the last four months of her pregnancy. Ever since the night she packed a bag and walked out on him.

She sighed and reached for the blue medical bag sitting in the centre of the large desk in the corner of the room. Afternoon sunlight cast its warmth into the area through the large window that faced out onto the clinic's car park, illuminating the normally invisible dust particles floating in the air. She empathised with those twisting and turning specks. Existing, yet not really having somewhere special to land and make a long-term home. A particular spot where they were really wanted.

Shoving several folders into the bag, Gila searched for the rest of her belongings. She was due to finish working at the clinic the following week, but each day she gathered a few more of her bits and pieces to take home rather than leave everything to the last day. She'd enjoyed volunteering at the clinic, but as her pregnancy advanced she found her energy sapping quicker with each passing week, often returning home utterly exhausted. She still had so much to organise before the baby came. Things she'd purposely put off, unwilling to do them alone. Hoping the situation with her baby's father might change and improve. But it hadn't, so it appeared that alone was exactly how she would be doing everything from now on. At least until the little one arrived.

She picked up her diary from the desk, her eyes falling onto the slim white band of skin on her left third finger. The place where her wedding ring once encircled. She'd removed it a week ago during a bout of tears and self-pity. One long lonely night, when the sight of it and everything it once represented mocked her one time too often for ever believing in happiness and love.

Her disruptive and unconventional childhood should have taught her better than to imagine that a normal happy life could finally be hers. That the pipe dream of a perfect marriage was actually achievable. Surely her own father's many destructive short-term relationships and incessant itch to wander the world, pursuing one false dream after another, should have taught Gila that simple truth didn't exist?

Yet despite knowing better, she'd hoped her relationship with her husband would be different. That it would last for ever and show everyone around them that she wasn't an undependable relationship car crash like her father, but a responsible adult who lived an ordinary, contented life. After all, she'd witnessed her parent's slip-ups so often, there was no chance she'd commit similar ones, was there?

Only, despite everything she'd thought and believed, it seemed she stupidly had.

In spite of all the promises she'd whispered to herself as a child on those nights when they'd slept on the pavements of unfamiliar streets because her father's money had run out and the hotel they'd been staying in had evicted them. Or the days when she would sit alone on a balcony while her father spent time with yet another woman he'd met and tumbled into mock love with. Left and ignored while they made love in another room. Gila had forgotten all of those promises and naively fallen in love with a man who turned out not to love her as deeply as she thought. And now she was weeks away from having their child and the solitude of the situation she found herself in seemed to increase with each and every passing day.

As she closed the bag, a knock on the door drew her attention from her sombre contemplations. Forcing a lightness she wasn't feeling into her tone and mood, she called out, 'Come in.'

Trudy, the afternoon receptionist, who dressed similar to a nineteen-fifties Hollywood starlet, opened the door and flashed Gila a cheerful smile. Tall and stylish, she reminded Gila of everything she was not.

'All finished for the day?' Trudy asked.

'Just packing up,' Gila replied with a smile she wasn't feeling. 'I'm glad it's nearly the weekend, though.' No longer working full-time at the hospital, she had the rare luxury of the whole Easter weekend free and she intended to enjoy every minute. Well, perhaps enjoy was too ambitious a goal, considering the wreck her private life was in, but she refused to spend further time wallowing. She intended to finish the lemon baby's blanket she'd started knitting a few weeks ago, despite the fact it looked nothing like the pattern's picture, and then make sure she'd bought everything she needed for the baby's imminent appearance.

'I've a ton of things to do,' she continued. Which wasn't quite true, but she doubted Trudy wanted to hear that her weekends were actually the worst part of the week because the days dragged like old arthritic toes through a puddle of treacle and gave her the unwanted opportunity to lull over how everything in her life had changed from being perfect and wonderful into a huge dreadful and horrible mess within the matter of months.

'I thought you'd want to know Reese Newman has walked in with her boyfriend, complaining of stomach pains. Any chance you can assist the doctor dealing with her? She behaves better with you.'

Reese, a teenager who was five months pregnant, struggled with every aspect of her pregnancy. She'd spent half of her life in foster homes and had been expelled from two schools, a fact she'd proudly informed Gila of the first time they met. She was also unfortunately rude and at times aggressive. She ignored most medical advice and spent her time following her on-off boyfriend as he committed one crime after another. She also had no settled home life or relationship with her birth parents, and loved nothing more than causing a scene.

Gila groaned softly and swung the bag onto her shoulder. Any other day she'd willingly deal with the girl's abrasive manner, but today she was just too exhausted. 'Must I?'

'She's with the new doctor right now,' Trudy said, leaning against the door frame. 'I doubt it's going well. You know what she's like with new people.'

'New doctor?' Gila asked, only half listening. Because a portion of the clinic's staff consisted of volunteers, it wasn't unusual for medics to come and go. Some stayed for a few months, others only a few days or weeks.

'Wait until you see him,' Trudy said with a grin. 'The man's gorgeous. Sexier than a top-ten heart-throb.

Has lovely wavy dark hair that hits his shoulders.' She tapped her own and smiled dreamily. 'Makes a woman think all sorts of naughty thoughts about tugging it.'

'I thought Dr Peters worked on Friday afternoons,' Gila said, walking towards the door. Dr Peters headed the Accident and Emergency department at the local hospital, but volunteered several days a week at the clinic. She knew him well, but so far they'd both covered different shifts, so she hadn't seen him during the weeks she'd been working at the clinic.

'Normally he does, but he's had to rush off to America to be with his daughter. Something about her child's been taken ill and it's not looking good. So he's arranged for this new doctor to step in for a couple of weeks to cover his Tuesday, Wednesday and Friday shifts. I swear my knees shook when the man walked in and spoke to me. Gorgeous brown eyes. Like pools of melted truffles. Rich and completely bad for a female's peace of mind. And his deep voice—wow.'

'Really?' Gila asked, mostly because Trudy expected it than any real interest in the new doctor. She was off men for good and wasn't in the mood to drool over another handsome one. Besides, this advanced in her pregnancy the only salivating she did involved toffee-covered edibles. Doctors were especially off her menu.

'How about a cup of raspberry tea before you go?' Trudy suggested, moving back so Gila could step out of the room and into the corridor.

Gila winced at the idea, sickness creeping up her throat. She swallowed away the undesired taste and shook her head. She really wanted to go home, but, conscious of not wanting to be considered grumpy, she said, 'If you have ginger and lemon, I'll consider it. Raspberry tea just reminds me of morning sickness.'

Trudy laughed as they walked along the corridor and headed towards the consultation rooms. 'It's jam sand-wiches for me. Someone told me during my pregnancy that they helped with alleviating morning sickness when I was carrying my twins, and to some degree they did, but now I can't stand the smell of strawberry jam with-out wanting to run for the nearest bathroom. So are you looking forward to becoming a mum?'

This time Gila's smile was genuine. 'I can't wait.'

'Do you know what you're having?'

'No, I want it to be a surprise,' she said, and in an effort to change the subject before it became even more personal, she asked, 'Which consultation room is Reese being seen in?'

Trudy pointed to the one at the far end of the cor-ridor. 'Room three. Don't forget to pop into the staff room before you leave. No sneaking off home hoping I won't notice.'

Gila forced another smile, and promised, 'I won't.'

Moving in the direction of the consultation room, she rubbed a hand over her stomach once more. If Reese was in an awkward mood, Gila would need a ton of pa-tience, because a sixth sense warned her that the next few minutes were going to be tough. She just didn't realise how right that prediction would actually turn out to be.

Leo Wright listened to the pregnant patient and frowned. Both she and the young man who'd accompanied her had continued to complain and bicker since stepping into the consultation room. Despite several attempts to intervene and discover the reason for their visit, Leo still had no idea what ailed the young woman. The only clue he'd gathered while observing her movements was the way she kept wincing and placing a hand to the right side of her stomach.

'Reese, perhaps if you'd just compose yourself,' Leo suggested, keeping his voice low, patient and friendly. 'Then we might be able to work out what it is that has brought you to the clinic today.'

'In other words, stop whingeing, and let the doctor help ya,' her boyfriend grumbled, his eyes not shifting from the screen of his phone.

Leo sighed when the young couple resumed arguing. The only reason he stood in this bland, unfamiliar room was because he owed his boss the biggest favour and he secretly wanted a chance to see his wife. Small glimpses from the window of his home were usually all he caught thanks to the fact that, despite leaving him and their home, she still resided close by. Brief moments where he mostly stared at her back as she walked away. For the last few weeks he'd suspected Gila of avoiding him. They needed to sort things out between them soon. The odd text and email concerning their unborn baby was not enough. This lack of real communication had continued for too long. Their baby's birth was mere weeks away and it was vital for him to be involved. He desperately wanted to be closer than he was right now. In what capacity he didn't care, but this silent stand-off and purposely skirting around each other wasn't helping either of them.

The time had come to try and fix the wrong he'd committed. He now understood that, without meaning to, he'd hurt the one precious person in his life. His wife. His Gila.

Every part of him wanted to beat and howl against the agony of knowing that he'd shattered her trust. That he alone had caused the anguish in her beautiful grey eyes and broken her world apart. He'd damaged their marriage and taken the most wonderful, tender woman and wrecked her. And why? Because the turmoil that had developed inside his heart after his sister's death had grown so big and powerful, he'd pushed everyone who mattered away. Not capable of dealing with the overwhelming guilt that had consumed him, he'd retreated into himself, when he should have clung to his wife, the way a dying man clutched to breath and hope.

Last November his kid sister, Jodie, died from a drugs overdose. One he'd failed to save her from. All the years of learning and practising medicine. Years poring over medical books and passing practical tests and for what? So he could help strangers, yet when his own sick sister had desperately required his help, he'd been useless to stop her addiction and keep her alive. Even worse, guilty of turning her away when she'd needed him the most.

For three days, Leo had sat by Jodie's hospital bedside, praying for her to wake up from a coma, but in the end she'd silently given up and slipped away. Leaving this world without giving him the chance to say sorry or goodbye.

And for weeks after, the sorrow and the misery had swamped everything in Leo's life. Catching him at quiet moments, the remorse had chewed at his conscience and gnawed at his heart.

Instead of seeking comfort in his wife's arms, Leo

had turned from Gila, not wanting to drag her into the bleak levels of despair that ate at him. Reluctant to admit his part in Jodie's death to anyone. If Gila had learnt the truth, she would have stopped seeing him as a protector, and viewed him as nothing but a failure. He would cease to be the hero he suspected his wife secretly viewed him as, leaving him exposed as nothing but a useless man incapable of protecting and helping a loved one. An incompetent doctor unable to heal.

Then after weeks of his pretending that everything was fine, hiding the agony inside him, everything had finally tumbled down and smothered Leo completely, ridding him of sane thought and normal behaviour. He'd withdrawn into his internal hell of regret and blame until he'd become aware of nothing but the darkness and the shame.

Even now, months later, he didn't understand why he'd reacted in that way. Or why he'd hurt the one person he truly loved.

Closing his eyes, Leo silently repeated the words his grief counsellor suggested he say every time the past's emotions threatened to resurface. With his counsellor's help he'd started the journey through the self-reproach, depression and sorrow. It wasn't an easy or fast process, but with each weekly session he was slowly accepting Jodie's death and putting everything into its proper context. His behaviour and the decisions he'd made before his sister's passing hadn't cause Jodie's death. With his counsellor's help, he was beginning to see that.

A counsellor his boss, Dr Peters, had insisted he visit, after recognising the signs of anxiety and depression in Leo. Without his boss's help, Leo doubted he'd still have a career or his job at the local hospital's A & E.

It was also Peters who'd come to him the previous day, in a terrible state, and begged him to temporarily take over his weekly shifts at Mart's, so that he could leave the country to be with his daughter and seriously sick grandchild. Without hesitation, Leo had agreed. Happy to do whatever favour the man asked, though how his estranged wife was going to react when she found out he would be working at the clinic, Leo didn't want to consider. But the chance to help and repay his boss as a work colleague and a friend took priority.

Returning his attention to the young woman sitting on the examination table, he suggested, 'How about you tell me why you're holding your hand to your side?'

Again she ignored him.

'Does it hurt there?' Leo coaxed.

'I ain't talking to you,' the teenager snapped.

A knock on the door prevented him from replying. With a curt nod at the female, he strolled over to the door and flung it open. And finally encountered the woman who haunted his every thought.

Gripping the handle, Leo lowered his gaze and took in the shape of their growing child beneath her too large, shapeless blue uniform. A child he desperately wanted to be close to. His flesh and blood, his contribution to his future family. Boy or girl, he didn't care. He just wanted to be its father. Somehow, he had to repair his relationship with Gila enough to be able to do that. He just hoped for their unborn child's sake it wasn't an impossible mission.

'Hello, Gila,' he said softly. 'Won't you come in?'

'Leo?' Gila's heart stopped as her brain tried to make sense and acknowledge the man standing in the doorway. For the last few months she'd avoided him, other than the odd text to keep him up to date on the baby's health and development, but here he was in the one place she'd considered herself safe from his presence.

Gripping the canvas straps of her bag, she forced her legs to keep her upright and not collapse into a crumpled heap the way the rest of her body suddenly longed to. How would Leo react if she did? Would he care enough to scoop her up from the floor, or would he leave her where she landed in a pool of shock and body parts and ignore her as he'd done for the last few months? Just pretend she didn't exist and was no concern of his.

She didn't trust in coincidences. She did however believe in bad luck, and it appeared that life had again chosen to dump another reeking bucketful slap bang in her path.

'Finally,' a female voice complained behind Leo. 'Someone I know. Here, Miss Wright, will you tell this man to leave me alone?'

'Sorry,' Gila stammered, her heartbeat thundering like a thousand drumming fingers. 'I must have the wrong room.'

Trembling, she half turned, desperate to get away from the man and the swoosh of memories initiated from one glance of his handsome face. Strong features whose hard plains she'd once traced and scattered with kisses and reverence. Bronze skin, sometimes smooth, occasionally covered with dark bristles that tickled her fingertips and prickled her own flesh in places only he had ever uncovered and explored.

'Gila.'

She stiffened at the sound of her name falling from his lips after so many weeks of silence and glanced back. The bright artificial light in the corridor giving her a view of the man she'd once adored, before he'd destroyed all that they'd shared.

She shook her head and moved away. Not even for Reese and her baby's well-being could Gila walk into the room and pretend that the man she'd once loved wasn't there with them. That he didn't stand less than a foot away. That his familiar body didn't dominate the space, reminding her of things she'd spent weeks and days deliberately closing her mind from. No, she couldn't do it. Not even for a patient. For once, not this time.

For long torturous weeks, she'd worked to regather the fragments of her shattered life. With no other choice, she'd forced the pain of Leo's abandonment to one side, refusing to face it, instead throwing herself into her work. And now, when she'd finally believed she had found a balance, here he appeared to upend and unsettle her calmness once again.

'No. I'm sorry, I must—'

'Gila, wait.'

The deep words wrapped around her, tempting and provoking. Wasn't it enough that Leo tortured her dreams, causing her to continually replay their last conversation when he'd proven that everything she'd imagined true about their relationship was nothing but a lie?

'No,' she whispered again, lowering her eyes. She couldn't do this. It was too late, or maybe too soon for this encounter.

He reached for her, but she jerked away, not wanting his touch. Once she'd craved his fingers on her body, desired the firm stroke of his caress upon her skin, now the thought made her stomach ache and her skin prickle.

This man once slipped a gold ring onto her finger in front of a church full of family and friends. A church not three miles from here. Then he'd professed to worship and love her for six wonderful months of perfect marriage, before discarding her from his life like an unwanted curio he'd simply grown bored of playing with.

'Oi, Miss Wright,' Reese called, oblivious to the tension between the two professionals. 'I want to speak to you.'

Leo stepped back and refocused on the patient. 'Miss Newman, you came here because you said you required help. Other patients wait in Reception. Ones who truly want our assistance. So unless you wish to sit for hours in the nearest hospital's A & E, I suggest you tell me exactly what is wrong.'

Pushing all emotions and private desires aside, Gila swallowed her reluctance and pride and stepped into the room. Moving over to where Reese waited, she took control of both the situation and the argumentative teenager. 'Reese, tell Dr Wright, what's the problem? He can help you.'

Reese pouted and folded her arms.

Gila sighed softly and used her best no-nonsense midwife voice. Knowing this was the best way to deal with the girl. Not taken in by the tough front Reese frequently hid behind when scared. She recognised the insecurity and self-doubt in the young woman as the same form that once sat in her own uncertain heart. Convinced that the world viewed you with disdain and disgust, simply because your home life differed from the standard model. What she'd learnt through her work as a midwife was that there was no standard family. Every single one was different.

'Because you're here for a reason,' she continued. 'And I'm sure it isn't to waste our time. So, are you in pain? You're very pale. Are you taking the iron tablets I prescribed for you?'

Reese shrugged guiltily. 'I lost them.'

'I'll write you a new prescription before you leave. It's important that you take them. So, where's the pain?'

Reese sighed, then, with a resentful glare at her boyfriend, stated, 'I'm not being a baby. Everyone thinks I am, but it really hurts here in my side. I vomited several times, too. I thought it was just the pregnancy, but I don't know. Something don't feel right.'

Leo moved closer but continued to let Gila lead the consultation.

'Reese, will you allow me to check you over while Dr Wright observes?' Gila asked.

'Go ahead.' Reese sighed, amazingly complacent now someone was listening to her fears. She glanced worriedly at Gila, vulnerability shining from her young, troubled eyes. 'Do you think there's something wrong with the baby?'

'Let's not worry yet,' Gila soothed, patting her arm. 'Now lie down and can you tell me exactly where the pain is and how it feels? Is it a dull pain? Or perhaps a stabbing kind of pain?'

She gently placed her fingers to the teenager's stomach on the right side, below her baby bump. 'If I press here, does it hurt more when I pull my fingers away or less?'

Reese gasped as Gila drew her fingers away. With a glare, she answered, 'More.'

Gila glanced at Leo, seeing the same suspicion in his eyes. 'And you say you've suffered bouts of sickness?'

'Yes.' Reese nodded.

Leo smiled reassuringly and glanced at Gila. 'Okay, well, I suspect it's a grumbling appendix. What do you think?'

'Highly likely,' Gila agreed with the prognosis, having come to the same conclusion.

Leo took over now they'd both agreed on the possible cause of Reese's pain and discomfort. 'I'm going to call for an ambulance to drive you over to the main hospital and once you're there the doctors can run tests and find out exactly what is going on.'

'Is it dangerous?' asked Reese's boyfriend. 'She ain't going to lose the kid, is she?'

Leo faced the man. 'I'm not going to lie to you. In severe cases it can be life-threatening. It's important Reese goes to the hospital and gets it checked out. This isn't an issue you should ignore or leave.'

Gila helped Reese down from the examination table. 'I'll write out a new prescription for the iron tablets and meet you in Reception. Do not leave before I give it to you. Okay?'

Gila followed the young couple out of the room, ignoring Leo, who stood watching her. She'd done her job and helped with Reese, but that was all she owed the man who didn't care that he'd broken her heart. Or that he'd taken all her stupid secret precious daydreams and shattered every single one.

CHAPTER TWO

'SURPRISE!'

Gila jumped and stared at the small group of colleagues crammed into the tiny staff room, and almost gave into the urge to run for the closest exit. She wanted to flee from the building, or in her case waddle quickly away from all the people now grinning expectantly at her.

Doctors, nurses, receptionists, even the clinic's office staff gawked back at her with bright eager faces waiting for a reaction. She immediately regretted not leaving after seeing Reese into the ambulance, but her conscience had battled against the impulse and she'd reluctantly headed to the staff room intending to drink a cup of fruit tea with Trudy and leave as quickly as possible.

But that resolution wasn't going to be doable now because it was clear that any chance to escape for home was a long way off.

So this was the real reason why Trudy had insisted she join her for refreshments, despite it being the end of Gila's shift. The other woman obviously planned to inflict social hell, wrapped up in a thoughtful act, on her. Gila's gaze flickered to the brightly wrapped pile of gifts in Trudy's hands. Oh, great, another baby shower. She'd already endured this public agony with her other colleagues at the hospital before starting her official maternity leave. When she'd had to pretend that everything was hunky-dory in her life, and not show any hint that their act of kindness made her want to buckle into a pile of uncontrollable sobs. And now her colleagues at the clinic, with this touching and sweet deed, left her feeling the same way. Only this time, thanks to her recent run-in with Leo, she feared she didn't have the strength to hide her inner heartache.

Forcing back tears, she forced her mouth into a wobbly smile and hoped her acting skills weren't too horrendous or lacking. 'I don't know what to say.'

'It's just a few small things for the baby,' Trudy quickly explained as she crossed the room and gently drew Gila inside. The firmness of the woman's grip on her arm hinted that Gila's acting skills must really suck. 'We wanted the baby to have something special, so we all clubbed together and purchased these few gifts for you to remember us by.'

Touched, Gila sensed movement behind her and almost let the tears fall when she turned her head to find Leo staring at her. Standing in the doorway, his white doctor's coat now replaced by a familiar black jacket and faded blue jeans. Part of her yearned to rush across the room and bury herself in his arms.

Trudy was spot on when she described Leo as gorgeous. Handsome in a rough, square-jawed kind of way. Brown kind eyes, thick wavy brown hair that curled on his shoulders. His nose slightly crooked, thanks to a moped accident as a teenager. In truth, his features should have created a face full of imperfections, yet the opposite was true. They sat together in perfect accord. As though the clever fingers of a super-talented sculptor had carefully and lovingly carved them over long hours and many days. Not stopping until the features were perfect.

Gila turned away and allowed Trudy to hand over the presents and lead her towards the others. She dragged up her fake and much used, though utterly despised, happy face. The one she'd formed as a second skin over the last few months. The expression she only dropped when alone, so no one would guess her true internal misery.

Stammering, she said to the group, 'Y-you shouldn't have gone to all this trouble.'

Though her attention appeared to be on the others, her mind crammed and twisted with questions concerning the man standing behind her. Even with space between them, she could feel his presence as though he were imprinted on her flesh like a permanent mark. What was Leo doing here at the clinic? Trudy had mentioned Dr Peters had asked him to take over, but Leo wasn't some junior doctor, eager to do his boss's bidding to win favour or promotion. He'd worked his way to the position of Dr Peters's second in command and he loved his job in A & E. So why come to the clinic? It didn't make any sense. Surely someone else could have taken the man's place.

She again caught sight of the man troubling her thoughts. He'd moved further into the room and now held a very large, ultra-adorable cuddly toy giraffe half tucked underneath his arm. Its sweet furry face stared back at her.

Everything was wrong with this scenario. Fresh tears

threatened to overflow as she regarded the man she'd until recently loved. She yearned to leave this room full of happy, cheerful people and crawl into some private, hidden hole, because the man who'd helped create their baby now stood holding a toy giraffe looking as uncomfortable as she was, but also meltingly gorgeous. No one at the clinic knew who her husband was, and she didn't intend to admit the new doctor standing paces away was the father of her unborn child, or that their marriage sat in tatters. Right now all she wanted to do was get through the next ten minutes without having an emotional meltdown.

How would she survive working at the clinic and seeing Leo? Maybe she should leave today and let the clinic find another midwife to take over her last two days. Use the frequent bouts of tiredness that constantly dogged her as an excuse to finish a week earlier than planned. This clinic for the last few months had become her sanctuary, away from her worries and concerns. Where she dealt with other people's problems and health concerns. Each patient an ideal distraction from the mess of her own life.

And Leo wasn't just any man or doctor. He was so much more than that. He'd once been her everything. Her life. Her dreams. Her all.

Biting her lower lip to stop herself from bursting into tears, Gila pulled her gaze from Leo. She knew more than anyone that crying was a waste of time. Did tears bring relief and peace? No, all they achieved was to lower her mood and leave her miserable.

Leo and Trudy rejoined them. Handing Gila several cards, Trudy explained, 'Dr Peters bought and sent over the giraffe that Leo is modelling so well.'

Gila smiled and for the first time in weeks a small wave of pleasure ran through her. She'd met Dr Peters many times through Leo and his work. Goodness knew what the man thought of her now. Did he consider her a dreadful woman for walking out on her husband so soon after the loss of his sister? People tended to take sides when a couple parted. Had he taken Leo's? But if so, why buy the giraffe?

'How kind of him,' she said, turning to the cuddly toy. Careful to avoid making eye contact with Leo, she slid a hand over it, gasping softly when her fingertips unexpectedly brushed his own hidden beneath the plush fur.

'Sorry,' she whispered, conscience of the wave of spiralling heat travelling up her arm from the contact. Snatching her hand away, she turned her attention back to the others stood close.

'Leo,' Trudy gushed, focusing her attention on the silent man. 'Why don't you rest the giraffe on a chair? Now your shift is over, I can introduce you to everyone. You've already met Gila, of course.'

Gila stayed silent as the couple moved away, dropping the huge giraffe onto a vacant plastic chair on their way. She didn't need to watch Leo making friends to know the concept of continuing to work here would be too hard to endure. Even for a few days. If one of her patients faced a similar situation, she'd recommend either they talked to their boss about a replacement for the newcomer, or that they consider leaving their job.

Somehow, she didn't think the clinic would accept her not wanting to work in the same building as her estranged husband as an acceptable excuse to ask Leo to leave. Not when Dr Peters obviously wanted him here.

And as she was a volunteer midwife, on the verge of leaving, it made more sense that she'd be the one to go.

She sighed and glanced down at the pile of presents and cards. Why did Leo have to turn up a few days before she was due to leave? Had he done it on purpose?

Someone handed her a plastic cup filled with weak orange squash. Accepting it, she glanced casually at the clock on the wall. How long before she could leave without appearing rude? Would fifteen minutes be enough? Or should she stay longer?

'Don't worry,' Trudy said, joining Gila once again. 'Cluster of new patients just walked into Reception eager to keep this lot busy, so you'll be able to head off in a few minutes.'

Gila sighed and asked guiltily, 'Am I that obvious?'

'No, but you're eight months pregnant and I remember how that feels. I spent the last few weeks of my pregnancy switching from wanting to organise my entire house and taking naps whenever the chance arose.'

Gila smiled, liking the woman a little bit more. 'I'm ready for one right now, to be honest.'

Trudy laughed, then pointed across the room at the male conversing with two female staff members. 'Well, Leo's proving a hit. I sense he is going to be a great asset to the clinic.'

Which made Gila want to weep as the two women vied for her husband's attention. How would they react if she marched over there, grabbed Leo by the face and kissed him fully on the mouth? Or shouted across the room that he belonged to her and she wanted him back?

Which, of course, she didn't. Not any longer. But even so.

A silly hysterical giggle worked up her throat and

she coughed to cover the sound before she embarrassed herself. The bleeping of her phone distracted her from the trio across the room. Retrieving it from her bag, she glanced at the screen and saw the alarm had gone off even though she couldn't recall setting it.

'I'm sorry, Trudy,' she lied. 'But I really must leave. I'm meeting someone.'

Trudy nodded and smiled. 'Let me ask Leo to carry the giraffe out for you.'

'No, really, I can manage,' she insisted, not keen to spend any more time around the man. She planned to enjoy her maternity leave and focus on nothing but the baby. Any decisions about Leo and the future could wait. She had some savings, and living rent-free on her uncle's narrowboat while he toured the wineries in France kept her expenses low and affordable.

'Nonsense,' Trudy dismissed. 'To be honest, I rather like seeing him carrying it. The giraffe suits him. I wonder if he has any children. Do you think he's married? Since my divorce I've been off men, but for him I'd dust off my sexy undies.'

'I doubt it,' Gila said, throwing him one last glare before gathering up the large toy with her free arm. 'He looks like the type of man who would be all words and empty promises.'

Trudy glanced back at her with a frown. 'Do you think so?'

Gila nodded. 'Only a fool would fall in love with a man like him. Trust me on that.'

'Gila.'

Gila's heartbeat skipped, but she ignored the man walking beside her along the long corridor that led to the clinic's front reception. Surely, he'd get the hint if she didn't speak to him? She'd made a point of keeping all contact between them centred only on their unborn child.

'Gila, please. I want to talk to you.'

'Sorry,' she stammered, her heartbeat thundering harder. Hugging the giraffe to her front, she said, 'I need to be somewhere. I don't have the time.'

It was all a lie, but she certainly didn't have the inclination to talk to him. Why didn't he just return to the staff room and resume his conversation with the other staff members? Go and bother them instead of her?

Trembling, she increased her speed, desperate to get away from the man and the swoosh of memories initiated from being around him. Memories of happy times when everything on the planet was wonderful and she believed she'd found a good man. Long before he ruined it all.

'Gila, please.'

Frustrated, she asked, 'What do you want, Leo?'

For weeks, she'd desperately worked to pick up the slivers of her splintered life and carry on. To put his rejection to one side and move forward. And now she refused to allow him to drag her backwards into the tempestuous well of emotions she'd spent so long battling to survive. Some days she'd wondered if she ever would. On others, why she even cared. So why now did Leo suddenly want to talk? Why not months ago when she'd knelt in front of him, clutching his hands while begging him to speak to her? When it might have mattered and made a difference?

'Please, Gila. Give me a chance to explain.'

The words enveloped her, tempting and teasing her

with the past. Wasn't it enough that he still occupied her thoughts too much. 'No,' she whispered. She wasn't ready to do this. She didn't want to face anything, especially not here at the clinic. She refused to become the latest gossip amongst her colleagues.

Leo raised his hand as though to touch her, before dropping it again. Once she'd hungered and revelled in the firmness of his stroke, now she resented the idea.

Leo moved closer, his firm, square chin lifting in determination. 'It's time for us to talk, Gila. Really talk. Not by texts or emails the way we have been, but a proper face-to-face conversation. We need to reach some sort of understanding before the—'

She clasped the cuddly toy harder, her fingers crushing its plush softness. Trying hard not to breathe in the familiar woody aroma of Leo's aftershave as he invaded her area. An expensive brand she'd once saved all her spare money to buy him not long after they'd first met. 'Why your sudden need for a discussion, when for months you've ignored my existence?'

'That's not true,' he denied. 'I haven't ignored you. I've answered every text or question you've sent. I thought only to give you time and because my—'

Gila closed off his excuses, no longer interested. This man whom she'd handed her heart, together with her trust, didn't deserve her time. This man whose laughter and lovemaking once filled her body and spirit so completely had let her down. Badly. He'd done just as everyone else in her life had. Abandoned her when things became hard.

A deep frown creased Leo's forehead. 'This stand-off between us is helping no one.'

'Whose fault is that?' she hissed. She swallowed,

her stomach rolling with fresh anger and resentment. Shaking her head, she closed the space between them and spat, 'How long are you going to be working here?'

Wasn't letting their marriage go enough of a crime to commit against her? Did he truly expect her to meekly work alongside him as though nothing linked them? As though he hadn't ripped her heart from her body and almost obliterated her?

'Let's go somewhere private and I'll explain everything,' he suggested. 'Once we talk—'

'How long?' she demanded again, refusing to move until she got an answer from him.

He sighed. 'I'm not sure. For the next few weeks at least. Dr Peters needs to be with his family.'

'Haven't you hurt me enough, Leo?' she asked. 'How dare you come to the clinic where I volunteer? Wasn't there someone else who could have stepped in? Didn't it occur to you that I wouldn't want you here? Is that why you didn't tell me? Well, I refuse to work in the same building as you.'

'I know it's not ideal, but I owed the man, Gila.' He stepped closer, dark brown eyes clashing with hers. 'Just let me explain.'

'No!' she snapped, her chest heaving as her legs wobbled. Stepping away, she bumped back into the edge of a table placed against the wall. A couple of leaflets stacked on top fell and floated to the floor.

Leo shook his head. 'Look, I'm sorry, Gila. For being here, for not thinking to tell you beforehand and for… well…everything.'

'I don't care,' she replied coldly. She didn't. Not any more. His apology meant nothing. Where was he during those first few days after she'd left? When she'd sat like an idiot in her uncle's narrowboat, constantly listening for the sound of his footsteps or his knock on the door? Convinced it would only be a short while before he came and begged her to go home. The anxious ritual of waiting for his appearance night after night, day after senseless day, now seemed ridiculous and infantile.

While she'd whispered a thousand prayers into the dark, silent hours, hopeful that they could mend what had torn them apart, he'd done nothing but shatter the few illusions she'd had left by staying away. Not once making contact during those first few days. Leaving her to wallow in pain and confusion.

Every emotion, all her devotion, every drop of her love for him had slipped away over those first few weeks apart. Running into the invisible drain of yet another broken relationship. Yet another let-down by someone who'd lied when they'd said they cared.

'I hate you,' she whispered. 'Don't you get that? What I once felt for you is gone. Now I simply hate you for proving what a fool I was to trust you.'

He flinched at her soft words, his expression turning emotionless and hard. 'I understand, but…'

She walked away, despite her unsteady legs still threatening to give way. She refused to crumble here in front of this man. This time there would be no crying or pleading the way she had before. This time she would walk away with her head held high, her future safe and protected deep inside her body.

Instinctively, she touched a free finger to her stomach, vaguely aware of the baby inside reacting with a gentle kick. Did her child sense that the man who had helped to create its life now reminded Gila of everything she'd lost? Of a love she no longer retained and suspected she never really had? That the true affection in their marriage had only come from her? And that fact hurt more than any of the disappointments from her past. The bitter, cruel knowledge that, yet again, neither she nor her love had really mattered.

Leo gazed after Gila as she rushed down the corridor. A piece of his heart slowly tearing at the speed she used to get away from him. Once they'd hurried to meet each other, now the woman raced away as though he risked her very existence.

She hated him. He'd expected it. Understood her anger, but the words she'd spat at him still pierced his soul. Seeping into the broken joints and cracks that continuously craved for her healing. A cure only she could instigate and perform. And something he now knew he would never obtain.

He should have called her when he'd found out yesterday that Dr Peters needed him to cover his shifts, but he hadn't thought—no, that wasn't true—he hadn't allowed himself to consider the complications his arrival here at the clinic might cause for his wife. Preferring to wait and deal with Gila's reaction in person instead of over the phone or through a text or email. In retrospect it had been cowardly and a mistake. Not warning her had just delivered another bad mark against himself when he already bore so many.

How could he make things right when she refused to listen? When she loathed being anywhere near him, and love no longer shone from her pretty grey eyes, which now held mistrust, dislike and pain.

He had caused the damage to their relationship and instead of rushing after her when she'd left, that night four months ago, he'd buried his head in his own agony and blocked out anyone else's wishes and needs. He'd acted like a selfish fool. A person he'd never believed he would ever become. Someone he didn't even understand or recognise.

He'd treated Gila as though she didn't matter, and that was what she couldn't forgive. He saw it in every movement and glance she sent his way. The hurt and disappointment of his being just another person who'd let her down after solemnly promising on their wedding day that he never would. Through her eyes, he saw her heart shouting out the unforgivable truth that he'd failed her.

Lowering his own gaze, he frowned at the small gift lying on the floor where, moments ago, Gila stood. Crouching, he picked it up, smiling at the cuteness of the bright yellow wrapping paper printed with orange rabbits. This gift had been bought for his child. Yet he'd stood in the staff room moments ago and watched everyone congratulate Gila without saying a word while the impulse to yell that he was the baby's father had almost crushed him. To let everyone in the room know that he was not some faceless stranger, but Gila's husband. The man who, in spite of his thoughtless actions, had never stopped loving her.

He clutched the gift and glanced in the direction that Gila had disappeared. She'd obviously dropped it in her rush to get away. To escape him and everything between them.

Straightening, he followed the same path. Determination in each stride. With luck he'd catch up with his wife before she left the car park. Whether she wanted it or not, they were going to talk face to face and not through some electrical means the way they had for the last few months. For the sake of his future relationship with his child, he'd fight for more.

Pushing open the clinic's glass entrance door, he paused to search the parked cars in front of him. Catching a glimpse of a familiar blue uniform, he headed after Gila, concerned when he spotted her resting against a black vehicle. He frowned as he took in the way she leaned over, one hand on the car's bonnet, head bent over as though having trouble breathing.

Quickly weaving through the remaining cars that separated them, he finally reached her side and demanded, 'Are you all right?'

Gila glanced up, her cheeks drained of all healthy colour. 'Leo?'

'What's wrong?' he asked, closing the gap between them. Something ailed his wife or their baby. Either way, he refused to leave them until he'd found out what.

'Nothing. I'm just feeling a little faint,' she answered. The words reluctant and dragged out as though she'd prefer to admit to anything else but the truth to him.

'How long?' he quizzed, reaching for her elbow.

'Just a few moments.'

'Why don't we go back inside the clinic and sit for a minute? Just until the feeling passes,' he suggested, relieved when she didn't pull out of his hold. Though the fact that she was letting him touch her at all increased his concern.

She shook her head. 'No, I want to go home, and my bus is due soon.'

'Forget the bus,' he dismissed, troubled by this unexpected show of vulnerability from his wife. Gila's unsettled and unconventional childhood had taught her to guard her feelings with a hard outer shell. She rarely showed her softer side, unless she was truly comfortable with a person. 'There's always a later one or I can give you a lift home.'

She sniffed and shook her head again. 'No, thanks. I'd rather walk.'

'Don't be silly, Gila,' he scolded gently. 'It's not as if we're not going in the same direction, is it? Besides, aren't you meeting someone?'

She ignored his question and replied, 'It makes no difference. I'll get the bus.'

'Gila…'

'Don't,' she warned. 'I just want to go home.'

'Okay,' he said, noticing how weary she looked. 'You clearly want no part of me and I understand that.'

'Good of you,' she said scathingly.

He lowered his head, until it stopped inches from her own. Secretly pleased by her returning smart attitude. A sign she was feeling better. 'But that baby you're carrying so beautifully is mine too, and as both a parent and a doctor I cannot leave you here by yourself. Tell me what I can do to help?'

'Perhaps I should sit down for a moment,' she conceded.

Leo glanced around for a bench or wall low enough to sit on. 'I'm not sure there's anywhere suitable. Would you be willing to sit in the passenger seat of my car until you're ready to catch the bus?'

After a few seconds, she agreed. 'Okay.'

With care Leo led her over to his vehicle, unlocking it before opening the passenger's door to help her down onto the leather seat.

'Why are you doing this?' she asked, pushing the large giraffe at him to take.

'Because you need help.'

'Of course,' she muttered, not covering the bitterness in her tone. 'Why else? It isn't as though you care for me, is it? I'm just the dispensable wife. The woman good enough to impregnate, yet not come after.'

Leo flinched at her words, but this wasn't the time to correct her assumptions concerning their marriage and his true feelings for her. Soon the time would come for their inevitable heart-to-heart, despite what she said. But getting Gila home tonight so she could rest mattered more.

'Now tell me again what happened,' he gently quizzed.

She huffed, but answered, 'I told you, I became dizzy.'

'Has it happened before?' he asked, concerned that her midwife had somehow missed a problem with Gila's health and well-being.

She gave him a wry glance. 'Back off, Leo. You're not the only medical expert here. It's nothing to be concerned about. All my fault for rushing around when I'm so far along in the pregnancy.'

'How's your blood pressure?'

'Usually fine when I'm not bumping into ex-husbands,' she relied tartly.

'I know you may wish differently, but I am still your husband and both your and the baby's health are important to me.'

'My husband in name but nothing else,' she replied.

'You left me, remember,' he reminded her. 'Not the other way around.'

Leaning into the car, Leo opened the glove compartment and retrieved a bottle of water. Unscrewing the sealed cap, he handed it over. 'Drink this.'

Without complaint she took the bottle from him and took a small sip. After a few seconds, she took another. 'I really need to go.'

'A few more moments won't hurt. Stay there and rest.' He ached to touch her. To lay his hand upon her skin and breathe in her scent. The sweet exclusive one, that no beauty company or perfumer could recreate, because it was Gila's natural aroma. The very essence of the woman she was. As individual and unique as she. Just another thing he loved about her.

But his love or desires were no longer relevant. He'd lost the right to do any of the things he used to do. Their relationship no longer close or intimate.

For the last few months he'd fought other demons, but now he faced the shredded scraps of their marriage with no idea how to piece together a new kind of relationship between them from the fragmented remains.

'Is there anything else I can get you?' he asked softly. 'Something to eat, perhaps? The mini market is just over there.'

Gila glanced towards the shop across the street and groaned.

'What's wrong?'

'I'm pretty sure my bus just pulled away from the stop.' She sighed, her unusual show of vulnerability returning. 'I just want to go home and sink into a bath.'

Leo nodded, searching her face. Seeing again the tiredness in her pretty features. Gila needed to rest. 'Then let me drive you home.'

Amazingly, she stopped arguing and gave in. Giving

Leo a stronger indication of how exhausted she really was, and a clue that perhaps the dizzy spell had frightened his normally resilient wife.

'Okay, but only because carrying the giraffe and my bag would be awkward on the bus and slightly embarrassing.'

He smiled and stood. He deposited the giraffe on the rear seat, a stirring of hope whispering through him for the first time in months.

When he'd first set eyes on Gila two years before, she'd been crouched in front of a young woman in the latter stages of giving birth in the unexpected surroundings of the hospital waiting area. While people around them had panicked and fussed, Gila had taken the woman's hands and calmly helped her through the birth, aware that any chance to get the patient into a birthing room or on a bed had long gone.

He had fallen in love with Gila that afternoon. But none of that mattered right now. Today the only thing that concerned him was getting Gila home to rest and making sure the baby was okay. Tomorrow could take care of everything else.

CHAPTER THREE

HOME SWEET HOME.

Gila managed to scramble inelegantly out of the car moments after Leo parked in the small residents' car park situated not far from the back street canal. She didn't want or need any assistance from him, well, no more than she'd already accepted, anyway.

Sitting beside him during the twenty-minute drive had turned into a form of emotional and physical torture. Every second fighting the urge to reach out and lay her hand upon his arm and gather strength and reassurance from the muscle beneath. Wanting to slide her fingers over the curve of his thigh and feel the heat coming through the material of his age-worn jeans.

'I would have helped you,' Leo said, rounding the car's bonnet and coming to a halt next to her. But Gila ignored him. As an independent woman, she needed no one. Hadn't she always known that? Hadn't life always indicated that to rely on others was nothing but a mistake that led to regret and disenchantment?

'I can manage,' she murmured, opening the back door to retrieve the oversized giraffe, suddenly craving the comfort of its soft squidgy body. Straightening, she slammed the door and waited for Leo to move out of the way, not inclined to give in over anything else. No matter how trivial or unimportant.

'Okay,' he said, backing off.

Her back ached and her shoes hurt. All she craved was a bath, a bowl of ice cream and a good weep. In exactly that order.

Shaking her head, she shoved past Leo, heading along the narrow, cobbled lane that led down to the canal that ran along the city's hidden back streets. Edged on both sides by a short, wide strip of forest, despite being so close to the hustle and bustle of busy London, it gave a tranquillity of calm that few in the city were privileged to live near to or experience.

Situated behind a row of expensive terrace houses in an area history once deemed a slum, this canal and many others had kept London and its many thriving businesses running during the industrial period. Separated from the houses by the high brick wall that ran along the bottom of the properties' small gardens.

These days the canal mostly accommodated holidaymakers and permanent residents who lived in the brightly decorated narrowboats. Just as Gila had since she turned fourteen years old and moved in with her uncle Art after her father became unable to care for her.

'Gila, will you please stop being so—?' Leo protested, hurrying after her.

She stopped, suddenly ready for a fight if it was the only way to get rid of him, and demanded, 'So what?'

He sucked in a breath, before replying, 'Nothing. I just want to make things better between us before the baby comes.'

To her shock and shame, she answered with a frustrated and irritable growl. Like something a bear cub would make.

Leo blinked twice, before asking, 'Did you just growl at me?'

Not wanting to admit to such odd behaviour, she swung around and stormed away. When had she started to growl at people? Was this a pregnancy thing, or a dumped and abandoned wife trait? Was she tumbling down the precarious tunnel of a disgruntled crazy ex? And was this only the start of such erratic behaviour?

Deciding not to dwell on the strange growling, Gila fixed her attention on the narrowboat moored up ahead. Finally, she stood close to her destination and a fridge with the tub of vanilla ice cream she'd been fantasising about for the last few hours. A handful of steps away from her home.

Home?

She took in the muddy brown painted narrowboat and silently sneered at the notion that this space was home. It wasn't. Not any more. In truth, not for some time. Not since the day she and Leo had moved in together.

Her eyes slowly and reluctantly slid to another narrowboat moored a few feet away, lovingly painted in a cheerful lilac colour with small pale blue wooden shutters. She let out a small sigh of pleasure at the heart-shaped cut-outs in the centre of each shutter. Ones Leo had handcrafted last year during one lazy summer afternoon. Baskets of orange and blue winter pansies sat on the roof and pink primroses mingled with purple heathers planted in traditionally painted barge ware buckets sat beside them.

When the narrowboat moored next to her uncle's

had come up for sale several months before their wedding, she and Leo had jumped at the chance to buy it. House prices in the area were crazy and Gila had known she would miss the friendly community of friends and neighbours she had found since moving in with her uncle as a child. This place was more than just somewhere to live. Luckily Leo hadn't cared as long as she felt happy and settled. Yes, space was limited and the practicalities of everyday living on a narrowboat could be different from those of a house, especially once the baby arrived, but she didn't require a home full of furniture and filled with belongings she rarely used. Life on the narrowboat was simpler. And where else could you be so close to nature?

She glanced once more at the lilac narrowboat. That was her *real* home. The home she and Leo had so lovingly renovated from an unloved shell. Where they had spent their wedding night and subsequent months of their marriage, cocooned in their love and happiness until it all fell apart and collapsed. Their so-called wonderful relationship in truth an unstable construction built from rotten material and false dreams. Unable to withstand the first major hit life struck against them.

A time before Leo's sister, Jodie, took a fatal overdose of drugs and through her death destroyed Gila's marriage, too. Before Leo did nothing to prevent all they were from becoming waste and dust. Or perhaps the splinters had already been present in their marriage, hidden and ignored, but under the pressure of Jodie's demise they grew and widened leaving nothing but shattered hopes and spoilt wishes.

'I'll see you inside,' Leo offered. She nodded, figuring he simply wanted to do his duty and then leave for a date or something. She'd noted he popped out a couple of times a week when he wasn't working. Not that she'd purposely been spying. She certainly wasn't some estranged wife stalker, desperate to know her husband's every move. She didn't care where he went or what he did, she'd simply noticed that he went out two evenings a week for about an hour. Maybe he'd chosen to move on, even though they'd only split up a few months before. But time didn't matter to some men, did it? He worked with plenty of nurses and doctors who'd all be willing to give him comfort and understanding over a failed marriage.

Not that she cared. She didn't. Not really. What Leo did in his spare time was his prerogative. Just as if she wanted to date a million men, then she could. But no man was asking her out. And she might not be living with her husband any longer, but she still felt married. The stupid white band on her finger from where the sun had never got through her wedding ring still marked her as someone's partner. She still used her married name, too. She still felt like Mrs Gila Wright.

'I'd prefer you didn't,' she replied, not unkindly, but wearily. She couldn't stand any further time together. Not at this minute when the lonesomeness stung stronger than ever. Sitting next to him in the car had been hard enough, without him entering and invading her last small refuge. If he came inside the narrowboat, his presence would taint the area and leave her imagining him standing in a certain spot or sitting on a certain chair for the next few hours.

'Gila, we need to talk sometime. Please, just give me a date and a time. That is all I ask,' Leo persisted.

When hell became a favourite holiday destination,

she almost replied. Why did they need to talk? She quite liked not talking. Why wasn't communicating through electronic impersonal means, each rigidly sticking to the subject of their baby and nothing else, enough for him? Besides, weren't brief, impersonal emails and texts better than the arguing they'd pursued for weeks after his sister's death? When the realisation that Leo wasn't just grieving, but slowly and determinedly shutting her out, had become clear.

Not talking didn't move their relationship backwards or forwards. It kept it stagnant. She wasn't ready or prepared for any new changes. Did he have a reason for suddenly wanting to talk? Like another woman? Was that behind his desire to converse? Had he met someone and wished to finish with his old life before moving on with a new one?

She shook the thought away. Nothing mattered but preparing for the arrival of their child. She didn't want to think about what Leo wanted or what he considered important. She wanted to be left alone with peace and quiet.

'Not today, Leo,' she said. 'I'm tired and all I want to do is lie on my bed and rest.'

'Are you taking enough iron?' He asked the same question she'd asked Reese earlier. 'You're very pale.'

'You're not my doctor,' she reminded him, all too aware she was every bit eight months pregnant and showing it in all ways. Not all of them appealing or attractive.

'I care—' he began, but stopped when she glared at him.

'But not enough, Leo,' she said, stepping onto the

narrowboat. 'In the end, you proved that you didn't care enough, didn't you?'

'That is not true, Gila. Let me explain—'

She moved forward, but her foot caught on a piece of wood and she stumbled. Two arms wrapped around her from behind, pulling her into a close embrace. A stupid, traitorous part of her soul desperately yearned to lean back into the warmth of Leo's hard front, but the pain of the last few months and the way he'd shut her out returned to mock her. Silently questioning what the heck she was doing.

When she'd packed her bags, she had hoped the extreme action would shock Leo from the numb state he'd slumped into after his sister's death. Instead, he continued to live alone on their narrowboat, while she stayed on her uncle's. The gap already present between them broadening with each passing day. Leo had done nothing to show that he wanted her. Absolutely nothing.

And for the first time since they'd met, Gila had finally faced the cold harsh truth that while she loved Leo with every part of her heart and soul, he obviously didn't feel the same. Why else had he left her alone? What other possible reason could there be to explain why he mentally and physically did nothing to save their marriage?

'Let me check you over,' Leo said, helping Gila onto the small green sofa pushed against one wall. Bright yellow and green velvet cushions sat in each corner. Reaching behind, he tugged one from its place and propped it behind her back, then, with gentle fingers, pushed her against its softness and straightened.

'I'm fine,' she insisted, flustered by his caring manner. She didn't want him here or for him to see how sparse the narrowboat was despite the fact she'd been living there for weeks. When she'd left their home, she'd taken one small suitcase of clothes and nothing else. None of her silver thimble collection or the small assortment of art deco vases Leo had bought her over the months. Other than a few throws and some cushions, she'd not bothered to create much of a home. Initially, because she'd honestly believed her stay would be short-term. Then, when it had become clear that Leo no longer wanted her and their marriage, she'd lacked the energy to care about her surroundings. Besides, she doubted her uncle would be pleased if he returned from his six months touring wineries in France to find his home redecorated in soft and feminine colours. As a diehard bachelor he'd probably keel over from a coronary.

'It won't hurt to make sure, will it?' Leo said, ignoring her complaints.

'I'm sure you're busy,' she remarked, again attempting to get him to go.

He stared down at her, his mouth a flat, determined line. 'You and our child will always top anything else I am doing or have planned.'

She sighed and rested her hands on the top of her bump. Was he avoiding giving any hint to his plans for the evening, or was that just her suspicious mind? 'You really don't have to—'

'I do,' he insisted, cutting her off. 'I'll just go home and fetch my medical bag. It won't hurt to check your blood pressure.'

With a huff, she pointed to a plastic box in one corner. 'There's a sphygmomanometer in there you can use.'

Leo nodded and fetched the blood pressure kit and a stethoscope from the box.

Gila glanced around, her gaze falling on the toy giraffe now sitting on a small stool across the other side of the room. Was she imagining it, or was the stuffed toy grinning at her?

Crouching in front of her again, Leo said, 'Stop sulking.'

'I'm not sulking,' she denied, giving the giraffe one last look.

He smirked but let the subject drop. Instead, he wrapped the cuff around her arm, and asked, 'How often are you losing your balance and feeling dizzy?'

'That's the first time I've stumbled, but the dizzy spells are on and off. They only last for a few seconds, though. You know as well as I do that it happens sometimes in pregnancy. I've spoken to my midwife about it.'

'Good.' He pumped air into the cuff, before slowly releasing it, using the stethoscope to listen to her pulse. After a few seconds, he mused, 'Your blood pressure is a little raised.'

'I know. I check it regularly at the clinic. It's to be expected. My midwife feels it's nothing to be concerned with.'

'Even so. A few days of rest and relaxation will probably do you good.' He glanced up and searched her face. 'You look tired, Gila.'

'Thanks. I'm pregnant, what do you expect?' she grumbled, not in the mood to hear comments on her terrible appearance. Especially from a man who made most of the male population seem dull. She certainly wasn't going to admit she rarely slept through the night either. Not when dreams of him were mainly the reason.

'I'm not being unkind,' he said, but stopped when she glanced away. Instead, he asked, 'Do you have the weekend off?'

'Yes,' she said, then frowned. 'Look, you can go now. I'm feeling fine.'

He removed the cuff and dropped it onto the sofa. After asking her several further questions, he leaned back on his heels.

'I only have a few days left to work at the clinic,' she said, hopeful that there might be a way for them both to work there without her needing to give up before she intended. 'Can we at least agree to keep out of each other's way?'

'Is that what you want?' he asked quietly.

She forced every emotion, doubt and disappointment burning inside her not to show on her face. Desperate to hide the fact that having him this near broke her heart all over again. 'Of course.'

He sighed and stood. Returning the sphygmomanometer and stethoscope to the box, he headed for the entrance.

At the door, he turned back. 'That's not just your child you're carrying, remember? It's ours.'

'Get out,' she choked, too furious to say more. Leo needed to go before she grabbed every small object in the room and threw them at him. How dared he? He'd caused the breakdown of their relationship, yet he dared to stand there as though he were in some way the injured one. She'd made a point to keep him informed on the baby's development and welfare during the last four months, when plenty of other women wouldn't have bothered. Keen to show that her baby's needs and happiness would always be her priority, even if it meant involving him. She loved her child. Real heart-thumping love and not the kind that disappeared under pressure.

'Get out!' she repeated, through clenched teeth, already knowing it would be hours before she could breathe without taking in the familiar smell of his damn lingering aftershave. 'Just, get out!'

Leo shut the wooden doors and stepped onto the narrowboat's deck. Stepping off and onto the path that ran along the canal, he glanced up at the sound of approaching footsteps, his heart sinking at the sight of the old man marching along the same lane he and Gila had used only minutes before. Could this afternoon deteriorate any further? Not only a stupid row with Gila, but now her uncle's unexpected return.

'Leo.' Art stopped several steps away. Both his tone and expression neutral and friendly. But Leo wasn't fooled. Art Brown had raised Gila for a good part of her childhood and they shared a close relationship. The man was as protective as any birth parent. 'Have you and my niece finally made amends?'

Leo shoved his hands into his jeans pockets. With a long glance at the narrowboat, he shook his head. 'No. Let's just say negotiations are still hostile.'

'Oh,' Art murmured, following it with a heavy sigh.

Leo decided to change the subject, not seeing any point in raking over a situation that wasn't about to change soon. 'You should know, Gila recently experienced a funny turn at the clinic where she volunteers. I brought her home and checked her over, but she needs to rest. Perhaps you can convince her to take it easy for the next couple of days.'

'You happened to be at the clinic, did you?' Art

asked, his expression curious. 'Lucky you were there to help when she needed it.'

Leo shrugged, not about to get into the hows and whys of his attendance at the clinic. Dr Peters's family business wasn't for broadcasting to everyone. He just hoped the man reached the States in time to see his grandchild. The accident and injuries she'd suffered were severe and life-threatening. Personally, he thought the prognosis wasn't good.

Art's gaze slid to the narrowboat they stood beside. 'I guess Gila's home. I need to speak to her.'

'Yes,' he confirmed, before moving to leave, but Art stopped him.

'You might want to join us.'

Surprised by the invitation, Leo shook his head and declined. 'I doubt Gila will appreciate my presence considering she's just ordered me to leave. We've had a row of sorts. I said the wrong thing.'

Art chuckled. 'Yeah, well, sometimes we men do that. The truth is, Leo, you may be interested in what I have to say.'

After a few seconds, Leo followed Art onto the narrowboat. Not looking forward to his wife's reaction, he hung back. Whatever the reason for Art's return, he wasn't sure he wanted to get involved and risk upsetting Gila more.

CHAPTER FOUR

'ART!'

Gila shifted on the sofa and pushed to her feet as warmth and surprise bubbled through her. The last thing she'd expected after Leo's departure was for her uncle to appear within minutes. But she was glad he had, because she needed the man's kindness and comfort right now.

She smiled as her uncle crossed the small space and grabbed both her hands, planting a noisy kiss to her knuckles, in the same way he'd always done since Gila was a child.

'Goodness, you've grown bigger in certain places since I last saw you,' he teased, drawing her back down onto the sofa and taking a seat next to her. He smiled at her very round and obvious baby bump, before gently resting an aged hand upon it. 'Looking gorgeous, sweetheart.'

Her smile bloomed into a full grin. No matter how low she felt, whenever her uncle was close, he always put brightness into her day and filled her with love. Something definitely lacking from her life for some time. 'Yeah, well, a growing baby isn't one of those things you can really hide.'

Art laughed and silently regarded her. 'You really are beautiful,' he complimented. 'Isn't she, Leo? Pregnancy never looked so good on a woman.'

Gila frowned and glanced from her uncle to find Leo once more standing across the small space. Arms crossed, he leaned against the kitchen opening. He nodded in answer to her uncle's question, his gaze slowly dropping to rest on her bump. The optical trace an invisible caress that left her skin and nerves tingling.

'Yes, she is,' he finally replied.

Her heart squeezed at his words, but she ignored her body's disloyal reactions and turned her full attention to her uncle. The confidence bash of a failed marriage had left her feeling unattractive and undesirable, yet the sensation of Leo's intense gaze dispersed all those feelings and left something very different pacing through her body. A feeling she reluctantly liked.

Ignoring the man across the room, she stared at her uncle, noticing how happy, healthy and relaxed he looked. His tour around France had obviously done him good, though the fact he'd returned early was concerning.

'I thought you planned to return to England at the end of June,' she said, hoping there wasn't anything wrong. He'd suffered a small health scare the year before, but nothing that wasn't easily treated and cured.

'I did, but an unexpected situation has cropped up and changed my plans,' Art answered, his fingers slipping away from hers.

A shiver of apprehension tickled along Gila's spine and for a moment the old, dreaded sensation she remembered from her childhood returned. When her father would utter similar remarks before dropping a bombshell into their already chaotic life. His idea of child-care invariably involved carting Gila off to unknown places, often with newly met acquaintances, with little thought to stability or adequate schooling.

Her lone parent had fallen in and out of love with the ease and regularity of a passing season. Gila was the result of one of those doomed love affairs. Her mother had disappeared out of their lives before Gila was six months old and never returned. Though having a small daughter never curbed her father's natural inclination to drift from one relationship to another, or to travel from country to country. She'd lost count of the many homes and cities they'd briefly lived in. Sometimes invited and legally, other times not so. He'd liked to call himself a free spirit, whereas others had labelled him an unreliable and incompetent parent.

'What's wrong, Art?' Without meaning to, she shifted her gaze to Leo. Was her uncle ill? Was her estranged husband here to ease the sharing of bad news? What did Leo know that she didn't? Were the pair keeping secrets from her?

Art sighed, his fingers claiming hers again. With a slight squeeze, he said, 'I need to come home, darling girl. To the narrowboat.'

'What?' she gasped. What did he mean? Was he home for good? If so, that was wonderful, but they'd shared the space while she was growing up, so she didn't understand his words or his serious manner. As though he feared telling her more.

'I have something of an emergency—'

'What emergency?' she demanded, preventing him from finishing. 'Are you sick again?'

'No, no, nothing like that,' he soothed, patting her hands. 'You see, I've met a woman called Maggie.'

'Oh,' she said, her heart sinking as that much despised awareness crept through stronger at the mention of this stranger. It and the happy glint in her uncle's eyes. 'And?'

'She was part of the group I toured the wineries with. She's a lovely lady. You'll love her. The thing is we've come back early because she needs to have an operation, but she's not allowed to travel home to Devon straight away. Something about needing to see the specialist afterwards. The hospital had a cancellation and brought the date for her operation forward. Anyway, she needs a place to stay. It's only for a week, and I would like to help her. She really is a wonderful woman and we've become very close over the weeks in France.'

Gila couldn't believe what Art was saying. While one part of her was pleased to see how happy her uncle was, she couldn't help wondering how they were all going to live on the narrowboat when there were only two small bedrooms. 'Couldn't Maggie stay at a hotel?'

'Not really. She hasn't much money and it's only for a week,' Art insisted. 'I'm sure we can manage. Maggie can sleep in my room and I'll sleep on the sofa. She's very funny and I'm certain you'll get on.'

Three people living in the tight confines of her uncle's narrowboat, which was smaller than the one she'd shared with Leo, would be snug. Having to spend time around two very cheerful and, from the silly smile on Art's face every time he spoke about this Maggie, loved-up people sounded dreadful even if it was only for a week.

'Perhaps I can find a hotel room,' she suggested, determined to find an alternative. 'Though with it being Easter weekend it might be hard to find somewhere with a free room.'

'You can move back in with me, if you want,' Leo quietly offered. 'It's only for a week. You're right—all the hotels will be fully booked with tourists and people attending the sports event that's taking place in the city on Saturday.'

'No, thank you,' Gila refused, not interested in the offer. She would *not* go back to the narrowboat they'd once shared. How could he suggest such a thing? She'd find somewhere else to stay. Not that she could really afford the expense of a hotel room for a week, not when she still needed to buy a couple of expensive items for the baby.

'I should probably mention that Maggie is arriving tonight. I'm collecting her from the train station in an hour. She wanted to pop home to Devon first and collect some extra belongings.'

'I see,' Gila said, shocked by the short notice her uncle was giving her to find alternative accommodation. It wasn't as if she could call a friend for a favour, because she had purposely kept quiet over the breakup with Leo.

'I should leave,' Leo said. 'You two need to discuss this on your own. Just let me know if you change your mind and want to stay with me, Gila.'

Art stood and nodded. 'It was good to see you, Leo.'

'And you.' Leo glanced at Gila, and asked, 'Are you okay?'

No, she wasn't. She wanted everything to go back to how it was a few months before. But fairy tales were for children and she'd never bothered to trust in them anyway. Had always known they were nothing but a fantasy created by adults. What she wanted to do was crawl into bed and not get out again until she'd dreamed a life where fathers, uncles and husbands didn't repeatedly let her down. 'Yes, I'm fine.'

Art waited until Leo's footsteps sounded on the path outside the narrowboat, before turning to Gila. 'I'm sorry about the short notice, but I'm sure we can manage for a week.'

Seven long days playing gooseberry to her uncle and this mysterious new woman he was so taken with. No, thanks. She'd prefer not to be an up-close spectator of her uncle's love life. 'No, it's fine. I'll find somewhere else and give you both some space.'

Her uncle stared at her for several moments, before he gently asked, 'Honey, why are you still here?'

She sighed. 'I told you on the phone. I've left Leo.'

'But why? I know things became tough after his sister died, but to leave the man when he was grieving.'

She stiffened. 'You make it sound like I wanted to.'

Art tilted his head to one side. 'When you were a child and you found life at home too hard, what did you always do?'

She shrugged and lied. 'I can't remember.'

'You used to run away,' Art said. 'Always hid here until I found you. Seems to me, you did the same thing this time. Trouble was Leo didn't come to find you, did he?'

Gila's lips trembled and she whispered, 'He didn't even come knocking on the door. And I left him a note telling him where I was.'

Tugging Gila gently to him, Art kissed her forehead. 'You need to stop running away when things are hard or scary. You're a beautiful, wonderful woman, who needs to learn to stand your ground and demand better whenever you're upset with life or people.'

'I thought if I left him he would realise how bad everything had become between us. I kept asking him how I could help, but he just refused to talk to me.' She turned her face into her uncle's shoulder. 'He didn't love me enough to come after me, Art. He didn't even try.'

'You sure?'

'I'm still here, aren't I?' Waiting and lonely. Wondering what else she could have done and what it was about her that made her so unlovable.

'I'm not saying the man hasn't acted like an idiot,' Art said. 'He has. But sometimes life is hard work and people…people you love do things you don't understand.'

'Don't you think I already know that?'

'This situation with Leo is not the same, kid. Your husband is not your father.'

'Isn't he? He's let me down too, hasn't he? Just the same as Dad.'

'Did he or did you just expect too much from someone who was in the worst kind of agony? And believe me grief is no easy gig to come out from. I've suffered a long spell there myself.'

It wasn't often her uncle mentioned the woman he'd loved and lost many years ago. A woman who died too young. Before medicine had advanced enough to help her. 'I don't know.'

'Honey, Leo isn't going to go away. For the next eighteen years at least he's going to be in and out of your life. You two need to come to a decision on how to share your child's future and upbringing.'

'And then what?' she asked, almost frightened to hear Art's reply.

'Move on and rebuild. But between you and Leo, that child you're growing deserves a safe and happy childhood. With parents who can be civil to each other. At some point, I'm afraid, you're going to have to face that.'

Gila snatched the pink jumper from the bed and threw it into the bag, along with the rest of her hastily packed clothes.

This morning when she'd rolled, literally, out of bed, her concerns had amounted to whether she could get through the day without thinking about her marriage or manage an hour without the desire to empty her bladder. Now she faced not only the idea of seeing her estranged husband at work, but also that for the next week she was homeless.

Okay, perhaps not exactly homeless, but almost as bad. Though being homeless did come with the bonus of being able to choose whose company you kept. She'd spent the last half an hour searching the Internet for nearby hotels with a free room, but every single one was full. Leaving her with no choice, for tonight at least, but to accept Leo's offer rather than stay here and suffer the discomfort of being the spare part to a happy couple. And the sofa was just too old and uncomfortable for her seventy-five-year-old uncle to sleep on.

Plonking down onto the bed, she lowered her head, squeezing her eyes shut as the weight of the forthcoming situation engulfed her. Not only was she going back to the lovely home she and Leo had shared, but the close confinement and situation would necessitate time in each other's company. Close periods together, which was fine if they liked and loved one another, but when their relationship was strained and in pieces, the idea sounded horrific.

As if she didn't already have enough stress in her life, wondering over the future, without this added complication. Seven days with a man who'd made it clear he didn't love her.

Standing, Gila grabbed the bag. The same one she'd used the night she'd left Leo when she'd still clung to the hope of salvaging her relationship. What a fool she'd been to hope for a positive resolution. Instead of the loving reunion she'd wished for, she and Leo had shifted from not talking, to only conversing over the baby and its needs. She guessed she should be grateful he still showed an interest in their child, even if he no longer cared for *her*.

Leaving the bedroom, she made her way through the narrowboat. Her uncle had disappeared, no doubt to let Leo know she had no choice but to move back in with him, before heading to the station to collect Maggie.

Walking the short distance to Leo's narrowboat, Gila concentrated on slowing down her suddenly erratic breathing. Perhaps the nervous buzzing in her stomach was indigestion due to the baby? The whole situation certainly soured her mood, so why not her stomach?

With a shake of her head, Gila stopped and drew in a deep breath, her gaze returning to the lilac narrowboat. What was the matter with her? Seven days wasn't so long, really. And a hotel room might become free before that. She intended to check the hotel sites each day just in case. With luck she and Leo would aim to avoid one another as much as possible. With his shifts at the clinic and the hospital, and her last two days volunteering, it shouldn't be too hard. And on his day off, she'd make herself scarce. Go into the city and visit a museum or two. Enjoy lunch at a local restaurant. She still needed to shop for the baby, and she also had an appointment with her midwife next week. Yes, with so many things to do, they'd hardly see each other. She'd make sure of it.

Maybe she could use the time to finally call an end to her marriage for good. Spend the next few days letting go so she could move on with the rest of her life. Build a new base for their future relationship. One that saw them putting their child before anything else. Before each other. Surely that wouldn't be too hard?

Her uncle was right. It didn't matter whether it was hard or not. It was how things were going to be and something they were going to have to do. Better to start by making that clear to Leo. They might no longer be lovers in any sense, but they would soon be co-parents, after all.

It was also time to stop acting like a naive, trusting fool and admit that, where relationships were concerned, the rainbows quickly disappeared and left nothing but oily puddles. And never again would she be stupid enough to fall for a so-called handsome hero. Not now she knew they truly didn't exist.

Gila's stomach tensed as she stepped onto the narrowboat and caught sight of a small wooden heart nailed above the two wooden doors that led inside. A pathetic lump of heartache mixed with fury destroyed all her freshly made decrees. Ignoring the burn in her chest, she reached for the door handle.

For over a year this had been her first true home.

Hers and Leo's. Their love nest, as they'd fondly named it. Where they'd shared their first night together, yelled through their first argument and kissed beneath the stars on their wedding night, desperate to be alone after a wonderful day surrounded by friends and family. And where the child she now carried was lovingly and passionately conceived.

Despite the passing weeks since she'd last stepped onto the boat, an odd and unexpected sense of homecoming threaded stronger around all the other emotions humming through her. Surely time apart should've changed how she viewed this place and what it once represented? Given her a better clarity on her marriage, instead of this sudden swell of aching regrets and yearnings.

Stepping down the narrow steps into the tiny kitchen, she was shocked to find none of the mess or disorder she'd anticipated. A secret part had imagined Leo falling to pieces without her. Obviously, just another thing she'd been mistaken about.

She moved into the small, but welcoming lounge, her nerves easing at the sight of the familiar soft chalky blue walls and the teal velvet Chesterfield sofa. With a quick scan around, she noted everything was as she'd left it. Why she'd half expected changes, she didn't know, but the odd buzzing inside her stomach started to settle.

Passing through this room, too, she only stopped when she reached the bedroom. Leo stood inside, gathering several items of clothing from a small chest of drawers. He glanced up when she hovered in the open doorway.

'Art's spoken to you?' she asked.

He nodded. 'Yeah.'

'As soon as I find somewhere else to stay—' she started to explain.

'It's fine. Stay as long as you want. I'll sleep on the sofa,' he said, picking up a blue woollen jumper and adding it to the items already hanging over one arm. He glanced meaningfully at her bump and smiled softly. 'You need the bed far more than I do.'

'I don't want to inconvenience you,' she said, in two minds over whether sleeping in the bed they once shared was a good idea. But slumming on the sofa didn't appeal as an alternative, either. These days she found it hard to get comfy wherever she slept. Besides, Leo had regularly fallen into a contented sleep on the sofa in the past, so he'd probably be fine. 'I'm sure I can manage for a week.'

'No, you need a comfortable bed. You won't get enough sleep on the sofa. Besides, the bed is every bit as much yours as it is mine. You discovered it in that old antique shop, remember?'

Memories of that day wandering around the nearby antiques centre floated through her mind. Pure art deco in every straight line and angle of the old bed, she'd fallen in love with it the moment she'd seen it. In excitement, she'd phoned Leo at work and sent photographs. Within minutes, he'd agreed it was ideal and Gila had made the seller an offer. They hadn't worried about how they'd fit the large bedframe into the narrowboat's cramped bedroom space. They'd just known they had to own it.

Leo finished collecting his belongings and moved to slip past where she still hesitated on the threshold. How easy it would be to reach out and slowly run her fingertips over the contours of his T-shirt. Rest her palm flat in the centre of his chest and experience the steady dull thud of his heartbeat against her hand. How she longed to lean her head against his shoulder and breathe in the scent of the one place in the world she'd ever felt completely safe and secure.

How effortless it would be to indulge herself in what they once were, but she couldn't do that. Just as she refused to forget the painful, empty weeks they'd been apart. Or the events that led to her departure. How he'd allowed the horrid wordless stalemate in their marriage to become bigger than anything else. So huge and dominant that it drove her from their home.

Home. That annoying word again. A fantasy she had spent most of her life without.

'Please, just make yourself at home,' he offered politely.

Wondering if her thoughts had shown on her face, she snapped, 'But it's not my home. Not any more.'

A gigantic lie, considering the contentment soothing into her soul since returning.

If she'd slapped him across the face, Gila doubted the impact would have been as robust. The shutters in Leo's eyes returned and closed her out. Those same much-hated shutters she'd seen so often during those last weeks before she left. Barring her from his internal thoughts and feelings, only this time she didn't blame him. Her remark was both cruel and unnecessary, and she hated how it sent him into retreat.

'I need to go out,' Leo said, stepping away. 'I've a meeting and a patient to check. I'll see you tonight, unless you're already in bed.'

'I will be,' she said, her eyes drifting again to the bed. The one they'd shared for over a year. Where they'd laughed and made love. Where they'd confessed secrets and shared Sunday morning tea mixed with buttered toast and laughter. The place where she'd believed they were their true selves. Where she'd sworn their love grew stronger.

And once again the overpowering sense of returning home caused another break in her already battered heart.

CHAPTER FIVE

GILA WOKE UP tired the following morning, having spent the night twisting and turning as best her bump would allow. Her back still ached, adding to her night of discomfort. Though, she wasn't convinced the main reason for her physical unsettledness came down to only lack of sleep. Knowing Leo lay a few feet away in the lounge didn't help her peace of mind.

Staring at the ceiling, she slid a hand tenderly over her child, alert to the sounds both outside and inside the narrowboat. Birdsong mingled with the occasional soft thump from the room next door, which indicated Leo was awake and getting ready for work. Going through his usual morning routine. When he'd returned last night, she'd still been up reading a book, and he'd mentioned having an early shift at the hospital.

Had he eaten his customary breakfast of cereal drenched in milk before having his shower? Or had he changed his daily habits in the last four months? Formed new ones that she wouldn't know or recognise.

Sighing, Gila rolled onto her side, purposely diverting her thoughts from the man she spent too much time thinking about. If she didn't find some way to occupy herself over the next few days, she would go mad counting the hours and minutes before she could leave.

This was all her uncle's fault. And she had a feeling the fates and the universe were involved, too.

And what about Leo?

She sighed as her wandering mind returned to the man in the next room. What was she going to do about him? As much as she'd happily defer it to some time later, a decision did need to be made about the future. She'd purposely ignored the idea of a long-term separation and the hassle of organising a divorce, but he said he wanted to talk, to explain things. What things? And did she really care any more? The past couldn't be erased and changed. So what was the point?

She opened her eyes and silently repeated the dreaded word. Divorce. Such an ugly-sounding term. She didn't really want one. When she'd uttered her vows to love, honour and cherish, she'd meant them for life. But only an obstinate idiot held onto a broken relationship. And she might be a fool, but she refused to be a totally hopeless one.

With a divorce came arguing over possessions and money. Wrangling over who got what and why. So far, they had sidestepped both subjects. All interaction they'd shared for the last few months had centred only on their unborn child. If she shifted the focus to include more practical, home-life stuff, then she would need to think about where she wanted to live and that all sounded like too much work right now.

Art's words from last night filtered through her thoughts. She didn't need a week to sort out her true feelings for Leo. She no longer had any. Well, okay, she did still experience anger and frustration, but that was to be expected, wasn't it? And those feelings were because of how stupid she felt, not because of something more powerful. Absolutely nothing to do with bruised love or crushed ego.

No, she did *not* love Leo Wright. Not any more. Not for weeks, in fact. Where love had once beaten and grown, numbness now filled its hollow space.

She rolled over and shut her eyes. Perhaps if she said the words with more gusto, they might sound more convincing? God, she truly was pathetic.

The too familiar pressure of her bladder became uncomfortable, giving her no other choice but to close down her internal reflections and rise from the bed. Pulling on her yoga outfit, she gave herself a quick pep talk and then grabbed her blue rubber yoga mat. With luck, Leo would be heading out soon and she could complete her morning's yoga stretches alone before her shower.

She groaned and left the room. The following days were going to be hell, she just knew it.

'Morning,' Leo greeted the second Gila stepped into the lounge. Forcing his feet not to move, he privately fought the temptation to race over and grab Gila in a bearhug. Kiss her full pretty mouth, the way he used to every morning. God, she looked so good standing in their home.

For the last few months, he'd missed seeing her every morning. Pined like a sad dog for the way she filled a room with her company just by stepping into it. His gaze ran over her, taking in the sleepy sheen to her eyes, the haphazard ponytail her hair was pulled into and the flushed rosy tinge to her cheeks. His gaze lowered, skimming down over the tight-fitting yoga top, boldly hugging her generous pregnancy curves until it settled on the large arch of her baby bump.

'You are…' His words trailed off as he dragged his gaze from her stomach and returned to her face. Smiling softly, he finished, 'Nothing, forget I spoke.'

He'd intended telling her she was beautiful, but he suspected she wouldn't appreciate the compliment and he didn't wish to see the sharp flash of pain and distrust the words would produce in her grey eyes. A simple compliment from him now had the power to hurt and offend her.

His stomach jerked and the never-ending rush of self-loathing returned for the irrational way he'd handled his sister's death, and the damage he'd allowed it to cause to his marriage. For the thoughtless and unintentional way he'd hurt Gila.

Gila waved the mat in her hands towards the floor, not acknowledging or questioning his comment. 'I need to do my morning stretches. I won't be long.'

He nodded and reluctantly finished his mug of cold tea. The last thing he wished to do was leave, but watching Gila in that outfit, while she ran through her morning workout, threatened to undo all the promises he'd made in the early hours while trying to get comfortable on the sofa. He refused to do anything to spook Gila into leaving before they talked. Not before he told her everything and exactly what he'd been doing for the last few months, when she imagined he'd done nothing but let their relationship go.

Taking a last sip of his drink, Leo murmured, 'I'll

get out of your way. I'll probably be late tonight. I have to go somewhere after my shift.'

Gila kept her attention on performing her yoga sequence.

Leo grabbed his car keys, his attention sliding back to his wife as she quickly settled into a series of poses. Something he'd witnessed many times, yet today, with the changes to her body, it felt different. Like watching a familiar stranger. The grace and poise she exuded as she moved through each different position—the Tree, the Half Moon and his own personal favourite, the Cat-Cow, always fascinated him.

He smiled as she moved into the Warrior position, his humour turning to concern as she suddenly gasped and straightened. Slamming the mug down onto the worktop, he dropped his keys and was beside her within seconds. 'Are you okay? Can I help?'

She shook her head and stammered, 'I—I…'

Night and day, from a distance he'd observed her growing their child, hungry for the chance to touch Gila. To explore the changes of her new and unaccustomed shape and run his hands over the precious life developing inside her body. To reconnect in some small physical way with the woman who owned his soul and the child he didn't know.

But his hands stayed by his side where they now belonged. He'd lost the right to touch her months ago.

Gila stiffened and shuffled away. 'I'm okay, thanks. Just baby deciding to shift positions. I think I'll go shower now.'

Leo swallowed the burst of disappointment and nodded. He waited until she'd disappeared into the bathroom before letting out a shaky breath. Want and desire raced through him, mingling with intense pain. How was he going to mend things when she flinched away from his presence? How was he going to gain her forgiveness when he knew he didn't deserve it? He'd treated her badly after Jodie's death. He'd not acted cruelly or physically harmed her, but he had turned away from her love. Away from her and her concern. He didn't blame Gila for not wanting to let him close again. She had every right to mistrust him. To despise him for mentally locking her out.

He retrieved his discarded car keys from the floor, his hands still tingling from aching to touch the woman he loved. His heart heavy of all that he had lost. Somehow, he had to accomplish the impossible and prove to Gila that he'd never hurt her again or disappoint their child. Regain her trust. The problem was he didn't know if either one was even possible.

Leo parked his car outside the old city cemetery and strolled towards the large ornate black gates. His thoughts were troubled as he passed row after row of graves, many from the previous century, until he eventually reached a large marble angel.

This grave stood out amongst the weathered gravestones because of its newness. Lichen, weather and time had yet to age and mute it into its green and peaceful tree-lined surroundings.

Linking his hands, Leo bent his head for a moment, before his eyes moved to read the still bright gold lettering on the stone. His heart pinching hard at the sight of the name: *Jodie Margaret Wright*.

His kid sister. His only sibling, born twelve years after his own birth. A young woman he'd spent most of his life trying to protect from herself, and yet had failed atrociously when it really mattered.

Crouching, he brushed his fingertips tenderly over the name, similar to the way he once wiped away her childhood tears whenever life turned cruel.

'Hey, kid,' he said softly. 'How's it going in heaven? I bet you're giving all those saints a hard time, eh?'

He visited his sister's grave once a week since she'd taken her own life in a drugs and drink overdose. Once a bright, happy young woman determined to conquer the world and pursue her chosen path as a dancer.

But then a tragic accident had killed her boyfriend. A boy she'd grown up loving, and it had tipped her into the world of despair and drugs when she'd met a group of people who handed out narcotics like harmless snacks that wouldn't ruin her life and rob her of her precious dreams.

Instead of throwing herself into her career to soothe the pain, Jodie had slowly melted into the destruction of being an addict. Concerned only with her next high, rather than pirouetting across the world's dance stages.

The years of trying to get Jodie clean had been a nightmare. The worrying times she'd disappeared for weeks on end, then reappeared sick, staying in Leo's company long enough to steal items of value, before leaving again. A pattern that had gone on for years, until Leo had finally found the strength to stop it. To halt the never-ending repetition that had disrupted their lives.

Unable to cope with the shame of having a drug-addict daughter, his parents had moved away from the city to their villa in Spain several years before. Leaving Leo once again with the responsibility of his younger sibling.

When he'd met and married Gila, he'd purposely pulled away from his sister's problems and her destructive lifestyle, not wanting it to taint his and Gila's relationship. But Jodie had grown to resent Gila and had often caused trouble to the point where Leo had been forced to choose between them. Pushing him until in the end he'd chosen the woman he loved the most. Gila.

Two months later Jodie lay in this grave and for weeks the guilt of wondering if his rejection had pushed his unstable sister over the edge had consumed and hounded his every thought until he could barely think or act.

'Gila's come home,' he said quietly, rubbing his fingers across the angel on top of the headstone. Her shaped wing cold beneath his touch. Aware his sister would not share his happiness at the news. But he no longer cared. He wanted his wife and child back in his life in whatever arrangement Gila chose.

'She didn't want to come home,' he continued, his fingers pausing against the marble. 'But she has. I guess I'm preferable to a park bench.'

The sound of a jackdaw calling in the late afternoon answered his words and he smiled. 'I'm not going to mess things up this time, Jodie. I'm sorry I let you down and told you to stay away from my home, but I couldn't risk you around Gila. You'd become so unpredictable and when she became pregnant, I didn't trust you not to become angry and violent. If you'd ever hurt her or the baby…'

He swallowed hard, their last angry conversation replaying in his mind. When he'd made it clear to his sister that he would no longer put up with her demands for attention or money, he'd not said why, but she'd known

Leo well enough to guess his reasons for forcing her away from his family.

By protecting his wife, Leo had failed his sister and it had taken him a long time to accept the responsibility of that decision. One he now understood and recognised as his only choice in the circumstances. To protect one female, he'd had no choice but to reject and hurt the other.

Reaching into his pocket, Leo withdrew a small crème Easter egg. Rubbing the pad of his thumb lightly over the pink foil wrapping, he crouched and positioned the egg onto the grave, pushing it gently into the soft soil.

'Happy Easter, Jodie. I hope you are happier in heaven than you ever were on earth.'

Straightening, he walked away, determined to fight for his relationship with his unborn child and for the friendship he used to share with his wife. The one thing he unthinkingly threw away and wanted back more than anything.

CHAPTER SIX

GILA SHIFTED THE floral bouquet and considered for the hundredth time whether a friendship could withstand a small let-down like bailing on an engagement party. But she knew if she didn't make an appearance, her friend Bea would insist on tracking Gila down, whether her fiancé minded or not. Though knowing the man, he'd probably be leading the needless search party.

In truth, she didn't want to celebrate anything, but she and Bea had been friends for years so, despite her reluctance, Gila didn't want to disappoint the other woman. Or hear the lecture she'd no doubt receive if she did bail. Besides, Gila figured she only needed to stay long enough to hand over the flowers, offer her congratulations and then disappear into the crowd before sneaking off home. Confident she wouldn't really be missed with so many other people to distract her friend's attention throughout the afternoon.

So here she stood at the entrance of a local restaurant's tiny outdoor garden area, searching through the sea of friends, relations and diners for sight of Bea and her wonderful fiancé, Nick.

Feeling unhospitable, though a common occurrence for Gila lately wasn't the main reason for her lack of enthusiasm for the get-together. Her reluctance for the occasion had more to do with the knowledge that she suspected Leo would arrive at some point during the afternoon, considering that Bea's fiancé also happened to be his best friend and that was enough to crush any of Gila's excitement and eagerness for the celebrations.

She and Leo had actually brought the couple together, when Bea and Nick had separately gatecrashed their third date. Their excuses, when they had turned up within minutes of each other, had been simply to check out their best friend's date, whom they had been sick and tired of hearing brilliant and unbelievable things about. Both long-time dating cynics, neither Bea nor Nick had believed such a fabulous person existed, or that their friend had been dating them. So they'd both arrived with the intention of finding fault with their best friend's new other half, and instead had found themselves drawn to each other. By the end of the evening they'd arranged to go on their own date the next night.

Gila sighed, frowning at the strong scent coming from the flowers. As if seeing Leo at home weren't hard enough. Seriously, she could do without constantly encountering the man outside the narrowboat and clinic, too. The last thing she felt inclined to do was spend the afternoon watching all the unmarried women gush around Leo once people learnt they were no longer together.

Despite her hostile attitude towards Leo, she couldn't deny his attraction. She'd fallen for his handsome looks on first sight and then toppled into love after one single conversation when his charming personality had totally floored her. Her uncle had insisted for years that when she met the right man she'd know. And she'd fallen for

Leo like a storm-split tree crashing onto shaky and unknown ground. Full force and with a vibrating boom. He'd amazed her with his funny attitude to life and the sweet way he could tug a smile from her no matter what mood she was in or how bad her day.

'You came!' squealed a female voice from across the garden, causing several people to jump and spill their drinks.

Startled from her musings, Gila chuckled as her best friend rushed from a group of guests to wrap her in an awkward hug. 'My God, the baby is growing huge. How on earth are you managing to lug it around?'

'The miracle of pregnancy.' She laughed, not offended by her friend's tactless remark. Bea was famous for speaking without thinking. The knack of saying what she thought without filtering or considering others' sensitivities just a part of her charm. 'Though sometimes I do wonder at it myself.'

Bea shifted and flicked a stern gaze over Gila's face. 'I fully expected you not to come. To find some flimsy excuse to sit at home and mope.'

'*Me?*' she quizzed innocently. Heat warmed her cheeks and gave her away, but she continued with her guiltless act. 'Why would I do that?'

'Because your delightful other half is here and I expect you to want to avoid him. When are you two going to sort yourselves out?'

'How do you like being engaged?' Gila asked, changing the subject, before she shoved the flowers into Bea's mouth to stop her talking. Couldn't she have a few hours where she didn't have to do a thing but enjoy herself? Was it really such a tough ask?

'Love it,' Bea replied, taking the bouquet from her.

'Now tell me the truth. How are things between you and Leo really? Come on, tell me. Do I need to get Nick to challenge him to something exciting and dangerous, the way they used to in the Regency period whenever a female was wronged by a man?'

'Pretty much the same as when you asked last week,' Gila replied, not about to inform her friend that she and Leo were once again sharing a home. Obviously Leo hadn't told Nick about the change so she wasn't going to. The last thing she wanted was for Bea to start imagining reunions and happy ever afters.

'Oh, Gila. I know he's a dolt, and you're hurt, but is there really no hope? I mean, let's admit the truth, men are on the whole pretty useless when it comes to the sharing and caring stuff—'

'Bea, don't,' Gila warned quietly.

'Okay, I'm being my usual insensitive self, aren't I? But it's only because I love you so much and want you happy. Would you like me to punch him hard on the arm next time I see him? Just like I used to with the mean boys at school when we were kids.'

Gila laughed and shook her head. 'I'm fine, honest.'

Bea let out a heavy sigh, then tensed. 'Prepare yourself, then. Leo's about to stroll by.'

Gila almost snatched the flowers back to use as a barricade between herself and Leo, but then sanity returned. The man would no doubt walk straight past. Nothing to worry over. If she just kept her head and acted relaxed and indifferent everything would be good.

'Bea,' Leo greeted, halting to stand beside them.

'Leo,' Bea greeted politely. 'If you're looking for Nick, he's inside playing darts with a cousin. How are you keeping?'

'I'm fine—'

'Bea, quick, Mum needs you.' Bea's teenage sister, Lola, joined them and started to drag Bea away. 'Quick, it's important.'

With a worried look at Gila, Bea reassured her, 'I'll be back in a moment, I promise.'

Several moments passed, before Leo remarked, 'So how shall we do this? Any suggestions?'

'This?' Gila quizzed, pretending not to understand. She refused to reveal her own discomfort. Not until she knew how he felt. Since yesterday morning when he'd shown concern when the baby surprised her by shifting during yoga, she'd become more unsure about things. All of which unfortunately centred around him. Probably an effect of being around each other again.

'Should I stand on one side of the garden and you on the other, while we carefully avoid coming into contact? Circulate with each of us heading in different directions? Perhaps we can time slot for when each of us buys a drink or grabs food from the buffet inside.'

'I'm sure we can be adult about this,' she said, not feeling a bit mature. All she did was remember every time she was in his company. Each one centred on a man who'd left her feeling unloved and unwanted. Where had this undiscovered sadistic streak come from?

'Of course,' Leo agreed. 'We share a home after all. Attending this party and being civil should be easy.'

'For seven days only,' she reminded him. Though now it was only six days and counting. 'Or until a hotel has a vacant room.'

He nodded and glanced down at the drink in his hand. 'I hadn't forgotten, Gila. Trust me, I haven't.'

Gila's gaze narrowed and she huffed under her

breath. What exactly did he mean by that? Was he also counting the hours until she left? Was he already regretting his offer for her to stay?

A commotion by the restaurant's patio doors caught her attention and halted her spiralling thoughts. Shifting to one side, she frowned when she spotted someone sprawled out on the ground.

'I think Nick's aunt Tom has fallen,' Leo murmured with concern. He placed his glass down on a nearby table.

Without exchanging another word, they hurried over to the woman and the small group already gathering around her. Their private dispute forgotten while someone hurt required their attention and help.

'Hey, Aunt Tom,' Leo greeted the old lady dressed in her usual navy jumper and skirt, spread-eagled on the patio. Looking like a small, dazed baby bird who'd just fallen out of a nest. 'Suffered a bit of a fall, I see?'

'Caught my foot on the chair and came down hard. Stupid new shoes, I knew I shouldn't have worn them. I never really got on with heels even as a young girl. You'd think I'd know better at eighty-five.'

Thomasina March, or Tom as everyone called her, flashed Leo and Gila a faint regal smile. 'How lovely to see you both again. Do be sweet and help me onto a chair, will you? These patio slabs are rather hard on one's bony posterior and the cold is starting to seep into my bones.'

Leo crouched and shook his head. 'Let's check you over first, shall we? Just in case you've broken something important. Now, does anything throb or hurt?'

'Mainly my pride, young Leo,' Tom answered with

a resigned sigh. 'I haven't quite trumped the aging with dignity bit yet. I do try, but it's a struggle.'

'How about any bones?' Gila asked, squatting next to Leo. She instinctively rested a hand on his shoulder to help with her balance, glad she'd chosen to wear her jean dungarees and not a dress to the party. Less chance of dragging her hem along the ground or flashing her unattractive practical pregnancy underwear to innocent onlookers by mistake.

Aunt Tom snorted. 'I may be a clumsy old whatnot, but I'm pretty sure I mostly bumped, not snapped, when I hit the ground.'

'Best we check you for anything broken, though,' Leo said, trying not to laugh.

Aunt Tom stabbed a long bony finger into his arm. 'Young man, I've known you since you were a small boy. You will keep your hands to yourself. Instead, your darling wife may check my body for anything amiss or displaced.'

Unable to stop her own laughter, Gila gently pushed Leo to one side and slowly but carefully checked Aunt Tom's small frame for any serious damage or cuts. Finally, she gently prodded the lady's right arm, concerned by the sight of swelling around the delicate bony wrist.

'Does your wrist hurt, Aunt Tom?' Gila asked, glancing at the woman for an answer.

'Unfortunately it does appear to,' Aunt Tom replied. 'Classic thing of putting my hand out to stop myself when I fell, I'm afraid. It's a bit tender.'

Gila nodded and examined it once more. 'You've probably sprained it. Though I can't rule out that there might be a break with the way it's looking.'

Aunt Tom huffed. 'I'm such a silly old woman.'

'No, you're not,' Gila soothed. 'You tripped over, which can happen to any of us, but I think a trip to the hospital is best just to be certain. They'll also be able to give you something for the pain.'

'Oh, what a bother,' Aunt Tom complained. 'I'm sure it isn't broken. It just feels a bit achy and tender.'

'Best to be sure, though,' Leo agreed.

'I suppose, though I do hope not. I've the WI coach trip to Torquay next week. I can't miss it.'

Gila mollified her with a smile. 'I'm sure you'll be able to manage the trip with one arm working.'

'Even if it's a sprain, you'll need to rest the arm, though,' Leo added cautiously, his caring concern for the old woman apparent. 'Now Gila's given you the once-over, let's get you onto a chair, shall we?'

Nick and Leo gently and slowly lifted Aunt Tom off the patio slabs and settled her onto a nearby plastic chair. Softly squeezing the old lady's shoulder, Leo said, 'I'll go and fetch some ice for the wrist.'

Gila straightened and rechecked for any other signs of injury to the arm. Once she was sure there were no protruding bones or wounds, she helped Aunt Tom position the damaged limb across her body.

'I can see why you married him,' Aunt Tom said, her eyes following Leo as he walked away. 'Has a lovely manner. So caring. Always was a sweet child.'

Gila almost snorted. Caring? She'd once thought so too, but now she knew better. She sighed. 'He's a good doctor.'

'A good man, too,' Aunt Tom insisted. 'How much longer until baby arrives?'

Gila happily grabbed at the old lady's change of topic. With another smile, she replied, 'Just under four weeks.'

Aunt Tom raised her thin white eyebrows, her mouth puckering together in contemplation. 'So long? Are you sure? Don't be shocked if the baby isn't earlier. I inherited the gift from my grandmother. And she got it from her mother.'

'Gift?' Gila asked curiously.

'Of knowing when a baby is coming. I've never been wrong.'

Gila frowned, but dismissed the old lady's words. She knew her dates were right, thanks to her monthly cycle being regular. And first-time babies were commonly late in arriving.

'I always felt a little sorry for Leo, you know?' Aunt Tom said, changing the subject for the second time. Gila stiffened, not sure what to say. Surely Nick had informed his aunt that she and Leo had separated? He and Bea were the only friends who knew. Though the way the man was so happily in love with Bea, it might have slipped his mind.

'You did?'

'Yes, his childhood wasn't an easy one. Oh, his family were what many would call privileged, I suppose. Wealthy and liked people to know it. But from the age of twelve, when his sister arrived, he became a sort of surrogate parent. Leo's mother and father both worked very demanding, high-profile jobs in the city. Worked hours on end, often seven days a week. Left the children in the care of one nanny after another. Some well trained, others not so. Young women who grew to resent the long hours Leo's parents expected them to work. In the end they left it to Leo to bring Jodie up. A lot of responsibility for a young boy. Far too much. Social services should've stepped in, but his parents were well off and middle class, so of course no one questioned it at the time. No one looked beyond the respectable front door, I suppose. I wonder if anyone in our street even noticed.'

'*You* did,' Gila pointed out, reluctantly intrigued and concerned by the picture the old lady was providing of Leo's childhood. Although they'd discussed their pasts, Leo had always made his upbringing sound normal and similar to other people's. Yet, it seemed as though neglect and too much responsibility had filled his early years. Why hadn't he told her that?

'Nick tells me that his sister's death hit Leo hard. You know, I guess he must have felt as if he'd lost his own child in a way. The sibling he raised and loved. The guilt must have hurt worse though. As a doctor unable to help her fight her addiction. I understand his parents blame him. Still as self-centred as ever. Easier to blame someone else than admit your own failings. But the truth is his parents neglected both their children.'

Leo reappeared holding a red checked tea towel and carrying a plastic bucket of ice. 'Here, Tom, let's wrap this around your wrist. It will help with the swelling and numb some of the pain.'

Working together, Gila and Leo slipped the tea towel around Aunt Tom's arm and packed several ice cubes each side of her wrist to help ease the swelling. Once done, Leo gently returned the injured limb to its former position across her body. His movements slow and considerate. Never rushed or impatient. Just the way a good doctor treated his patients, but there was more to his actions. His genuine care and concern for the old lady was obvious and Gila could see how much he thought of Aunt Tom. But then patience was one of the things she always admired in Leo. He rarely became ruffled by events or situations. Always a clear practical mind when required. Her father had always lived by whatever twist or turn his emotions or moods took him, so Leo's cool level-headedness was always a comfort to her jaded soul.

'Keep your arm in this position to support it,' he advised with a smile.

Nick appeared once more at his side. 'Dad's going to run you to A & E for an X-ray, Aunt Tom.'

The old lady huffed, but allowed her brother and nephew to lead her from the garden and into a waiting car. With a quick thanks, she bid Leo and Gila goodbye.

Alone again, they watched the car drive away, before Gila turned to Leo. 'I think I'll head home. I'm afraid I'm not really in the mood for socialising. Hopefully Bea will be too distracted to notice my absence.'

Leo nodded, shoving his hands into his trouser pockets. 'I know what you mean. Do you mind if I come too?'

She hesitated for a second before answering, 'No, I don't mind, Leo.'

She smiled awkwardly, suddenly not sure how to act around him. Her conversation with Aunt Tom still lingering in her mind. Why did Leo's parents blame him for Jodie's death? Important information he'd never told her. Why not? Had he worried about her reaction, or, worse, felt he couldn't talk to her about it? Was that why he'd shut her out those weeks before she'd left?

Not once had she ever considered that his perfect life might not have been what it appeared or thought to look beyond the fancy background to the real layers beneath Leo's family. On the few occasions she'd met his parents, she'd felt intimidated and inadequate. They'd never hidden their disappointment in their son's choice of wife and Gila's unforgivable lack of social connections.

But, thinking back, had she been so wrapped up in the negativity of her own past that she'd not contemplated Leo's early life might not be as flawless and perfect—well, apart from Jodie and her issues—as she thought? Leo had kept any time she'd spent with his parents brief and infrequent. Was that because he'd been concerned that she might find out the truth behind the swanky glint of his family's middle-class shine?

Perhaps it *was* time they talked. After all, how could she make a decision about her, Leo's and the baby's future when she suspected she didn't know everything from their past?

The narrowboat was delightfully peaceful after the noisy party. Gila kicked off her shoes and wriggled her toes, enjoying the freedom. Grabbing a ripe peach from a china bowl on the side, she padded into the lounge as Leo came from the opposite direction.

'I've started a bath for you. Your back's hurting, right?'

She nodded and smiled, refusing to be awkward or argumentative. Leo's ability to read her moods and body had always fascinated her. His knack of being able to tell when she required a hug, or to be left alone to brood, was surprisingly instinctive. No one in her life had ever bothered to read her that way. No one else had ever cared to.

'It's killing, to be honest. Pressing up against my spine must be baby's favourite position.'

'Go and grab a towel while I pour a glass of orange juice for you. You can sip it while you soak away the aches.'

She hesitated, then nodded, happy to do as he recommended. 'Thank you, Leo.'

He smiled softly before leaving to organise her drink.

Padding into the bedroom, Gila stripped out of her dungarees, top and underwear and wrapped a clean towel around her body. For the first time in months it felt nice to have someone fuss over her. Her father and Art had done their best over the years, but they were both old-school men who had struggled with the emotional needs of a young child. Leo, though, had always managed to make her feel secure. That was until Jodie's death, when he'd shut down and left her wondering what to do or how to help. She'd never faced a situation like it before and she'd panicked, convinced he was letting her go. Deserting her the way so many others had.

Heading for the minuscule bathroom, she found Leo waiting outside the room.

'Here's your drink,' he said, handing over a fresh glass of cold juice. His fingers bumped hers as she took the glass from him. Condensation ran down its sides and pooled against her sticky peach-juice fingertips. Running her tongue over her top lip, she hesitated, before asking, 'Leo, can we talk?'

Leo stared down at her for several seconds, before nodding, 'Okay. How about I sit out here while you bathe? If you leave the door open, we'll be able to hear each other. Is there something in particular you'd like to discuss?'

She moved towards the bathroom, but just before stepping inside, she glanced back over her shoulder. Not certain if it was a good idea or not, she said, 'This might seem odd, but will you tell me about your childhood?'

Leo slipped to the floor and rested his head against the plasterboard wall separating them. He'd expected Gila to ask something mundane or general, but her question about his childhood threw him. What caused her to want to delve into a time in his life he rarely considered or discussed these days? He almost wished she'd asked anything but that.

He closed his eyes and the smell of roses and cucumber drifted through the half-open door. The aroma courtesy of the bar of soap Gila always bought from a local health shop. She rarely wore perfume, preferring a simpler, cleaner scent. Something that didn't overpower the senses. It reminded him of long-ago nights in bed, snuggled together. The two of them wrapped completely and wholly into each other. Skin touching skin, their heartbeats twinned in a matching rhythm.

He'd give anything to enter the bathroom and kiss her. To sink into her body and return to the special place where he was simply Leo. Not the husband, brother, son or doctor. But just Leo, the man.

'Leo?'

He heard her gentle prompting for him to start. Not wanting to disappoint Gila now she was finally talking to him without looking as though she wanted to grind him into the ground, he faltered for a moment, uncertain how to begin.

'I'm not sure where to start,' he admitted. 'You know

most everything about my childhood. My parents were two very successful city—'

'No, not the boring stuff,' she interrupted. 'But your day-to-day life. Nick's aunt mentioned your parents employed nannies. You never told me that.'

Her sudden interest in his past started to make sense. Obviously, Aunt Tom had said something to Gila when he'd left them alone while he'd fetched the ice and towel. He wasn't sure he liked the idea of them discussing his family. He'd made a point to keep Gila away from his parents, knowing what hard work they were to be around and their prickly attitude towards her because of their own prejudices. They viewed his and Gila's marriage as a temporary inconvenience. His father had even given Leo the number of a solicitor who specialised in divorce the morning of their wedding. A number Leo had immediately thrown away. So what had the old lady said to raise Gila's curiosity?

'Yeah, a lot of nannies, until the agencies stopped sending them amid complaints of exploitation. My parents took advantage of their employees. After all, why care for your own children when there's more interesting and entertaining events like meetings or parties to attend?'

'But it's what parents do,' she argued. 'They look after their babies.'

He chuckled dryly. 'You know yourself that parents come in all guises. Some adequate, some less so.'

'And yours?' Gila probed.

'Absent mostly,' he said with a heavy sigh. 'They never considered their children as a barrier to living the life they really wanted. We were not a responsibility, they believed, who had the right to disrupt the freedom of their social lives. Jodie and I were just two events they ticked off a pre-prepared life list. Their friends had children, so of course they had to produce some, too. Only they preferred the type of offspring who stayed behind a nursery door and never cluttered the house with their barely tolerated presence or belongings.'

'But that's terrible,' Gila said, disapproval lacing her voice.

'It's what it was,' Leo murmured. 'We move on, don't we? Make sure we do things differently in our own lives, with our own children. Never repeat our parents' mistakes and faults.'

'Yes, I suppose. But...'

'What?' he coaxed, hearing concern in her tone. Did hearing about his upbringing cause her to worry over whether he was capable of being a good parent to his own child? He'd already botched up being a husband and brother, hadn't he? Was she now doubting his ability in the role of a father? Was there any way he could prove he'd never be like his own parents when he'd already bombed so badly in other relationships?

'*We* both have busy careers...' she pointed out.

So it wasn't just him she was concerned for, it was both of them. 'I'll give up my career if our child needs more. I'll never put my job before our son or daughter.'

'I won't either,' she promised solemnly. 'Oh, Leo, what happened to us?'

Leo closed his eyes and breathed slowly. The one question he had asked himself so many times. Finally, he acknowledged, 'I shut you out, Gila. After my sister's death. I'm sorry, I did that.'

'Did I do something to make you?' she asked. 'Did I not support you? Not show you how much I cared?'

Fresh pain shot through him at her soft anxious queries. The slight tremble in her voice shaming him. Breaking him apart a little bit more. 'I swear you did nothing wrong, Gila. It was all me. Not you.'

'I didn't help you much, though, did I?' she said. 'When Jodie died, I mean. I wasn't any real comfort to you other than staying with you in her hospital room. In nursing college they teach you how to be kind and supportive to patients and their family members. But it's easy to be that way with a stranger, because it doesn't truly affect you, does it? Things may upset or sadden you at work, but the training helps you to deal with it. To put it in a place where your raw emotions are protected and you can keep some perspective. You have to otherwise you wouldn't be able to do the job, or at least not for long. But I didn't know what to do when confronted with your pain. I had no idea how to reach out or help you. I tried, but you refused to let me in.'

Horrified by the way she was blaming herself, Leo searched for the right words to explain. To find a cohesive way to describe that period in a way that would make sense to Gila and stop any ill-founded guilt she might carry. 'I believe Jodie never wanted to stop being an addict, or for the pain of losing Russ to leave. It was the only connection she had with him. The truth is the Jodie I knew died the day Russ did. The woman she became was nothing but a stranger I was related to.'

'I always felt she resented me in your life,' Gila admitted quietly. Revealing a feeling she'd always kept to herself, not wanting to upset him. 'Especially in the beginning when she made it clear she didn't like me.'

Leo nodded even though Gila couldn't see him, recalling the arguments his sister had caused between them. The way she'd ignored Gila whenever they'd met. Or the lies she would tell when Leo left the room. Lies created in the hope that Gila would believe them and leave Leo. So Jodie could once again have him all to herself.

'I think she was jealous at times. I had a career, a home and you. She in turn had drugs and sad, old memories. She'd never really shared me with anyone else. She grew up with me on one side and Russ on the other. Always there to support her when she found things tough and struggled. Then Russ died and everything she viewed as safe suddenly ended.'

The sound of trickling water drifted from the bathroom. Leo imagined Gila shifting in the warm bath, conjuring images of it running over her sleek, pale flesh as she moved around the bathtub.

A noise brought his head up and he found she now stood beside him, wrapped in a pink towel. Her cheeks rosy from the bath and tiny tendrils of her damp hair curled against her neck. His fingers itched to play with the curls, but he didn't dare.

Crouching, she said, 'I'm sorry about Jodie, Leo. I really am.'

He nodded, squeezing his hands into fists to stop them from reaching out and sliding over the curve of her shoulder. His fingers tingled with the need to brush away the drops of bath water scattering the skin around her collarbone. Every part of him yearned to lean forward and kiss her soft mouth and make the pain and the hurt of the last few months melt away for just a few seconds. 'Me, too.'

'It's all such a mess, isn't it?' she whispered.

He nodded and glanced at her bump covered by just

the towel. 'Yeah, but we have the baby to look forward to. I swear I'll do a better job as a father than I have as a husband.'

She tensed slightly and then nodded. 'Let's just take it slowly. Yes?'

Leo nodded, grateful for the chance she was offering.

Gila reached out and grabbed his fist, uncurling it. She placed it flat against her stomach, keeping her eyes lowered as though fearing he might pull away. 'Would you like to feel the baby move and kick?'

Leo swallowed, his eyes stinging, and whispered back, 'Yes, Gila. I'd love to.'

She looked up then and met his gaze. Her grey eyes holding his own. 'There…can you feel that?'

Leo grinned and a single tear rolled from the corner of his eye as a firm thud vibrated through the towel and hit him in the centre of his palm. His unborn child's kick. The baby he'd helped to create. 'Yes, sweetheart. I can.'

CHAPTER SEVEN

GILA LIFTED THE small glass dome-shaped cloche and watered the barely sprouting onion seed inside the black plastic pot. Replacing the cloche back over the container, she slowly moved on to the next veg box, this time mini beetroot, and also gave it a decent drenching of water from the pink watering can.

She'd come out onto the narrowboat's roof garden to think and the slowly encompassing darkness as the late afternoon eased into early evening created the perfect place to mull over her troubled and confused thoughts.

What was she supposed to do about Leo? Everything she'd thought over the last few months suddenly felt irrelevant now she'd discarded her own hurt feelings to one side and observed the situation from his point of view. Had she really not done that before? Not even once? The awful truth was, she hadn't. Not really.

She watered another box of barely grown vegetables and sighed at her own self-centred behaviour. When had she become so uncaring? Surely it wasn't her true nature to see everything from only her own aspect and disregard other people's? But thinking back to after Jodie's death and the following horrible weeks when Leo slowly circled away from her, emotionally pushing her aside with his continued silence and indifference, she couldn't recall one moment when she'd stopped and fully reflected on his feelings, or pondered on how deeply his grief truly went. Oh, she wasn't completely insensitive and cold-hearted. She'd known he was upset and miserable, but she'd never questioned that there could be more behind the expected stress and emotions that everyone suffered when going through the initial stages of mourning. Not once had she suspected his grieving might also be mixed with guilt because he'd virtually raised his sister from birth and then found himself unable to help her in the end.

But then how could she have known when he'd never told her? Not once had he revealed the truth concerning his and his sister's early relationship, or how he'd taken on the role of parent. And how could Gila have helped him when Leo had never reached out to her? Never made that initial move or effort to communicate the pain inside him. Pain he had to endure and come through if they were ever going to move forward.

Gila thought back to the hours she and Leo had sat in Jodie's hospital room. She'd thought it strange that his parents hadn't travelled over from Spain, and now she knew the reason why. They were indifferent to their own daughter's welfare, and also too selfish to concern themselves with the pain Leo was going through.

And her? Wasn't marriage supposed to be a partnership where each person committed to the other through good and bad? Had she only played at the good and when the bad had come hurling along to test her, she'd failed dismally? Hadn't she in fact without meaning to, like Leo's parents, neglected him? The man she had sworn to love and help. The male who'd been her world.

So was the truth not whether he had abandoned *her*, but that *she* had actually abandoned him, too? Somehow, they had both lost one another and their closeness due to their inability to talk honestly to each other?

Gila sighed, shaking her head. Her thoughts leaving her more confused than ever. Which one of them was guilty of letting the other down? For the first time in months, she wasn't so sure of the answer.

Placing the empty watering can down beside the box, careful not to catch either the hem of her night-dress or dressing gown on the dripping plastic rose, she rested her hands on her hips and stared along the canal's length.

Several ducks swam past, sending a quack of hello in her direction. A robin flew out from a tree to land on a narrowboat further along, much to the surprise of the passengers sitting on the roof enjoying an evening cocktail. Gila chuckled and turned away, before resuming her silent wonderings.

Was she culpable of failing to see and put Leo's heartache before her own wounded feelings? Allowing him to disappear alone into his sorrow because she hadn't known how to deal with it or him? Giving into the old habit of running away rather than stay and face a situation she had no idea how to react to?

A thread of guilt-ridden shame twisted through her, prodding at her conscience. Well, she hadn't provided much help during that time, had she?

She reflected back on their courtship. That period of their relationship had been both quick and intense. Both had been eager to spend what little free time they had with each other. Each purposely giving only sketchy accounts of their family backgrounds when questioned. Was it because they were equally ashamed of their childhoods and hoped neither ever discovered that they were less than the person they liked to portray to the world? That semi-perfect character an individual showed when desperate to hide their imperfections, but keen to impress someone new into liking them.

Was that yet another mistake they'd made in their relationship? Had they never revealed their true selves to the other? Never taken the time to really discover the people deep inside their hearts? She didn't have an answer to any of her ponderings, but what she *did* understand was that her husband's relationship with his sister had been more complex than just siblings. Was Aunt Tom correct when she stated that Leo must have felt as though he'd failed as both a doctor and a brother when Jodie died?

When Gila and Leo first started dating, she'd tried to reach out to Jodie, wanting to help the younger woman with her problems. But Jodie had quickly made it clear that she'd neither sought Gila's help nor liked her existence in her brother's life. Initially, not upset by Jodie's resistance, Gila had waited several weeks before trying again. Keen to help both Leo and his sister in any way she could, eager to become the girl's friend, but Jodie had resented and blocked every attempt and eventually accused Gila of harassing her.

And then the lies had begun. At first silly things like saying Gila had made nasty comments when Leo was out of the room. Then she'd call Gila's mobile at night when Leo was working a shift and say she'd seen him with another woman. Trying to worm doubt and suspicion into their relationship whenever she could.

Unsure how to handle the situation, and not about to

believe anything Jodie said, Gila had stepped back when Leo had suggested she wait until Jodie had a chance to get to know her better. The excuses Leo had made for his sister's behaviour had sometimes been frustrating, but she'd trusted that he understood Jodie best and that things would eventually improve. Unfortunately the opportunity to get closer had never materialised because the other woman had suddenly insisted on meeting Leo alone and often away from the narrowboat.

And truthfully, Gila had felt relieved not to have to deal with Jodie's spiteful and childish behaviour any more. As much as she'd wished to help her, Gila had never expected when she married Leo to have the shadow of Jodie's dislike, resentment and addiction hovering over them.

But how painful for Leo to lose his sister. Not having grown up with siblings, Gila struggled to grasp or appreciate how such a connection worked between people. Those close complexities that only brothers and sisters understood. But she did know Leo was not a man who walked away from his responsibilities easily. Even when *they'd* split up, he'd still made certain she was cared for financially by depositing money into her bank account every month. She hadn't asked him to and had even demanded he stop, but every month the money arrived for her to use.

Folding her arms, Gila glanced at the darkening sky, taking in the way the clouds sat in a mass of small puffy balls above her. Though singular in shape they were all connected to each other, unlike her and Leo.

When Leo's sister had passed away, instead of clinging to one another the way the clouds overhead did, they'd slowly and painfully glided apart.

Was she a terrible person to put her feelings before the person she loved? Wasn't that a big no-no rule when in a committed relationship? To be honest, she didn't know. Leo was the only man she'd ever fallen in love with. The one male she'd allowed herself to trust completely. The whole romance game totally unfamiliar and confusing to her. An emotional and sexual maze of wrong turns and dos and don'ts. Most of which she didn't understand. But she did recall reading a book years before, one she'd borrowed from a library, which stated certain important rules in love. Had putting your partner's needs first been one of them?

Perhaps she wasn't cut out for love? Maybe seeing and living through her father's many failed attempts had crushed all emotion and compassion inside her? Was she as flawed in the love game as he'd been? Chasing after some fantasy sentiment that in truth didn't exist. Just as incapable of experiencing it for longer than a few weeks, several months or at the most a year.

A sound from the other end of the narrowboat attracted her attention and she glanced up to see Leo climbing the steps to the roof. He paused, his hands gripping the metal rails on each side. Rails he'd fixed there when they'd first learnt she was expecting the baby, after declaring he didn't want to risk her falling or hurting herself whenever she went onto the roof.

Her heartbeat increased as she stood silently taking him in. Why did the sight of him still ignite such a warm sensation deep inside her? Surely her body should know not to skip or respond every time he came into her vicinity? When would her fingers stop wanting to brush his thick dark fringe from his face, or her disloyal lips lose the urge to kiss his?

Gila forced a smile as he stepped onto the roof and walked towards her. His easy, long strides so memorable and comforting. She loved the way he walked. It caused her to think of hazy summer afternoons and warm smooth brandy with just a hint of walnut and black pepper. Earthy tastes with a kick of heat.

'How's the gardening going?' he asked, glancing to where the watering can dripped a small puddle.

'Want one?' she asked, pulling a cherry from her dressing-gown pocket. She'd grabbed a handful before leaving the kitchen, figuring it was better to eat these than the cream cake she really craved.

Leo nodded and reached for the offered fruit. Taking it, he popped it into his mouth and murmured, 'Hmm, nice.'

She agreed, her traitorous eyes watching his mouth as he chewed the cherry. How her tongue yearned to lick the corner, just by the faint small scar he'd received a couple of years before after attempting extreme cross-country running for the first time and colliding with a tree halfway round the course.

But that would be a mistake and she'd already made plenty. Ones she'd learnt to regret. At this moment, she didn't know what to think. She just knew that the past wasn't as simple as she'd thought.

'I'm amazed the plants are so healthy—' She suddenly broke off. Out here in the semi-darkness with the peace interrupted only by the sound of classical music and laughter drifting from a couple of the nearby houses, it seemed wrong to drag up all the unpleasantness between them. Not when they'd achieved some kind of unspoken truce for the evening.

'I've tried my best to keep the garden going for

you,' Leo murmured, obviously guessing her unspoken words. He shifted closer but didn't touch her.

She glanced around at the plastic boxes filled with winter vegetables and the young tender shoots of spring and summer ones. Plants she'd sown and tended before she left, not thinking she wouldn't be around to maintain or harvest them. Yet the plants were healthy and happy because Leo had taken the trouble to care and water them. Why? The garden had always been her interest and hobby. Was it really as he said and he'd done it for her? Had he wanted to show that he cared enough to keep her small winter garden going?

She hadn't bothered to grow anything on her uncle's narrowboat. Her enthusiasm for everything had waned during the long weeks living there. But Leo had fussed and cared for this mini garden, never knowing whether his efforts would be wasted or not. It touched her heart that he'd done so.

'Want another?' she asked, pulling a second dark shiny cherry from her pocket. Unsure whether to thank him or demand answers. Tonight they'd talked but so many questions still plagued her mind.

Leo chuckled and accepted it. Glancing around the surroundings, he said, 'It's so calm out here, isn't it?'

Gila gazed at him, taking in the long line of his neck and the way his hair curled against the loose collar of his T-shirt. He appeared relaxed and content. Happy in himself. Was it how he felt inside, though? Or did deeper emotions bubble beneath the skin in readiness to spill out?

'Unlike life,' she murmured.

He nodded and turned her way. 'It's certainly not

been quiet and uneventful recently, has it? For either of us.'

A hard kick from the baby prevented her from replying. Gila laughed and placed a hand to her stomach. 'I think little one has woken up again.'

'Do you have everything you need for the baby?' Leo asked, shifting the focus from the past and to the future. 'Is there anything I can help with?'

She rubbed a loving hand over their child. 'There's a few things I need to pick up. Last-minute stuff, you know? Items I've hesitated to buy in case I jinxed things. Silly superstitious nonsense, really.'

'I don't think it's silly. Are you excited?' he asked.

'Yes,' she admitted. 'And a little scared, too. I mean, of course I've studied the subject for years and helped countless women through their births, but it's still the first time for me. I'm going to find out how it really feels to give birth to a baby, instead of reading and learning by observing others. How about you? Are *you* excited?'

He hesitated for a second before solemnly declaring, 'I can't wait to be a daddy.'

She licked her lower lip. 'I suppose we should think about what's going to happen after the baby's here. How we co-parent.'

He touched her other hand, his fingers loosely linking with her own. 'There's plenty of time for those decisions.'

She frowned, her brain silently shouting to pull her hand away, but her body hesitated. 'Is there? The weeks are whizzing past.'

His fingers squeezed hers lightly. 'Look, Gila, there's something I want to tell you.'

A cold trickle travelled slowly along her spine, her brain yelling at her to be wary because when a person said those words it rarely brought joy to the receiver. Was this when he admitted he wanted a divorce? That he no longer saw a future together for them? This sweet moment ruined by the intrusion of ugly realism.

'There's no rush,' she began.

'No, it's important you hear this,' he interrupted her, his tone firm and determined. Making it clear he wasn't going to be put off by any attempt she made to redirect the conversation. The expression on his face reminded her of the times when her father would inform her that, yet again, they were going to live with another woman or move to a different country.

She glanced away, her eyes falling on a passing insect. How she'd love to swap bodies with that creature and scuttle away into a small hole or deep crevice. Or jump overboard into the water and swim somewhere new. But she'd tried to do that when she left months before and she'd discovered life refused to be so easily avoided, so instead she nodded. 'Okay, tell me what you wish to say.'

'The thing is, I've been seeing—'

She yanked her hand from his, not intending to hear any more. Resisting the impulse to cover her ears and sing loudly like a hysterical child, she snapped, 'Don't, Leo. Please, don't. I can guess what you are about to say and I don't want to know. Not tonight.'

Not when she was just accepting that the faults in their marriage might not all be his.

Leo grasped her arm to prevent her from moving

away. His hold firm but not painful. 'Gila, what is it you think I'm going to say?'

She sucked in a deep breath and tried to bury the fear that had plagued her most of her life. How many more times would a male insist on influencing the course of her life without regard for her feelings, just so they could have everything their own way? How many times had her own father put a woman he hardly knew before *her* safety and welfare? His own child's needs irrelevant when matched against his own. Did Leo now intend to add yet another fracture to her already sore and shattered heart? Did he plan to show her yet again how unimportant she was?

'If you want a divorce, then I'd prefer you didn't tell me until after the baby is born. Let me have time to concentrate on our child and forget everything else for a while. *Please*, Leo.'

Leo was stunned at her words. A divorce? Was she kidding? Did she really think he was going to tell her such rubbish only weeks from their child's birth?

God, did she not realise how utterly in love with her he was? How he didn't see other women because she'd ruined him for anyone but her? No one smiled the way she did, nor caused his heart to flip, or even roused his temper the way only she could. For him there was no one else, but obviously she no longer trusted what he said. All his fault and his problem to mend.

Tonight he'd waited before searching Gila out. His concentration refusing to settle on the work papers he'd tried to bury himself in after their earlier conversation. The memory of his palm placed over their growing child, and the delightful shock when the baby kicked, one he would always treasure.

But a feeling of unfinished business remained since they'd parted. A strong sense that there was so much more to share. Now he'd finally started to open up to Gila and admit the secrets in his heart, he yearned to get it all out. To tell her everything and let her hear exactly what he'd tried to protect her from and why. Why now when he couldn't before, he didn't know, but it just felt time to at least try.

How could they find a pathway towards any honest future, no matter how they raised their child, if the prior secrets still clung and stuck to him with the same tenacity of a rampant vine intent on smothering everything? Wasn't it crucial to expose and deal with the past for good if they hoped to rebuild?

Deciding to get the conversation started, because circling around sent them in the wrong direction and hurt Gila unnecessarily, Leo gathered his courage. He saw the clear desire to run in his wife's guarded wary gaze, but gently drew her towards him, until her body stopped next to his. The curve of her stomach nestling against his flat one. Cupping her cheek, he whispered, 'You think I want a divorce?'

'Don't you?' she stammered. 'Don't you want to finish everything with me and start again?'

'No, my darling. Besides we'll never be finished when we share a child.'

Or while every part of my heart still belongs to you.

He shook his head and insisted, 'I don't want a divorce. Why would you think I would?'

She shrugged and flushed. 'I don't know. I suppose

it came into my head when you said you wanted to talk. I thought that maybe you'd met someone.'

'Well, please allow that thought to leave because there's no one else I'm interested in and any decision we make about divorcing can wait.'

'Good,' she said shakily.

Leo smiled and probed, 'Good?'

She stiffened and glanced away. 'Well, yes. Separation can be hard without other people becoming involved and confusing things. Or so others say.'

His thumb gently caressed the corner of her mouth. 'I get that you're not ready to hear that you're the only one I want because I've hurt you. That's my sorrow to carry and I always will. But what I want to share with you is this. I *have* actually been seeing someone, but it isn't for any romantic reasons or intentions. It's simply to do with my mental well-being.'

She frowned and met his gaze. Her grey eyes searching his face for clues to what he meant. 'I don't understand.'

He sensed her tension and confusion. Not wanting to prolong the moment now he'd started, Leo continued, 'For the last few months I've had weekly sessions with a grief counsellor. Basically, since you walked out on me.'

She stared at him trying to make logic of his words. Opening her mouth, she shut it again, before finally asking, 'A counsellor? You?'

He nodded, feeling a self-conscious flush warm his skin. He didn't know why he felt so awkward talking about this, he certainly wasn't ashamed of seeking help. But this was the woman he'd always longed to astonish and amaze. The female he'd wanted to be a hero to. 'Yes.'

'But why?'

'Because when you left, I finally admitted to myself the mess I was in, and I understood that if I ever hoped to right things between us, I needed to make sense of the anguish consuming me.'

'Oh, Leo,' she said, placing her hand over his where it still rested against her face. 'I thought... I...didn't...'

'What?'

'It doesn't matter. I suppose I never thought you would visit a counsellor.'

He let out a sharp noise that was neither a laugh nor a groan. But definitely a sound of discomfort. 'Why—because I'm a doctor? A man?'

'No,' she said. 'Because you constantly refused to talk to me.'

'Only because I wasn't sure what to tell you,' he confessed. 'Truth is, I'm exactly the person who needed to find help and I'm not too proud to say so. But before you left, I couldn't see it.'

Gila stared at him. 'We've created such a muddle of everything, haven't we?'

'But we're trying to mend it, aren't we?' His gaze held hers, his question hanging between them. What if Gila viewed his reaching out to a professional as a weakness? What if she concluded that she didn't want him any more because of it? Now she knew about the counselling sessions would she see him as broken and flawed? Less of a person? A sad image of a man? Resent him for talking to a stranger when he'd stubbornly shied away from opening up to her?

'Isn't that all that matters?' he asked, concerned when Gila stayed silent. 'That we at least try to make amends for the confusion of the past.'

CHAPTER EIGHT

GILA STEPPED OFF the bus and stared at the large post-war concrete hospital situated across the street. People streamed in and out of the main entrance, dotted by the odd white-coated medic. A couple of paramedics, distinctive in their green uniforms, wheeled a patient stretched out on a trolley from the back of an ambulance, closely followed inside by a trio of chatting nurses, possibly returning from their lunch break.

Gila breathed in a deep, fortifying breath and then crossed the road and walked towards the building, heading for the hospital's main section, where Leo worked his morning shift.

She'd travelled to the hospital on a whim and now she desperately prayed she wasn't making a mistake. During the bus journey into the city, she'd silently debated with herself, unsure whether her trip would end with a positive result or a negative one. But after last night, when Leo had stated his eagerness over the baby's arrival, she'd woken up this morning with the idea that he might like to join her on her shopping trip to buy the last few things she needed before their baby's birth.

Heading along the wide and long hospital corridors in the direction of the A & E department, Gila passed streams of hurrying people, many with tight, worried faces as they headed to appointments or visited sick friends and family. Each in a bubble of their own thoughts and fears.

Reaching A & E, she took in the full and busy seating area, before making her way over to a harassed-looking middle-aged nurse sitting behind the main desk, glaring at a computer screen.

'Hi, can I help you?' the nurse asked with a distracted, weary smile. She took in Gila's pregnancy bump, and immediately declared, 'If you're searching for the maternity unit, I'm afraid you've taken a wrong turn. We're Accident and Emergency. So unless you've broken, burnt or cut something or worse, then you're in the wrong place.'

Gila shook her head and rested a hand on the desk. 'Actually, I'd like to speak to Dr Wright.'

The nurse shot her a surprised look before glancing around. 'He should be here somewhere. I think he's recently finished with a patient. As you can see, we're really busy today. Are you a patient's relative? Only he won't be able to talk to you about them if you are.'

'No, I'm not,' Gila replied, before the woman could come up with any other reason to shoo her from the department. She hesitated, not sure whether to admit her marital connection to Leo or not. Did she still maintain the right to call herself his spouse when they were no longer romantically involved? Though last night he'd insisted he wanted to sort things between them, what did he mean by that? Did he want their lives to go back to how they were or create a new link? Did he see their future separate, but joined by their child, or as a couple living together? Was it even possible to do so after the hurt and misunderstanding they'd experienced? And say they tried again, what would happen next time a problem or dilemma blotted their lives? Because she never wanted to experience the same sickening feeling of dismissal and abandonment from him again. She'd faced many tough hardships in her childhood, but to lose Leo twice would destroy her.

'Gila?'

She sagged with relief when a familiar male voice prevented her from having to explain further to the woman behind the desk. Turning, she came face to face with the man she'd come to speak with. Wearing his doctor's coat over blue scrubs, Leo resembled every bit the medic he was. Tall, capable and distractingly handsome.

He moved closer, touching her elbow. His hold gentle through the thick layer of her coat. A concerned frown creased his brow. 'Is everything okay? The baby?'

She nodded, instantly wanting to ease his worry and concern. 'We're both fine. I just wanted…' Her words trailed off as she realised the nurse behind the desk was blatantly listening to their conversation. 'Can we talk somewhere private for a moment?'

'Of course,' he said, glaring at the nurse. 'Excuse us, I need to speak to my wife for a few moments.'

'Wife?' the woman repeated, but Leo didn't wait around to confirm, intent only on gently directing Gila over to a quiet corner in the room, close to a large window overlooking a small garden. Several patients were sitting on benches, enjoying the peaceful surroundings.

'The reason I'm here is to…' Gila stopped, suddenly unsure whether this was a good idea. A wave of self-consciousness consumed her. How to explain her reason for asking without making herself sound desperate for his company? Because she really wasn't. She just thought he might like to help choose the last few items. She was doing her part to be nice and accommodating. All she needed to do was make it sound as though she wasn't the least bit bothered either way by his answer. If he declined the invitation or had other plans, then she'd just leave and do the shopping on her own. No big deal. Nothing to get worked up over. Just ask the question and leave the rest to him.

'The reason I'm here is…' she began again.

And stopped for the second time and contemplated him. What if he didn't want to come with her? What if he thought it best to go back to scarcely communicating? He'd said he still wanted her, but in what way? After the last couple of days, when they'd begun to share how they felt, a part of her secretly hoped to find some new balance in their relationship. Urgh, she was starting to get a headache from all the indecision.

'Gila? What is it?' Leo asked, gently nudging her arm.

Shaking away the doubts, she accepted it was too late to change her mind. 'I'm going shopping for a pram. I haven't organised one yet, you see. And time is running out and—I've put it off, to be honest—bad luck and all that business new mothers-in-waiting are warned against and I thought maybe you would like to—'

'I'd love to come with you,' Leo smoothly butted in. A twinkle of pleasure glimmering in his eyes. 'When do you wish to go?'

'Today,' she said, ignoring the burst of happiness his acceptance caused to bloom. How ridiculous to be so pleased by his agreement to join her in a task tons of people performed every day. Yet, she was. Why it meant so much to her she'd mull over later, but now she just wanted to leave the hospital and head to the shops before Leo changed his mind or an incoming emergency prevented him.

Leo checked his watch. 'I finish my shift in ten minutes. Why don't you wait here for me?'

She nodded, resisting the urge to clap her hands in excitement. They were going to pick out a pram, for their baby, together. For the first time in weeks exhilaration fizzed like sparkling giddy bubbles inside her. 'Sounds great.'

Leo nodded before turning away. Suddenly he stopped and spun back. Shooting her a grin, he said, 'Thank you, Gila.'

Confused and slightly dazed from his smile, she stammered, 'What for?'

'For including me,' he said simply, before walking off.

'This pram is so cute,' Leo declared, rolling the pink pram back and forth across the shop floor. His large hand out of place on the immaculate rubber handles. Very soon that same hand would hold their child. Enfold its small, delicate body in his strong grasp. Cradle their son or daughter in the protection of love. The thought sent goosebumps scattering over Gila's skin.

'Not so cute if the baby is male, though,' Gila mused, taking Leo's elbow and manoeuvring him over to a row of neutral-colour prams and pushchairs neatly displayed on the other side of the baby department in the well-known London store. 'We need a pram which is both colour neutral and also converts into a pushchair as the baby grows and their requirements change.'

'So no pink or blue,' Leo said. 'Unless you know what sex the baby is?'

'I don't, and definitely not,' she agreed, turning her attention back to the prams in front of them.

The sound of laughter and cooing coming from a couple standing a few feet away drew Gila's attention. The way the pair tenderly smiled to each other while searching through a rail of brightly coloured baby clothes made her heart twinge. Wasn't that how parents-to-be were supposed to behave when buying for a new baby? All joyful and happy. Perhaps she and Leo would have participated in similar tender moments if she'd stayed a little longer and seen the depth of his sadness. If only he'd talked to her when she'd asked him to.

But they hadn't done either. Instead she had deserted him, wrapped up and troubled with her own dissatisfaction and bewilderment. Concerned mainly with making her husband see the damage to their marriage his rejection was causing.

She glanced away, her gaze falling on a black pram with soft grey lining close to where she stood. Stylish in its simplicity, it drew her. The colours suitable for either a girl or boy. Neutral but not bland and boring. Tasteful and not garish and patterned like some of the other prams. Walking over to it, Gila hesitantly placed her hand on the handle and gave it a small push, instinctively knowing that this pram was the one for them as it smoothly rolled back and forth on the tiled floor.

'This one's nice,' she murmured.

Leo joined her, placing his hand next to hers. Gila resisted the urge to release her hold on the handle, and instead took in the physical differences between their hands. Hers, pale and slim, Leo's long, dark and strong. Heat radiated from his skin, mutely enticing her to touch him. To feel the comforting heat from his body.

'What do you think?' she asked, shifting her hand away. If she left it there any longer, she'd give into the temptation to stretch out her little finger and touch his thumb. To connect with him in some small way.

'You're right,' Leo said. 'It's lovely. Perfect, in fact. Do you like it enough to buy it?'

She nodded, already visualising their child laid out inside it. Dressed in a cute all-in-one, kicking its little legs in the air. A flutter of longing tumbled through her and she touched her stomach. Soon she would be able to hold her baby. See its sweet little face. Soon they would both meet their child. And what kind of relationship would they be bringing their innocent son or daughter into? Where its parents lived separately? Where they behaved like polite strangers towards one another, both wary of upsetting the delicate equilibrium between them?

Pushing her silent contemplations to one side, she answered his question. 'Yes, I do.'

'And it converts into a pushchair?' Leo checked, glancing at the large information label hanging from the handle. A minute later, he grinned and nodded. 'It says it does.'

'Good,' Gila said, relieved it suited all their needs.

'Then this is the pram for us,' Leo agreed, giving the handle a final fond pat. 'Let's go and ask someone about it, shall we?'

Gila hesitated, then reached out to stop him from moving away. 'But do *you* like it, Leo?'

'Does it matter?' he asked, giving her a questioning glance.

Stunned by his question, she paused. Was that what he thought? That his opinion didn't matter? Was that why he'd never reached out to her when he required help? Did he believe his wants and needs were less relevant or important? That she wasn't interested in his wishes?

It wasn't true. She wanted to know exactly how he felt or what he thought. She always had. She hated the idea that he might be holding back from airing either. Shouldn't sharing their views and beliefs with each other be easy and natural?

'Of course,' she replied. 'The decision over which pram should be both of ours.'

Leo gave the pram another once-over, then shoved his hands into his trouser pockets. After a second, he asked, 'What's this really about, Gila?'

'The pram,' she said, but he stopped her with a shake of his head.

'No, why are you really asking if I like it? It's more than this being a joint choice, isn't it? What's truly bothering you? Have I said something to upset you?'

She shrugged, irritated by his accurate observation. Of course, he would search beyond a simple question for deeper information. His mind trained to view every topic from all angles and levels. 'I just don't want you to think I don't care about your opinion, that's all. Thinking back over our marriage I realise I may not always have considered your view on things, and I don't want you to feel that I don't respect or value it.'

Leo listened, then placed an arm across her shoulders and drew her close. Bending his head, he whispered, 'I've never felt you didn't care, Gila. Not once.'

Glancing up, she ignored the tickling warmth of his breath against her skin. She refused to be diverted by physical distractions when his comments were too important. Or rather he was too important. 'Honestly?'

He nodded and repeated, 'Not once.'

'But when I left—' She frowned, not finishing the sentence. How could he not feel some sense of resentment?

He held her tighter and continued, 'You left because you *did* care. I've always known that.'

Relieved, she said, 'Good.'

He pulled her closer for a second before easing back slightly.

'So can we go and buy the pram now?' he asked, sending her an indulgent smile. His arm still lingered casually on her shoulders. Its hold comforting and informal.

'Yes, I think we should. There's still a few other things we need to pick up, though.'

'Good,' Leo said, dropping his arm to grasp her hand. Silently, he led the way towards the counter, where a smartly dressed staff member stood speaking with a younger woman similarly dressed, but who sat on a chair. The younger female appeared to be having difficulty speaking and kept shaking her head at the other woman's questions.

With a heavy sigh, the older woman turned to Leo and Gila and forced a polite smile in their direction. 'Hello, can I be of assistance?'

'Hi, we'd like to buy one of your prams. The black and grey one that converts into—' Leo broke off as

Gila tugged on his sleeve. Glancing down, he asked, 'Is something wrong?'

Gila nodded towards the shop assistant sitting on the chair. 'I think someone else might need our help first. She seems to be struggling to breathe correctly.'

Leo shifted his attention to the young female, before flicking his gaze to her colleague. 'Excuse me, but is your friend all right? She seems to be in some physical distress.'

'She's new. Started today, but she is feeling a little unwell,' the woman said, glancing worriedly at the younger woman. 'I've suggested she go to the staffroom and grab a drink of water but she refuses to listen and insisted on staying in case we become busy.'

Gila rounded the counter and stopped at the young assistant's side. Squatting, she studied the woman's pale face and figured her to be somewhere in her early twenties. 'A drink won't help if she's struggling to breathe. Hi, there. What seems to be wrong?'

The young assistant gave Gila a shaky smile and gasped, 'It's…an asthma attack. I'll…be…all right in…a moment.'

'Where's your reliever inhaler?' Leo asked, joining them. Squatting on the woman's opposite side, he also ran his expert gaze over her, silently searching for clues for how bad the attack was.

She lifted her hand and showed them both the blue inhaler she clutched.

'How many puffs have you taken?' Leo quizzed, his tone relaxed and patient. Though Gila guessed he was mentally working through and ticking off his internal doctor's list. The one every trained medic used when dealing with a new medical situation. Going through a pre-set format of questions and observations as he calmly attempted to make a diagnosis and subsequent decision for the best treatment to give to the patient.

'Nine…' The woman gasped. 'It doesn't seem…to be working.'

'It's not making much difference?' Gila asked, turning to Leo. The woman's breathing continued to worsen. If the reliever inhaler wasn't doing its job, then it was best to get further medical help via the hospital.

Gila gently grasped the woman's hand and quietly reassured her. 'My husband is a doctor and I'm a midwife. We're going to help you, okay? I'm Gila and this is Leo. Can you tell me your name?'

'Kate.' The young woman wheezed before taking a last puff from her inhaler.

Gila smiled. 'Well, Kate, do you mind if my husband and I quickly check your vital signs? I'm sure you're used to doctors troubling and fussing at times like this, right?'

She nodded, giving her agreement, and for the next few moments between them Leo and Gila checked Kate's pulse, level of response, her nails and finally her breathing, which was still very laboured.

'How long have you suffered with asthma?' Leo asked as he finished his last check.

'Since…a toddler,' Kate replied.

'Do you know what triggered this attack?' Gila asked, aware sometimes an attack transpired because of environmental and emotional influences. If the problem was still present, it could be preventing the young woman's breathing from improving.

The woman glanced at her colleague, then whis-

pered, 'Perfume. There was…a customer…just now…
wearing…a ton… I served her….'

'That's it, slow, deep breaths,' Gila coaxed, wanting
to ease Kate's struggle when talking, but also needing information about what had set off the attack and
whether it was still a risk to Kate.

Leo nodded and made a decision. 'Right, Kate. I
think we need to call an ambulance to transfer you to
the local hospital.'

The woman frowned and started to argue. 'I can't…
first day…won't look…good…boss will…be—'

Gila cut her off, not about to leave the woman in dire
straits when she required further medical help. It was
obvious Kate was tiring. 'I'm sure your boss will understand how important it is for you to go to the hospital, where they can regulate your breathing and monitor
you. You realise the risks involved to your health if you
don't get help, especially as your reliever inhaler isn't
helping you.'

Her colleague stepped forward and nodded. 'Of
course she must go. I'll clear it with the store manager.
I'm sure he'll understand. He has a small daughter who
suffers with asthma.'

'I'll ring for an ambulance,' Leo said, standing and
pulling out his mobile phone from his jacket pocket and
shifting several paces away. 'Breathe slowly and deeply,
Kate. You know what to do. I'm sure this isn't your first
time dealing with such a severe attack.'

Kate nodded and did her best to stay calm and do
as Leo advised.

Gila continued to monitor Kate, searching the woman's face for any concerning grey-blueness around the
lips, but, luckily, they showed only a little pale. With

Leo on the phone, she asked, 'Kate, is there anyone you want me to call to let them know that you're going to the hospital?'

Kate produced her phone and quickly pulled up a number. Handing it over to Gila, she rasped, 'My... mum. She'll worry...if I don't arrive...home on time.'

Gila nodded and pressed 'call'. Placing the mobile to her ear, she waited for someone to answer. After a few rings a female voice finally spoke. 'Hello?'

'Hi, is this Kate's mum?' Gila enquired.

'Yes, it is,' Kate's mother replied. 'Who is this?'

'My name is Gila Wright. I'm with your daughter Kate at the baby department where she's working and I'm calling to inform you that unfortunately she has suffered a severe asthma attack.'

'Oh, my goodness,' the mother gasped. 'Is she okay?'

'My husband's a doctor and I'm a midwife, but we both feel it's best if Kate heads to hospital as her reliever inhaler isn't helping to ease her breathing. We've already called for an ambulance, but your daughter has asked me to let you know what is going on.'

'I—I...yes, oh, thank you. Do you know which hospital she is going to?'

Gila glanced up to see two paramedics strolling into the department looking completely alien amongst all the cute baby paraphernalia. 'The ambulance is here now. I'll just ask the paramedics.'

She quizzed one of the men as he passed, explaining how the patient's mother needed to know where to pick up her daughter. She relayed the information before bidding Kate's mother goodbye and handed back the mobile to the young woman.

'Your mother will meet you at the hospital,' she said,

giving Kate's shoulder a comforting squeeze. Relieved that she'd finally agreed to further help. Another job could always be found, but a life couldn't. Once at the hospital, the doctors would soon aid and monitor her breathing. 'Everything will be fine now.'

'They got here quick,' Gila murmured to Leo as the paramedics took over Kate's care.

'Just around the corner, apparently,' Leo replied. 'Ideally placed for when the call came over the radio. This is the third asthma attack they've dealt with today.'

'Thank goodness they were close. Last thing Kate needs is to be waiting ages for the ambulance to arrive.'

'Thank...you,' Kate gasped minutes later as the paramedics led her from the department.

'Our pleasure,' Leo said with a wave. Staring after the paramedics as the trio left the floor and headed into the store's main lift, he added, 'Well, that was unexpected.'

'It seems to be becoming a regular thing when you and I go out. Aunt Tom the other day and poor Kate today.'

'Curse of being medical practitioners, I suppose.' Leo sighed, placing an arm around her shoulders once again. The action both pleasant and relaxed. They'd always touched one another freely and easily during their marriage and she had missed it during their weeks apart. 'How about I buy you a cup of something warm and milky and include a sugary treat with it once we finish here?'

Her stomach rumbled at his offer and she smiled. Hunger dictating her answer to his suggestion. 'Sounds lovely.'

'But first,' he said, turning her back around, 'we've

our baby's pram to buy. Let's do it quickly before another emergency occurs.'

Gila laughed, not complaining when Leo steered her back over to the counter and the assistant still waiting to help them.

'So, the counsellor?'

The idea of Leo talking to someone—a stranger—sat odd with Gila. Especially now she'd had time to think it over. Ever since he'd mentioned it last night, questions had surfaced in her mind as she tried to imagine how it felt to visit a complete outsider and expose all your deeply hidden fears and feelings to them for an hour each week. In the medical profession seeking help of any kind was encouraged and championed, but to actually do so—for *Leo* to—secretly shocked Gila.

Leo leaned back in his chair and sighed heavily. The sound saying a thousand things without the need for words or syllables. Other diners surrounded them in the rooftop café, drinking and eating, chatting and catching up with friends and family. But Gila hardly noticed them or the background hum of their conversations. Her whole attention instead on the man sitting across the small table from her with a slight frown creasing his brow.

'Yes?' Leo asked, weariness creeping over his features at her query.

Gila stirred sugar into her large mug of hot chocolate and shifted closer to the table, wanting to keep their conversation as private as possible despite their busy background. Her curiosity pushed her to ask for details, specifics, anything that would help her understand. But how to query without upsetting or offending Leo?

'What made you go?' she asked, meeting his gaze. 'I mean, we suggest to our patients to do this sort of thing when we think it will help them, but often medics are the worst people for following their own advice. So what convinced you to visit a counsellor?'

Leo half chuckled and shrugged. 'Mainly because my boss, Dr Peters, threatened to sack me if I didn't visit someone. I'd lost you, so I didn't want to add my job too. And then once I went, it helped me to reflect on the situation with Jodie and see it differently. Rather than repeatedly beating myself up over the decisions I made at the time, the counsellor forced me to question what else I could have done. And the conclusion is there was nothing else I could do. Viewing the whole situation today, I honestly don't believe I would've reached that conclusion alone or at all.'

He took a sip of his coffee and continued, 'I'd spent so many years trying to push away feelings and anger over Jodie and her life, and I guess it all just built up until it refused to stay silent any longer. Jodie's death was just the pinnacle where it all broke through, I guess.'

'And you're happier now?' she probed curiously.

'No, not happier,' he said. 'Because to get to where I am, I lost you in the process. So no, I'm not happier, but I am calmer and more accepting that I'm not to blame, not really. That no matter how much I tried or what I gave, it would never have helped Jodie fight her own struggles. The parts of her were just too damaged.'

Gila reached across and grasped his hand, clutching it tightly. Glad he'd finally acknowledged the truth and found peace with it. 'You never were at fault, Leo. Not about your sister. Never that.'

He smiled softly and placed his other hand on top of hers. His thumb slowly stroking across her skin, causing it to tingle. A shiver of awareness shimmered over her wrist and up her arm.

Leo leaned forward and squeezed her hand, his skin warm against her own. 'Drink your hot chocolate. And then I think we should spend what's left of the afternoon at the pictures.'

'You want to go to the cinema?' she asked, stunned by the suggestion. She'd half expected them to go their separate ways now they'd completed their shopping. Yet it appeared Leo wished to prolong their afternoon together.

'Yeah, why not. Fancy it?'

Yes, she really did. She nodded and smiled. 'I think I do.'

He tilted his head to one side and regarded her. 'It's what we did on our first date, wasn't it? Do you remember?'

She smiled and lifted her mug. Glancing at him over the rim, she replied, 'Of course I do. You chose a horror film and then spilt your popcorn all over the floor when one of the ghosts jumped out of the box in the cellar.'

'I never jumped,' he denied. 'My arm jerked, nothing more.'

She scoffed, not believing his excuse any more today than she had back then. 'At exactly the same time?'

He smirked. 'Damn muscle spasms. Never sure when they're going to happen. One moment you're absolutely fine, the next, *wham*, it hits you.'

She laughed and placed her mug down on the table. Wham was kind of how she'd felt the first time they'd met. One minute she'd taken in the unknown doctor offering his help during a woman's labour, and the next she'd fallen full heart in love with him.

Trouble was, she wasn't sure if a part of her didn't still feel the same way, no matter how much she desperately warned her tattered, beaten heart to protect against it. Because second chances might sound wonderful and achievable, but it still meant putting your heart back where it risked being hurt all over again. And she wasn't sure she would ever be brave enough to do that.

CHAPTER NINE

'GOOD MORNING.' LEO stepped into the kitchen from outside, accompanied by a chilly blast of early morning spring air. In one hand he carried a brown paper bag and his car keys dangled from the other. 'Sleep okay?'

Gila nodded and resumed spooning tea leaves into the vintage china teapot. Her movements fluid and relaxed. The initial tension that had throbbed between them during the first few days had disappeared completely after yesterday's trip to town, and being around each other now felt more regular and normal. Like old times, but not quite. Enough to get them smoothly through the next few days, though, she hoped.

And then what? her annoying internal voice quizzed. At the moment, she couldn't answer that question. There was still so much to think about.

Tipping the last heaped teaspoon into the teapot, she said, 'Yes. You?'

'Like a baby,' he joked. 'Baby shopping is definitely a good cure for insomnia. I'll remember so in future.'

Gila screwed the lid back onto the tin and reached for the recently boiled kettle. From the corner of her eye she observed Leo as he opened a cupboard and withdrew a small plate, searching for obvious signs he wasn't sleeping well. What kept him awake these days? The unsettled state of their marriage, or did remaining stress from Jodie's death still haunt him? She wanted to ask, but faltered, not sure if he would tell her considering she'd refused to listen to him for so long.

But wasn't that exactly the problem that had plagued them before she left? The fact that she'd stepped away from asking uncomfortable and personal questions. Drew back from demanding answers, because she was half afraid to hear their subsequent replies. If she'd stayed and continued to prod and poke, would the depth of his grief and depression eventually have surfaced through his silence and become evident?

'What are you planning to do today?' Leo asked, placing the bag on the counter top. He leaned over to retrieve a second plate from the wooden rack above her head. The smell of fresh morning air and his spicy aftershave encircled her as he stretched close. Its crispness enticing her to lean into its invisible swirl.

She tilted her head to one side as she pondered her day's plans. Did he ask because he wished to include himself in them? The time they'd spent together yesterday was both fun and enjoyable. The film they'd watched at the cinema funny and light-hearted. Did he seek more togetherness or was she just secretly hoping so?

'I figured I would try and finish the blanket I'm knitting and then go through the list I made and see if I've forgotten anything for the baby.'

'Sounds a good idea.'

Popping the lid on the teapot, she gave it a swirl, careful not to spill liquid from the spout, and then glanced at Leo. Placing the teapot down again, she turned to him. 'Leo, about yesterday.'

He pulled a pastry slice scattered with almonds and white icing from the brown bag and dropped it onto a plate. 'Yes?'

'I just want to say how much I appreciate you telling me about the counsellor and Jodie. I realise it isn't easy for you—'

He reached out and grasped her hand, staring down at it thoughtfully before he spoke. 'You're right, it's not. I find it hard to open up and just let everything out. Even though it's all inside, saying the words out loud is tough.'

'But it helps?' she asked. 'Talking?'

He nodded. 'Yeah. After years of suppressing stuff, it does. I just wish I'd tried it before you left. Maybe then things between us wouldn't have gone the way they did. I've always admired the way you've always spoken so honestly about your own childhood. Never hiding anything. I guess being raised by parents who believe appearances are more important than the truth they conceal has unfortunately left its mark on me.'

Squeezing his fingers, she encouraged, 'If it makes you feel happier, then keep letting it out. It's obviously working for you.'

'What if what I say makes no sense?' he quizzed, self-consciously.

'If it's what's in your heart, then it will,' she reassured him. 'And it doesn't matter as long as you get it out.'

He nodded, then slowly met her gaze. 'I loved Jodie, but when you've spent so many years protecting and helping someone, which in the beginning you're happy to do because you care for them, but the longer it goes on and nothing helps or the situation never changes, that love dies inch by inch and resentment and tiredness replaces it. The simple reality was that no one could help Jodie. Not me, not you, not anyone.'

'I see,' she said, her heart breaking at the sadness clouding his eyes. Admitting such a bleak truth must be hard. No matter how much a person might want to fight for the hope of improvement and change, sometimes it turned out to be a struggle that could never be won.

Leo sighed, letting go of her hand to roll one shoulder. 'I'm probably not explaining any of this very well.'

'You are,' she soothed, instantly missing his contact. Before she would have reached out and pulled his hand back, but now she hesitated over doing such a thing.

'Really?'

She nodded. 'I've shared with you before how much I hated the way my father dragged me to yet another town or a different country. What he viewed as adventure, I perceived as hell. I never understood his excessive need to travel somewhere new. He loved new sounds, new people and new sights. Whereas I craved the regular pattern of school terms and sleeping in the same comfortable safe bed every night. In the end, I couldn't stand it and begged Art to give me a home. I think it broke my father's heart when I told him I didn't want to live or travel with him any more. He barely spoke to me again, and when he died of heart failure in Africa it was too late. He just never understood how I felt.'

'Families can be tough work sometimes, can't they? Always putting their own wants and wishes first,' Leo mused. 'I'm barely speaking to my parents.'

'Aunt Tom mentioned you'd fallen out with them.'

'She did?' Leo asked, then sighed. 'They blame me for Jodie's death. The fact that I didn't find some cure to turn her back into the perfect and presentable daughter they'd imagined having is just another disappointment they hold against me.'

'That's ridiculous,' Gila said. 'You're a doctor, not a magician. Addiction doesn't work like that.'

'I know it doesn't. But in their eyes failure is unacceptable. No matter whose or the reason why.'

'Surely you explained to them—'

Leo snorted. 'They refused to listen. The same way they always dismiss anything that doesn't fit into their nice orderly lifestyle. My parents have never dirtied their own hands when it involved Jodie and me. I don't think either of my parents ever changed a nappy or comforted us when we were ill. Why do the menial tasks of parenthood when they can pay someone else to do it?'

'But those are the most important jobs, aren't they?' Gila argued. 'Being there for your child whenever they need you. Kissing their hurts and loving them.'

'They are. And the reason my parents never bothered to visit Jodie in hospital before her death wasn't because they couldn't get a flight over in time.'

'It wasn't?'

'No, it was because they said there was no point since she was in a coma and wouldn't know if they were there or not. Truth is, they didn't want the embarrassment of the hospital staff knowing they were the parents of an addict.'

'Oh, Leo,' Gila sighed. 'Why didn't you tell me?'

He looked away. 'Because I didn't want to drag you into it.'

Gila desperately longed to wrap her arms around

him and absorb some of his pain. It throbbed so intensely from him, she ached to soothe it. Instead, she said, 'Your parents are fools. And I'm glad you found help, Leo. I really am.'

She meant it. Where she hadn't pulled Leo from the pit of his grief, someone else had managed to succeed. Despite the knowledge leaving her feeling completely incompetent as a partner and a wife, she was grateful that he'd found the help he required from someone.

Lifting his gaze, he found hers. 'For years I tried to hold Jodie up and not let her sink completely, but it was hard and tiring. Juggling my career and life while trying to shore her up whenever she needed it. Helping her and knowing that if I didn't nobody else would. That no one in her life loved her the same. But when we found out you were pregnant, I decided I couldn't do it any more. I just didn't want to. And I didn't trust her to behave around you. She already begrudged your place in my life and heart. And you and the baby need all of me, not just a share. So I told Jodie that if she didn't try to get clean for good, then she was on her own.'

'How did she take it?' Gila asked softly.

'Badly.' He sighed heavily and confessed, 'After I gave her the ultimatum, I felt ashamed.'

Confused, she asked, 'Ashamed? Why?'

'Because when she refused, I felt an overpowering sense of relief. Like something huge and crushing had been removed and, honestly, it felt so good. For the first time since she was born, I didn't have to be responsible for her and her problems or wants. I could finally concentrate on just us and the baby. Something I *wanted* to do, rather than something I felt I *had* to do.'

* * *

Leo shut his eyes, recalling that day with familiar old regret. Jodie had reacted the same way she always had when denied her own way. She'd hated the idea that she and her issues were not the most important thing in his life. The truth was Jodie had been dramatic and selfish. Only ever concerned with herself. She'd accused him of hating her. Of letting her down. Said *he* was the real reason that she took drugs. That if he'd been a nicer, more caring brother, then she would have had a better life. If he had done more to help her, loved her more, then she would have had everything he did.

But it was all lies and wishful thinking. Jodie had made her own mistakes and never wanted to face them or admit that she was at fault. If anyone quizzed her or tried to make her see the truth, she turned on the tears and cried. Threw a tantrum and then sulked rather than see and accept that others saw things differently. She was bone-deep self-centred and jealous and it was always someone else's fault.

And then she turned her bitterness and anger onto his unborn child. The hateful words she said that day a poisonous memory Leo would never forget or forgive. One thing to tell him that he was a rotten brother who'd make an even worse father, but to wish harm to his child was something no decent person ever did or wished. Anger and resentment were no excuse for what she'd said, especially when it had later stirred up doubts inside him. Deep, dark worries that questioned whether he was capable of becoming a decent and loving father, if he couldn't save his own sister.

'But then she overdosed,' Gila reflected quietly. Breaking through his recollections.

'Yes.' Less than two months later he'd received a call from a colleague at the hospital informing him that Jodie was in a coma. By letting go of his sister and wanting a life for himself, he'd sent her hurtling towards a grave. At least that was how it had felt for a while. When the uncertainties and Jodie's last angry remarks had continued to echo loud and strong in his ears during the weeks after her death.

'I wish I'd known,' Gila said, grabbing his arm.

Leo frowned and quizzed, 'Why?'

'Because sometimes I felt shut out of your relationship,' Gila admitted. 'I'd always envisioned an in-law would become a close friend, but when that didn't happen with Jodie, I felt excluded from your bond. I longed to be a part of you two, but, no matter how I tried to help, I couldn't find a way in.'

Leo shook his head. 'I never meant for you to feel that way. I simply wished to keep you clear from all the chaos of Jodie at her worst. I wanted you and I to stay free from the added drama. We—our marriage—were a sanctuary filled with light and joy. I didn't want to spoil that.'

'If you'd just told me,' she said, not able to hide the reproach in her voice, 'I would have understood.'

He shrugged and nodded. 'I know that now. I made a lot of mistakes and not talking to you is my deepest regret. I suppose I gave into fear and let it control me. Half convinced that I had pushed Jodie to her death, and worried that I'd lose you and your respect if you ever discovered what I'd done. Which is ironic when you think how I lost you anyway by not telling you.'

She lowered her hand. 'I didn't know what to do when you drifted away from me.'

Leo groaned. 'I'm so sorry, Gila. Even though I could see what I was doing, I just couldn't stop and was ter-rifi—'

The sudden violent jerk of the boat prevented Leo from finishing. Instead he watched in horror as Gila went flying into the cupboards on the opposite side of the small galley kitchen before he could stop her.

'Gila!'

'What the…?' Gila gasped as intense pain shot through her stomach. Grasping the counter to steady herself, she cradled her stomach. Her instinct to protect the child inside her body stronger than any concern for herself. Wincing, she tried to straighten and catch her breath.

Leo reached for her, pulling her from her spot by the cupboard and into his arms. Clasping her in his warm embrace as though he feared a further attack from out-side and aimed to shelter her from it and any additional injury. His automatic reaction to protect and keep her safe pleased and reassured Gila.

'Are you okay? Did you hurt yourself?' he de-manded, his hands going to her bump.

'I'm fine, I think,' she said, reluctantly pulling back from his hold. She didn't want to. She'd rather stay se-cure in his arms until the shaking and trembling scram-bling through her body ceased. But their relationship was already so confused and complicated, muddled to the point of total confusion, that to allow herself to in-dulge in things that threatened to make it more com-plex would be foolish and completely wrong for both of them.

'I hit my hip and stomach against the cupboard. It hurt for a moment, but it's subsiding now,' she said.

Leo immediately touched the mentioned area. His examination gentle and comforting as his fingers moved over the still throbbing tender spot. 'And the baby? Is the baby okay? The way you went flying across the space and smacked into the cupboard I thought…' His words trailed off but she understood his meaning. She wasn't the only one shaken from the unexpected bang against the boat's side.

Placing a reassuring hand on his arm, she smiled up at him. Her heart tugging at the genuine fear and distress shadowing his gaze. Turning his normally brown eyes to almost black. Quickly, she soothed, 'None the worse, I promise. We're both fine, Leo. Honestly. Just a touch wobbly and stunned.'

'Are you sure?' he persisted, rubbing his hand over the curve of her stomach again. As though, by caressing it, he could comfort both her and the baby. Guard them from the unforeseen hazards in the world.

She nodded and attempted to draw some normality into the moment, because if she didn't force her thoughts to move in a different direction, she might do something stupid like kiss her estranged husband fully on the mouth. 'Do you think another narrowboat hit into us?'

Moving narrowboats banging into moored ones often occurred during holiday periods and summer, when holidaymakers hired a boat for the first time and took to the water with very little training or skill. Usually plates or cups became the casualties of such comings together, but this time it was her pregnant body that took the full brunt of someone's thoughtless and unintentional mistake.

Leo frowned and his mouth thinned. With a gentle squeeze to her side, he declared, 'I'm going to go and find out. I won't be a minute. Perhaps you should sit down.'

He disappeared before Gila could stop him. Wrapping her arms around herself, she tried to calm the still present shaking. Moments later, she heard the low mumble of Leo's deep voice talking with someone outside. No, it sounded as if he was scolding someone. Sometimes the doctor's authoritative tone worked for situations other than when dealing with a disruptive or confused patient.

Gila shakily finished making her tea and sat down on the sofa. Holding the warm mug with both hands, she slowly breathed in deeply. Despite her assurances to Leo, the knock had shocked her and her hip still smarted from its forceful impact into the cupboard. Though the backache she'd woken up with that morning bothered her more. Different in sensation from the normal pregnancy aches she'd experienced for the last few days. She'd done her best not to dwell on it, but it wasn't easy when the area throbbed constantly. Aunt Tom's words floated through her mind again, but she quickly dismissed them. This baby wasn't going to be early. The old woman wasn't a medical expert or a midwife. She hadn't spent years studying the subject. She was just a sweet old woman who'd worked at the local library before the council had closed it during a round of cutbacks in the early nineties.

Taking a sip of her milky tea, she glanced up when Leo returned, his expression grimmer than when he'd left. The slamming of the door behind him an indication his mood hadn't improved after his conversation outside.

'Is our boat still in one piece?' she asked curiously. Be just her luck if the narrowboat suffered serious damage and required her to move somewhere else for the rest of the week. Where she'd go, she didn't want to consider.

'Fortunately,' Leo said, sitting down next to her. 'And to add to this morning's drama, apparently a lorry has just overturned and blocked the canal path's entrance. Thanks to a spilt cargo of oranges we're all trapped here on our boats, with no other way out for some time.'

She laughed, glad for the distraction from the pains of her body. 'Oh, dear. It appears to be one of those days, doesn't it? Good thing we both have today off *and* that you managed to get to the cake shop before the lorry's accident.'

He agreed, then searched her face. 'Are you sure you're all right? No pain or twinges? Cuts or stings?'

She smiled and gave his hand a pat. 'Leo, I'm fine. At the most I'll probably end up with a couple of bruises to show for my unexpected flight across the kitchen.'

Leo gave her a wry glance. 'Well, you may be fine, but I'm not sure I am. All I keep recalling is the way you banged into the cupboard. Our son or daughter must be wondering what is going on. Lying there all contented one second, the next thing bam!'

She chuckled, the concern in his eyes too sweet to resent. Perhaps this was their way forward. A close and comfortable friendship instead of the lingering anger and disappointment of their marriage. For their child's sake they had to form a platonic relationship if nothing else.

She rubbed the top of her stomach. 'Luckily he or she is well protected in there.'

'Thank God,' Leo said. 'With the canal entrance blocked and no other way out for at least half a mile, the last thing we need is a medical emergency.'

Gila murmured in agreement, ignoring the discomfort in her back. It was just pregnancy aches, nothing else. Just normal third-trimester niggles and twinges. And definitely nothing to do with labour.

The dull ache in Gila's lower back hadn't eased by late afternoon and neither a bath nor lying flat out on the normally comfortable bed helped ease it. For the umpteenth time she turned onto her side, hugging a pillow close, in the faint hope of finding a smidgen of relief from the persistent torment.

Just stupid pregnancy discomfort and certainly no reason to panic and start thinking crazy thoughts. First babies always arrived late. They really did. Occasionally mothers would even require inducing to get a way too contented baby to give up their comfortable home of nine months and join the world outside. Yes, the odds were definitely piled in that direction. This baby wasn't coming yet. The uncomfortable feeling was nothing but the delightful joys of late pregnancy and nothing more. There'd been no signs that her pregnancy would differ from most other first babies. She just needed to relax and stop thinking the worst. If Aunt Tom hadn't mentioned the baby arriving early, then she wouldn't be having any doubts. It was all the old woman's fault, muttering ill-informed, old-wives'-tales nonsense. At least she'd spared Gila the ring-dangling-off-a-piece-of-string theatrics in an effort to guess the baby's sex.

Leo stepped into the room then paused. His gaze slowly running over her. Folding his arms, he said, 'You're glaring. Is something bothering you?'

Yes, everything. Pain made her seriously grumpy and she hated being in a bad mood. It made her even more irritated. 'It's my back. It's really hurting and I can't get comfortable no matter how I lie.'

He mumbled something under his breath and drew closer. Sitting down on the bed, he asked, 'Do you want me to rub your back? It might help.'

The offer sounded nice and the thought of his fingers magically massaging her tender sore muscles had her nodding in agreement. 'If you don't mind.'

She tried not to sound too eager, but she longed for his strong digits to alleviate her pain. She was desperate for it to go or at least lessen, and if he achieved a few moments of respite, she was beyond caring about any rightness or wrongness of whether he should be doing it. She just craved some relief.

Leo smiled softly and coaxed, 'Why don't you roll over onto your other side for me?'

Without a word, she did as he suggested, groaning when his hand slowly stroked over her hip before moving lower towards her throbbing spine. She sucked in a breath, as he pushed down the waistband of her leggings and caressed her bare flesh. 'Is this where it hurts?'

She groaned and purred, as his thumbs tenderly pushed into her flesh and moved in small circles. 'Oh, yes. Just there.'

Leo chuckled and massaged the area for several minutes, easing the tension out of the tight muscles. His fingers lightly resting against her lower back. His touch firm but gentle. 'Does that help?'

'It feels *so* good,' Gila moaned, snuggling her face into the soft pillow to muffle a whimper of pleasure that escaped. But after several hours without a break from the constant pain, the momentary relief felt heavenly and lovely. 'So very nice. The NHS should hire you out to pregnant women. You'd be booked up for years.'

He snorted at the idea, and asked, 'You'd give me a reference, then?'

Gila silently gave the idea more consideration. Leo's hands all over other women when everyone knew that pregnancy hormones often increased a woman's sex drive. The thought of amorous women enjoying her husband's soothing and wonderful backrub suddenly horrified her. His hands weren't going anywhere. They were hers to keep and use.

'Actually, it's a terrible idea,' she determined, realising only seconds later that she'd said the words out loud.

He leaned over, his breath warm and carrying the faint whiff of coffee when he spoke. 'It is?'

'Yes,' she replied, burying her face further into the pillow without smothering herself. Not wanting him to see the flush of embarrassment warming her cheeks. Such honest thoughts were best kept to herself.

'Why is that?' he teased, his tone indicating he had guessed the reason for her sudden change of mind. His fingers increased their pressure, extracting another moan of pleasure from her.

'Oh, God, that is nice,' she groaned. Reluctant to confess the idea of him touching other women sent her stupidly possessive. No, she didn't intend to admit a thing. His ego would grow to gigantic proportions if she did.

'Because…' she hedged, searching for another plausible reason—one that didn't make her sound like a jealous wife. Because she wasn't jealous. She just didn't like the thought of Leo touching other pregnant women when his hands had far more important tasks to do as a doctor. Because to be jealous meant she still held feelings for the man and she wasn't sure what they were, and she refused to explore them in case she found the answer and didn't like it.

'Ow!' Gila gasped, her thoughts scattering as a new, different pain, unconnected to her back, ran across her stomach. Was that a contraction? She stared at the cotton pillowcase, once again glad Leo couldn't see her face from his angle.

'What's wrong?' he asked, his hands pausing as he waited for an answer. One hand holding her hip. 'Did I hurt you?'

'No,' she denied, trying to keep her voice steady and normal-sounding. Better to keep quiet until she'd worked out what was going on with her body and exactly what that last pain was. No reason to concern Leo yet.

'You gasped as though in pain. Are you sure you're okay?'

'Absolutely,' she lied. Probably nothing more than Braxton Hicks, the pre-contractions all women experienced as their bodies readied for labour. Unquestionably nothing to worry over. She was *not* in labour. She wasn't.

'Perhaps you should try to sleep,' Leo suggested, replacing the band of her leggings over the area he'd just massaged. His fingers paused as though hesitant to break their connection.

'Is the path still blocked with oranges?' Gila asked, trying to sound more curious than desperate.

Leo patted her hip. 'Yeah, apparently there's a bad accident on the other side of the city, which takes precedence over this one. It could be several more hours before the recovery truck arrives to clear our entrance.'

Gila swallowed and pushed the terrifying feeling climbing up her throat back down. Not normally prone to panic, she forced her thoughts to settle. It was just Braxton Hicks. Nothing else. Just her body preparing itself for birth. One that would happen sometime in the next few weeks. Because there was no chance that this baby was on its way today. Absolutely none.

Oh, God, there was no denying it, even though Gila had frantically tried. The pains shooting across her stomach and in her back were definitely more than just practice contractions. As a midwife she knew about these things. She'd helped other women through their own labour and recognised the signs, even if a very big part of her had refused to admit it.

Shuffling to the bed's edge, she swung her feet to the floor and padded to the door. Leaving the bedroom, she headed for the sitting room, pausing on the threshold as she pondered the best way to announce the news to Leo, who sat reading on the sofa and hadn't yet noticed her.

Silently, she ran through several different options.

Leo, I'm in labour.

Leo, the baby is coming.

Guess what, Leo? In a few hours we're going to be proud parents.

Hey, Leo, how do you fancy spending your day off at the maternity unit? That's if we can get there considering the path is blocked and we're kind of trapped here.

She closed her eyes and shook her head.

Gila, just stop messing around and tell the man. It's not as though you created the situation. No, that was down to nature and their child. Opening her eyes, Gila coughed to get her husband's attention. 'Leo?'

'Hey, you didn't sleep long,' Leo said, tossing the medical journal he was reading to one side and getting to his feet.

'I kept waking up,' she said, figuring it best not to just announce the news.

He folded his arms and regarded her. A flicker of worry in his eyes. 'Is your back still hurting?'

'Yeah, but…well, it's not like normal back pain.'

That was good, Gila. Several obvious hints should ease the telling.

'Really? What do you think it is?' he asked, raising an eyebrow.

'I wonder if it might be…' She trailed off, hoping he'd catch on, but the lack of suspicion in his expression that her pain might be something more serious than random aches killed all hope. And he called himself a doctor.

'Yes?' he queried.

'Oh, dear,' she gasped, her eyes widening as another contraction ripped across her lower body. She glanced at her watch, horrified to see the contractions were getting closer in time to one another.

Leo reached out and grabbed her arms. 'Gila, what is it? What's wrong?'

'Well, I'm pretty sure that there's a chance I'm experiencing contractions,' she said, trying to soften the news, but knowing she failed dismally when she heard his sharp intake of breath and saw the startled widening of his eyes. 'I've been having them for a while.'

'What?' Leo repeated sharply. 'How long? Not since the boat hit us?'

'No, sometime after.'

'Why didn't you tell me?' he demanded.

'I wasn't sure—' she started.

'But you're a midwife,' he declared, placing his hands on his hips. With a confused frown, he asked, 'How can you not know? You're the expert.'

'But I've never given birth, though,' she reasoned back. 'Yes, I've read all the textbooks and helped out practically, but, in case you've forgotten, I've never gone through the actual physical process myself. It's one thing to read and learn about it from books and stuff, but another to do it. You know, a person can only gain so much understanding from helping women in childbirth. I mean, as a doctor you're aware of what occurs during an amputation, but it doesn't mean you know exactly what it feels like to have one.'

'You're right,' he agreed, then asked, 'You don't think these pains are simply practice contractions?'

Gila almost laughed at Leo's hopeful expression. So similar to her own for the last few hours. But there was no more ignoring or denying the truth. This baby was coming no matter how early or inconvenient it might be for them.

'No, I'm sure it's the real thing—' She stopped, her mouth falling open and her eyes widening in horror.

'What's wrong?' Leo demanded.

Colour flooded her cheeks and she shook her head. 'Nothing.'

'Gila,' he said more gently.

She sighed and slowly glanced down, taking in the puddle of amniotic fluid now soaking her feet and oozing into the carpet. 'Looks like my waters have just broken.'

Leo's gaze shot downwards, before he swallowed hard and agreed, 'Hell, Gila. You really *are* in labour.'

CHAPTER TEN

GILA'S STOMACH DROPPED as reality leached into her brain.
They were stuck on the narrowboat and she was in labour, and all she could think to do was wrap herself into
Leo's body and hide. Snuggle into his chest and close
her eyes until it all went away.

But she couldn't do any of that, because this baby
wasn't playing around and she and Leo were—who
knew what? God, why were relationships so hard to
work out and keep straight? Perhaps it would be best
if they just forgot the past for the next few hours and
concentrated on getting through their child's birth. Together. As a couple but not a couple. Just two close
friends, helping each other out. Because despite all her
training and knowledge, she felt the same as any other
female in labour. A tiny bit anxious and worried over
what was to come in the following hours.

'The recovery truck is still at the site of the other accident. Once it gets here, it will take a while to shift it
to a safe position before they can remove it,' Leo said,
placing a towel over the puddle at her feet. 'But we
probably have plenty of time before we need to leave
for the maternity unit.'

'Then we'll wait,' she pronounced with more conviction than she felt. Her labour would in all probability last for hours. First babies were rarely quick births. Everything would be fine. The blocked entrance would be a blip they'd laugh over later from the comfort of a hospital bed. No reason to panic. Seriously, there wasn't. None at all.

'Okay, then can I get you anything?' Leo asked.

Shaking her head, she sucked in a calming breath. Determined to act tranquil and chilled. No hysterical mother-to-be was she. Oh, no. Mother Nature could learn from her. So, ignoring her racing heart and the nerves busily rock-and-rolling in her stomach, she smiled brightly. 'No, thank you. I'm good.'

Leo walked over to the sofa and started throwing cushions in random directions. One flew over his shoulder and landed on the floor by her feet. 'Perhaps you should sit down.'

Gila crouched and retrieved the cushion from the floor, biting her lower lip to stop herself from laughing at Leo. But honestly when a person stopped and considered the situation it was funny. Separated couple stuck on their narrowboat, dealing with the onset of wife's unexpected labour.

Another cushion dropped off the sofa and onto the floor. What exactly was he doing? If she didn't know him so well, she'd believe he was rattled. But Leo never—'

Ow, that hurt.

She grimaced and clutched the cushion tight against her body as another contraction hit.

Gasping, she concentrated on breathing through the pain. Trying to recall everything she told her expectant mothers during their labour. Something pacifying and comforting. But no matter how hard she focused, her mind refused to conjure up the words of advice she'd spoken hundreds of times in the past, and instead fixated on the pain and nothing else.

With a quick glance at Leo still beating cushions into haphazard new positions, she checked her watch. Oh, dear, the contractions were getting closer. This baby wasn't playing. It appeared their child was eager to greet the world and it wasn't waiting for the vehicle-recovery team to turn up. Perhaps it would be best to consider the possibility that they were not going to make it to the hospital and instead ready themselves for having the baby here at home.

'Will you rub my back, please?' she asked, hoping to distract Leo. If she didn't, he might start rearranging the furniture next. Wasn't it supposed to be the mother who displayed the nesting urge, not the father?

Leo straightened and rushed to her side. 'Yes, of course. Where does it hurt?'

Another contraction hit Gila hard. Yep, definitely getting closer. Groaning, she did her best to breathe through the pain. First-time babies were supposed to come on time, late even, certainly not early. And not this quick once they decided to. Why couldn't one thing follow the book? Was this a sign of this child's personality? Did it intend to always ignore the rules of life and do its own thing?

'You're doing great,' Leo encouraged, rubbing her back and holding her hand as she blew through the contraction. 'That's it, deep breaths and—'

She was in agony and probably going to give birth here in their home, without any pain relief or familiar colleagues hanging around to help. Not even her own midwife. Just her and Leo. The two of them, and, yes, they were capable and fully trained, but this was the birth of *their* baby and that alone rendered it different from any other.

Letting out a long sigh as the contraction receded, Gila puffed away a stray strand of hair from her face and glanced at the man holding her. 'Ah, Leo.'

He continued to rub her back, but leaned in. 'Yes, sweetheart?'

'I think we'd better get several blankets and shake them out onto the floor.'

He frowned and repeated, 'Blankets?'

'Yes.'

His frown deepened. 'Are you cold?'

She almost laughed at the innocence of his question. 'No, but I don't think our son or daughter is going to wait until after the recovery truck arrives. My contractions are getting closer and closer. This baby is coming soon and it looks like it is up to us to bring this little one into the world.'

Every healthy trace of colour drained from her husband's face, and he stammered, 'What? But your waters have only just broken.'

Gila sent him an encouraging smile. 'Yeah, that sometimes happens. Childbirth likes to liven things up occasionally with the unpredictable.'

'But—'

She grasped his hand tighter. 'We're professionals, Leo. We can do this. We've no other choice.'

'I guess—' he started.

'And giving birth is a beautiful and natural experience,' she said, repeating the words she always said to her mothers-to-be. She just hadn't expected her childbirth to be this natural, but, hey, life handed over the occasional surprise and a person had no choice but to face it.

'But it's *our* baby,' Leo stated, his hand tensing around her fingers.

She knew exactly what he meant. One thing to help strangers give birth, but completely different now they were the ones going through the whole procedure without any kind of medical back-up. 'I know.'

He swallowed hard, then asked, 'Are you worried?'

She glanced at him, desperate once again to throw herself into his arms and vanish. To submerge into his body and disappear. 'No, of course not,' she lied. When in truth, she was just a little bit petrified.

Leo gathered the blankets and other items Gila asked for. His mind spinning like a fairground ride dipping and diving all over as he struggled to concentrate on the chore and not the situation.

Gila was in labour. Apparently, she'd been having contractions for hours and never said a word. Not a single one. How had he missed the clues? Hadn't she complained about backache for the last day or so? And now they were stuck on the narrowboat with no way out, unless a person wanted to hike for half a mile to the next exit, or until both the lorry and the ruined fruit were scraped up from the road and removed.

Sinking onto the bed, he cradled his head in his hands. Nausea turning in his stomach. This couldn't happen and certainly not here. When women gave birth, especially for the first time, it was best they did so in a nice clean hospital, with all the specialist equipment on hand if things went wrong.

Went wrong? Where did that thought come from?

Leo stood and began to pace the floor of the small bedroom. God, what if something went wrong? It was possible. There was always a chance the baby could become distressed or it would be a difficult birth. What if the baby was breech? What if Gila haemorrhaged? Saving her would be down to him alone. With no back-up or equipment how could he do that? How would he manage? With the road blocked, there was no way to get her and the baby to the safety of a hospital if they needed to in an emergency.

He groaned and buried his face in his hands again. It wasn't supposed to be like this. This was the day he'd looked forward to for months. The moment when their family grew from a duo into a trio. Not once had he imagined it would occur in their home, with only him to tend and help Gila through the birth. And he'd certainly never pictured they would still be in a romantic deadlock when doing it.

He swallowed the bitter acid taste coating his mouth and pushed all emotional thoughts to one side. He would not fall apart. He was a doctor from his fingernails to his toes. Some people even called him an excellent doctor. He faced and thrived in stressful situations. Never knowing what to expect each time he started a shift in A & E. And today Gila needed him. She was his emergency. He'd treat her the same as he would any other patient. They were both medical professionals with plenty of experience between them and, whatever happened, they'd find a way to cope. There was no other choice. Their child was determined to appear soon and nature would dictate everything from here, as it already was. He just had to hang around to keep things going smoothly.

Rubbing his face one last time, he quickly gathered everything they required, then changed his mind and deposited the items onto the small chair near the bed. No way was his wife giving birth on the lounge floor when she could do it on a comfortable bed. The actual bed where they'd conceived their child. Somehow it seemed the perfect place.

Women all over the world gave birth outside hospitals and they did it just fine. Frequently without the help or interference of a medic. He prayed it would be the same for Gila and their child. Together they would be able to do this.

Rushing back to the lounge where Gila was now sitting on the sofa breathing deeply, he said, 'Why don't we do this in the bedroom?'

Gila considered the question for a moment, then nodded. 'Yes, good idea. Much more relaxing. Better than spread out on the floor. But we'll need to cover the bed with something waterproof to save the mattress from getting ruined.'

Leo nodded then hurried back in the bedroom's direction, spending the next few minutes stripping the bed, before heading through the lounge and continuing on to the door outside.

'Where are you going?' Gila called out.

'There's an unopened tarp in the storage box. We can spread it over the bed before replacing the sheets. It might rustle a bit, but the mattress will stay stain-free and clean.'

Gila nodded and Leo disappeared outside, before returning minutes later with the tarp. In no time the bed was remade and ready for her.

Leo returned to Gila's side and gently helped her to stand. 'How are you doing, darling?'

'I'm fine,' she replied. 'You?'

'Great,' he lied. Perhaps it wouldn't hurt to head back outside and get an update on the lorry's expected arrival time.

'I think I'll have a quick shower,' Gila said, interrupting his racing thoughts.

A shower? She wanted a shower? What if the baby shot out while she was in there? Yes, he was a doctor, but childbirth wasn't his speciality. He could get her through the birth, but this was all Gila's expertise. He'd prefer she climbed into bed and stayed there, cutting down the risk of any unexpected surprises. If they were going to do this, couldn't they at least do it the simplest way?

'Do you think that's a good idea?' he asked. 'Can't we just head for the bed and stay there?'

She smiled slightly and shook her head. 'Leo, there's no reason why I can't move around or take a shower. It's good to keep moving. I've read a lot of studies on it. Besides, a shower will help me to relax. It's perfectly fine. We've loads of time before things pick up.'

'Okay,' he said, already deciding it would be the quickest drench under the hose she'd ever taken. 'If it's what you really want.'

She smirked and patted his chest. 'Everything is going to be fine. We can do this.'

Leading her to the bathroom, he helped Gila remove her top and leggings, before stepping back. 'Can you manage from here?'

She nodded, but stopped him when he turned to leave the room. 'Where are you going?'

He pointed towards the corridor. 'I'll wait in the hall until you've finished. Give me a shout if you want any help.'

'No, I want you to stay with me,' she said, the expectation and hope in her expression almost Leo's breaking point. Didn't the woman realise how close he hovered to the tip of anxiety?

He glanced longingly at the open bathroom door then back at Gila. Careful to keep his thoughts from his face, he asked, 'Are you sure it's what you want? You know, with the way things are between us.'

She hesitated for a moment, before saying, 'Please, Leo. I need you. Although I'm doing my best to stay calm, it's mostly an act. I'd really appreciate your support.'

Shame, anger and fresh determination pumped through him at her words. Softly spoken, they still had the power to annihilate him. Of course, she was scared, because this was her first time. Not giving himself a chance to question the sense of his actions, he tugged her to him and kissed the top of her head. 'I'm here, baby. I'm not going anywhere. I swear.'

'I can't do this,' Gila panted as yet another contraction ran through her body. She wanted to yell and weep all at the same time, but a part of her mind also told her to stay quiet and not make a fuss. She wasn't an outgoing, dramatic kind of person. The idea of screaming like a banshee was completely outlandish to her. But this had gone on long enough and now she was done.

'Gila?'

'Yes?' She winced at the sharpness of her tone, but found it impossible to regret. In the centre of the bed, on all fours, she tried to go with the pain, silently repeating to herself how childbirth was natural and survivable without the inclusion of drugs, but it wasn't easy when it hurt *so* much.

'Gila?' Leo repeated.

She sighed and rolled her eyes. Couldn't the man see she was busy? She didn't have the time or the desire for chit-chat. 'Yes?'

Leo touched her side and coaxed, 'You're doing beautifully, darling. Just a little longer. Your progress is perfect. Totally textbook, you'll be happy to hear.'

'How do you know it's going to be a little longer?' she demanded, suddenly angry. 'The baby's not inside you, is it? Doing its best to rip you to pie—'

Leo dunked back towards the bottom of the bed away from her complaining. Rubbing a comforting hand on her right leg, he soothed, 'But I am a doctor. So I outrank you even if you are doing all the work.'

'Pfft,' she dismissed. 'You mend broken bones and save people from life-threatening complications. You do *not* regularly bring new life into the world the way I do. *I'm* the baby expert here, Dr Wright. Understand? I make all the decisions. You just keep telling me what everything looks like down your end.'

He laughed and commented, 'Childbirth is making you grouchy, I see. Would you like more ice to suck on? Or do you fancy sitting up for a while? Shall I get the mirror from the bathroom so you can see what's happening, or do you trust me to do everything right?'

'I trust you,' Gila panted, because she did. Every question she asked, Leo answered with patience. When she demanded information, he gave it without hesitation. So far, he'd acted the perfect birthing partner. 'What I need is for this to be over and the baby in my arms.'

Leo again stroked his hand over her leg. 'You're doing really well and you're totally beautiful, too.'

'I'm not beautiful,' Gila dismissed crossly. 'I'm tired, on all fours and sweaty. In no realms of someone's imagination can I be viewed as anything but a hot, hormonal mess.'

'I think you're amazing,' he added, ignoring her complaints. 'And I'm so proud of you. You're doing brilliantly, Gila.'

'I'm being a nightmare patient, aren't I?' she suddenly sobbed, rubbing her hand against her forehead. 'I'm a terrible person, Leo. You're trying to help me and I'm being mean and angry and so flipping emotional and—'

'Our child's giving you a hard time,' Leo interrupted softly. 'You're allowed to be all of those. Besides, I've borne worse patients than you, trust me. You're in the minors league when it comes to awkwardness and bad behaviour.'

She snorted, wiping away a stupid tear. 'Thanks, I think.'

He smiled and rubbed her behind. 'But I've never had a patient as brave as you're being. Are you sure I can't fetch you more ice?'

'No, just stay here with me,' she begged as another contraction hit her. 'I need you.'

'Of course,' he said, reaching out to rub the base of her spine. Their purpose linked as their child fought in its journey towards life. 'We can get through this. Now a gentle push, that's it.'

Once the contraction eased, Leo checked her once more, struck speechless when he spotted the top of the baby's head. 'I can see the head. Oh, God, Gila. I can see the top of the baby's head.'

Gila chuckled. 'Really?'

'Yes, and it's amazing. A bit mucky, but amazing. Here comes the rest of it.'

'It's going to be soon,' Gila warned. 'I need to take a breath. Don't forget you'll need to check that the cord is not around the baby's neck.'

He shifted to the top of the bed and grabbed her hand and squeezed it. Smacking a loud, sloppy kiss to her damp forehead, he said, 'I'm ready when you are. Nice and slow, no rushing for this next part. The baby's head is out. You're doing really well.'

She laughed helplessly when he dashed away. 'I want to push.'

'Okay, but don't use too much pressure. The baby's coming. There's no sign of the cord. The shoulders are out, I'm ready to receive, sweetheart. Yes, that's it. Yes. Yes. Oh, my God, she's beautiful, Gila. Our daughter is utterly beautiful.'

CHAPTER ELEVEN

A FAINT ANGRY squall filled the bedroom moments later. Leo lifted his child and didn't bother to wipe his falling tears as he cradled her to his body. This angry, irritated miracle of a baby, created from his and Gila's love, was their child. And between them—together—they'd brought this wonderful small bundle into the world.

And she was perfect. Their sweet, precious daughter, only seconds born and a little mucky, was absolutely and completely perfect.

'Is everything okay?' a weary voice enquired from the other end of the bed.

Leo nodded, unable to find words, his throat and eyes full of more tears, and stepped closer to where Gila, exhausted, but beautiful, waited for them.

Grabbing a towel, he quickly wrapped it around the baby to keep her warm, before carefully laying her onto Gila's naked body, all the time careful to keep the cord, still attached to baby and placenta, free from tension. He would cut it in a second, but, first, it was time for mother and baby to get acquainted.

Gila gave him a tired smile, her eyes curious as she took in their daughter now placed against her stomach and breast. A tear of her own rolled slowly over her cheek. With shaky, hesitant fingers, she softly touched the baby's face. 'We have a little girl, Leo.'

Leo sat on the bed next to them. Aching to stretch out and hug the two most precious females in his life, but aware he still had work to do. There'd be plenty of time and occasions for cuddles. In fact, the rest of their lives.

'Oh, Leo. She's so...' Gila's words faded off as she stared at her baby. Love and wonder shining from her, as she gently stroked a finger across a precious cheek.

'Isn't she?' he agreed, placing his arm around Gila's shoulders. Together they silently took in the marvel of their newborn daughter. No words needed as they acquainted themselves with this longed-for stranger, who, since pushing her way early into the world, was now and would always be the centre of their lives.

Gila rubbed a light finger over the baby's hand. 'Look at how tiny her fingers are. Oh, Leo. Her nails are minuscule. I never imagined I would ever experience this moment. I always thought I would be alone in life. Until I met you.'

Leo gave into the urge and slipped his other arm around the baby, where Gila held her. Fresh tears fell, but he ignored them, too. For the first time in many months he was happy and he meant to enjoy it. Here with his wife and daughter. The one place he truly wished to stay. 'She's adorable, isn't she?'

There were no words good enough to describe their daughter. Beyond adorable or astonishing. Just perfect and theirs. How on earth they'd managed to create a child so breathtaking, he didn't know, but he thanked all the saints for gifting her to them.

'She looks like you,' Gila whispered, lightly rubbing the dark wisps of their daughter's hair.

'Really?' He frowned, not seeing it. Surely not. The baby was beautiful and he definitely wasn't. Rugged, some people liked to call him, but he just saw the same old beaten-up face he'd always owned, whenever he looked in a mirror.

'I think she resembles you more,' he said, touching the baby's lower lip. His heart melted as his daughter tried to capture his finger with her mouth. 'Especially her mouth. Such a pretty one, isn't it? Just like yours.'

Gila smiled and continued to gaze at their daughter. 'Perhaps she simply looks like herself? A mixture of us, but totally individual.'

Leo liked that idea. Made by them, but original. 'Yep, I think you're right. Anyone looking at her can see she's amazing and unique. Shall I give her a quick wash, before you try feeding her?'

Gila nodded. 'Good idea. There's a blue bag in the bottom of the wardrobe at my uncle's. It contains baby stuff and a few newborn outfits. Though she's pretty long despite being a few weeks early, the all-in-ones should fit.'

Leo leaned over and gave into the urge before he stopped himself. Closing his eyes, he kissed Gila fully on the mouth, lingering for several long seconds before pulling away. He loved this woman and he hoped she understood exactly how much from that kiss. 'Thank you for our daughter.'

She smiled back and whispered, 'Thank you, too.'

Leo quickly dealt with the cord and placenta. Helping Gila to the chair, he quickly changed the sheets, before easing her and baby back into the bed.

Gathering all the dirty linen, he glanced at the

woman and child sitting in the centre of the bed. His family. His girls.

Gila looked up and smiled at him. 'I guess despite everything we did something right.'

He nodded. 'We did. I'll go and get the bag from your uncle's place.'

Stepping outside the narrowboat, Leo paused and glanced up at the sky. Somehow, he had to put his marriage back together. He didn't want to be just friends or polite acquaintances with Gila. He craved more. He wanted his family living with him.

Tilting his head further back, he whispered, 'I'm a daddy, sis. I've a daughter and she's incredible.'

Leo wrapped the soft knitted cream blanket around their daughter and walked over to the bed.

'Make sure to hold her head—' Gila stopped and winced, knowing she didn't need to tell Leo what to do. The gentle, careful way he held and tended to the baby's needs showed he was more than capable. 'Sorry, I just…she's so dear and I want to be a help.'

Leo grinned. 'You're a protective new mum, you're allowed to fuss. But I know what I'm doing. Besides, you did all the work bringing her into our lives, enjoy a minute's rest while she lets you.'

Gila sighed and leaned back against the clean pillow he'd switched when he changed the bedding earlier. The man hadn't stopped since their little one's arrival. Not only had he been the best stand-in midwife, Leo had helped her birth the placenta, cleaned her and the bed, and had just finished bathing their daughter. Without doubt a human dynamo of a man.

'Of course you do. Thanks, Leo. For everything.'

'My pleasure. Hey, I did the easy work. You're the one producing miracles today. Besides, can't have either of you going for a check-up at the hospital all messy, can we?'

Her second sigh filled the room as she snuggled into the pillows behind her back. 'I suppose it's best to get checked out.'

'If you want to stay home, you can, but I think all your friends at the maternity unit are hoping to see both you and baby. They were very excited when I phoned in and told them the news.'

She grinned. 'No, we'll go. We can grab some take-away on the way home. Besides, I want to show off our baby girl.'

Leo chuckled and rocked their whimpering daughter. Washed, dressed and, by the sounds of complaint coming from her, more than ready for a feed. 'Have you thought of any names?'

Content, Gila shrugged. 'A few. You?'

Leo bent over and placed their daughter down onto the mattress, close to the foot of the bed. Reaching for the stethoscope he'd fetched at the same time as Gila's baby bag, he placed one end in his ears and then blew on the other end to warm the metal, before bending over his wriggling baby.

'What are you doing?' Gila frowned as Leo partly unwrapped the blanket and pressed the stethoscope's end to their child's chest.

He straightened slightly and turned his head Gila's way. 'Thought I'd give our daughter a quick check over. So…names? How about Arabella?'

Gila tilted her head to one side and pondered the

name. 'Arabella Wright. I like it. Actually, I love it. What about a middle name?'

Leo frowned and replaced the stethoscope back on the same spot on the baby's chest and listened once more. His frown deepening as he shifted the instrument slightly without saying a word.

'What's the matter?' Gila asked, seeing his concerned expression. She knew Leo well enough to know when he was troubled over something. Tautness radiated from his body so strongly that she could practically feel it pulsating across the space between them.

'I—'

The sound of her uncle calling their names interrupted Leo and together they glanced towards the open bedroom door.

'We're in here,' Leo called back, picking the baby up and handing her over to Gila. With a lingering kiss to Arabella's head, he straightened as Art rushed into the room.

'Oh, it's true. Maggie said Leo called in to collect your bag,' Gila's uncle gushed, moving closer. 'Oh, my goodness, you've really had the baby.'

Gila reached out and caught Leo's fingers. Smiling at him, she searched his face, but found nothing to indicate something was amiss. Perhaps she'd imagined his worried expression and tightness in his movements.

Turning back to her uncle, Gila laughed. 'We did. Come and meet your great-niece.'

Art walked nearer and glanced down at the baby. 'Oh, she's a darling, isn't she? I also wanted to tell you that the road is clear and free from oranges.'

'Finally.' Leo chuckled, removing the stethoscope from his neck and dropping it onto the chair.

Art nodded, his eyes not leaving Arabella. 'She's so small. Are babies always this tiny?'

'She is,' Gila agreed, then reassured him, 'She's early, but she'll soon gain weight. Apart from that, she's fine.'

'Congratulations, both of you,' Art said. 'Your baby is beautiful, but your lives are about to get noisy and busy.'

Gila laughed and glanced at Leo, her heart hitching when she noticed that he wasn't laughing with them, instead his thoughtful gaze was fixed firmly on their sweet baby daughter.

Leo hadn't heard wrong. He'd prayed during the car journey that he had, but the sound he'd picked up when he'd listened to Arabella's heart was just as he thought. When they arrived at the hospital, the doctors soon confirmed his fears. Their daughter had a suspected heart murmur.

Pushing open the door to the room Gila had been allocated, Leo paused on the threshold taking in his wife as she nestled Arabella in her arms. Rooted to the floor by the sheer scene of love before him. A true and pure love. A mother and child's love. Clear in the way Gila held and looked at their daughter, softly whispering comforting words to her.

Love.

That special sentiment that filled a person's life with meaning. A reason for living each and every day. Possessions might look fine and pretty, but they didn't fill a person's heart with light and laughter. They didn't calm a man's soul the way true love did.

The news he'd come here to give Gila would test

that connection of love and probably theirs as well. He wasn't too conceited to admit it scared him. He'd already let this woman down. He'd promised Gila a life of happiness, when all he'd managed to do was inflict heartache on her without meaning to. He'd emotionally locked her out when he should have smashed through the difficulty and found a way to say the words crammed inside him.

'Hey,' he greeted, stepping further into the room. He wasn't going to avoid this moment any longer. He suspected Gila already sensed something was off because of the way she'd kept glancing at him during the car ride to the hospital. Plus, he needed to make a phone call after he spoke with her. One that wouldn't wait.

She smiled, her beautiful smile that always hit him hard in the centre of the heart. The one that had captured him the first time she sent it his way. The one he'd fallen in love with.

'Gila, we need to talk.'

Apprehension erased the happiness from her expression and he faltered as he crossed the room. Here was his small perfect family. His purpose for waking each day. The real reason his heart took each single beat. He hated doing it, but she had to know the truth. He refused to keep secrets from her. He'd done it once and look at what happened. It was time to find out her thoughts, before someone else accidentally let slip about the murmur. And she would hate him if that happened.

He reached the bed and sat down. The thin mattress giving underneath him. Swallowing, he took a moment, before he said, 'Gila, the doctors have checked over our sweetheart.'

Gila frowned and waited for him to continue. 'Yes,

the midwife who brought her back just now told me
they'd finished, but she never said anything else. Is everything okay?'

Leo hesitated, before meeting her gaze. Seeing the
concern in her eyes, he stiffened his spine. God, how he
loved this woman. How he ached to protect her from any
worries, but this was their child and she needed to know.

'Leo?' she quizzed.

His eyes moved to their daughter. The corner of his
mouth twitching as he took in her sweet baby face. How
could anyone think babies were ugly when they were
born? His little girl wasn't. Without thought or effort,
love flowed through him with more force than a mon-
soon. There wasn't anything he wouldn't do or give for
his little girl.

'Something's wrong, isn't it?' Gila whispered.

He nodded, not surprised by her question. As a midwife, she'd easily recognise the signs when the medical
staff were concerned for a baby's well-being. No doubt
she'd already figured out the truth. 'Yes.'

She sighed impatiently. 'I'm not stupid, Leo. I know
the protocol, and from what I can tell you're all keeping
something from me. Something concerning my child.
And I want to know what it is. In fact, I insist you tell
me right now.'

He grasped her hand and cradled it in his own. Cupping the warm palm with his cold one. Clearing his
throat, he swallowed the dryness in his mouth and said,
'Arabella has a suspected heart murmur.'

She stared at him for a moment, before nodding and
shifting her gaze to their daughter. 'Are they sure?'

He gently squeezed her hand. 'Yes.'

'I see. And why wasn't I told?'

Her lack of surprise told Leo his instinct had been correct. She'd guessed something was wrong. Probably worked out what it was during the car journey and before they reached the hospital.

'You knew,' Gila accused, pinning him once again with her gaze. 'At home when you listened to her heart. You knew then, didn't you? And yet you never said a thing. Why not?'

He held up a hand, to stop her from continuing. 'I suspected, but I hoped I was wrong. Cardio is not my speciality. But, yes, I thought I could hear whooshing as I listened to her heart. But I wanted a second opinion first.'

'I don't understand why you didn't tell me,' she said. 'At least mention your concerns. I'm Arabella's mother. I'm your wife.'

'I didn't want to worry you until I knew there was a definite reason to,' he repeated, desperate to reassure her. To explain there was nothing thoughtless or calculated behind his thinking. He merely thought it best to be sure.

She tutted and pulled her hand away. Averting her face, she tightened her arms around their child, as though to shield and defend her from Leo and the world. 'Keeping things from me again, Leo. Is this how it's always going to be?'

He winced as he took the hit. Yes, it hurt but he deserved it. Of course she'd think the worst, and he couldn't deny it. But this time he'd kept quiet because he'd wanted to be sure of his facts first. To save her from unnecessary worry. She'd just given birth and was so happy. The notion of having to crush her delight and replace it with anxiety, even for a while, when it might be unnecessary had kept him quiet. Nothing else. 'This isn't the same, Gila.'

She glanced back to him, her grey eyes flashing like lightning in a stormy sky. And mingled in the silvery depths was another emotion. One he recognised easily because he'd seen it so many times over the last few months. That unwelcome companion that often seemed to shadow his wife's estimation of him. Disappointment.

'Isn't it?' she asked quietly. Her anger from moments before disappearing as resignation replaced it. The sigh that followed both heavy and tired.

'No. I just wished to make sure first,' he insisted, hoping to make her understand. This really wasn't the same as when Jodie died. He wasn't turning into himself, unknowingly pushing everyone—her—away. He'd just figured waiting until he could give her more information was a wiser decision.

She shook her head. 'Doesn't this sound familiar, though?'

He reached for her hand again, but she shifted it away, tucking it underneath Arabella's bottom. Hiding it from him and making it plain she didn't welcome his touch. 'Don't do this, Gila. We're both emotional and worried right now, but—'

'There's nothing wrong with my daughter,' she insisted, her grey irises daring him to argue. 'I don't care what you or any other doctor in this hospital thinks. My baby is perfect and she will be fine. I'm her mother and I know it's the truth deep down inside. I would sense if something was wrong with her.'

'Gila, please. You may well be right, but—'

'I *am* right!' she vowed, glancing down at Arabella.

She fiddled with the pink knitted hat their daughter was wearing. 'I know I am.'

Leo nodded, accepting it was what she believed and refusing to argue with her. He had no reason to until they knew what they were dealing with. 'All right, but we have to do the checks.'

She huffed and twisted further away. Closing herself off from him and what he was saying. Doing to him what he'd not so long ago done to her. Was this immense pain ripping through his heart how he'd made her feel?

'You should go now,' she said quietly. 'I need to sleep.'

'Would you like me to put Arabella in her cot?' Leo asked, nodding towards the hospital cot at the side of the bed.

Gila shook her head and hugged their daughter closer. 'No, I can do it.'

Leo stood, deciding it best to leave her alone while he made his phone call. They would talk when he returned, but first he had to make the call. It was important. 'Okay.'

Walking away, he paused at the door. 'Please don't shut me out, Gila.'

She waited until he'd stepped through it, before replying softly, 'That's your forte, Leo, not mine.'

CHAPTER TWELVE

LEO PUSHED OPEN the glass doors, exiting the baby unit, and finally allowed hope to ease its warmth through his cold, numb body. Since confirmation of his initial diagnosis, he'd switched into his detached and cool professional doctor vibe, instead of giving into the out-of-control parental worry hovering and threatening to wipe away some of the joy of his daughter's unexpected arrival.

Their precious little girl had a congenital heart defect, or, in layman's terms, had been born with a heart problem and while his clinical brain focused on the fact that many babies were born with heart murmurs and lived perfectly normal, healthy lives, his same rational mind refused to forget that there was a rare but slim chance that a defect could turn out to be a major issue for his child.

It all depended on what type of heart murmur Arabella suffered. After leaving Gila in her room, he'd immediately telephoned a friend—a heart specialist—and asked him to examine Arabella. It wasn't that he didn't trust the hospital's doctors, but this man was one of the top cardio experts in the world and his little girl deserved to see the best if Leo could pull the strings and make it possible. He didn't care if it ruffled egos or upset any member of the staff. He was doing this for Gila and Arabella. Doing everything he could to make sure he didn't let another person down. That he didn't let Gila down again.

Fortunately his friend had readily agreed and was right at this moment examining Arabella. Leo had chosen to leave the room and wait outside, not trusting himself not to give into the impulse to snatch his child away from the people who were trying to help.

Suddenly exhausted, Leo lowered onto a nearby chair positioned against the corridor's wall. Closing his eyes, he blocked out the sounds of the busy hospital all around him, his thoughts shifting to his wife and her earlier reaction to the news.

Recalling the stubbornness in Gila's tone and the protective flash in her eyes caused him to smile despite the gloom of his mood. She was right when she insisted their daughter was perfect. Arabella was, no matter what was going on inside her tiny, delicate body. Seeing Gila so defensive and dismissive of any criticism of their baby filled him with strength and wonder. Amazed yet again by the intensity of a mother's love for her child.

Gila would never reject or feel inconvenienced by her child the way his parents often had. She'd fight any battle, big or small, to protect their daughter. Because despite her knowing the medical realities and possible ins and outs of such a condition, the fierce glimmer in her eye showed clearly that she thought he and the doctors in this hospital were all fools. When she looked at Arabella, she saw only a beautiful newborn baby. She would never view her as a problem or an inconvenience.

Opening his eyes, he tilted his head back against the wall. Yes, a mother's love was a powerful thing, and today Gila had displayed its real and full magnificence and he felt privileged and proud to have witnessed it.

She'd also made it clear how unimpressed she was with him and the way he'd kept quiet about his concerns over Arabella's heart. Yet again he'd chosen the wrong course when hoping to safeguard his wife. But he honestly hadn't wanted to scare or worry her until there was cause to.

Instead, though, he'd given her a new motive not to trust him. After everything they'd been through today, bringing Arabella into their lives. The fragile bridge they'd created working together for their child's sake, he'd broken by staying quiet. When she'd asked what was wrong why hadn't he just told her? When he'd heard the whooshing noise, a sign of turbulent blood flow, while listening to Arabella's heart, why hadn't he asked Gila's opinion? Included her in the discovery. Because the old part of him wanted to shoulder all the stress and save her from it. And if he was really honest, he didn't want to accept that there might be a problem with their daughter's health, either. Didn't want to face that stark reality when, as Gila had already stated, to them Arabella was perfect. Or allow the idea that someone he loved might be snatched away again, and him incapable of doing anything to prevent it.

And now he sat here alone waiting for the specialist's verdict because he'd messed up for the hundredth time. Or so it felt. Praying for a positive outcome, while people passed by, concerned only with their own problems and troubles. Knowing that there was nothing he could do to aid his child except beg whatever God cared to listen to his pleas to save his baby from the worst possible scenario as he impatiently waited to hear how poorly his baby girl really was.

How many more times must he stand alone? Always unassisted and solitary. Helpless to change the inevitable. He was tired and fed up with dealing with problems without someone to turn to. Without a shoulder to rest upon. His counsellor during their sessions encouraged him to share his feelings, but Leo didn't really want to talk to the man. It was Gila he yearned to unburden his soul to. Gila he wanted to hold close and confess his inner fears to. She was the one whose opinion he longed to hear. Whose arms he craved to encircle him when his body threaten to buckle. But how could he expect her to be there for him, when he shied away from letting her in? From accepting her strength and wisdom when his own faltered.

The sound of a door opening and heavy footsteps drew his attention from his bleak thoughts. He turned and watched his friend, the specialist, walk briskly towards him, tweed jacket flapping, his expression void of any clue or indication whether the update he brought on Arabella was bad or good.

A shiver prickled over Leo's neck and his mouth dried. His gaze not leaving his friend's face even though his eyes burnt from watching him. Rubbing his clammy hands against his jeans, Leo ignored the increasing dense thud of his rapid heart pounding in his ears.

Reaching Leo, his friend stopped and removed his silver glasses. With a sigh, he took the seat next to him and cleared his throat before meeting Leo's gaze. 'Let's go somewhere private and talk, shall we?'

* * *

Gila wasn't sure how she ended up sitting in the hospital garden. After she'd been checked over, the doctor on duty had happily declared she was fine and fit for a woman who'd recently given birth and discharged her. The fact she lived with a doctor no doubt eased any of the man's concerns, but Gila couldn't leave because half an hour ago a midwife had arrived at her room and whisked Arabella off for further checks and tests over at the special baby unit.

Gripping her hands together, she sighed. At least this time she knew why they had taken her and wasn't left frustrated and wondering why the midwives wouldn't give clear answers to her questions.

The fragrance of the plant to the left of the bench filled the air. Gila didn't recognise the shrub, but the fragrance reminded her of the baby lotion she'd bought for Arabella. One she hadn't yet used. Same as all the other items she'd gathered over the last few months for her baby.

Dashing a tear away, she folded her arms and fixed her gaze on the trickling water bubbling from the stone fountain in the centre of the garden. The sound was supposed to be comforting and relaxing, but Gila found it annoying and wished it would stop. How could she feel calm when her mind resembled a mixed pot of disturbed thoughts?

A heart murmur wasn't so worrying. Not always. Babies were often born with them and no one really understood why. Many were nothing to be concerned over and disappeared within days or weeks.

But every time Gila considered it, all she could

see was the image of Leo's face when he'd listened to Arabella's heart, followed by his lying. He'd said he'd wanted to save her unnecessary worry. Huh! Just the same way he'd wanted to protect her from his depression after his sister's death. But was it protection or simply lying? She wasn't some innocent who needed hiding from life and its ugliness. She was a trained midwife, who understood how these things happened sometimes. Leo should have respected her rights professionally as a midwife and Arabella's mother, and as a new parent to hear the truth straight away. But no, he'd made a decision and done everything his own sweet way. Was the pattern of Leo shutting her out repeating itself yet again? Had all their talking over the past few days meant nothing? Had his ears been as muffled as they had been in the past? Did he still harbour the misconception that she needed to be screened from the world and its harsh realities? Hadn't she experienced and dealt with more than her share of unpleasant things during her childhood?

She sucked in a breath and made herself view the situation from his perspective. Maybe that last one was partly why he did it. He'd said he wished to wait until he had all the facts before including her, but did he also hope to save her from facing it because she'd been subjected to so much trauma and upset during her early years?

Well, she didn't require gentle handling when it concerned their daughter. The child her empty arms seriously ached to hold but couldn't because her poor little girl was undergoing more tests. Gila had asked which ones, but the midwives on duty, supposedly her friends and colleagues, were decidedly vague and rebuffed her questions with lectures on her need to rest and sleep. They were kind, but she knew when she was being brushed off. She'd done the same to her own patients in the past, usually when they didn't have the medical answers and were shy of causing the parents unnecessary apprehension. Now having experienced how annoying it was to be the parent being fobbed off, she vowed never to do it again. From now on she would be straight with all her mums and dads. It wasn't nice being kept in the dark and treated like a breakable new mother on the verge of shattering. She hated it. No, she *resented* it. How dared they treat her in such a way? They should know better. As Arabella's mother, she had more rights than any other human being in this hospital.

She also wanted to yell and scream because once again she was going through a horrible confusing hell and doing it completely alone. Leo had disappeared and her child was having who knew what done to her and no one, not one single person, thought that she might want to be with her. Or how *she* might be terrified and feeling utterly useless and superfluous while others fussed around her baby.

'So this is where you are.'

A familiar deep voice spoke behind her. One she wasn't particularly keen on hearing right now. Reluctantly, she turned her head and took in her husband, standing with both hands resting on his hips. Tiredness lined his face, and there was something in his gaze she couldn't decipher.

'They've taken Arabella again,' she said, suspecting he knew already. But she didn't know what else to say to him. What did a wife say to the husband who dashed off and left her on her own? Earlier, during Arabella's birth, they had been as one, so together, a proper couple again, but now she could hardly stand to look at him.

'I know. She's in the baby unit waiting for us to collect her.'

Leo strolled over and settled next to Gila on the bench. Without saying a word, he reached over and hauled her into his arms, and whispered, 'I called a friend—a cardiologist—he knows his stuff. One of the best. I asked him if he would come to the hospital to examine Arabella and he did.'

'Is that where you've been?' she asked, scared to hear the rest of what was coming. Hiding from the inevitable was irrational and impossible, but suddenly she desperate wished to delay it. She'd imagined Leo somewhere else, doing other things, *what* she wasn't certain, but she'd never considered he'd be calling in favours from medical associates or friends.

Leo kissed her head and squeezed her tighter. 'Yes.'

So instead of abandoning them as she'd feared, Leo had been making sure their daughter was seen by an expert in the field. 'When you disappeared, I thought… I know I told you to go, but—'

'I'm sorry I left you for so long, but I realised I wasn't your favourite person and I wanted to speak with the man. He's a friend and I knew he was only in London this week, visiting family. Normally he's based in Scotland. When he agreed to come to the hospital straight away, I figured you'd want me to find out his prognosis immediately.'

She nodded and asked, 'What did he say?'

Leo cuddled her tighter. 'He suspects the problem lies with a leaky valve. There are no guarantees, but he's pretty confident that over the next few months

Arabella's heart will mend itself. She'll need regular check-ups to monitor her heart through follow-up appointments, but he sees no reason why we can't all go home and let nature do its own healing with no other interference from us.'

Gila smiled and then burst into tears. Their little girl wasn't completely out of danger, but the murmur wasn't so serious it required an operation. With time the heart would mend allowing Arabella to enjoy a full and normal life. They weren't going to lose her. She was going to be all right.

She smiled through her tears. Wiping at her damp face with the cuffs of her jumper, she sniffed. 'Oh, Leo, that's wonderful.'

He chuckled and agreed. 'It is.'

Quietly absorbing the good news, Gila slowly leaned her body into Leo's. She turned her face into his chest, the thick material of his blue-checked shirt rough against her cheek. But she didn't pull away, the feel of it and the firm wall of his body beneath too comforting to leave. For the last few hours she'd refused to listen to the hateful voices whispering inside her head, goading her. Voices whose only aim was to fill her with doubt and questions. But she'd adamantly refused to listen to them. Deep down inside she'd known her darling baby was fine, and now Leo had confirmed that belief. Her mother's intuition spot on when it came to her daughter.

'Leo,' she said, fiddling with one of the buttons on his shirt. 'I have a confession to make.'

Leo shifted and tilted her face upwards. 'You do?'

'I owe you a big apology because I'm guilty of believing the worst of you. I'm ashamed to admit that for the last half-hour I've been thinking the most terrible things about you. Really awful thoughts.'

To her surprise he laughed. 'You have?'

She nodded. 'I asked one of the midwives where you were and she'd said you'd gone. I felt so alone after you left my hospital room and I assumed you'd left Arabella and me because of the way I reacted...'

'You thought I'd deserted you both when you needed me?' he asked, guessing the rest.

She nodded and dropped her head to his shoulder. Not eager to see his displeasure. 'I did.'

Leo sighed and tugged her closer. His strong arms wrapping her in the cocoon of his embrace. 'Sweetheart, it's going to take time learning to trust one another again. But we've the rest of our lives together to do so. I'm not worried, nor should you be. We just need time.'

She glanced up at him and quizzed, 'You're not mad?'

He thought for a moment, then shook his head. 'If you'd disappeared after our conversation about the heart murmur, considering the last few months, and the way I behaved before, I probably would've deduced the same thing. But I swear to you, on this old thing called my heart, that you and our daughter are everything I want in life, and I'm not going anywhere without you both. I promise, I'll never leave you physically or emotionally again. All I'm guilty of is wanting to get the specialist here and I'm afraid I pushed everything and everyone else from my thoughts while I did so.'

Gila sighed. 'I hate being like this...doubting you and—'

Leo put his finger on her lips. 'It's understandable. Just give me the opportunity to dispel those fears. It's all

I ask. I love you, Gila. Please give me a second chance to prove how much. You know, the counsellor helped me with accepting that nothing I did would ever have helped my sister, but on those hard dark days when I struggled, it was the thought of you that got me through them. I didn't know if you'd ever forgive me or even if we would have a future together, but just the notion of you being in my life in any small way was what pushed me to fight. You are the splendour in my life. These last few days together have been precious to me. Living together, properly talking to each other. Admitting feelings I've never told another soul. And now we have Arabella. If you decide that all you want is to be friends while we raise our child, then I'll accept that. I'll take whatever you feel able to give.'

Gila stared into the face of the man she still loved, suddenly convinced a life minus him would be nothing but an empty one. One lived but never fully enjoyed. Like the sky without rain, or grass without soil. She'd tried for four months to give up their love and hated every minute. Four long months merely existing through each day. She refused to live the rest of her life in such an empty way. Not when she didn't have to.

'Is that what you want?' she asked. 'To be friends and nothing else?'

Leo shook his head. 'No. I want to come home… to you.'

'You do?' she whispered.

He placed two fingers against her top just where her heart lay beneath. 'In there. I want to go home inside your heart.'

Gila swallowed hard. She'd thought to use their week together to say goodbye to their relationship, confident she already understood the wishes of her own heart. What a stupid arrogant fool she was. No, not a fool, but a coward. Running away, instead of fighting for her marriage. Brooding when Leo's own strength called for bolstering. He'd fallen, and instead of picking him up, she'd walked away and sulked.

Please give me a second chance to prove how much.

And he'd asked for a second chance, when *she* should be asking for the same. No, not asking, but begging. She'd picked the easy choice and left their marriage because she hadn't liked the unfamiliar turn it had taken. Like the insecure child she'd once been, too scared to stand and face a situation she found uncomfortable, she'd packed a suitcase and left. But she wasn't a child any longer. She was a strong woman and Leo had helped her become *that* woman with his love and understanding. He'd encouraged and filled her with confidence, yet when he'd needed her the most, she'd failed in not returning that same self-belief.

So yes, she too needed to plead for a second chance. Not just Leo. Because her insecurities had almost robbed them of something very precious. Their marriage. And now it was time for her to be brave and fight for it. Fight for him.

Licking her lips, she said, 'I have a condition first.'

Leo's gaze searched her face. 'Which is?'

'That you give *me* a chance to prove to *you* how much I love you. I let you down, Leo. So I have as much to prove as you.'

'You didn—' he began, but she stopped him.

Covering his mouth with her finger, she shook her head. 'I did. The truth is, I don't understand how love works. Perhaps you can teach me how to do it properly.'

A faint smile tugged at his lips. 'I can do that. It might take a lifetime, though. Loving someone is a special art and should never be rushed.'

She smiled and laughed. 'I promise to be a good pupil, teacher.'

'I need a promise from you,' Leo said, kissing the pad of her finger, still resting against his lips.

'Yes?' she asked.

'Help me learn how to open up when I need to talk. The counsellor's fine, but he's not *you*. You get me better than anyone. It's *you* whose judgement I respect and desire. The last four months have been hell and lonely. I miss you, Gila. Help me learn how to be a better, more open man. One who deserves your love.'

Ignoring her sudden tears, Gila nodded. She could do as he asked. It might take time and many mistakes, but she promised to love this man the way he desired. The way she desperately wanted to. Their relationship had stalled because they'd both made mistakes and resorted to old familiar habits. Ones learnt before they'd ever met. But the best thing with bad habits was that they could be broken and new patterns learnt.

'There's something I'd like you to do,' she said. Reaching into her coat pocket, she took out a ring. A plain simple circle of gold whose symbolism carried so much.

Leo frowned at the sight of it, and then met her gaze. 'Your wedding ring.'

She nodded and held it up between them. 'I kept it under the pillow during Arabella's birth and brought it with me. Like a lucky talisman, I suppose.'

It didn't make sense considering their recent separation, but right now little made much of any. Her fingers were trembling as she held it out to him. 'Will you please put it back where it belongs?'

His eyes widened as he absorbed her words. 'Are you sure it's what you want?'

She nodded. No doubts or concerns murmured to her, just clear certainty that this was the right decision. Every part of her soul urged her to return home in every sense. To repair the broken pieces of their relationship, not with unstable, flimsy patches of promises, but with firm and strong reinforcements made from sturdy and formidable love.

'If you need more time,' he offered.

She shook her head. 'I don't.'

'If I replace the ring then you can't leave again. Whatever problems come along we deal with them by staying under the same roof,' Leo said.

She smiled. 'I agree. I promise to stay put if you promise to talk to me. We're stronger together, Leo. It's taken me a long time to understand that I am no longer alone and I'm determined to make sure that you never will be, either.'

She lifted his hand and placed it against her chest. 'I'm asking you to come home, Leo.'

Leo took the circle of gold from her, and slowly and carefully slid it back onto her finger. Lifting her hand, he kissed the band where it sat snuggly against her skin. 'I'll never give you another reason to take it off again, I swear. You're right. Together we're whole.'

Gila sighed, content and happy. Glancing at the man she loved so desperately, she said, 'Let's collect our daughter and take her home.'

Leo smiled and kissed her hand again. 'With you

and Arabella it's the only place I ever want to be. But first I have to do something.'

'What?' she asked.

'Kiss you,' he said.

And so he did. And together they finally returned home to that place they were always meant to be.

EPILOGUE

GILA KISSED ARABELLA'S dark head and breathed in the mixture of soap, baby lotion and sweet little girl that made up her daughter's unique smell. As she rearranged the long ivory-coloured antique gown her daughter wore, a happy peacefulness slipped through her. A familiar feeling these days and she treasured it.

At six months old, her gorgeous baby girl glowed with health and, so far, it appeared her tiny little heart was doing as the doctors hoped and mending naturally. Yet again the human body's ability to heal amazed Gila and she thanked the heavens for the miracle.

Glancing at the clock on the tall city church tower, she smiled when it struck one o'clock. All around friends, family and colleagues manoeuvred their way inside the church building, all there to witness and celebrate Arabella's christening.

After several days of rain, the sun had chosen to reappear that morning and its warm rays heated the busy city and put everyone in a good mood.

'You okay?'

Gila leaned into the man whose arms encircled them. 'I'm a mixture of excited and nervous. How about you?'

'Nah, our Arabella's got this,' Leo answered. 'She's a

scene stealer whatever she does. I can't see today being any different. Not our little star.'

All the troubles, disappointment and fears were behind them. These days they continued to move forward, building their relationship and family. Both having learnt from the mistakes they'd stupidly committed. Each determined to make a life together where they talked to one another, even when it was hard and tough. And sometimes it was, but together they managed and worked through it.

They were a family who'd learnt to share and grow. More so since Arabella's arrival. They'd fought their wobbly beginning and survived. No more hiding or trying to shield the other and especially no leaving. Oh, no, her suitcase stayed under the bed and she planned for it to remain there gathering dust, between holidays.

She grinned and turned slightly in Leo's hold. In his dark suit he made her mouth water. Later, she would definitely be helping him out of it when they returned home. His shirt and tie, too.

'You know I love you, don't you?' she said.

Leo's eyes glimmered with happiness and mischief. 'Behave, Mrs Wright, or I'll ravish your pretty mouth right here in front of everyone.'

'In front of a church?' she teased, arching her eyebrows. 'What a naughty man you are.'

Leo chuckled. 'I'm pretty sure the guy in the sky will understand. You're my soulmate, why wouldn't I want to kiss you?'

Gila smiled and hugged their precious daughter closer. Yes, they'd all be having an early night. When she'd met and fallen in love with Leo, he'd given her more than just a love affair. Right here in his arms he'd given her somewhere to belong, a place that would always be her true home.

'Are my special girls ready?' Leo asked, dropping his arms to offer her his hand.

Gila took it and smiled up at the man she adored. 'Always, Leo. For you, always.'

* * * * *

COMING SOON!

We really hope you enjoyed reading this book.
If you're looking for more romance, be sure to
head to the shops when new books are
available on

Thursday 18th August

MILLS & BOON®

Coming next month

HER SECRET RIO BABY
Luana DaRosa

The door opened, interrupting their conversation, and Dr Salvador strode back into the room. The fierce protectiveness in Diego's eyes vanished, leaving his face unreadable.

Eliana's eyes were drawn to the emergency doctor, who stepped closer. She was wearing an expression of medical professionalism on her face that quickened her pulse. She knew that look. She had given it to patients herself.

She whipped her head around, looking at Diego, and whatever he saw written in her face was enough to make him get off his chair and step closer to her side. A similar look of protectiveness to the one he'd had a few moments ago was etched into his features.

'Would you mind giving us some privacy?' Sophia asked him, and a tremble shook Eliana's body.

The nausea came rushing back, her head suddenly felt light, and Eliana reacted before she could think, her hand reaching for Diego's and crushing it in a vice-like grip.

'It's okay if he stays,' she said, in a voice that sounded so unlike her own.

Something deep within her told her she needed him to stay. Whether it was premonition or just a primal fear gripping at her heart, she didn't know.

Diego stopped, giving her a questioning look, but he stayed, and his hand did not fight her touch.

'Well, it looks like it's not a stomach bug, but morning sickness. Or, in your case, late-afternoon sickness.' She paused for a moment, before confirming the absurd thought that was rattling around in Eliana's head. 'You're pregnant.'

Eliana opened her mouth to speak, but no words crossed the threshold of her lips. Pregnant? How was she pregnant? Her head snapped around to Diego, and whatever expression she was wearing on her face seemed to convey to him all the words she didn't want to say in front of the doctor.

The baby was his. They were pregnant.

His hand slipped from her grasp as he took a step back. The shock she felt at the revelation was written on his face.

'How long?' she asked, even though she knew it didn't matter.

Eliana had only slept with one person in the last six months, and that was the man standing here in the room with her.

Continue reading
HER SECRET RIO BABY
Luana DaRosa

Available next month
www.millsandboon.co.uk

MILLS & BOON

THE HEART OF ROMANCE

A ROMANCE FOR EVERY READER

MODERN

Prepare to be swept off your feet by sophisticated, sexy and seductive heroes, in some of the world's most glamourous and romantic locations, where power and passion collide.

HISTORICAL

Escape with historical heroes from time gone by. Whether your passion is for wicked Regency Rakes, muscled Vikings or rugged Highlanders, awaken the romance of the past.

MEDICAL

Set your pulse racing with dedicated, delectable doctors in the high-pressure world of medicine, where emotions run high and passion, comfort and love are the best medicine.

True Love

Celebrate true love with tender stories of heartfelt romance, from the rush of falling in love to the joy a new baby can bring, and a focus on the emotional heart of a relationship.

Desire

Indulge in secrets and scandal, intense drama and plenty of sizzling hot action with powerful and passionate heroes who have it all: wealth, status, good looks…everything but the right woman.

HEROES

Experience all the excitement of a gripping thriller, with an intense romance at its heart. Resourceful, true-to-life women and strong, fearless men face danger and desire - a killer combination!

To see which titles are coming soon, please visit

millsandboon.co.uk/nextmonth

JOIN US ON SOCIAL MEDIA!

Stay up to date with our latest releases, author news and gossip, special offers and discounts, and all the behind-the-scenes action from Mills & Boon...

 @millsandboon

 @millsandboonuk

 facebook.com/millsandboon

@millsandboonuk

It might just be true love...

MILLS & BOON
True Love

Romance from the Heart

Celebrate true love with tender stories of
heartfelt romance, from the rush of falling in
love to the joy a new baby can bring, and a
focus on the emotional heart of a relationship.

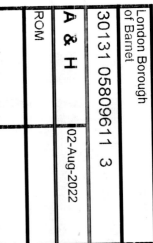